Windrush: The City of Dreadful Death

Windrush
The City of Dreadful Death

Jack Windrush Series – Book VIII

Malcolm Archibald

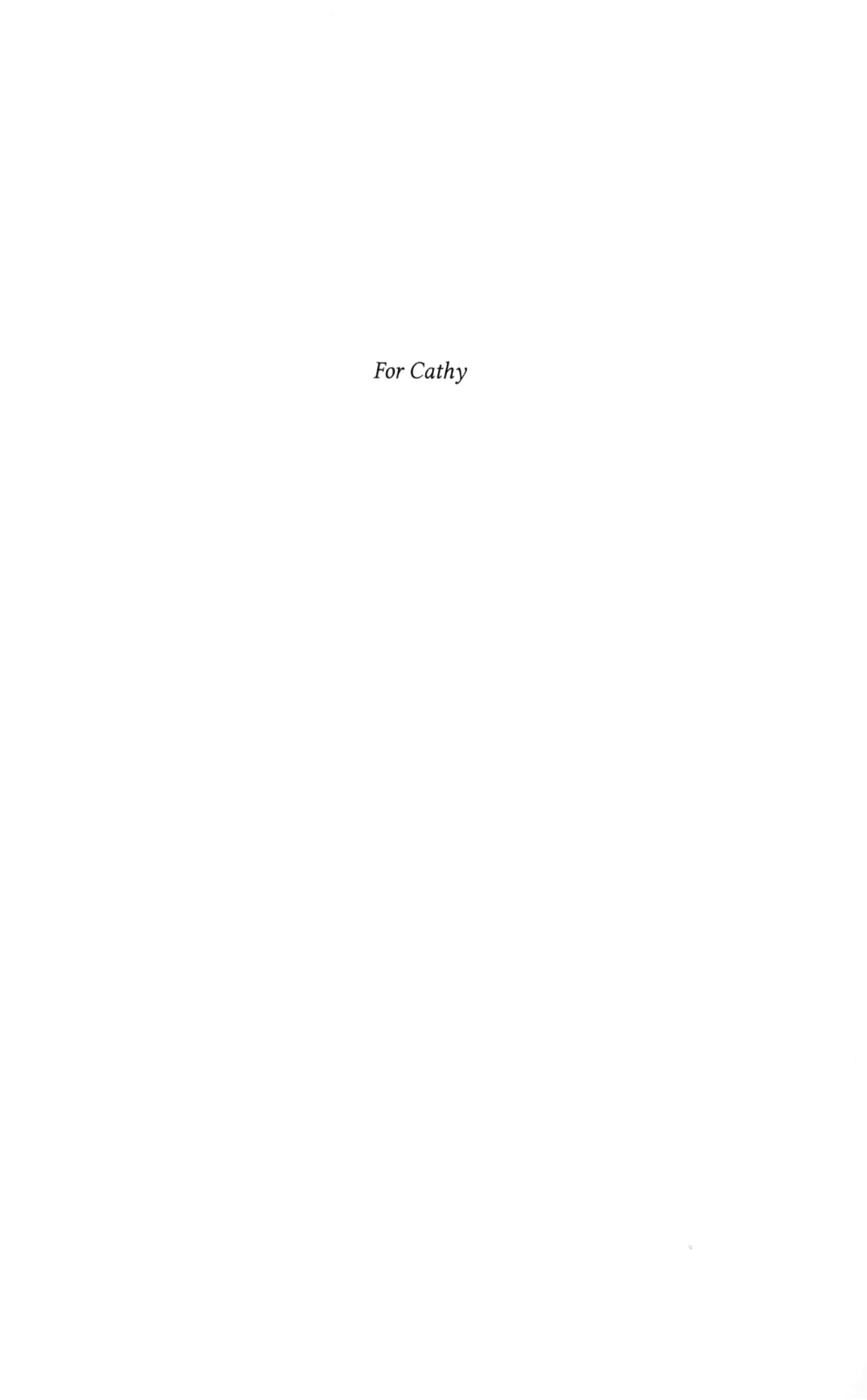

For Cathy

We could not move in that city of dreadful death without coming across signs of human sacrifices and suffering.
Sergeant J. Flynn, Rifle Brigade

Wha saw the Forty Second?
Wha saw the Forty Twa?
Wha saw the bare ersed buggers
Coming frae the Ashanti War?
Traditional

Acknowledgement

I would like to thank Dr Zachary Beier of the Department of History and Archaeology, University of the West Indies for clearing up a couple of historical points.

Prelude

DENKYIRA, WEST AFRICA, SUMMER 1800

The family sat together in the courtyard of their house with the wind rustling the leaves of the palm tree in one corner and the food set up before them. Kodzo knew that with the first harvest of the year successfully gathered, there was plenty for everybody, plantains, yams and manioc, together with sweet potato and gourds of beer.

Koshiwa Badu sat at the head, joking with her family, chiding where necessary, allowing the children all the freedom of childhood while keeping them from danger, as was the Denkyira tradition. Beside Koshiwa was Yawo, her daughter, and Kofi and Fifi, her sons. Further away, Kwabena and Kodzo, her grandsons, played happily with the fowls, not caring about the conversation of their elders. They were at home and life was as it had always been.

Koshiwa looked up when she heard the frantic barking of a dog. She glanced at Kofi, who pulled a face and continued to eat, while Fifi reached for his second gourd of beer. A shift of wind rustled the palm leaves and brought the sound of a man shouting in the distance.

"That's Kwasi Bekoe," Kofi said. "He's probably drunk again." He laughed, with his family joining in. Kwasi Bekoe was something of a standing joke in the village, always getting drunk and falling out with his wife and anybody else who had the misfortune to meet him.

When the dog's barking ended in a high-pitched squeal, Fifi lowered his gourd, wiped the beer from his chin and smiled. "Kwasi has kicked the dog!"

"I wish he would shut his teeth," Koshiwa said, as the shouting continued. "Kofi, go and tell him to keep quiet. Either that or I will."

"You would start a quarrel," Kofi said. "I'd better go." Taking a sip at Fifi's gourd, he stepped outside the courtyard, walked through the open front room and into the village. He saw Kwasi running towards him, his legs blundering as if he were exhausted, and blood sliding down his face.

"Kofi!" Kwasi said. "Run! Run now!"

"What is it?" Kofi dropped his smile as he saw what was behind Kwasi. "Edwesu Asanti slave hunters!"

"Mother!" Kofi only had time for one word before the rush of men overpowered him. Knocked to the ground, he struggled for only a moment as two men held him, and a third cracked a heavy stick on the back of his head. Other men rushed past him and into Koshiwa's house.

Koshiwa rose from her seat, screaming as the Edwesu warriors charged into her courtyard. Naked except for white loin-cloths, each man had two white stripes painted down each side of his face, and carried a heavy club in his hand.

Fifi was first to react, throwing his gourd at the first man and leaping for the long spear in the corner of the courtyard. The gourd caught the striped man square in the face, sending him staggering back. His companions blocked Fifi's path, swinging their clubs, knocking him to the ground. The white striped Edwesu circled the courtyard, grabbing everybody, smashing their clubs on the heads of those who tried to resist.

Only Kodzo managed to escape, ducking under the long arms of one Edwesu warrior and side-stepping another to run into the street outside. Panting with fear, he saw more of the white striped warriors all around the village, gathering together the Denkyira people and shoving them under the fetish tree in the small village square. Sliding into a patch of bushes, Kodzo watched the Edwesus grab the Denkyiras and manacle their ankles and wrists, hugged his knees to his chest and lay still, sobbing in fear.

As soon as night came, Kodzo slid free from his hiding place. By that time the Edwesus had marched the Denkyiras away, leaving the village deserted. Wiping away his tears, Kodzo ran home to search for food. He did not notice the man with the white stripes until it was too late.

"Another for the slave market!" The Edwesu said. "Come with me, little slave."

Kodzo began to scream. It was a sound he would grow used to in the long, bitter years ahead.

Chapter One

"The barometer's falling fast." Harry Young, mate of the three-masted barque *Lady Luck,* tapped the glass, swore softly, and checked the set of the sails.

"Aye," Captain Hobson glanced aft, where dark clouds piled up from the darkening horizon, and a greasy sheen tinted the sea. "We're in for the very devil of a blow, I reckon, Mr Young."

"Best get below, Mary." Lounging by the rail, Jack Windrush had been listening to the conversation. "If the captain thinks there's a storm coming, I don't want you swept overboard."

Mary smiled. "It's not stormy yet, Jack. All we have is a fresh breeze."

Jack grunted. "Aye, but a fresh breeze can soon turn into a howling gale."

"If that happens," Mary said, "I might go below." She stepped along the deck with the wind whipping her long hair around her shoulders and threatening to lift her straw hat. "I can't stand being cooped up in that tiny cabin, Jack. I'll stay on deck as long as I can."

"You're a stubborn hussy, Mary Windrush!"

Mary gave a small curtsey, with a stray shaft of sunlight reflecting from the silver Celtic cross she wore around her neck. "Why, thank you, Captain Jack. Coming from you, I'll take that as a compliment."

"That's Major Jack, hussy, and I'll thank you to remember it!"

Mary laughed. "You've been Captain Jack to me for too long to change now, *Captain* Jack!"

The wind increased, coming from the south-west, cracking the canvas against the spars and whistling through the standing rigging. Jack put a protective arm around Mary, who shook it away. "I can stand on my own two feet, thank you!"

"All hands aloft!" Captain Hobson roared. "Make fast the skysails, royals and royal staysails!"

Mary watched the seamen scramble aloft with the wind flapping their loose clothing and shirts and threatening to blast them from their precarious hand-and-foot-holds. "Brave men up there," she said, tucking her purple-and-gold scarf around her neck.

Jack tapped the glass. "The barometer is still falling."

"Aye," Harry Young glanced at the gathering clouds. "We'd better shorten all sail before we're caught out here." He watched the seamen return to the deck, some to slip below to the foc'sle.

Captain Hobson grunted, paced the deck for a few moments, checked the sea and made his decision. "All hands!" he roared. "All hands shorten sail!"

"Time for us to get below," Jack said as a rush of nimble-footed seamen filled the deck and once more swarmed aloft.

"It is getting blowy!" Mary grabbed at her hat a second too late as the wind finally whisked it from her head and tossed it overboard. She watched as if floated for a moment then was lost in the rapidly rising waves.

"The lads are struggling up there," Jack gestured aloft, where the seamen balanced on the footropes fought with the gaskets. Unfurled, the heavy canvas of the sails billowed and bellied as the wind rose. One bald seaman momentarily lost his footing and wrapped both arms around a spar as the rising gale blasted the sails from the gaskets, thrashed the canvas to pieces and hurled the ragged remnants into the heaving sea.

"Mary!" Jack grabbed his wife as the deck heeled to starboard. After stripping the canvas from the masts, the wind pressed down on *Lady Luck*, forcing Jack and Mary to hold onto anything solid. The bald seaman slipped and nearly fell until one of his mates hauled him back to comparative safety.

"I can hardly breathe!" Mary gasped as the wind clutched at her.

"Get that woman below!" Jack could hardly hear Captain Hobson's bellow above the howl of the wind that was now forcing the ship further and ever further over. Waves leapt up the side of *Lady Luck*, reaching for the frail life on board.

"She's broaching to!" Harry Young yelled as *Lady Luck* tilted onto her beam ends, with her lower yards dragging in the frothing white water to leeward. Her seamen held on with white-knuckled hands, while their feet scrabbled for purchase on ropes that were no longer taut.

"Hold on!" Jack held Mary, who had wrapped both arms around the mizzen mast. He saw the white faces and gaping mouths of the helmsmen, both unable to move as the wind pressed them against the wheel.

"Dear God help us!" a half-shaven seaman yelled.

"Aye, Peter," a rough voice replied. "I knew you were a Christian at heart. I told you before that there are no atheists in a storm."

After that, there was no speech as the gale mounted, and the waves broke green and white over the heeling deck. Unable to speak, scarcely able to breathe, Jack fought to see through the curtain of spindrift and driving rain. The light had died, with the occasional burst of lightning the only illumination, each flash revealing a nightmare of leaping dark water topped with crests of foaming white. Looking aloft, Jack saw the storm had carried away the main topmast, while the mizzen topgallant hung in the rigging, threatening to fall with every fresh assault of the wind.

Sodden, with her dress and hair slicked close to body and head, Mary wrapped her fingers around Jack's thumb. He met her gaze, saw no fear in her brown eyes, and tried to muster a smile.

Then the wind died. A great sea broke over the stern, sweeping up the length of the ship, carrying away the steering and standard compass, splintering the ship's longboat into a thousand pieces and breaking the cover of number two hatch. As that wave receded, *Lady Luck* dipped by the head, thrusting her bowsprit underwater.

"Are we going to sink?" Mary asked with surprising calmness.

"No," Jack said. "The storm's easing. I can hear you talk."

Mary nodded. "So you can." Her smile did not look forced. "I can hear you as well."

Although the wind had receded, *Lady Luck* still wallowed in a tremendous sea, with waves around her higher than the broken mizzen.

"Sound the well!" Captain Hobson ordered the carpenter. "See how much water we're making."

"I tried, sir," the carpenter was a balding, middle-aged man with a worn-out face. "There's too much water slopping in there to get an accurate reading."

"Try again." The captain stepped aft to examine the damage aloft, holding onto the rail to keep his balance on the heeling deck. "You're still with us I see, Major and Mrs Windrush?"

"We're still here, Captain," Jack confirmed. "How's *Lady Luck?*"

Captain Hobson grunted. "Deserted us, Major, deserted us." He continued his scrutiny of the masts and rigging. "The cap of the lower masthead is broken," he said to the mate, "and the storm's wrenched the masthead around. The main yard and both topsail yards are also down." He nodded to the splintered spars as they lay across what remained of the rail, "and the topmast, topgallant mast and all the upper yards and their gear are floating to leeward, hammering at our hull."

"Yes, sir," the mate nodded to the ten-foot-high tangle of broken spars, cordage and various pieces of ship's timbers that lay across the main deck. "There's that, too, and the mizzen topgallant mast and yards could fall at any minute." He raised his voice slightly. "Major Windrush, you and the missus would be better moving elsewhere. If that raffle falls, you are right underneath."

Jack looked up at the mess above, with only the straining lower rigging holding it in place. He shifted further along the deck as Captain Hobson watched, unsmiling.

Brushing wet hair from her face, Mary looked around *Lady Luck*. "What happens now, Captain? Can you repair your ship out here at sea? Or do we continue the voyage with only half our masts and no sails?"

The captain glanced at the mate, who screwed up his face.

"We'll set up a temporary jury rig," Captain Hobson said, "but we're making too much water to sail right to London. No, Mrs Windrush, we'll have to head to the nearest land to fix her up. I'm sorry, but your journey home will be delayed by a few weeks."

"Sir!" the carpenter appeared from below, "we're making water fast. About two feet since I checked below. I reckon we're stove in below the waterline."

"Well, that confirms it," Captain Hobson said. "We head for the nearest sheltered anchorage."

"That would be somewhere in West Africa," Jack said. "Over there beyond the horizon."

"Aye," the captain said. "The Gold Coast; Cape Coast Castle if we can make it, although it's not the best anchorage in the world."

"And if we can't make it?" Mary was still calm. "We don't seem to have many boats left."

"We make for Elmina."

"I don't know that place," Jack said.

"It's part of our Gold Coast colony," the captain's eyes were never still, check-ing the rigging, the set of the masts, the actions of his crew and the slowly decreasing swell of the sea. "It used to be Dutch, but we took it over last year. I'm surprised you haven't heard about it."

Jack frowned. "Our regiment has been in Ireland, dying of fever in Hong Kong and doing a little soldiering in Penang. I've not had much interest in politicians redrawing maps in West Africa."

"Well, Major, you'll see it for yourself soon, if the old *Lady* holds out until we get there." Captain glanced looked aloft as another line parted. "I believe the anchorage at Elmina is more sheltered than Cape Coast although I've no charts."

"No charts?" Mary began to look worried.

Jack glanced at the waves, marbled grey-and-white and still as high as the mizzen-mast, their tips white and curling, with the remnants of the storm flick-ing spindrift onto *Lady Luck*. "We'd best leave you to carry on."

"Jack?" Mary clung to his arm as they inched along the deck. Pieces of loose gear rattled above them, with a block swaying precariously a few feet above the deck.

"It's as bad below," Jack said. Their cabin was a wreck, with seawater swirling three feet deep through a smashed porthole.

"All our possessions are in there," Mary gripped Jack's arm.

"The sea chests are water-proofed," Jack held her tight as the ship rolled from side to side. "Everything will be fine."

Captain Hobson shouted orders which saw the crew working aloft, clearing the worst of the mess and tossing cordage and splintered spars overboard. As the wind kicked up again, *Lady Luck* lurched, with seawater surging over the port quarter.

"Come on, old *Lady!*" Captain Hobson revealed a tenderness towards his ship that surprised Jack. "We'll get you sorted out."

With the south-west wind driving her on, *Lady Luck* plunged over the sea, raising clouds of spray as the crew worked frantically to save the ship. Captain Hobson and Harry Young nursed *Lady Luck* towards the shore, chasing the hands from difficulty to crisis as spars broke and water surged through holes in the hull.

"We won't make Cape Coast," Harry Young shouted. "We'll be lucky to reach Elmina."

"We'll be lucky to reach anywhere," Captain Hobson said.

With the waves only gradually decreasing and the masts creaking ominously, Mary lifted her head. "Can you smell that?"

"I can," Jack said.

"It's like the Indian jungle," Mary said, "yet different." She drew a hand over her head, pushing back her long black hair. "It's wilder."

"Aye," Jack peered eastward, trying to see through the curtain of spray.

"Have you ever been to Africa?" Mary asked.

"Never to stay," Jack said. "I passed through Egypt on my way to India back in '52, and touched at Cape Town a couple of times, but that's all."

"We're both strangers here, then," Mary said.

Battling against the offshore wind, *Lady Luck* limped closer to the shore, hour by wave-battered hour until Jack heard the call from the wreckage aloft. "Land ho!"

"We're going to make it," Jack said.

"I've never doubted it." Mary had somehow rescued Jack's sole remaining dry cheroot and lit it with a salvaged Lucifer. Waving the match in the air to extinguish it, she drew on the cheroot. "So that's Africa."

"That's Elmina," Captain Hobson said. "Thank you, Lord, for small mercies. If we can cross the bar, we might find the river there a better anchorage than Cape Coast."

"It's not what I expected." Borrowing the mate's telescope, Jack studied the large white building that dominated the town of Elmina. "It's like a mediaeval castle." He checked to ensure that it was the Union flag that hung from the flagpole. "Aye, it's British, thank God."

"It's charming. I'd like to visit that place." Shifting the cheroot to the corner of her mouth, Mary relieved Jack of the telescope. "I wonder if the captain will allow us to land."

"How long will repairs take?" Jack asked.

"Weeks," Harry Young said. "You'd be as well taking Mrs Windrush ashore as letting her remain here in a flooded cabin."

"We're making water fast," the carpenter looked even more worried than he had with his previous report. "There are more planks stove in."

"Let me see." Without hesitation, Captain Hobson swung down a length of rope to inspect the hold. He emerged swearing and sodden a few moments later, and in that short space of time, Jack saw the ship had settled further into the water.

"She waited," Mary murmured, still studying Elmina.

"Who waited?"

"*Lady Luck*," Mary said. "She waited until we were close to shore before she decided to sink. She was looking after her crew and passengers."

"Aye," Captain Hobson said. "The old *Lady* would do that." He gave Mary an approving nod before raising his voice. "Get the hands together! Salvage all that can be salvaged and then abandon ship."

Chapter Two

The news spread through *Lady Luck* in seconds. Most of the seamen looked over the side and towards the land, calculating how far they could swim.

"Are there sharks?" The carpenter asked.

"Not that I am aware of." The mate raised his voice to a roar. "Come on, lads; get what you need from the foc'sle and off we go."

"Wait here," Jack said and splashed down the companionway to the tiny cubicle he had shared with Mary for the past three months. Seawater lapped nearly to the deck above, ruining the bedding and any loose clothing. Fortunately, both he and Mary were experienced travellers and had packed their essentials into two sea-chests, with the remainder of their possessions travelling separately. Both chests were floating, chest-height in the cabin, washing back and forth with the movement of the ship.

Calling on a reluctant seaman to help, Jack hauled the chests on a deck which was now nearly on a level with the waves.

"Major Windrush," Captain Hobson said. "Take your wife ashore at once. You're no good to us here."

"How the devil do we get the chests to land?" Jack stared at the heaving sea between *Lady Luck* and the shore, and the white line of surf that crashed on the beach, a quarter of a mile distant.

"These men may help." Mary pointed the stump of her still smouldering cheroot at the half dozen canoes that came out from the shore, their prows rising high with the waves. "They seem to know what they are doing."

Propelled by two grinning, near-naked men, the first canoe came alongside, with the men handling their paddles with unconscious skill.

"Kroomen," Harry Young said. 'They're everywhere on this coast."

"Are you going ashore, my lady?" One youngster asked Mary.

"Yes," Mary said. "Our ship is sinking. Have you room for two people and two sea chests?"

The young Krooman said something to his companion, who swarmed on board without hesitation and helped Jack lift the chests into the canoe as if it was something he did every day.

"Your ship is sinking fast," the younger Krooman said. "Better hurry, my lady."

The second paddler waited until Jack helped Mary into the canoe before he joined them. "Sit in the centre," the paddler said, still smiling. Jack noted that his teeth were filed to sharp points, and close to he looked older than he had appeared from the deck. The Kroomen pushed off without another word, guiding the canoe through the waves to the beach beside the castle where tall palm trees waved in the breeze, and the surf boomed like thunder.

"Hold on," the leading paddler steered the bow of the canoe up the next wave. The muscles in his back shone like oiled ebony as he dug in the paddle, then abruptly changed hands and paddled from the other side. For a minute the canoe rode the surf, with growling waves on both sides of them and the beach approaching at a terrifyingly fast pace, and then they were hissing onto the sand with the roller breaking around them. The whole operation from boarding the canoe to fetching up on the beach had taken less than fifteen minutes.

"Welcome to Africa," Jack said.

"Elmina," the leading paddler said, as he leapt from the canoe, nimble as a youth although the more Jack saw him, the more he realised the Krooman was well into his middle age.

"Elmina," Mary repeated, stepping clear of the canoe into knee-deep water without turning a hair. She curtseyed to the paddlers. "Thank you, gentlemen. My husband will pay you."

Jack fumbled in his pocket, produced a silver crown and pressed it onto the first paddler's eager palm.

"Five shillings for twenty minutes work," he said. "That's good wages."

"Yes," Mary said absently. "I am not so sure I like this place, now I am close to it. There's a sinister atmosphere."

"Maybe so," Jack agreed.

The castle loomed above them, its white walls reflecting the sunlight while the snouts of cannon poked menacingly toward the sea. Whoever had built this place knew his job, for it stood securely on an outcrop of black rock at the end of a peninsula of sand. Jack saw the scarlet splash of military uniforms on the walls, and the multi-crossed Union Flag alternatively straining at the rope or hanging limp against the pole, depending on the vagaries of the wind.

"It's very impressive," Jack said, watching as the Kroomen unloaded the chests and carried them above the high-water mark. "I wonder what it was for, and who built it."

"So do I," Mary said. "Look, Jack, the ship's going. The old *Lady*."

As Jack looked out to sea, the last of *Lady Luck's* masts dipped underwater, leaving only a litter of wreckage. A dozen canoes ferried most of the crew towards the land.

"Nobody has drowned, at least." Jack watched as an unmistakable Royal Navy ship pulled alongside the canoes, and bluejackets shouted out to the survivors. Captain Hobson and Harry Young were last to be rescued, clambering on board the naval ship as a host of bluejackets clustered to help.

"Jack," Mary nudged Jack with her elbow. "We have company."

"Halloa!" The man wore a uniform that reminded Jack of the French Zouaves he had seen in the Crimea. "Castaways are you?" He glanced at Mary. "Venus rising from the waves, no less!"

"How do you do?" Jack extended his hand.

"Welcome to Elmina and all that." The man was about twenty-five, with an open, freckled face and the voice and bearing of an officer however unfamiliar his uniform. He wore baggy blue trousers below an open scarlet jacket, while on his head he wore a turban wrapped around a red fez. His handshake was firm and vigorous. "You'd better get off the beach and into the castle." He glanced at the chests. "I'll have some of the lads bring your kit up. I'm Walter Hopringle by the by, or Lieutenant Hopringle, 2nd West India Regiment if you're interested."

"I thought the uniform was unfamiliar," Jack said. "I've never met your regiment before. I am Major Jack Windrush, 113th Foot."

Hopringle's smile vanished. "Major!" He straightened to attention. "My apologies, sir. I had no idea."

Jack glanced down at his civilian clothes. "There is no reason to apologise, Hopringle. You could not have known."

"Thank you, sir." Hopringle gave an awkward bow to Mary. "Mrs Windrush."

"Lieutenant Hopringle." Despite her sodden clothes and sand-stained boots, Mary still managed to make an elegant curtsey.

"This way, if you please," Hopringle spoke over his shoulder. "You might have chosen somewhere quieter to be shipwrecked, sir, and Mrs Windrush. We expect all sort of excitement here over the next few days."

"What sort of excitement?" Jack's military eyes noted that the fort had a river on one side and the sea on the other. It would have been a secure defensive position except for the ramshackle village that straggled along the spit to within pistol-shot of the castle walls. A curious crowd gathered at the edge of the settlement, watching the drama offshore.

"Oh, the Ashantis, of course."

"The what?"

"The who," Hopringle corrected. "The Ashantis are the dominant people of the Gold Coast area."

"The local tribe," Mary said.

"The Ashanti are a bit more than a tribe," Hopringle led them to a flight of steps ascending to a gateway in the white wall of the castle. "This is the Door of No Return," he said, "from the old slave trading days."

Mary lifted her head. "Slave trading?"

"Yes, Mrs Windrush. This castle, St George's, was a major slave trading post for the Portuguese and the Dutch."

Mary looked around her in disgust. "I knew I didn't like this place."

"I'll have your baggage brought in." Hopringle lifted his voice. "Sergeant Wickham! Bring four men!"

They entered a long chamber, dimly lit by flickering lamps. The arched ceiling seemed to press down on them. Mary shivered as the echoes of their voices seemed to waken memories of past suffering. "I like this place even less," Mary said.

A file of a sergeant and four West Indian soldiers clattered into the chamber, all wearing the same Zouave uniforms as Hopringle. The sergeant saluted Hopringle while the men looked sideways at Jack and Mary.

"Go to the beach, Sergeant Wickham," Hopringle said quietly. "You'll find two sea chests there. Take them to the officers' quarters."

"Yes, sir." The sergeant was a broad-shouldered man with two scars on his left cheek. He glanced at Mary as he hurried past, with his men as smart as guardsmen.

"This chamber is where the Dutch and Portuguese held the slaves," Hopringle said. "Some of them may have been the ancestors of my men."

"I can feel them," Mary shivered. "Their sorrow is still here." She felt for Jack's arm.

From the slave dungeons, Hopringle escorted them to the sun-blessed castle courtyard, from where tall white walls, punctured by shuttered windows, rose all around. Stairways led to defensive platforms, wrought iron railings, partly rusted by the salt air, eased around balconies and soldiers of the 2nd West India Regiment spoke to blue-coated Royal Marines. Jack was relieved to escape from even that brief visit to the dungeons.

"That's the church," Hopringle nodded to the most significant building within the fort.

"Shackle the slaves and pray for forgiveness," Mary did not hide her distaste.

"And up there," Hopringle said, "is where you will be staying." He led them up a flight of wooden stairs to the upper stories where the rooms were lighter and airier, with an onshore breeze ruffling the cane curtains.

"I hope you're comfortable here," Hopringle opened a heavy door to a surprisingly fresh chamber. "I only pray you have time to get used to it."

"Why is that?"

"The Ashantis," Hopringle's grin merged his freckles into an orange mass. "They don't want us here."

Jack grunted as his mind took stock of the situation. "You have an impressively strong fort here. How big is your garrison?"

"We can rustle up a couple of hundred on a good day, including Hausas, that is native police from Lagos, further up the coast, plus bluejackets, Royal Marines and my own Wests."

Jack nodded. "Two hundred men behind the walls of a strong fort. How many men can these Ashantis muster?"

Hopringle stepped aside as the Wests bustled up with his men and the sea chests. "We estimate around fifty thousand."

"So many?" Jack did not hide his surprise.

"So many," Hopringle said. "And they also have allies and friends among the neighbouring tribes." He nodded to the small window. "If you look out there, sir, you'll see Elmina village."

"I noticed it when we arrived," Jack said.

"The Elminas are staunch allies of the Ashantis." Hopringle said, "which could be awkward as they're so close to the fort."

Jack became aware of Sergeant Wickham listening at the door.

"You'll have duties to attend, Sergeant," Hopringle acknowledged Wickham's salute with a nod.

Jack felt Wickham's gaze as the sergeant left the room. He raised his head and stared back until Wickham dropped his eyes and withdrew.

"Why allow the natives so close to the fort if they are hostile?" Jack surveyed the native village, estimating the numbers. "There must be a few thousand people there."

"The village was there long before we took over Fort St George," Hopringle said.

"I see." Jack accepted the explanation. "How effective are your men, Hopringle? I confess I know nothing about West Indian soldiers."

Hopringle's smile was back. "They are about the best in the business, Major. Loyal and brave to a fault."

Watching as Mary inspected the room, Jack invited Hopringle to sit on one of the three cane chairs. "I have not heard anything of them, Hopringle."

"No," Hopringle suddenly sounded defensive. "As they are black troops, they don't get the credit they deserve. Our lads serve in the worst conditions and have the toughest and most thankless tasks in the British Army."

"Where do they serve?" Jack sank into a second chair.

"In the fever jungles of West Africa, the White Man's Grave," Hopringle's smile had vanished as he spoke of his regiment, "and across the West Indies and Central America. My lads did a lot of good work against the French and Americans last century, and Private Hodge of the 3rd Wests won a Victoria Cross in the Gambia only a few years ago."

Mary had stepped closer to listen. "Why are these things not better known?"

Hopringle shrugged. "Either because we're a regiment of black soldiers, or because British newspapers don't write about regiments where there is no local interest." He leaned back in the chair. "Newspapers exist to make money, and where there is no interest, there are no sales. So my Wests are destined to work without recognition."

"Except by their officers and the men who fight alongside them," Jack said. "A bit like the 113th Foot or the Sepoys from what they call non-martial races."

"Quite so," Hopringle said. He rose from his seat. "Now, if you'll excuse me, sir and Mrs Windrush, I am sure you'll want to get settled in. Colonel Festing will no doubt wish to see you later."

"Thank you, Lieutenant Hopringle," Mary said. "It was very kind of you to help."

Jack heard the distant thud of a musket but said nothing. A shipwreck and a slave station in one day was sufficient drama for Mary.

Chapter Three

ELMINA, GOLD COAST COLONY, JUNE 1874

The setting sun brought the drums. Mary heard them first, lifting her head and frowning as she walked to the window.

"Can you hear that, Jack?"

"I hear them," Jack said. He remembered the drums beating out their warning along the North-West Frontier of India. "There is something ominous about drums at night. They sound more menacing when you can't see the drummer."

"I wonder what they are saying." Mary stood at the window for a few moments with her head cocked to one side.

The drumming increased in volume, seeming to penetrate the walls of the fort and creep into Jack's head, so they became part of his mind, rhythmic, alien and intrusive. Lying on the hard bed in the heat of the night, he swatted at the circling insects, listening to the insistent beat.

"I can't sleep either," Mary threw herself on the bed.

"The drummers are trying to unsettle us," Jack said. "Don't allow them."

"I'd be unsettled even without the drums," Mary said. "This is a bad place, Jack, worse than any we've been in."

"The slave chambers?" Jack asked.

"I can feel the slaves, Jack," Mary said. "I can feel the despair down there. The people have gone, but they left something behind them. It's as if a part of them never went away."

Jack pulled her closer. "It's nearly seventy years since we stopped the slave trade. It was all a long time ago."

"How much time doesn't matter, Jack. That depth of hurt doesn't disappear. It haunts the place," Mary said. "Some people can sense the tragedy on places of distress. Others, such as you, Captain Jack, are cold-blooded Englishmen with no sense of the spiritual at all."

"Not all Englishmen are cold-blooded," Jack said quietly. "Anyway, I'm part Indian, remember?"

"You know what I mean!" Mary moved to the edge of the bed and sat up.

Aware of the effect the idea of slavery had on Mary, Jack decided it was best to say nothing.

"I've had a recurring nightmare ever since I was small," Mary spoke so softly that Jack had to strain to hear her words. "I dreamt I would be a slave, being led away in chains. I used to wake up crying and in a terrible state. I can't imagine anything worse."

"It won't happen," Jack assured her.

"It happened here," Mary said. "It happened to hundreds of thousands of people right in this building."

"It's stopped now," Jack said.

"No, it still happens," Mary contradicted him. "The Arabs still have slaves and so do some tribes up there," she jerked her head towards the interior of Africa. Rolling over, she clung to him. "Promise me something, Jack."

"What's that?"

"Promise me that you'll never let anybody take me as a slave."

"That's an easy promise to make, Mary. You know I wouldn't let that happen."

Mary nodded. "I know, but that place scared me. I could feel the anguish of these poor people."

The drumming continued, a resonant throb that seemed to echo around the room, rattling the pitcher and ewer on the dressing table, making it difficult to think.

"I thought I'd sleep after all the excitement of the day," Mary rolled back to her side of the bed and lay back, watching the stars through the open window. "I was wrong."

"Maybe you're overtired," Jack said.

"I don't like this place, Jack. I hope we can get a ship home soon."

"So do I," Jack realised that the drumming had stopped as suddenly as it started. Somebody shouted, high and clear, and then there was silence except for the distant crash of surf.

Mary was asleep, with both hands behind her head. Smiling, Jack rearranged her to be more comfortable, eased out of bed and stepped to the window. In the open ground on the other side of the Benya River, beyond a suburb of Elmina village, Jack saw moonlight gleam on something. Although he could not be sure, he thought it looked like an umbrella, but why anybody should be walking in the night under a yellow umbrella, he could not imagine.

Pulling the shutters closed, he lay down beside Mary. He was an old enough campaigner to grab sleep whenever he could, for the morrow could bring unpleasant surprises. In his head, he still heard the drums.

* * *

"Major Windrush!"

"Sir." Jack drew himself to attention, with the air already stuffy in this small room.

"Lieutenant Colonel Francis Festing, Royal Marine Artillery." Heavily bearded, the colonel stood erect beside his desk. He surveyed Jack through level grey eyes on either side of a straight nose. "I heard you were shipwrecked here yesterday."

"That's correct, sir." Jack knew that Festing was a veteran of the Baltic and Crimean campaigns and the Chinese War. Festing knew his business.

"Well, that was a piece of damned bad luck for you, but could be opportune for us." Festing remained standing as he spoke, forcing Jack to do the same. "You have some experience in action, I believe."

"Yes, sir, Burma, Crimea and the Mutiny, as well as the North-West Frontier."

"I remember hearing about a Windrush in the Crimea. Royal Malverns was it not?"

"No, sir," Jack said. "That was my half-brother. I was with the 113th Foot."

"I don't know them," Festing dismissed the subject. "What do you know about Africa?"

"Not much, sir. I've never served in Africa."

"Well, now is your chance. I am requisitioning you for my little army. Do you know of the situation here on the Gold Coast?"

"Only what I've picked up since we came ashore, sir. We bought Elmina from the Dutch a few years ago, and now the Ashantis are massing to attack us."

Festing managed a small smile. "I suppose that's all a soldier needs to know. However, I'll give you a little more background information. Sit down, Windrush."

It was an hour before dawn, and they were in a small office on the upper floor of St George's Castle. From the window, Jack had a view to a starlit beach, festooned with waving palm trees and a few canoes, while a line of phosphorescence marked the crashing surf. Successive occupiers had furnished the room with a very ornate desk that looked as if it had been in the castle since the Portuguese were in charge, a heavy Dutch armchair and half a dozen cane-chairs. Jack settled on one of the latter, feeling the structure creak under his weight. Festing positioned himself behind the desk.

"The Portuguese built this fort back in the fifteenth century," Festing said, "and the Dutch grabbed it, either by agreement or war, I don't know or care which." He shrugged his shoulders to show his contempt of other European nations. "However the Ashantis – I'll come to them later – claimed the place, and rather than fight, the Dutch paid them about £9000 a year rent or tribute. That suited both parties, for the Ashantis were the chief suppliers of slaves, so the Dutch were guaranteed a steady supply and the Ashanti, a regular customer."

Jack nodded. "Thank God we stopped that hellish business."

"Aye," Festing looked up. "Thank God we did, but in doing so, we made some dangerous enemies. When we ended the Slave Trade back in '07, the Ashantis, and other tribes who had made a good living supplying European states and others with slaves, got a rude shock. The Ashantis had expanded their empire at the expense of neighbouring tribes partly to capture slaves; it became the reason for the Ashantis' existence."

Festing fixed Jack with a long look. "As you can imagine, the Ashantis were displeased when we stopped the slave trade and instituted anti-slavery patrols along the coast."

"I imagine so, sir," Jack said.

"We've had a few difficulties with them, including a war back in the twenties when the Ashanti killed our Sir Charles McCarthy, cut off his head and made the skull into a drinking cup."

"Charming people," Jack murmured, wondering where Festing was leading.

"Oh, absolutely delightful," Festing said. "Just the sort you wish to bring home to tea with mama."

Jack decided he could smile.

"We had another Ashanti war in the 60s, and then, a few years ago, the Dutch transferred Elmina to us. King Kofi Karikari of the Ashantis, or the Asantahene, as they call him, claims he owns the place and wants us to continue the payments that the Dutch made."

"And will we pay them?" Jack asked.

Festing visibly stiffened in his seat. "Her Majesty will not pay a penny to people who use the heads of British generals as drinking cups."

"No, sir," Jack said. "Of course not." He paused for a few seconds. "Although paying the rent might save the treasury a fortune. Wars tend to be expensive in currency and lives."

"National prestige is more important than mere money," Festing said. "If one foreign potentate gets away with it, who knows who'll try it next? Perhaps Spain will demand tribute for Gibraltar, or Prussia for Heligoland." He shook his head. "No, Windrush, Great Britain cannot go along that road. We don't want war, but we'll draw a line in the sand. If the Asantahene wishes to co-operate, then we can all be friends. If he chooses war, then war it shall be."

"I believe we only have a few hundred men in the colony, sir," Jack said.

"The bulk of the Second West India Regiment is coming from Bermuda to re-inforce us." Abruptly standing, Festing walked to the window. "Ah; that's what I like to see. Come here, Windrush and I'll show you Her Majesty's response to demands."

The ships sailed past the coast in line astern. Even without the White Ensign at the masthead, there would be no mistaking them for anything except Royal Navy warships, with the neatness and precision that Jack expected from the Senior Service. There were only two warships, a sloop and a gun-vessel, with their size hardly impressive by navy standards, but each towed several ship's boats from which a cannon or rocket-trough projected, and they joined another sloop off Elmina.

"HMS *Decoy*, *Druid* and *Argus*," Festing indicated each vessel in turn, "towing boats from the squadron we have at Cape Coast Castle, eight miles up the coast."

"Yes, sir."

"You must have noticed the native town beside the castle wall," Festing said.

"I did, sir," Jack said.

"The men of Elmina have openly supported the Ashantis, and they want the Dutch back here," Festing explained. "The Ashantis store weapons in the town and the Ashantis strut around with great arrogance as if they rule the roost. Now that the navy's here, I can do something about it."

"Yes, sir. What do you wish me to do?"

"I want you to go along with the 2nd West India," Festing said. "A man with your experience could be a steadying influence." He looked at Jack. "I am well aware that you have never worked with West Indian soldiers but the more British officers, the better."

"Yes, sir." Used to army life, Jack accepted the command without expression although internally he felt the old familiar slide of mixed dismay and excitement.

"Captain Brett is in charge of the West Indians; report to him and offer your services." Festing sighed. "I hope there won't be any awkwardness because you outrank him."

"None at all, sir," Jack said. "It is his regiment."

* * *

From the battlements of St George's Castle, Jack looked down on Elmina, a village of brushwood and timber houses that had grown up in the lee of the castle. While the larger section of the town, the King's Quarter, was on the same side of the river as the castle, the smaller, the Garden Quarter, was on the opposite side, across a low, broad bridge. Jack watched the navy's boats take up their positions on the river, with their cannon pointing toward the King's Quarter.

"What about that part of the town?" Jack indicated the Garden Quarter.

Captain Brett was a steady, sober man with the lines of responsibility etched deeply in his face. "The people there are friendly to us."

Jack nodded, noting that the Garden Quarter had some decent stone-built houses.

"And there?" Jack indicated a smaller fort further inland.

"That's Fort St Jago. We don't have the manpower to occupy that." Brett shrugged, "we've scraped up all our reserves for this little operation today, let alone garrisoning anything inland."

"What's out there, Brett?"

Brett screwed up his face. "Past St Jago, there is a lagoon and a chain of small hills; I've never been out there, but I hear the local people are hostile.

They preferred the Dutch, who did not interfere with their quaint local customs such as slave-owning and human sacrifice."

Jack grunted. "I see."

"Here we go," Brett said as Festing stepped into the courtyard of the castle, where a score of the local chiefs and dignities had gathered. Some sat on elaborately carved stools, others sheltered under elaborate umbrellas and two had little boys at their feet, either their sons or for purposes that Jack did not wish to consider.

"You are all welcome," Festing said. "Her Majesty, Queen Victoria, who owns this castle and this town, is displeased that some misguided people in Elmina have been openly aiding the Ashantis."

The chiefs and dignities looked at him without expression.

"Some foolish men in this town have been giving the Ashantis arms, ammunition and gunpowder, with the Ashanti have been using to kill, terrorise and enslave Her Majesty's subjects."

A few chiefs nodded sagely, although Jack was unsure if they agreed that such events had taken place, or the opposite.

Colonel Festing continued: "I will shortly fire a cannon. You have one hour after that signal to hand your weapons to St George's Castle, or I will bombard the town."

"Well, that was short and sweet," Brett said as the chiefs turned and left, most without saying a word. "They won't believe the colonel, though. The Dutch were forever making empty threats."

Jack remembered Festing's level gaze and fighting experience. "I think they'll find that Colonel Festing is no Dutchman." He nodded. "Now, Captain Brett, where do you want to place me?"

"This is most awkward as you outrank me, sir."

"I am here by mischance, Captain. You know your regiment best, so where would I be most useful?"

Brett looked embarrassed as he spoke. "If the Elminas don't hand in their weapons, Major, could I prevail upon you to take half a company and hold that bridge?" He pointed to the bridge across the Benya River that linked both quarters of Elmina town.

"I'll do that willingly," Jack said. "Although we could be bolting the stable door after the horse has carried away the hay." He watched a trickle of men and women cross the bridge, most carrying household goods and some with bundles that looked suspiciously like firearms.

"Aye, that's so," Brett said, "but we've given a time, and we must stick by our word." He gave a twisted grin. "After all, we are British officers."

The bang of the cannon echoed across the castle and town, setting a score of dogs barking and causing some women to scream in alarm. White powder smoke drifted from the castle out to sea, where the Royal Naval vessels floated as a reminder that Britain's power extended everywhere there was salt water, and many places there was fresh.

"That's Colonel Festing's signal. We have one hour to wait," Jack watched the trickle of people across the bridge increase to a steady flow. "By that time there won't be many people left in Elmina."

"As long as the women and children are safe," Brett said. "We don't want to war on innocents."

Hopringle glanced at his watch. "I'll check on our men," he said. "They might be getting restless."

"I'll come along," Jack wanted to see the unit he was going to command.

The Second Wests looked like any other regiment that Jack had served with, except for the black faces. The sergeants barked them to obedience the same way; there was the same mixture of old soldiers with greying hair and young recruits desperate to prove themselves, confident men and men who jumped whenever a sergeant barked. Jack looked them over, aware that they were also inspecting him.

"We might be called upon to go on duty soon," Jack said to his half-company. "If so, we'll be holding the bridge against gun smugglers." He watched their faces, looking for the eager and the trouble-makers, marking his men.

One man looked particularly enthusiastic, nearly stepping forward when Jack passed.

"What's your name?" Jack asked.

"Private Samuel Stair, sir! Are we going to fight the Bushmen?"

"He means the Ashantis, sir. That's the rankers name for them," Hopringle explained.

"Good man, Stair. You'll get your chance. We'll all get our chance." Jack nodded to Sergeant Wickham. "Carry on, Sergeant."

"Sir!" Wickham gave a smart salute.

"They seem a decent bunch," Jack said as they returned upstairs.

"None better!" Hopringle was enthusiastic about his regiment. He checked his watch. "That's the hour about up."

"Give them another hour before we open fire," Festing had his binoculars trained on the town. "They seem reluctant to comply." One elderly man tottered up on matchstick legs, dropped off a broken Tower musket and wandered off, duty done. A young boy followed, threw a stick against the gate, lifted the Tower musket, sighted against the castle wall and dropped it in disgust.

The first hour passed, then the second. A second broken musket joined the weapon at the castle gate, but still, Festing hesitated to give the order to fire. He sighed, checked his watch, and shook his head. "I'll give them until noon."

"I'll get off to the bridge." Ensuring his revolver was loaded, Jack marched downstairs where his half-company of West Indians were waiting in the court-yard.

"Right lads! Are you all set?" Out of habit, he checked their rifles, noting that they were the old pattern muzzle-loading Enfields rather than the newer breech-loading Sniders. "Keep together now. Don't be too eager, Stair, trouble will come whether you seek it or not."

"Yes, sir!" Stair bellowed.

Jack nodded to Sergeant Wickham. "How are the men, Sergeant?"

"All set, sir." Wickham stood at attention.

"Stand easy man; we're not on parade." Jack faced the fifty men, noting the nervous eyes of two of them. "Right lads, you don't know me, I don't know you, and none of us knows what this day will bring."

The men watched him, expressionless except for Stair. Jack noted the smell of rum and wondered who had been drinking.

"In a few moments, we'll be marching out to guard the bridge between Elmina and the mainland. Our duty is to ensure that nobody carrying arms tries to leave, and no Ashantis enter." Jack recognised the excitement that ran through him. "I've heard that the 2nd West is as good a regiment as any in the British Army so we should get on fine."

"Sir," Sergeant Wickham spoke as if he was addressing a deaf man thirty yards away. "Permission to speak, sir?"

"You're my sergeant, Wickham. You don't have to ask permission. Speak, man!"

"Thank you, sir. Are you the Captain Windrush who fought through the Crimea War and the Indian Mutiny?"

"That was me," Jack said.

"I thought so. Thank you, sir." Wickham said.

"Right lads; follow me!" Jack led the way, wishing he led men from his 113th rather than these unknown West Indians. However, both Hopringle and Brett claimed the Wests were good soldiers when well-led, which could describe any regiment in the British Army or any other army, Jack guessed.

The Wests filed after Jack, each man with his Enfield at his shoulder. They looked smart enough, Jack conceded, yet he hoped he never had to fight the Ashantis with these raw troops.

Although Jack had spent much of his twenty-one years in the army in India, the tropical sun felt different in Africa. It was a damper heat somehow, less friendly. As he marched through the castle, he saw the Royal Marine artillerymen working on the castle's guns, training them to aim at the town. The artillerymen were sweltering, dripping drops of sweat onto the stone slabs.

Clattering from the castle, Jack led his men onto the wooden bridge. "Halt! Stand at ease! Stand easy!"

The Wests stood across the entrance to the bridge, Enfields in hands, sun shining on the red jackets and waving turbans. To Jack, they were unfamiliar, foreign-looking soldiers, and he wondered if he would ever get used to them.

Beyond the Garden Quarter, on a plain between the coast and the fringe of what appeared to be a never-ending forest, Jack saw a large number of men gathering, all carrying firearms, mostly muskets but a few with more modern rifles. They were bare-chested, some with kilt-like clothes of multi-coloured stripes, others with long white robes from the waist down. He frowned as he saw a group of men standing under a bright yellow umbrella.

I saw that umbrella last night, Jack told himself. *You were walking in the open, examining the castle of St George.*

"Sergeant," Jack nodded to the umbrella. "Do you know anything about that?"

"An umbrella is the sign of a chief or a nobleman," Sergeant Wickham said at once. "The Ashantis use umbrellas as we use regimental colours or flags."

"Do they indeed? Thank you, Sergeant." Lifting his binoculars, Jack focussed on the men beneath the umbrella. There were four. One held the umbrella; tall and muscular, he had the dull eyes of a menial. Jack ignored him. The next carried a long Tower musket and wore a bandolier across his shoulder. He was a foot soldier, a bodyguard perhaps, tough-looking and handy to know. Jack nodded and slid his attention to the next man, a slim, wiry young man with a strange cap on his head and a gold hilted knife at his waist.

"Now, you are somebody who matters," Jack said. "I'll watch for you."

When he focussed on the fourth man, Jack knew he had found a chief. Half a head taller than any of the others, he stood proud, nearly haughty, with a broad face under a leopard-skin cap adorned with ram's horns and eagle-feathers. A multi-coloured robe decorated in geometrical shapes descended from his shoulders, while around his waist, a gold –hilted sword hung almost to his ankles.

"'Sergeant Wickham." Jack passed over the binoculars. "What do you make of that fellow?"

The sergeant took the binoculars gently, as if afraid to damage them. He put them to his eyes and looked away until Jack showed him how to focus.

"The men under the yellow umbrella are of the Edwesu tribe of the Asante, the Ashanti as you call them," Wickham said. "Asante means 'because of war'."

"I thought the Ashanti was one tribe," Jack said.

"They are a fusion of many tribes of the Akan people," Wickham explained. 'The Oyoko and the Edwesu are the most warlike. I don't know that man's name." He handed back the binoculars.

"He's important, then," Jack said. "Thank you, Sergeant."

"He's a chief or perhaps a minor king."

Jack studied the group below the yellow umbrella again until the crowd surged and a score of men blocked his view. The umbrella remained in place, dominant above the mass.

Jack checked his watch. Noon: That was the final deadline. "Load, lads. Sergeant, check the rifles." He could nearly taste the tension in the air. The Ashantis had threatened war by invading the British colony, and now the British had retaliated. The next few moments would decide if this game of dare and bluff would escalate into war, or if Colonel Festing would back down.

"Sir," Wickham said. "The enemy is collecting."

"I see them, Sergeant," Jack said. "We may have to fight on two fronts here. Number the men from one to fifty, with the even numbers facing the town and the odds the plain." He watched as Wickham obeyed. "Make sure every man has his rifle loaded."

Jack looked up as a pair of vultures flapped clumsily past the castle to land on the ground a hundred paces beyond the bridge. With their long bald necks and predatory eyes, they looked like the scavengers they were.

Further to his right, a hundred and fifty of the Hausas lined the riverbank, their red fezzes distinct. Their officers seemed to have them well in hand, although Jack thought the men were excitable, like recruits on their inaugural Field Day. He glanced over his Wests, growling unnecessarily.

"Keep steady, men. Show these Hausas how real soldiers behave."

"Hausas are not soldiers," young Private Manning said slyly. 'They're Bushmen in uniform." He laughed, relapsing into silence when nobody else joined in.

Despite expecting the sound, Jack started when the cannon from the fort fired, with great tongues of orange flame and jets of dirty white smoke erupting across the town. The gunboats were next, fifteen seconds later, sending a storm of shot crashing into Elmina. The iron cannonballs smashed through frail walls, ripped at thatch roofs and cascaded along now-deserted streets.

We're at war, Jack said to himself. *My fourth official war and I should not even be here. Now the Asantahene will know that he cannot treat the British with the same contempt as the Dutch. I only hope I can send Mary to safety before this thing expands.*

Chapter Four

ELMINA, JUNE 1873

"Steady now, lads," Jack spoke above the bark of the artillery and the sharp orders of officers and NCOs. For a moment, he wondered how Mary was faring, told himself that she was familiar with army life and had lived through far worse than a minor native war, and watched the progress of the bombardment. The smoke already formed a white bank around the boats, so they fired blind, shot after shot and shell after shell howling into the King's Quarter of Elmina.

Within a few moments, a house exploded, with a sound louder than any of the British cannon. Broken pieces of timber and burning palm-thatch rose high above the smoke, hovered for a few seconds then drifted back down, setting fire to other thatched roofs.

"There must have been gunpowder stored there," Jack said, as his men openly wondered. Young Private Manning backed away until Sergeant Wickham roared him back to his position.

"You're a soldier, Manning, remember? Not a Bushman in uniform."

Jack wondered if Manning appreciated the dark humour as his initial doubts about bombarding what he had thought to be an innocent town faded a little, and vanished altogether when a second house erupted in fire and smoke, and then a third. "The colonel was right," he said above the crack of cannon fire and crackle of flames. "The Elmina men are storing arms and powder for the Ashantis."

"The Ashanti and Elminas are waiting to fight us, sir." Sergeant Wickham gestured to the men who continued to mass on the plain.

"Our duty is to guard the bridge, Sergeant," Jack said as Wickham moved forward as if to challenge the entire enemy host. "Keep vigilant in case the Elmina people try to storm the bridge."

There was no sign of movement from Elmina. Jack saw one of the boats fire a rocket, with the fiery trail glowing through the smoke before the missile exploded against the wall of a stone-built house. By now, most of the town was ablaze as fire from the burning powder-stores spread to the other buildings. Smoke rose in choking clouds, with the gunfire and rockets from the castle and Royal Navy adding to the confusion.

"Sir," Sergeant Wickham was tense, moving from foot to foot as he stared at the village and then at the mass of men standing in the clearing.

"The enemy is firing back, sir."

Peering through the smoke, Jack saw the flashes from the massed Elmina men and Ashantis as they fired at the naval vessels and the Hausas who lined the river bank. Although the yellow umbrella had advanced to the Ashanti front rank, the smoke was too dense for Jack to see the men beneath. He started when something struck the parapet of the bridge beside him, ricocheting away with a vicious whine. The bullet had left a raw scar in the wood and bent the top of a nail.

"The enemy's firing at us," Private Daley, a handsome young man, raised his rifle. Jack saw the beads of nervous sweat on his upper lip.

"Don't fire yet," Jack was not a believer in blooding his men by allowing them to take casualties, but that might have been a stray shot. By firing on the enemy, he would invite retaliation by a vastly larger force. "Lie down on the ground, aim at the enemy and wait for my orders. Nobody fire yet."

Jack looked up as something cooled his cheek. An offshore breeze was stirring the smoke, shredding it to increase visibility. He could see the wreckage of the village and the dull green of the forest. Two more vultures had arrived, waiting for the fresh meat that fighting humans always provided.

"Sir!" When Private Edward Ogston nodded to the enemy, Jack smelled the rum on his breath. "Over there."

As Jack watched, warriors filed from the forest to join the more ragged ranks of the Elmina men, with one entire company forming up around the yellow umbrella.

"Ashantis!" Sergeant Windham nearly hissed the words as he brought his rifle to his shoulder.

The Ashanti warriors moved in disciplined formations, most carrying long, old fashioned muskets while a few held more modern weapons. War captains, older men with long robes and an elaborate close-fitting head-dress, stood in front of each formation, clearly giving orders. One of these war captains approached the group at the yellow umbrella and then moved his company to the far flank of the Ashanti horde.

"They look a formidable bunch," Jack ran his experienced eye over them. "And the fellow with the umbrella appears to be in charge."

"The Ashanti are the best forest fighters in Africa," Windham's eyes were intent on the enemy as more emerged from the forest, including a man under a scarlet and black umbrella. "And they have royalty with them."

"Royalty?"

Yes, sir." Windham aimed his rifle.

"You're out of range, Sergeant," Jack said. "If they come closer, you can have a pot at them."

Jack glanced behind him. His half company of Wests was the only barrier between the Ashanti army and the castle. On one side of the river was the now fiercely burning town and on the other, the Garden Quarter, where the more loyal inhabitants watched proceedings from the doors of their houses or huddled in small groups. *They'll be praying to their ancestral spirits that the British can protect them from the Ashantis*, Jack thought.

As the boats continued their bombardment, the Ashanti army and their Elmina allies moved closed and opened a terrific fire. The slugs barely reached the navy boats, but the Hausas wavered and looked towards the bridge.

"I told you the Hausas are only Bushmen in uniform," Private Manning sneered. "We'll be shooting them soon." He lifted his rifle in readiness.

"Settle down, Manning," Jack said. "The 2nd West doesn't shoot our friends."

A bugle sounded, high and shrill above the barking of the guns and crackle of flames. Within minutes the castle gate slammed open, and the garrison marched out, with the Royal Marine Light Infantry, the Jollies, in front, followed by the bright colours of the 2nd West Indians and the more sombre Hausas. Amongst the troops, the bluejackets, the Royal Navy landing party, stood out with their peculiar rolling gate and the cutlasses hanging from their belts.

"Stand ready, men," Jack said.

"Windrush, isn't it?" Freemantle, the Royal Naval captain in command, stopped for a second beside Jack. "Leave half your men here, Major and bring the rest with us. You'll be eager to join the fun."

"Yes, sir," Jack said. "Sergeant Wickham! Remain in charge here."

"I'd prefer to come, sir." Wickham stood at attention, looking every inch the professional soldier.

"Not this time, Sergeant," Jack said. "I need you here. Don't worry; you'll get your chance." He frowned when he saw Wickham about to protest and closed off any possible insubordination with a quick. "Guard the bridge. That's an order."

Years of discipline snapped Wickham to attention. "Yes, sir."

"Fleet Marines and bluejackets," Captain Freemantle gave quick orders, "take the right flank. Marines of the garrison, 2nd West India and Hausas, take the centre and left." He led the way with a long lope, his sword dangling at his side.

"Come on, lads!" Jack marched towards the enemy, pulling his revolver from its holster. A glance over his shoulder revealed his Wests marching forward resolutely. Private Coffin was singing under his breath, Daley looked nervous, while Ogston was impassive. At their side, the garrison Marines had already fixed bayonets. On average the Marines were smaller and lighter than the 2nd West, lithe men with a swing to their step, hurrying forward towards the enemy.

"Halt!" Freemantle ordered.

The British force stopped amidst the smoke from the burning town. They remained static as the Ashantis fired at them, the deep thuds of muzzle-loading muskets sounding like artillery but most of the shots dropping short. Jack saw a single Hausa stagger and hold a hand to his chest as if in wonderment.

"Aim!" Captain Freemantle ordered.

Jack ran his gaze over his Wests. They lifted their Enfields handily enough, although some held them loosely, rather than cuddling them close to their shoulders. He pushed down the barrel of Private Stair's rifle. "Aim at the Ashantis, Stair, not at the sky. The clouds are not your enemy."

"Yes, sir," Stair said with a smile.

"Fire!" The Marines' Sniders and Wests' Enfields cracked out with jets of white smoke. As Stair stepped back with the recoil, Jack made a mental note to ensure the men cleaned their rifles later.

The front rank of the Ashantis wavered as the rifle bullets slammed into them, although the yellow umbrella remained proud above the smoke.

"Reload!"

The Marines inserted cartridges into the breech, with the sun reflecting on the brass. Armed with the muzzle-loading Enfields, Jack's half company were noticeably slower, with Private Daley fumbling the percussion cap, dropping it and stooping to pick it up.

"Advance!" Freemantle snapped, pacing forward five steps. The Wests moved without hesitation, with the powder smoke shredding around them.

"Halt!" The British line halted. Two deep, the British looked vulnerable against the mass of Ashantis and Elminas. Every yard they came closer to the enemy, the British bullets were more effective, passing through men in the dense mass of the Ashantis. Yet every step also brought them closer to the far more numerous Ashanti muskets. Gunsmoke rolled between both forces, with the deep roars of the Ashanti war-cry sounding as background noise, aided by the rattling thunder of the drums. Behind the warriors, Jack thought he saw a horde of women in bright dresses, urging their men on, and then Freemantle lifted his arm.

"Fire!"

Another British volley crashed out, with the 2nd Wests firing steadily, although Jack saw some of the Enfield barrels were still too elevated. *I'll sort out their marksmanship after this affair is completed.*

The smoke hid any results of the volley, and the Ashantis replied, their muzzle flashes showing as orange spurts.

"Load!"

There was another rattle of brass from the Marines, another flurry of percussion caps from the Wests. Jack saw his men knocking the butts of Enfields on the ground to drop the bullets down the barrels.

"Advance!"

Advancing and firing, the Marines and sailors of the centre and right faced the bulk of the enemy. Jack's Wests were on the left flank, slightly further back, slower to load but every bit as ready to take on the enemy. Jack watched his men; they were fighting well, although their marksmanship was shocking. It was relentless, this advance and fire against the enemy.

"Halt! Fire!"

Again the bullets smashed into the Ashanti ranks, shivering their morale, knocking down the warriors. Jack heard a Marine laugh. 'If you get two directly behind each other, Joe, you can bowl them over together.'

"I like to see the beggars jump when the bullets hit them. Make them dance for King Kofi!"

Seen closer to, even behind a blanket of powder smoke, the Ashantis looked frighteningly dangerous. They were big men, as tall as the Wests, taller than the Royal Marine Light Infantry, and held their muskets with the confidence of long practice. However, the Marines, West Indians and Bluejackets were more disciplined and had more modern weapons, with the Ashantis beginning to waver as their casualties mounted. They withdrew, step by step, towards the forest, still firing, but outranged by the British guns. Few of the Ashanti shots took effect although Jack saw one of the West Indians crumple to the ground and lie still while others fell, groaning or writhing with wounds.

The men under the yellow umbrella remained in the centre of the Ashantis, with the black-and-red umbrella slightly further back.

"Right lads," Jack shouted. "When we fire again, I want everybody to aim at the group under the yellow umbrella. Whoever these men are, they are organising the enemy."

Even as he spoke, Jack knew he was wasting his words. The Wests were such poor shots that targeting the men with the yellow umbrella was probably making him the safest man in the Ashanti army.

Behind the Ashantis, Jack saw the women again, urging their men on, cracking sticks over the heads and backs of any who turned away, pointing to the advancing British and yelling.

"Lieutenant Quinn!" Freemantle's voice carried even above the intermittent thunder of the Ashanti musketry. "Take your Marines and clear the bush running parallel to the beach. Windrush; your Wests go in support!"

Quinn was a young man, as eager as all these Marines seemed to be. He grinned at Jack. "Come along, sir! My lads will do the work, and your Wests can watch and learn."

Jack met Quinn's smile. "When the Ashantis chase you back, we'll be here to stop them."

The bush was thicker than Jack had realised, with a mixture of shrubs, plants and flowers intertwined beneath trees that soared up to 200 feet. Creepers barred the passage of anybody not equipped with a long knife while the atmosphere was stifling, with the air so dense Jack found it hard to breathe. He felt the sweat burst from his pores the second he stepped off the beach onto the narrow path, with its twists and turns and clouds of flying insects.

"Come on, men," Jack checked his revolver and strode, on with his Wests a few yards behind.

Facing the Ashantis in the forest was utterly different from fighting them in the open. When the Marines attempted to extend into skirmishing order, with two yards between each man, the thick bush impeded their vision, and they instinctively closed their files. The officer's orders echoed through the trees.

"Open your ranks, Marines! Skirmish order!"

Quinn remained on the path, giving sharp commands to his men as they pushed through the foliage. Thirty paces behind, Jack arranged his men, waiting for the first sign of the Ashantis.

"They've all gone, sir!" A Marine shouted in the hard accents of Northumberland. "They've run."

The response came almost at once as half a dozen Ashantis opened fire. They hid behind trees and bushes to fire their long muskets, but for every shot they fired, the Marines, with their faster-loading Sniders, could fire four, and British bullets were more potent than the slugs of the Ashantis. The British moved on, blasting at every gush of powder smoke and gradually driving the Ashantis out of the woodland. Jack followed the Marines, with his Wests hardly firing a shot, ensuring the Ashantis did not try to ease around the British flanks to take the Marines in the rear.

"There's one!" Private Stair lifted his Enfield and fired, with three more Wests following his example.

"Don't fire unless you're sure of your target," Jack shouted. "We don't want to pot a Marine. Their heads would be ugly decorating our wall."

Some of the Wests smiled, others looked puzzled, not understanding the humour.

There was a flurry of activity to the left as the Marines dealt with a nest of resistance, and a single Ashanti warrior ran toward them. Private Ogston knelt and fired, with the shot clipping a tree branch ten feet above the man's head. Private Daly tried next and missed by about three feet, so Jack aimed his revolver and fired three rounds, knocking the man backwards.

"We're doing target shooting once we've cleared away the Ashantis," Jack promised. "I've never seen such poor marksmanship."

As the British advanced on two fronts, the Ashantis melted into the main forest, only for a large formation to appear behind the British ranks.

"Bugger that!" A young Marine said as the Ashantis ran up an area of high ground beside the beach. "They're persistent buggers, aren't they?" He looked exhausted, with his face brick-red and his sweat-dark uniform clinging to his slight body.

"Clear them off, lads!" Thankful for something constructive to do rather than following Lieutenant Quinn's men, Jack led his Wests toward the high ground.

"Volley fire on my command," Jack said, stepping back to see how the men reacted. Their first volley was reasonably controlled, with a few shots finding their target, but after that, they lost cohesion and began to fire wildly, without aiming. The bullets whistled in all directions, including towards the other British soldiers.

"Right, that's enough!" Jack had to grab Private Jackson's rifle to prevent him from firing again. "Cease firing!"

The musketry had not dislodged the Ashantis from the high ground. They stood there with a colourful green-and-yellow flag flying, drums beating and, Jack noted with interest, the same two groups of chiefs standing together under the shade of umbrellas. High above the group, a man taunted the British with a Dutch flag.

"Bayonets, lads! And follow me." Reloading his revolver, Jack strode forward. As always in action, he felt a surge of elation, tempered by the dread he could be wounded and left a faceless, mewling cripple.

As soon as the Ashantis saw Jack's men marching forward, they began a fire that kicked up sand or hummed through the air around the Wests. Jack saw a slug burrow into the sand a few feet in front of him, like some fast-moving insect. Stepping over the little mound, he calmed his nerves with a deep breath.

"Come on, lads, the quicker we get there, the less time we're under fire!" Jack increased his pace, hoping that his men would follow. Instead, they gave a yell and charged forward, some overtaking Jack in their enthusiasm to reach the Ashantis' position.

"Damn your eagerness! Keep in formation!" Jack swore, realised the Wests did not listen to his words, swore again, and ran with them.

The Ashantis faced the West Indians for a few moments, still firing, with the flags waving and the nobles beneath the umbrellas standing firm. Only when the Royal Marines came in support did the Ashantis drift back towards the forest. Rushing forward, a Marine and a Hausa reached the Dutch flag together. As the Marine bayonetted the Ashanti, the Hausa grabbed the flag, only for the Marine to snatch it back. By that time the rest of the Marines, with the Hausas and Jack's Wests, pursued the retreating Ashantis into the fringe of the forest until the shrill notes of a bugle ordered them to return.

"Come on!" Jack dragged a snarling Private Stair back from the trees. "The Ashantis will be waiting for us!"

One by one, his Wests withdrew from the forest, with Manning taking a final shot and Private Coffin singing a quiet psalm as he reloaded his Enfield in the shade of a giant banyan.

"Form up!" Jack ordered. Pushing his men into a column of fours, he counted them. "One man wounded."

"Hargreaves, sir." Coffin said. "He's gone back to the castle."

Jack noted that some of the Marines encouraged captured Ashantis back at the point of a bayonet, while a blue jacket wiped the blood off the blade of his cutlass.

"Back to the bridge, lads." Jack stopped Private Stair from pursuing the entire Ashanti army into the forest and watched the orderly withdrawal of the Marines and Naval Brigade. Except for the litter of Ashanti bodies and the drift of powder smoke, nothing seemed to have changed.

"You did not bad," he said as they took up their former position guarding the bridge. "Except for your marksmanship." He nodded, grimly pleased. "We'll soon get to work on that."

* * *

"I wonder if anybody back home will ever hear of that battle." Mary watched the Naval Brigade and Marines from the fleet board the boats that took them back to their ships. In the few days since her arrival, Mary had altered their room to make it more comfortable, cleaned it of cobwebs and dust and put out a few of their possessions to look more like home.

"I doubt one man in a thousand could point to the Gold Coast on a map, let alone realise we have a colony here," Jack looked through the window at the dark forest. "I don't know why we are in this God-forsaken place."

Mary pulled on a cheroot and exhaled blue smoke into the room. "The name should give a clue," she said. "The Gold Coast. Gold is the local currency, Jack, with an ackie of gold worth half a crown and a periguin about ten shillings.

There is gold inland, and I am sure the Ashanti use slaves to mine it." She pulled a face. "I truly despise slavery. Imagine people owning a fellow human being. What sort of mentality is that? I can't think of anything more despicable than tearing somebody away from their home and making them a permanent chattel, yet it was a way of life and still is," she pointed to the forest with her cheroot. "In there."

"Aye," Jack nodded. "I once thought that only Europeans and Americans took slaves from Africa. I had no idea the Africans used slavery too."

"Aye, Jack, we were heavily involved." Mary glared at Jack as if he had been personally responsible for the slave trade. "But there has been slavery in Africa forever."

"I hope we can get away from here soon." Jack knew better than to challenge Mary when she was laying down her law. "I'll talk to Colonel Festing tomorrow, and if he doesn't need me, we'll hitch a lift on the first Royal Navy ship going back to Britain."

"The British and African Company has regular mail steamers that stop at Cape Coast Castle," Mary told him. "I'm sure we can get a couple of berths on *Loanda* if we can get to Cape Coast."

"Cape Coast Castle?" Jack said. "That's only eight miles away. We might manage that."

"We can walk that in a few hours," Mary blew out more smoke. "Hire some porters to carry our baggage, and we'll be there by this time tomorrow."

"There are about 50,000 Ashantis out there," Jack reminded. "They might not let us pass them."

Mary's look could have melted cheese. "Let them try," she said, "just let them try."

A bugle blared again, insistent, accompanied by the urgent shouts of officers and the drumbeats of boots.

"It looks like I'm needed again," Jack kissed her gently on the forehead. "Don't stray far, Mary. The Gold Coast is a dangerous place."

Mary nodded without looking round. "Take care of yourself, Jack." Only when Jack left did she take a deep draw of her cheroot to calm her suddenly trembling body. "And may God protect you, Captain Jack. Please bring him back safe to me, Lord. Don't let anything happen to my Jack in this terrible place."

Chapter Five

Colonel Festing stroked his whiskers as he spoke. "The Ashantis are back in force, gentlemen. It seems that we did not teach them a sufficiently severe lesson earlier today."

Looking around the gathering of officers, Jack saw the tired, wan faces and wondered if these men could fight for long in this tropical climate. West Africa seemed even unhealthier than India.

"Our friendly natives report that an Ashanti noble called Kumi Okese boasts he will burn the Garden Quarter of Elmina and capture Fort St George. I intend to stop him."

Kumi Okese. Jack repeated the name. He recalled the men beneath the two umbrellas, the black satin and the yellow, and wondered which one had issued the threat.

"Will the navy help again, sir?" Lieutenant Hopringle asked.

"I believe so, Hopringle," Festing managed a faint smile. "Otherwise they will have no fort to defend and no anchorage to call their own."

Jack thought of the handful of Hausas and West Indians, plus the few hundred bluejackets and very young Marines. They were brave enough, but when pitted against tens of thousands of Ashantis who were fighting for what they believed was their property, it was hardly a fair contest. The British would have to maximise their advantages of better discipline and superior weapons.

"The Ashantis are coming in force, gentlemen, and fast. They are about two miles north of the town near the salt ponds in the plain and heading towards us."

"Can we hold the fort, sir?" Hopringle asked.

"I will fight the Ashantis in the open," Festing said. "I don't intend to let them near Elmina. This Kumi Okese fellow promised to kill the white men and enslave the white women in the town."

Jack stiffened. "Did he now?" He thought of Mary's abhorrence of slavery. "I don't think we'll allow that."

Festing fixed Jack with a steady look. "No, Major Windrush. We won't allow that."

"Captain Freemantle, I want your Marines and bluejackets to remove any Ashantis from the Garden Quarter."

Freemantle nodded. "We'll do that." There was no hesitation in his voice.

"Windrush, you seem to have a bit of a roving commission. Go with the West Indians; they have a shortage of officers." Colonel Festing said. "You'll have to take a command beneath your rank, but in the present emergency, I am sure you will understand."

"Yes, sir." Jack nodded.

"Right, off you go and the best of British luck to you all." Festing managed another smile. "Shoot straight, gentlemen."

Once again, Jack felt the strange mixture of apprehension and excitement as he marched out with the West Indians. Sergeant Wickham marched with great determination, glaring at the Ashantis as if they were his personal enemies, while Ogston swayed slightly.

"Ogston," Jack stepped beside him, "lay off the rum."

Ogston's eyes were huge as he stared at Jack.

"Shoot straight," Jack said, marching ahead.

The Naval Brigade trotted out of the castle with their cutlasses bouncing at their hips, beards on their chins and straw hats at jaunty angles. Jack thought they were almost a throwback from an earlier age. He could imagine these men fighting alongside Nelson at Trafalgar, Duncan at Camperdown or even with Hawke or Anson.

"Come on, lads! We're not guarding a bridge this time," Jack said. "We're chasing the enemy back to his forest." He caught Sergeant Wickham's eye. "You'll get your chance to fight now, Sergeant."

Wickham nodded, fingering his Enfield. He looked very intense.

As the Naval Brigade and Marines spread into the houses and trees of the Garden Quarter, the Ashantis and Elmina men opened fire from behind a wall.

The deep thud of their muskets echoed from the buildings, with the crash of slugs against stone a second later.

Led by a young midshipman, the sailors and Marines gave a loud cheer and charged forward, with the sailors leaping over the wall, cutlasses flashing in the evening sun as they leapt down on the Ashantis. One sailor fell back, doubled up as a slug hit him.

Sergeant Wickham edged toward the fighting, his face contorted.

"Don't be distracted, Sergeant," Jack said. "There are plenty more Ashanti for us!"

Stiffened by a sizeable body of Royal Marines, the Wests and Hausas advanced against the Ashanti army. Ashanti drums sounded non-stop, with flags fluttering above the chanting warriors. When Jack swept his binoculars over them, he saw again that most carried long muskets with exquisite gold decorations, while umbrellas sheltered the captains and chiefs. As before, a group of women stood in the rear, singing and carrying powder horns and sticks.

"That's new," Jack passed his binoculars to Hopringle. "There's a bunch of lads right at the back."

"They're carrying whips," Hopringle said after an examination. "I wager they're to ensure nobody runs from the fight."

"That could be right," Jack said.

The main Ashanti army had split, with one section advancing in front of the main body and a third, ragged group of ill-armed men pushed to the van.

"Skirmishers," Jack said.

"Bushmen slaves," Sergeant Wickham grunted. "Musket fodder."

"You seem to know a lot about the Ashantis, Sergeant," Jack examined the enemy, searching for weaknesses.

"I know too much about them," Wickham said.

Jack spared him a glance. "After this battle, Sergeant, you can tell me more. In the meantime, keep the men in order."

"Yes, sir." Wickham continued to glare at the Ashantis.

Although Jack outranked Lieutenant Quinn, he was experienced enough not to interfere in other units, so he concentrated on his Wests and gave Quinn free rein with his Marines.

"Keep in formation, Wests," Jack said for the fifth time. "Don't break ranks even when the fighting begins. That means you, too Stair!"

"Yes, sir!" Stair responded with his usual smile.

When they were three hundred yards away, the Ashanti skirmishers opened fire on the British with a huge volume of smoke and noise.

"Never mind the shine, Wests!" Jack knew how alarming the first taste of action was for inexperienced men. "It's all noise and smoke. They're well out of range!"

The drums began again, joining the high-pitched singing of the women. The warriors increased the noise with a deep-throated chant that crossed the space between them and the British.

"If noise won battles, the Ashanti could conquer all Africa," Jack said. "I wonder what the words mean."

Wickham spoke quietly. "The Ashantis are saying: 'If I go on, I shall die; if I stay behind, I shall be killed. It is better to go on.'"

Jack glanced at the sergeant. "You're a man of hidden depths, Wickham."

"It is the Ashanti tradition," Wickham said. "If they run away, the chief's policemen will kill them, or the women."

"Interesting concept," Jack said, as the Ashanti fired another ragged volley, this time with some of the shots landing among the British.

"Keep in line, men!" Jack shouted. "Don't fire until I give the order."

The British moved on, mostly ignoring the torrent of slugs from the Ashantis, whose advance force had joined the skirmishers. When they were about 250 yards from the still advancing enemy, Lieutenant Quinn ordered the seamen and Marines to open fire. As the Sniders cracked viciously, the Wests looked hopefully at Jack.

"Wait," Jack said, acutely aware of the low standard of marksmanship among his men. Marching them on another twenty paces, he gave the welcome order. "Aim low and drive into the smoke, lads!"

Jack saw a pair of Hausas crumple to the ground without a sound. The British line marched on, halted to fire, loaded again, marched, halted to fire, loaded and marched on. Each volley felled a dozen or a score of the enemy without seeming to reduce their numbers or the volume of fire they returned. The hammer of the drums continued, with the blare of horns and the high screeching of the women.

Bedlam, Jack thought. *We are at the sharp end of soldiering, marching towards an enemy in an alien land.*

"I hope these Ashanti lads break before we reach them," Quinn said to Jack. "There are thousands of them. We must be outnumbered twenty to one, and I don't fancy charging them with the bayonet."

"It's not as bad as that," Jack said, checking his Wests, "here are our supports coming now."

After clearing the Ashantis from the Garden Quarter, the bluejackets and Marines hurried to the right of the main British body.

"That's much better," Quinn approved. "Now the odds are only ten to one."

"Advance!" When Colonel Festing gave the order, the British moved forward again, marching and firing in a succession of volleys that tore into the Ashantis, whose main force now merged with the advance guard, with the umbrellas visible above the smoke. Jack saw the familiar yellow umbrella prominent in the centre-right, with the red-and-black umbrella at its side.

Kumi Okese, he said to himself. *I'd wager my pension that's you under that umbrella. I thought you were going to capture Elmina! Not today, my friend; not today.* Beside him, Jack could feel Sergeant Wickham edging forward.

"Stay in formation," Jack shouted. "We have to meet them as a cohesive force."

"Yes, sir," Wickham growled.

The Ashantis withdrew a few paces, still firing until the yellow umbrella lifted high above the smoke.

"They're making a stand," Jack said as the Ashantis halted beside a large pool of salt water. The light was fading fast, eroding visibility, enhancing the muzzle flares of the Ashantis' muskets.

"Halt!" Festing ordered. "Fire three volleys. Fire!"

"Steady boys!" Jack said as his Wests began to rush to keep pace with the Marine's breech-loaders, going for speed rather than accuracy. "Keep the men in order, Sergeant!"

"Yes, sir!" Wickham said, and snarled at his men.

With British bullets tearing into their ranks, the Ashanti army began to disintegrate. As a rising wind cleared some of the smoke, Jack saw first one, then two Ashantis, and then groups of a dozen or more, turn away from the Sniders and withdraw into the thick forest. Only the men around the umbrellas remained, firing in disciplined volleys that would have done credit to any infantry in the world.

"You're a good soldier, Kumi Okese," Jack said, "whatever else you might be." He watched as Sergeant Wickham knelt to fire, aiming each shot and grunting with satisfaction when his chosen target crumpled to the ground. As he fired, he mumbled something in a language that Jack did not understand.

Lieutenant Quinn stepped across to Jack as the Marines took up position beside the Wests. "We're pushing them back, except for that group around the yellow umbrella. They're a stubborn bunch and no mistake."

"That's Kumi Okese, I believe," Jack said.

"It could be King Kofi himself, for all I know," Quinn said. "I don't believe in finding out about the enemy. It's easier to kill them when they're only targets."

"I like to know my enemy," Jack said. "The more I find out about them, the more I can work out their tactics." Lifting his binoculars, Jack studied the men beneath the umbrellas.

With the onshore breeze continuing to shred the powder smoke, Jack saw the two captains standing side by side. The man under the red-and-black umbrella was less tall than Kumi Okese, younger and festooned with golden jewellery. The warriors around the umbrellas remained static, each man sporting vertical white lines down his face and each arm.

"These must be the Ashanti equivalent of the Guards," Jack said, knowing the image would always remain with him.

Without saying a word, Wickham dropped a ball down the barrel of his rifle, rammed it home and carefully placed a percussion cap in place. Kneeling, he aimed at the younger captain, took a deep breath and squeezed the trigger. Jack knew immediately that the shot would go home. He saw the Ashanti captain stagger, saw the tall man beneath the yellow umbrella jump to his aid as a collective shiver ran through the Ashanti ranks. The man with the yellow umbrella seemed to stare directly at Windrush and Wickham, and then the breeze died, and smoke closed around the Ashantis.

"You got him," Jack said.

"I did," Wickham reloaded hurriedly. "I'll get that other fellow, Kumi Okese, now."

"Everybody aim beneath the yellow umbrella," Jack ordered. "That's where one of their chiefs stands."

As Jack spoke, the Ashantis fired in a torrent of smoke and flame. The slugs pattered around the West's ranks, hitting two men. One gasped, writhed and stood up, while the other felt the lump of ironstone that had lodged in his forehead.

"Thank God these Ashantis don't have modern weapons," Jack said.

"And they can thank God we don't have more men," Quinn said. "Or we'd burn their whole blessed country to the ground."

The Wests aimed and fired, and had time for a second shot, but the yellow umbrella remained in place, standing firm through the smoke. The black-and-red umbrella vanished.

"Some of them are running," a Marine with a Devon accent said, and Colonel Festing ordered the bugle to call cease fire. The bluejackets led the cheering, with the Royal Marines next and the Hausas and West Indians joining in enthusiastically.

"There goes the last umbrella," Quinn said.

Bright through the smoke, the yellow umbrella withdrew with a final blare of horns. The drumming continued for a few moments, slowly diminishing to a single beat that also stopped. Only the harsh breathing of the Wests and the soft moaning of wounded Ashantis disturbed the silence.

"By George's wig," Quinn said. "I rather think we've beat them."

"I rather think we have," Jack said.

Wickham reloaded his rifle, staring through the smoke. "I hope we got Kumi Okese, sir."

"So do I, Sergeant," Jack said. "Do you have some personal animosity towards the man?"

Wickham hesitated before replying. "No, sir. I only wished to test my shooting."

"Well, that's a damned lie," Jack said. "You're a good shot, the best shot in the company by far. What's the real reason?"

"There is no other reason, sir." Wickham remained impassive except for a single bead of sweat that ran down his temple.

Jack grunted. "Let's have a look then. You other Wests stand easy. We'll be back directly."

Scattered bodies showed where the Ashantis had stood, many with the white stripes down face and arms. One wounded warrior raised his musket and fired a last defiant shot at Jack, with the slug going nowhere. Wickham kicked away the weapon and allowed the man to die.

"I can't see Kumi Okese's body," Jack said. "Or the body of the man with the gold jewellery."

"The Ashantis retrieve the bodies of their nobility," Wickham said. "We may have killed these two chiefs.' He turned over one of the corpses with his foot. "Or they may be alive and well."

"I hope we've killed enough to persuade King Kofi, not to attack British territory again," Jack said.

Wickham shook his head. "No, sir."

"No, sir?"

"I know of the Ashanti, sir," Wickham spoke with perfect sincerity. "Unless they are utterly defeated, they won't give up. They will come again and again until they have swept every last British man, woman and child into the sea, and then they will enslave and slaughter every other tribe in the area." When he looked up, Wickham's eyes were clear. "They'll chop down the Fanti fetish trees – the sacred trees - to show they've defeated the Fanti gods, enslave the white women, decapitate any white prisoners and display their skulls on their war drums."

"Are they that bad?" Jack studied the forest edge. It was too dark to be sure, but he thought he saw movement there, as though the Ashantis were watching him.

"They are the devil's brood, sir; worse than anything you can imagine."

For a moment the forest leaves parted and Jack saw a man standing under the trees. Kumi Okese was staring directly at him, and without a word, he lifted his right hand and pointed. Jack felt himself shiver; he knew that the man had singled him out. Raising his binoculars, Jack stared back at the Ashanti, and even at this distance, he recognised the malevolence in Kumi Okese's brooding eyes.

Then the leaves closed and he was alone with Wickham, the bodies of the Ashanti and the drifting smoke.

Chapter Six

CAPE COAST CASTLE JUNE 1873

"So this is Cape Coast Castle," Mary said. "I think I preferred Elmina." She looked in distaste at the castle that rose from the shore, with the lines of high surf marking the beach. A ridge of reddish-brown clay stretched in both directions, with scrubby plants fighting for space under a weeping grey sky. In the centre of the ridge, crushed into a gorge, was the settlement of Cape Coast Castle. Three hills thrust up, each surmounted by a square-built fort, while the most significant feature was the castle itself, with the union flag hanging limp from its staff.

"Do the British deliberately choose situations with the most awkward places to land?"

"Of course," Jack said. "That's how we test British pluck, don't ye know?"

"No, Jack, that's how we test British stupidity," Mary was not in the best of tempers. "How do we get ashore? Will the navy take us?"

"I think we land by canoe again."

Mary sighed, looking at the heaving waves that ended in crashing silver-white surf. "If we must. Come on then, Jack. Let's get this over with."

A collection of canoes bobbed alongside HMS *Druid*, the wooden screw-corvette that had carried Jack and Mary from Elmina. Most were the native fish-canoes, little more than hollowed-out tree trunks, while a few were the more sturdy craft known as surf boats. Mary chose one of the latter and charmed a couple of seamen to lower their chests into the eager hands of the Kroomen paddlers.

"Hello my lady! Hello, sir! Thank you!" The Kroomen grinned as they helped passengers into the surf boats.

The closer they came to Cape Coast Castle, the less Jack liked it. There seemed to be a high number of decayed buildings with sagging roofs, and far too many people milling hopelessly on the shore. He was too intent on watching the town to realise that they were near the shore until the boat gave a massive lurch, her bow rose nearly vertically, and they were speeding with frothy surf on each side of them and the roar of a breaking wave in front. They beached with a crunch of sand, and Mary stepped unaided into the shallow water.

"That's us ashore again," Jack helped the Kroomen pull the surf boat further up the beach, where they unloaded the chests. "Now we'll see about getting you a ship for Britain."

"I'm not leaving without you," Mary said. "We're going on leave to visit our son, and I'm staying until your duty is done. There is no argument, Captain Jack."

People packed the streets, some evidently locals while most were refugees fleeing from the Ashanti invasion. They stood in huddled groups, staring at nothing, talking together or trying to beg food from equally unfortunate people.

"Look at that," Mary pointed to an emaciated woman carrying an ancient man on her back, "and that," a baby sitting in a puddle in the road, ignored by everybody.

Mary lifted the child. "Who's in charge here, Jack?"

"The Governor," Jack said, "whoever that may be."

"Why isn't he doing something about these people? They've starving!"

"I'm sure I don't know," Jack said.

"I'm sure you can find out and get something done," Mary said, with the light of battle in her eyes. "I won't see people suffering like this."

"We've only arrived," Jack said.

Mary shook her head, holding the baby close to her. "I know that, Jack Windrush. Find the governor and get him told."

"I will, as soon as we're settled." Jack looked up as a harassed Marine lieutenant rushed towards them.

"Major and Mrs Windrush, isn't it?"

"It is," Mary answered for them. "Who is looking after these people?"

The lieutenant looked at her. "Looking after them?"

"That's what I said."

"I've come here to take you to your accommodation," the lieutenant was about thirty, with a skin yellowed by fever. "I don't know about anything else."

"This gentleman is not the man to ask," Jack felt a mixture of pride for Mary's concern and embarrassment as her verbal assault on an evidently harassed officer.

"Where is the Governor?" Mary moderated her tone slightly.

"Colonel Harley, the Administrator-General might be in his office in Government House," the lieutenant gestured vaguely towards the town.

"Then that's where I'll see him." Mary stalked away, still carrying the child.

"Mary!" Jack shouted after her, knowing he was wasting his breath. Once Mary set out on a crusade, she let nothing stand in her way. Jack pitied Colonel Harley with an animated Mary crashing through his door.

The lieutenant glanced at Mary, decided to say nothing, and gestured to a group of watching Kroomen. "You, men! Take these chests."

Jack watched the Kroomen lift the chests as if they were feathers. "Where are we going, Lieutenant?"

"Green Lettuce Lane, sir. I'm afraid there is no suitable accommodation in the castle for a married couple."

"I am sure Colonel Harley will be pleased about that."

"Quite, sir! This way, if you please." The lieutenant led the way at a brisk pace that the Kroomen matched easily, despite the heavy chests. Refugees crammed in every street, staring at Jack with dull eyes and the occasional hopefully outstretched hand. Jack could taste the fear in the air. It was worse than the atmosphere in India during the Mutiny, for then there had been defiance and the anger of revenge. These people lacked even hope.

"Can we not band these men together?" Jack gestured to the staring refugees. "Arm them and train them to fight the Ashantis?"

"They wouldn't fight, sir," the lieutenant said. "They run at the first sign of the Ashantis. They need us to protect them."

"Surely some of them can be trained." Used to the sepoy regiments of India, Jack found it hard to believe that so many fit, strong young men would not wish to fight back. "They're a fine-looking people."

"They're cowards, sir," the lieutenant said. "It's as simple as that." He halted at the end of a street of flat-roofed, stone-built houses. "Here we are, Sir. Green

Lettuce Lane. It's not the most salubrious area in the world, but the best available at present."

Jack could see nothing green in the street and not a sign of a lettuce. "I've lived in much worse," he said as the Kroomen hefted his trunks into the house, laid them down with a thump and waited hopefully. Sighing, Jack passed over half a crown, knowing he was over-paying.

"A shilling is the going rate, sir," the lieutenant advised.

"Aye, but these lads might be paddling the canoe taking my wife out to the next ship," Jack said. "I hope to give a good enough impression that they take care of her."

"Yes, sir." The lieutenant said no more.

The house had four rooms and a kitchen, with windows on the upper storey that afforded a view of a lighthouse. Jack had barely settled in when Mary came to the door.

"Colonel Hartley wishes to see you," Mary said as she entered. "His official title is the Administrator-General of the West African Settlements, and he's very proud of his position."

"I hope you haven't upset him too much, Mary," Jack looked around for the child.

"Hardly at all. I handed over the baby to the local church; it's the best I could do." Mary smiled. "I'll get this town organised Jack, once I've cleaned up our house. Now go, and sugar talk the colonel. He's in Government House, top floor."

* * *

The Royal Marine on duty slammed to attention and called for the sergeant, who conducted Jack to a very airy room. Jack entered with a feeling of trepidation, wondering if Mary had angered Harley or if there was another reason the Administrator-General should want to see him.

As soon as he stepped inside the room, Jack knew there was trouble ahead. Three men stood in a small huddle amidst a cloud of blue tobacco smoke. One was Colonel Festing, who gave him a cordial nod, the second a man he did not know but guessed to be Harley, and the third advanced towards him with a broad smile and his hand outstretched.

"Windrush! Jack, my dear fellow! How good to see you again!"

"Colonel Hook," Jack felt the sick slide of dismay as he took Hook's hand. "I did not know you would be here." Jack had known Hook as the Head of Intelligence in India and later in Britain.

"Major General Hook, now, Windrush." Hook said. "As soon as your wife spoke to Harley, I knew you were in West Africa, and I thought to myself: Jack Windrush! The very man!"

Thank you, Mary, Jack thought.

"I'm a regimental officer now, sir," Jack reminded. "I haven't been involved in anything political since that Fenian business in North America."

"I know," Hook ushered Jack to one of the four seats that stood around a central table. "Cheroot? Drink? Whisky was your tipple, was it not?"

"It still is, sir," Jack admitted cautiously. He liked Hook well enough but knew that when any senior officer expressed such delight at a meeting, there was trouble in the wind.

"I understand you two know each other?" Colonel Harley was a tall, dignified man with straggly whiskers and hard eyes. In common with so many British on this coast, his skin bore the yellowish tinge of fever.

"Oh, we go back a long way," Hook said. "As far back as the Mutiny. Isn't that right, Jack?"

"Yes, sir," Jack said cautiously. "General Hook, or Colonel Hook as he was then, sent me on some political missions in India and along the Frontier."

"In North America too, old fellow," Hook murmured.

"North America, too," Jack said. "But now I am a regimental officer and thankfully no longer involved in such matters."

Harley and Festing looked at one another before Festing spoke. "I saw you in action at Elmina, Windrush. You are a fighting soldier who leads from the front. I had no idea you were also talented in other directions."

Jack sipped his whisky, watching a beam of sunlight seep through the window to highlight the amber liquid within the crystal of the glass. It was strange to think that a spirit distilled beside the Spey in the far north should glow with strong sunshine in West Africa. "I have little talent, sir."

"I've met your wife, Windrush," Harley said with a slight smile. "If you can control her, you have immense talent."

Jack smiled. "I have never managed to control that woman, sir."

"Fighting Jack Windrush, his men call him," Hook said, "and he's just the man for the job, although he'll deny it."

Jack sighed. "What job is that, sir? I'm only passing through Africa. My ship was driven in by bad weather, my uncontrollable wife is in a rented house in the town, and our son is waiting for us back home."

Hook smiled. "And how is the redoubtable Mary?"

Jack noted the oh-so-casual use of his wife's Christian name. "Mary is looking forward to going home to see our son, sir. We both are."

"Ah, David, isn't it? He'll be a fine young man now. I'll arrange for Mary to be on the next steamer, in a first-class cabin, paid for by Her Majesty's government. That should keep her happy and ease any worries you have on her part. If everything goes well, you'll be able to join her within a few weeks. I'll ensure you have passage on the first available steamer."

Acutely aware that three senior officers were watching him and assessing everything he did, Jack took his time with the whisky. *Is it worthwhile kicking against the pricks? No; they would only turn a request into an order, with bad feeling on all sides.* He had been a soldier for twenty years, long enough to know it was better to accept the inevitable with good grace.

"Thank you, sir," Jack said. "Mary will enjoy travelling first class after being squeezed into a tiny cabin in a sailing ship." He mustered what he hoped was a convincing smile. "What is it you wish me to do?"

Jack felt the atmosphere in the room relax.

"Good man, Jack. I knew we could rely on you. Tell me, what do you know about the Ashanti Empire?"

"Only what I've learned here, sir."

Hook nodded. "I'll try and keep this brief. The Ashanti are Akan people from further west and moved to this part of Africa about two hundred years ago. They started as a minor tribe, paying tribute to the then larger Denkyira nation until around 1700 a priest named Anokye summoned a golden stool from heaven."

Jack sipped at his whisky, raised his eyebrows and waited for signs of scorn from the other officers present. When they gave no indication, he took another sip and listened, aware that Hook would not talk of such things unless he thought them essential.

Noticing Jack's scepticism, Hook gave a small smile and continued. "The Golden Stool drifted down onto the knees of the then king, Osei Tutu. Anokye, the priest, claimed the stool held the spirits of the Ashantis' ancestors and as the king was its guardian, he was also the guardian of all the Ashanti tribes."

Hook paused for a moment. "In case you are unsure, Windrush, the Ashantis, like all the tribes in this area, worship their ancestors. That is their religion."

"I see, sir," Jack said.

Nobody else in the room spoke. Jack heard a sergeant's voice from the courtyard outside, and the crisp marching of a Royal Marine guard.

Hook continued. "The Ashanti kings used the Golden Stool to unify all the Ashanti tribes. It was not only a link between the king and his people but also a link to their ancestors."

Jack fidgeted on his seat, acutely aware of the importance of symbols to any nation.

Hook lowered his voice. "Unless you understand their beliefs, you can never understand a people. If we are to defeat the Ashantis, we must first know what we are fighting."

Jack nodded.

"United under the Golden Stool, the Ashantis began empire building. They imported guns and gunpowder from the Dutch who they saw as a tributary nation and conquered a host of Akim tribes, the Sefwi, Banda, Wassaw, Gyaman and others. They invaded the plains to the north of the forest belt and eventually controlled everything from the River Volta to Assinie, which is the westernmost port on the Gold Coast. Naturally, each victory brought them territory and slaves."

"Slavery seems to be endemic here." Jack sipped his whisky. "With us part of it."

Hook nodded. "What we did was appalling and utterly disgusting. We encouraged tribes such as the Ashanti who captured tens of thousands of slaves and sold them to the European and American slavers. It was supply and demand: the Ashanti wanted European goods and supplied slaves in return." Hook paused for a moment, staring at Jack. "The Ashantis also kept slaves for mining gold, clearing land and other purposes including human sacrifice."

Jack nodded; he did not wish to think about the slave trade.

"When Britain led the way in ending the slave trade in 1807, we immediately became unpopular in West Africa. Nations like the Ashanti and Dahomey had built up a culture based on catching and selling slaves."

"Yes, sir." Jack fidgeted in his seat. Not naturally a patient man, he wondered what this history lesson had to do with him.

"Nearly done, Windrush," Hook read the expression on Jack's face.

"When we outlawed the slave trade in 1807 the Asantahene, the High King of the Ashanti tribes, sent his army to the coast. They smashed the local tribe, the Fantis, and we agreed to pay the Ashantis rent for our forts and trading posts.' Hook paused for a moment. 'Remember the context, gentlemen. We were in the middle of a war with Bonaparte at the time, so a minor colonial skirmish in Africa was hardly important."

"Yes, sir,' Jack finished his whisky.

"That situation continued until the 1820s when the first crown governor, as opposed to a commercial trading company, took over the forts. Our man, Sir Charles McCarthy, refused to pay bribes to the Ashanti and tried to protect the Fanti chiefs. He brought a small army inland, but when he faced the Ashantis, the Fantis ran away. The Ashantis killed and decapitated McCarthy."

"Yes, sir."

"I have already given Windrush the background," Festing said.

Jack nursed his empty glass, hoping somebody would offer to refill it. Nobody did.

Hook continued. "The Fantis have constantly proved too terrified to fight. They know the Ashantis of old as slavers and killers."

"Yes, sir," Jack said. "I saw hundreds of young men in the town and wondered if we could form them into a regiment."

"We'd be as likely to find a regiment of abstainers in the British Army," Hook said. "Now then, you are wondering where you come in."

"Yes, sir," Jack said.

"Since Colonel Festing pushed the Ashantis back from Elmina, they have settled in a town called Effutu, about 10 miles inland. Their advance parties have occupied villages about six miles from Cape Coast. We estimate they are about fifteen to twenty thousand strong, so not quite the fifty thousand of rumour, but far too many for our handful of men to tackle, with or without the doubtful help of our native allies."

Jack felt the tension in the room rise as everybody looked at him.

"We might be able to defend Cape Coast and Elmina, and perhaps mount some limited attacks along the coast, where the Royal Navy gunboats will offer support. However, at present, we have given up control of the interior to the Ashantis. In effect, despite Colonel Festing's gallant victories, their General Amanquatia has won the first campaign."

Jack nodded. "We often lose the first battle sir, yet still win the war."

"We intend to win the war, Windrush." Hook leaned back in his chair. "We cannot allow such a dangerous enemy loose in our lands. Now, what I am about to say will not leave this room." He paused for a moment before continuing. "The government is so concerned about the situation here that they are sending out one of our best young generals. You may have heard of Sir Garnet Wolseley?"

"I met him in the Crimea, sir, and I heard he did great things in North America."

"That's the fellow. He's our brightest up-and-coming general." Hook passed over the whisky decanter, with the sunlight glittering on the crystal. "We also have the remainder of the 2nd West on their way from Bermuda."

Jack poured himself a generous tot of whisky, knowing that Hook was about to reveal what his duties were to be.

"Well Windrush, I want you to go to Effutu as our ambassador, see what's happening there and talk to them, palaver as they say here. Delay them until our reinforcements arrive. We could only defend Elmina by stripping Cape Coast and the fleet of every available man. If the Ashantis attacked both towns at once, we wouldn't have sufficient men to hold them."

Jack swallowed the last of his whisky in a single gulp. "I am no diplomat, sir, and I don't even speak the language."

"That's all right," Hook said. "We'll supply you with a translator and an escort of some of the 2nd West. Every day you gain will be invaluable as we strengthen our defences and await reinforcements." He paused for a moment. "Wear your medals and take your best uniform. That sort of thing might impress the Ashantis; they seem to go in for show."

"I might be better with a large umbrella," Jack said. "The Ashantis seem to like them, too."

"Very good, Windrush, I'm glad to see you've retained a sense of humour. The climate here drains that sort of thing."

"Yes, sir."

So I am being ordered to go to a village and palaver with the Ashantis, a people who practise human sacrifice and slavery, and try to persuade them not to attack until we can build up a decent force to fight them. Why me? Why a man with no African experience?

Because I have no official position, I am an extra man and therefore expendable. My loss would not weaken any British unit here.

"I can see you are thinking how best to proceed," Hook said cheerfully. "Oh, one more thing, Jack. Some European missionaries are being held in Kumasi; see if you can free them as well, or at least find out if they are still alive."

"How many missionaries, sir?" Jack asked, trying to gain time.

"We are aware of three, from the Society of Basle, worthy people who educate the youngsters as well as preaching the Bible. More importantly, they train masons, blacksmiths, and carpenters."

"I've never heard of them, sir." With Mary being Mission-educated in India, Jack knew what good work missionaries could do.

"They are among the best of people," Hook said. "And a great civilising influence wherever they are." He managed a brief smile. "I wish they could come into some of the back slums of London, but I suspect that would be too wild even for them."

"Yes, sir. I see you've retained your sense of humour as well."

Hook smiled. "These unfortunate missionaries have been held hostage since June 1869. We don't know what conditions they'll be in."

Without asking, Jack poured himself another glass of whisky. He had worked in some dangerous places before, but even the North-West Frontier of India had a veneer of civilisation. This King Kofi, with his slavery and human sacrifice, was something beyond his experience. He took a deep breath.

"When do I leave, sir?"

Chapter Seven

"That's another alert." Mary stood at the window, listening to the pandemonium in the streets outside. Shouts and wails reached the house, with one woman sobbing hysterically. "One only has to whisper the name Ashanti to cause a panic. If the Ashantis ever come, these people will be too petrified to put up any resistance."

"Aye, they're scared right enough," Jack gestured to the orange glow on the underside of the clouds. "Maybe with reason. That's the reflection of a large fire, probably the Ashantis burning a Fanti village."

"I've heard it's been like this for weeks," Mary sipped at a cup of tea. "The Ashanti general Amanquatia controls all the interior.' She faced Jack. "I hate this place, Jack. I hate all the memories of slavery. We did terrible things here."

"We did," Jack agreed.

"Now we have to do something to redress the evil to which we contributed," Mary said. "God knows I don't approve of wars, Jack, but the townsfolk and the Fanti people are terrified of the Ashantis, and we should protect them."

Jack nodded slowly. "I think we're going to."

"You must win this war, Jack, for me."

"I'll do my best," Jack said.

"I know you will," Mary came closer. "You always do. And I'll persuade General Harley to help the people in Cape Coast." She smiled. "He'll soon get so sick of me that he'll be glad to help them."

"That poor man," Jack said. "I feel sorry for him already."

Mary touched his arm and turned away. There was no need for any more words between them.

* * *

Sergeant Wickham threw an immaculate salute. "I am to lead your escort, sir."

"Glad to have you with me, Sergeant," Jack said. "I can't think of anybody in Africa I'd rather have."

"The good sergeant volunteered," Hook was puffing on a thin cheroot. "As soon as he heard what was happening."

"Sergeant Wickham fought at my side outside Elmina," Jack said. "He's the best shot in the company."

"I've detailed five privates of the 2nd West to accompany you," Hook indicated the men who stood rigidly to attention within the courtyard of Cape Coast Castle.

Jack nodded. "I know these lads: Privates Stair, Manning, Daley, Ogston and Coffin. They're veterans of the fight outside Elmina. We'll get to know each other even better on the journey to Effutu."

"They're only a token, of course," Hook said. "If the Ashantis decide to kill you, six soldiers or sixty won't make much difference." He gestured to a group of local men who sat or lay around a pile of baggage. "Those are your porters. They carry your tents, food, water purifying tubes and so on."

"I don't need the porters," Jack said. "I'm used to travelling light in India. Porters will only slow us down and give us extra mouths to defend."

"You'll take them," Hook said. "It's expected here. You know the old rhyme, 'beware and take care of the Bight of Benin, where one comes out for forty goes in'? Well, it's as bad here'. If the climate doesn't get you, the fever will, and if the fever doesn't, the Ashantis will." He paused. "We have the dangers of night-dews, soil-exhalations, unwholesome nourishment and heat exhaustion. Shall I order the porters to leave?"

"I'll take them then," Jack decided. "They might make me look more important."

"Making a show matters here," Hook said. "Show and noise. You'll have heard the drums already."

"I have," Jack said.

"Well, good luck, Windrush," Hook said. "Remember, you are there to stall, to play for time, nothing else. I don't want any heroics, no taking on the entire Ashanti army on your own."

"I won't do that," Jack promised.

"They know you are coming," Hook said. "And here is the interpreter. Akron Bekoh."

The interpreter was in his early thirties, with the bearing of a warrior and gold bracelets on both wrists, He gave an elaborate bow to Jack, ignored Wickham's hostile stare and waited politely for orders.

Having said his goodbyes to a staunchly cheerful, Mary, Jack felt self-conscious as he marched out of Cape Coast Castle with his tiny West Indian escort and a dozen Fanti porters balancing loads on their heads. *All I need now is a fife and drum, and I'd be completely ridiculous.* The castle garrison watched them leave, with the West Indians and Hausas saying nothing while the Marines gave cheerful advice and black humour.

"Good luck, sir," a Marine sergeant said. "Don't trust them Shantees. Leave an escape route back to the coast."

"Keep your gun handy," a young midshipman with basilisk eyes advised. "If in danger or in doubt, hoist the anchor, get off out."

"We'll watch for you coming back without your head," an Irish voice said. "I heard King Kofi likes souvenirs of his visiting British officers."

"Thank you, all," Jack lifted a hand in farewell and headed northward into the interior. He knew that Mary would be watching but refrained from turning to see her. Jack could picture her on the battlements, holding her straw hat on her head, lifting her chin and refusing to cry. Goodbyes were always the worst part of life and, God willing, he would only be a few days, a couple of weeks at most.

One hundred yards from Cape Coast, Akron stepped in front as if it was his right.

"Get behind me!" Jack ordered.

"I will have to speak to any Ashanti or Fanti we meet," Akron explained, smiling.

"You can speak to them from behind me as well as from the front," Jack said.

Akrom gave another little smile and slipped behind Jack, where Wickham pushed him to the side.

Aware that the Ashantis could be watching every step, Jack led his men on the short march across the open plain and into the first patch of forest. Almost immediately the path narrowed and deepened, with trees soaring on both sides and creepers coiling around their trunks like watchful serpents.

"Load your rifles, men," Jack said, "and make sure your bayonets are loose in their scabbards."

Well used to the forests of India, Jack expected the stifling heat and the green tinge to the light, the slanting sun-beams and the hum of insects. It was the atmosphere that was different. Even during the Mutiny, Jack had never experienced such foreboding, as if some great evil waited to unleash itself. He shook his head to clear away such fantasies. He was a British officer, not an impressionable Johnnie Raw.

He heard the regular thump of boots as the West Indians continued their parade-ground march. They remained at attention, with rifles shouldered and eyes firmly fixed in front of them.

"Break your formation, lads. We don't know if the Ashantis are waiting in ambush or not. Watch the trees for movement and if anybody fires, shoot the buggers flat." Manning and Stair grinned at that, as Jack had intended.

Behind the Wests, the porters moved with a regular rhythm, making light of the packs balanced on their heads. Jack gave them a few words of encouragement, nodded to Akron and returned to the front of the column. Moving slower now, they walked into steadily increasing heat with a shower of insects tormenting them.

How much time had passed since they entered the forest? An hour? Two hours? Three? Jack did not know. He could not work out time within the denseness of trees. He could only march, swat insects and watch for ambushes.

The Ashanti warrior stepped out of the forest in front of them with his long musket held butt up and muzzle down as a sign he came in peace. Bare-chested, he wore a patterned robe around his waist and a green turban on his head.

Jack halted his men, knowing that things were about to get interesting. "Akrom, go and do your stuff. Ask that fellow what he wants."

Stepping forward, the interpreter gave a broad smile before hurrying forward to speak to the Ashanti.

"Keep the lads alert, Sergeant," Jack looked around the trees. Where there was one Ashanti, there could well be more, hiding among the sheltering trees, probably with their muskets trained on the Wests as they stood on the path.

"This Ashanti warrior is a friend," Akrom said. "He says that the people in Effutu are waiting to welcome the brave Major Jack Windrush."

"Thank him, Akrom and tell him that we are looking forward to talking to Amanquatia as a representative of the Ashanti people."

There was an exchange of conversation for a few moments before Akrom spoke to Jack again. "This warrior will lead you to Effutu."

"Thank him kindly, Akrom, and say we will follow." Jack glanced at Wickham. "Make sure the men are alert, Sergeant."

"Yes, sir," Wickham said. "I'd like to speak to you, sir, where these two can't hear."

"We can't show mistrust on a diplomatic mission, Sergeant," Jack said. "Don't make it obvious."

"This way!" Akron said as the Ashanti warrior trotted along the track for another fifty yards before turning to his left, pushing aside a screen of palm-leaves and stepping onto a side path. They moved on for another ten minutes before they reached a village in a clearing. Jack looked around, for it was the first purely African village he had seen. Set on a slight rise, a score of houses lined both sides of a broad street, with a single mangrove tree in the centre. Half a dozen white-haired men sat under the tree, idly chatting, while bones and other objects hung above their heads. Dogs and children ran around, with hens scraping at the dust and the smell of cooking fires pleasant in the air. There was not a single warrior in sight, only a few brightly-dressed women and a dozen children. It all looked so peaceful that Jack felt himself relax.

"Bring up the porters," Jack said.

"They won't come, sir," Wickham said. "They're scared."

"Let me talk to them," Jack stepped back.

"Sir," Wickham spoke in a low tone. "Don't trust the interpreter. He's only telling you half what that Ashanti is saying."

Jack grunted. 'How much of the language do you know?"

"We spoke it at home as much as English. My mother insisted."

"You're an interesting man, Sergeant. Not many soldiers can speak two languages."

"Yes, sir." Wickham opened his mouth to say something else, changed his mind and looked away.

"Keep your skill to yourself, Sergeant. It might come in useful." Jack felt the change in the atmosphere a moment too late.

"Shantee!" One of the porters cried. "Shantee!"

"What the devil?" Jack looked up at the exact moment the first porter dropped his load, turned, and fled in the direction he had come. Without waiting for an explanation, the other porters followed, dropping their baggage on the path as a score of Ashanti warriors appeared from the forest. Tall men with impressive physiques, they stood around the Wests, fingering their muskets. Each one sported white stripes down their face and on both arms.

Kumi Okese's men. That is not good. Jack felt for the butt of his revolver.

Akron smiled. "Here is our escort, Major Windrush. Now we are safe from any unwanted incidents."

"You scared my porters, damn you!" Too angry to heed his safety, Jack strode to the warrior who seemed to be in command of the Ashantis. "What's the meaning of this?"

Seeing Jack's indignant advance, the Ashanti stepped back, pointing his long musket, which had Wickham calling the West Indians to ready their rifles.

"Back to back!" Wickham snapped.

For a moment, it seemed that Jack's mission would end there until he calmed himself down.

"Lead on then, Ashantis, and pray carry our baggage." He exchanged glares with the Ashanti leader, a man he judged to be in his mid-twenties, with a healed star-shaped bullet wound on his shoulder and gold inlays around the lock of his musket.

"Leave the baggage," Akron was still smiling as more warriors appeared until thirty Ashantis surrounding Jack's little band. "It will be safe here. Amanquatia has given orders that nobody will touch your possessions."

"You seem to know a lot all of a sudden," Jack said. "All right men, it seems that we have an escort. Shoulder arms and we'll go with the Ashantis. Be prepared for treachery."

"The Ashanti are known for treachery," Sergeant Wickham said. "Deception and lies are how they wage war. That is how they have managed to conquer their neighbours, deception, lies and savagery."

With the Ashanti warriors all around, Jack felt more like a prisoner than a diplomat as they hurried on narrow forest tracks to Effutu. After half an hour, one of the Ashanti began to beat time on a small drum he carried around his neck, and the others chanted, repeating the same refrain again and again until the rhythm felt imprinted on Jack's brain. The Ashantis increased the speed, with Jack's Wests keeping pace with them while the sweat beaded on Jack's forehead and rolled down his chin.

"How far is this place, Akron?" Jack asked.

"Not far now," Akron looked as uncomfortable as Jack felt. He was a translator, not a superbly fit warrior.

The number of Ashanti warriors surrounding them multiplied as they moved on until there were a couple of hundred, all carrying long muskets and looking askance at Jack and his handful of red-coated soldiers. The white-striped men kept closer to the Wests, glancing at them every so often.

"We'll be there soon," Akron promised. "Then you'll get a nice rest."

Not sure what to expect, Jack was surprised when their escort slowed to a walk. They climbed up a short slope, passed a cleared area that had once been used for agriculture and reached Effutu. Expecting a small village, Jack looked around at a town of three main streets that met at an open space in which stood a large tree. *That will be the fetish tree.* The roads were broad and clean, with large, square-built houses with an open frontage and roofs of overhanging palm leaves that provided shade from the sun and shelter from the rain.

Lining the streets, crowding every house and camping around the central tree, Ashanti warriors looked up curiously when the striped men escorted in Jack and his men.

"Keep your heads up, lads!" Jack said. "Remember you are soldiers, men of the 2nd West India Regiment! Show these Ashantis what that means!" Glancing over his shoulder, Jack saw that, despite the heat and the stifling dust raised by thousands of feet, his Wests were marching at attention, with their rifles at the slope and eyes facing forward.

Well done, lads.

Among the warriors were several chiefs or captains, sheltering under enormous umbrellas, every colour of the rainbow and decorated with dangling tassels, with gold figurines of various animals festooned across the peak.

Women emerged from the houses, pointing and shouting, yet without any overt hostility. Scores of Ashanti warriors kept pace with them as Akron led Jack and the Wests to the largest house in the town, opposite the fetish tree.

"Here we go, lads," Jack said.

Two massive umbrellas stood side by side outside the house. One was of scarlet silk, with gold elephants parading across the top, and the other was ominously yellow. Under the scarlet umbrella sat a very dignified woman who eyed Jack with curiosity from narrow eyes, taking in every detail of his dress and appearance. Under the yellow umbrella, seated on an ornately carved chair, was the man with whom Jack had exchanged glares outside the walls of Elmina.

"Major Jack Windrush of the 113th Foot, British Army," Akron said with elaborate politeness, "may I introduce Yaa Asantewaa, a lady of the royal household."

Jack gave a polite bow, "your ladyship," he said as Yaa Asantewaa responded with a slight nod.

Akron seemed pleased with the response. "And under the yellow umbrella, may I introduce Kumi Okese, the commander of this section of the army of the Asantahene, King Kofi Karikari."

Chapter Eight

Kumi Okese pushed aside the young slave who sat at his feet and stared at Jack through curiously clouded eyes. He was even more impressive than Jack remembered, a tall, broad-shouldered man with the horned leopard-skin cap and vertical white lines somehow enhancing the strong bones of his face. When Kumi Okese spoke, his voice was deep and crisp, with Akron translating almost instantaneously.

"That white man Windrush fought against us at Elmina. That man killed the nephew of the king!"

Jack knew that Okese referred to the man embellished in gold that Sergeant Wickham had shot. "I did fight against your army, Kumi Okese," Jack spoke directly to the Ashanti warrior. "As for the death of the king's nephew, well, he was a soldier, as you and I are, and dying in battle is part of the soldier's bargain."

When Akron translated, Kumi Okese stiffened and reached for the gold hilted sword at his waist. Jack put a hand on the butt of his revolver, knowing that if he shot this chief, the hundreds of Ashanti warriors would massacre him and his men. He held the Ashanti chief's glare, aware of the rising tension, and then Yaa Asantewaa spoke. Kumi Okese relaxed his grip on his sword, and Jack released the butt of his revolver.

"There is no need for killing, yet." Akron translated Yaa Asantewaa's words. "We need to hear what the British officer says."

"I will remind you," Jack strove to keep his voice calm although he could feel his heart racing, "that I am on a diplomatic meeting to ease our differences and free the hostages in Kumasi."

While Akron translated as quickly as before, Jack saw Yaa Asantewaa listening intently.

"There are no hostages in Kumasi." Kumi Okese was still on his feet, with his hand remaining close to the hilt of his sword. Around them, a score of Ashanti warriors waited to attack, while Sergeant Wickham and his men were equally prepared to fight.

Yaa Asantewaa spoke again, with Akron translating her words with genuine humility.

"Yaa Asantewaa says that neither she nor Kumi Okese has the authority to deal with such important matters." Akron nearly prostrated himself to the woman, hardly raising his eyes to meet her.

"You told me Yaa Asantewaa was of royal blood," Jack reminded, "and that Kumi Okese is the commander of this division of the army."

Akron turned mournful eyes on Jack. "They don't have the king's authority, Major."

"I can shoot them both, sir," Sergeant Wickham said softly. "Just give the order."

No; then they'll kill all of us. We have a mission here, Sergeant."

"They'll kill us all anyway."

"Don't fire, Sergeant. That's an order." Jack felt the tension rise further. He sensed that Wickham would willingly sacrifice his life to kill Kumi Okese. "Ground your rifle!"

Yaa Asantewaa spoke again, with Akron translating in a quiet tone. "Yaa Asantewaa said you have to go to Kumasi."

Jack started. "That's the Ashanti capital, right in the heart of Ashantiland. I am here to palaver with the commander of this army, not with the Asantahene."

Yaa Asantewaa listened to Akron's translation and gave a little smile. "You wished to discuss what you call the hostages, Major Windrush. We prefer to think of them as our guests."

"Discussing the hostages was one reason I am here," Jack agreed.

"Then you must come with us," Yaa Asantewaa said. "Our guests are in Kumasi, under the Asantahene's direct care."

"Will my men be safe?"

"If your men do not threaten us, then they will be safe." Yaa Asantewaa said, with Akron translating immediately.

Something in the woman's tone told Jack she could be trusted. "I am going nowhere until you give your assurance that my men and I will be permitted to return to Cape Coast Castle." Jack forced a smile. "I don't wish to add to the number of your guests in Kumasi."

Yaa Asantewaa nodded slowly. "If your men do not cause trouble in our land, they will not be harmed, and will return to the coast once your palaver is completed."

"Thank you," Jack said. "In that case, we are happy to accompany you to Kumasi."

Yaa Asantewaa lifted one finger. "Kumi Okese will take you." Moving with great dignity, she left Jack and his escort in the middle of the street, with her scarlet umbrella proud among the crowds. Kumi Okese and the white-striped Ashanti warriors stepped towards the Wests.

"We can fight! We can kill some of them," Wickham slid his hand closer to the trigger of his rifle.

"We'll accept the lady's word," Jack said. "Shoulder your rifles, lads."

"Don't trust them, sir," Wickham shouted as Kumi Okese yelled orders. A crowd of warriors closed on the Wests. Dozens of hands grabbed them, snatching their rifles and Jack's revolver.

"This wasn't part of the agreement!" Jack roared. "Tell them, Akron!" He saw Kumi Okese push Akron aside as the translator tried to speak.

"What the devil?" Jack thrust away a tall Ashanti who grabbed at his wrists, only for a warrior to pinion him from behind as a burly man fastened heavy metal shackles around his wrists.

"Thank you," Kumi Okese said.

"Thank you?" Jack lunged forward until a warrior cracked him over the head with a heavy stick. He winced, swung his manacles in the hope he might make contact and fell as two warriors pushed him to the ground. Within seconds, the same practised hands were snapping iron manacles around his ankles.

"Who the devil are you?" Jack glared at the burly man.

"He is a policeman," Akron spoke rapidly, his eyes wide. "He ensures the men don't run from battle and he looks after the prisoners."

Kumi Okese stared at Jack, his eyes smokier than ever. When he stalked away, two of his warriors hooked a stick through the shackles around Jack's wrists and hauled him upright. The Wests had been similarly treated and staggered behind the Ashantis, stumbling as they tried to keep their balance. The chains around their ankles clanked as they moved.

"We're slaves!" Wickham said in a tone of infinite horror. "The Ashantis have taken us as slaves!"

"Keep your head up, Sergeant!" Jack snapped. "You're a British soldier!"

"They'll sell us to the Arabs," Wickham said. "Or sacrifice us to one of their fetishes."

"They won't," Jack noticed that Manning appeared to be in shock, staring ahead of them without a word. "We're British soldiers. If we are maltreated, the British army will exact such revenge that the Ashantis will never recover."

I hope so, anyway. Not that it will help us much.

"We're the 2nd Wests!" Jack shouted. "Heads up, men! We'll get through this."

Akron appeared, wringing his hands. "I did not mean this to happen," he said. "I did not know."

"Tell Kumi Okese that he is foolish," Jack stumbled on the rough track. "Tell him that our queen will be displeased that the Ashantis are maltreating her subjects."

"I can't," Akron looked close to tears. "He is sending me away. I have to go with Yaa Asantewaa."

"Tell him!" Jack said, trying to kick out as the Ashanti policeman appeared, brandishing his whip.

"I can't!" Akron was near to tears as a press of warriors ushered him away.

"Tell him Queen Victoria will not be happy!" Jack's voice was lost in a roar of noise as the Ashantis surrounded the prisoners. The warriors pulled and pushed them onward, disregarding the shackles that rubbed the skin from their ankles and chafed their wrists.

"Thank you!" That phrase seemed to be the only English the Ashantis knew as they propelled the Wests along the track. "Thank you!"

Within an hour, Jack realised that even wearing shackles was torture that restricted movement and made every step painful. After two hours, he was breathing heavily, cursing the flies attracted to his raw flesh, and forcing himself to remain cheerful for the sake of his men.

"Keep your heads up, lads. We're the 2nd Wests. This situation won't last forever."

Jack was drooping with weariness when evening found them at a small village. Thrown into a filthy hut with his men, he checked their condition, thrust palm leaves between their wounds and the rusty iron manacles before he did the same for himself. The Ashanti policeman threw a mess of some vegetable stew onto the floor and watched dispassionately as the Wests scrambled to eat it.

"Officers first!" Sergeant Wickham roared.

"No," Jack shook his head. "Equal shares for all."

Unused to sharing with an officer, some of the men backed away.

"Come on, Daley," Jack urged. "You have to eat as well."

"It's not right," Daley said.

"It is right," Jack contradicted. "Eat, man."

Slowly, lying on their face in the filthy hut, the men took their share of the stew.

"Now sleep," Jack ordered. "We don't know what tomorrow will bring, so get whatever rest you can."

Lying on his side with the manacles biting into his flesh, Jack tried to sleep. He heard the rustling of rats in the hut, the clanking of iron every time one of his men moved, the stifled groans, and Coffin's quiet voice as he sang a psalm. *I can't help them. I'm their officer, and I've led them to humiliating captivity, perhaps slavery or worse. How can I make amends?*

Jack was not sure which was worse that night, the torment of the irons, the nibbling of the rats or the mental agony of knowing he had led his men into captivity. He lay as still as he could, aware he had made the only rational decision, and after a night of discomfort, rose bleary-eyed and unshaven to see two Ashantis at the door of the hut.

The warriors dragged Jack and the Wests outside and shoved them along the narrow forest path, with the brawny policeman slashing any who straggled with a hippopotamus hide whip.

"Keep moving men!" Jack swore as the whip curled around his shoulders. He stopped to stare at the policeman, remembering his broad face in case he ever had the opportunity to retaliate, however unlikely that seemed at present. When the man gestured with his whip, Jack turned away and limped after the others, dragging his feet with their heavy chains.

Every time they crossed a river, Jack and the Wests risked the whip to scoop up handfuls of water. Once, Manning delayed too long, and the policeman landed two heavy blows before Jack hustled him away. The Wests moved on, gasping with the heat, tormented by insects, drooping with exhaustion.

"We should have fought them," Wickham said.

"If we had, we'd all be dead now," Jack pointed out. "This way, we are alive and have a chance to survive."

"It's better to be dead than to be a slave of the Ashantis."

Jack did not reply to that. He kept moving, harbouring what strength he could. Each step was an ordeal, each hour seemed to stretch forever and the sun, green-tinged through the forest, beat on their heads with callous unconcern.

That second night, Jack and the Wests collapsed without thought into another hut. Heedless of the rats and other vermin, they slept, waking only when the burly policeman wielded his whip. The third day was worse than the second, and after that, life was only a torment of effort and pain until they reached the river.

"The Prah," Sergeant Wickham said. "Once we're over that, everything we see is Ashanti. No enemy army will dare to cross."

Jack nodded. The river was around seventy yards wide, hardly impressive, with the water sluggish and a dirty brown colour. "Don't give up, Sergeant."

With the police urging them on with their whips, the captives stepped into the river. Jack hoped there were no snakes or crocodiles, or whatever other predatory animal lived in this country. The Ashantis were all around, talking together, their faces devoid of pity or concern and the vertical white stripes somehow making them even fiercer.

The water was barely waist-deep, the current manageable, yet Jack felt he had crossed a significant barrier when he struggled up to the northern side of the Prah. Now he was in the territory of the Ashantis proper. Not even the most thrusting of British administrators could claim this land for the queen.

"Thank you." The policeman cracked his whip, pushing them on.

Wickham looked around him. "I've often dreamed of being in this land, but not as a slave."

"You've dreamed of this, Sergeant?" Jack asked. "Why?"

Wickham looked away. "Not as a slave," he repeated in a whisper.

"We're prisoners, not slaves," Jack said. "Colonel Festing will already be negotiating our release." He thought of the missionaries, held for years, and wondered what Mary was thinking. *Do the British even know we are prisoners? Or does General Hook think I am engaged in a long palaver with Amanquatia?*

Once across the Prah, the forest became denser, if anything, although the Ashantis relaxed a little. Kumi Okese visited the prisoners, prodding at them as he spoke to his warriors.

"What will happen to us?" Daley asked.

"I don't know, Daley," Jack said.

"Keep faith in the Lord," Coffin said. "He will get us through this."

"We're British soldiers," Ogston reminded. "We defeated Bonaparte at Waterloo. We can defeat the Ashanti Empire as well."

Jack felt a surge of pride for his Wests. "Well said, Ogston. We're British soldiers. Keep your heads up!"

After days of toil, the country altered, rising into a series of hills. Walking along the level was hard, walking up a slope was nearly impossible, particularly since the Ashanti road thrust in a straight line, whatever the gradient. Jack and the Wests, taking tiny steps with the constraints of the shackles, constantly under attack by flying insects, inched their way up the slope, gasping.

"Thank you!" The policeman plied his whip as young Private Manning collapsed.

"Leave him alone!" Jack snarled.

"Leave him!" Ogston stood over Manning, glaring defiantly at the policeman.

"Come on, Ogston, help me here!" Taking one of Manning's arms, Jack hauled him upright, gasping as the whip slashed across his back. "You'd better be careful, my man," he said to the policeman. "Once I'm free of this, I'll be coming for you."

Helping each other, dragging young Manning behind them, the prisoners ascended the hill, to find a much gentler slope descending northward, and then another steep hill rising behind.

"Keep going, Wests," Jack said, although his legs felt like rubber and his heart was thundering within his chest.

A crowd of warriors surrounded them, prodding with the barrels of their muskets, laughing, jeering.

"We're slaves," Sergeant Wickham said again. "You've led us into slavery, Major Windrush!"

"Keep your discipline, Sergeant!" Jack snapped, although he could understand Wickham's point of view. *I've failed these men. They trusted me, and I've failed them.*

Moving more slowly by the hour, the prisoners dragged themselves up the next hill, and then Manning dropped again.

"I can't go on, sir."

"You must," Jack said. "The Ashantis will kill you."

"Let them." Manning's face was grey with fatigue. He shook his head. "Leave me."

"No." Jack looked upwards, where the path cut directly upward. "I'll carry you."

"We'll carry you," Ogston corrected.

"No." Manning shook his head.

Working together, Jack and Ogston lifted Manning and carried on, fighting the slope, with their muscles screaming at every step. They reached the summit with the blood seeping over the shackles on Jack's ankles and Manning's weight pressing down on him.

"There are no more hills, lads," Jack was hardly aware of the sweat beading on his forehead and soaking through his uniform jacket. The Ashanti warriors stopped, with one man pressing the muzzle of his musket at the base of Jack's spine, shouting something that Jack took as an order to halt. A pleasant breeze up here kept the insects away and cooled the Wests, while a short distance away, a scarlet umbrella told Jack there was another group of Ashantis.

Lying on the ground, Jack wondered if he could walk any more. Between the ache of his muscles and the agony of his torn ankles, every step was a nightmare. He looked around. They were in a small clearing, with a group of three trees together, hung with low creepers. Behind them, the path undulated downwards toward the distant and unseen coast. In front was a deep forest, mostly hidden beneath a thin mist, through which forested hill-crests protruded like islands in a grey-green sea.

I'm in the heart of Ashanti-land, Jack said to himself. *As dark and mysterious as anywhere I have ever been.*

"Cheer up, lads," Jack croaked through a thirst-parched throat. "That's the hills behind us now. Better days ahead."

When three people left the shade of the scarlet umbrella, the warriors stepped aside to leave a distinct passage to the Wests. Yaa Asantewaa had returned, walking with dignity through the warriors, who reversed their muskets as a sign of peace and respect.

When Yaa came closer to Jack, speaking rapidly, Kumi Okese stood in her path. Yaa pushed him aside, evidently angry, and Kumi Okese reached for his knife.

For a second, Jack thought there would be a stabbing, until Yaa yelled at Kumi Okese, adding a full-blooded slap on the face, which resounded around the clearing. The Ashanti war captain recoiled, his eyes wild and murder in his face until Yaa's sharp order brought two policemen from the mass.

Yaa pointed to Jack's shackles and spoke sharply. The broad-faced policeman produced a key and opened the manacles around Jack's wrists, then the shackles on his ankles. When the policeman made to step away again, Jack shook his head and grabbed the man around the wrist.

"No," Jack said. "Free my men as well."

The policeman looked at Jack in total incomprehension. Pointing to his men, Jack repeated his words louder, wishing he had even a few words of the local language. Tempted to ask Wickham, he bit back the order, knowing the sergeant wanted to hide his knowledge of Ashanti.

As the policeman reached for the knife at his belt, Yaa stepped forward, gesturing behind her. Akron hurried through the ranked warriors, his eyes worried. Yaa spoke sharply, pointed to Kumi Okese and then to the West Indians.

"Yaa Asantewaa wishes to know what you said, Major Windrush."

"Tell Yaa that I want my men freed. They are British soldiers, not slaves. They are my escort on a diplomatic mission, and I demand that the Ashanti treat them with respect!"

Yaa spoke to Jack and gave a sharp order.

Akron translated. "Yaa Asantewaa said she did not wish you to be shackled. Now you will all be released."

The policeman immediately released their shackles, smiling obsequiously.

Jack stood, rubbing his ankles. As soon as his men were freed, he stepped up to the policeman and threw an uppercut. It was not the best punch he had ever landed, but Jack could think of few that had afforded him so much satisfaction. The policeman staggered back, astonished, with a hand to his jaw and murder in his eyes.

Although Yaa Asantewaa watched without saying a word, Jack suspected he saw a glint of humour in her eyes. He bowed to Yaa. "Thank you, Ma'am," he said. "I will return the favour if I ever have the opportunity."

Without a word or change in her expression, Yaa gave another order, turned around and walked to her umbrella. A moment later, three stony-faced Ashanti warriors brought fruit to the prisoners.

"I said things would get easier," Jack said as they began to move again, with Yaa's scarlet umbrella in front and Kumi Okese's yellow a hundred yards in the rear. Putting an arm around Manning, he helped him along the track.

"It's not right," Manning said. "You're an officer."

"We're all British soldiers," Jack checked his men. They looked more alert, watching the guards as they kept together. Only Sergeant Wickham walked apart, with his shoulders erect as befitted a soldier but his eyes fixed on the scarlet umbrella.

Chapter Nine

They heard the noise from nearly a mile away, a cacophony of horns, drums and human voices raised in either welcome or defiance, Jack was not sure which.

"They must know the 2nd Wests are coming," Jack said as Daley and Stair started. "They've never met such soldiers. Heads up, lads!"

"They're going to surrender to us." Manning's joke was feeble but welcome. He had recovered quicker than Jack had expected.

"That's what it must be," Stair agreed.

Akron approached them, with a body of slaves. "You must change."

"Change?" Jack looked at his much stained and battered uniform. "I have no other clothes."

Akron snapped an order, and the slaves hurried away, to return with the baggage Jack had thought long lost. "Well, that's a cheering sight." He noticed Yaa Asantewaa watching, stony-faced as he changed. Only when Jack was in his best uniform did Yaa walk away.

"Yaa Asantewaa wanted to see if white men were different from Ashanti men," Akron said. "We are approaching Kumasi."

A few moments later, they moved on, with the noise increasing with every yard. As they splashed through a shallow swamp, they saw a slope rising ahead, with a scattering of trees.

Coffin glanced upward. Two tall poles soared upward with the body of a dead goat suspended between them, wrapped in red cloth. "Good Lord, preserve us."

"What's that?" Jack asked.

"It's a fetish," Sergeant Wickham said. "The people worship such things either because it is magical, like a god, or because they believe a spirit lives inside it."

Jack raised his eyebrows without saying anything. He was familiar with the deities of the Indian sub-continent, but this was different from anything he had encountered before. *I am glad Mary is not here to witness such things.*

"And those," Wickham pointed to a pair of human skeletons, tied to the top of two separate trees. "Those men were slaves. The king must have ordered them fastened to the trees to die of starvation."

"Why?" Jack asked.

Wickham shrugged. "The Ashanti priests would study their deaths to work out the outcome of the war."

Jack grunted. "It makes our gipsy fortune tellers look innocent."

The noise rose to a frenzy as thousands of people banged drums, blew horns, shook rattles and clanged gongs. The instant Yaa Asantewaa entered Kumasi, scores of warriors added to the commotion by firing muskets into the air.

Thick powder-smoke and the dense crowd prevented Jack from seeing much of the town, although he noted a broad street of well-built houses before the mob rushed towards him.

"What the devil is this?" Jack asked as a group of colourfully-dressed men approached, amidst a riot of colourful flags, with the Union flag beside that of the Netherlands and Denmark. As the incoming column wound through the main street, the men within the flags began to dance.

"Those are the war captains welcoming Yaa Asantewaa back into Kumasi," Akron spoke with pride.

"I've never seen anything quite like them before," Jack said.

Like Kumi Okese, the war captains wore caps adorned with gilded ram's horns that thrust out from their heads, while plumes of eagles' feathers waved sideways above each ear. From waist to neck they wore a jacket of red cloth, adorned with dozens of objects that must have been sacred fetishes, while embroidered boxes rattled against their chests as they threw themselves around in wild dancing. Brass bells, animal horns, shells and cow tails completed their decoration in front, while behind, a profusion of leopard tails bounced in time with their movements. Below the waist, their cotton trousers ended at tall boots of red leather covered in shells and more brass bells.

Jack wondered if the captains wore such finery when they fought in the forest. He hoped so, for British soldiers could find them distinctive targets.

The bearer of a yellow and green flag waved it over the heads of the warriors as they fired a welcoming volley. When the muzzle flares set light to the flag, the bearer dropped it immediately, with a dozen sandaled feet eagerly stamping out the flames. "Nicely done," Jack approved as the procession continued. Surrounded by thousands of people, Jack still could not make out details of Kumasi, except to see the houses were large, with palm-leaf thatch.

More umbrellas appeared, some of them huge, rising and falling in time with the band, making an incredible spectacle as the sun reflected from the ornamental figurine on top of each umbrella. Some were animals; others abstract shapes without apparent meaning.

After ten minutes of walking through the crowd, the drums altered their beat to a slow rhythm.

"The drums are talking to us," Akron said.

"Talking to us?" Jack repeated.

"Yes, Major," Akron spoke with pride. "The drums send messages as fast as your telegrams, and more efficiently."

"You have an interesting culture," Jack said. "What are the drums saying?"

"They say that the king is coming. The Asantahene," Akron sounded awed. "There's King Kofi. He's under the black and red umbrella."

Jack squinted up the street, where the sun reflected from what he thought was a massive mirror.

"That's the king," Akron said.

As Jack's party moved through the crowd, Jack realised that his imagined mirror was the sun reflecting from a mass of gold ornaments that every man around the king wore.

"What do you think, Major Windrush? Is the Asantahene not the most majestic of kings," Akron asked, "with the most dignified of noblemen?"

Sitting under his red-and-black umbrella, the king was half-hidden, although the ministers and nobles around him were prominent.

"He is undoubtedly the finest king I have ever seen," Jack said solemnly. "Tell me, who are these people, these gold-encrusted noblemen, around the king?"

Akron looked pleased to educate Jack. "The tall man is the chamberlain, a very important personage. The man with the golden horn in the Gold Horn-Blower and, beside him is the Captain of the Messengers."

Jack tried to concentrate through the cacophony of horns and bells, with the hammer of drums a constant distraction. Anything he learned about the Ashantis might be useful in the forthcoming campaign if he managed to return to Cape Coast Castle before the Ashantis killed him.

Akron was still talking. "The Captain of the Messengers makes sure the drummers send the right messages." He gave a small laugh. "After all, it would not do to say the Asantahene was coming when all the time it was a British army at the sacred Prah River."

"No, indeed," Jack snatched at the words. "Is the Prah sacred?"

Akron gave a solemn nod. "Some say it is the outer border of our Empire. Sixteen years ago the British Governor Benjamin Pine failed to take his army across the Prah."

"Why was that?" Jack asked.

"Our priests cast a spell on him. He became confused and ran in circles before throwing away all his supplies and fleeing back to Cape Coast Castle."

"Ah," Jack said.

"No British Army will ever cross the Prah," Akron boasted. He continued, shouting above the discordant medley of sounds. "That gentleman there, the fellow with the golden wristband, he is the Captain for Royal Executions."

"That's an interesting title," Jack said. "I'll try to keep on his good side."

"And that gentleman," Akron was positively glowing with enthusiasm as he indicated a massively muscled man who sported an impressively large golden hatchet on his chest. "That gentleman is the Royal Executioner."

Remembering a similar man in Jayanti's realm in India, Jack repressed his shudder. However impressive and dignified a monarch, there was always an iron fist beneath the velvet glove. The gleam of gold could not hide the sinister threat of the hatchet.

As Akron continued to list the Asantahene's officials, Jack realised that the Asantahene's officials were men of responsibility and this kingdom was organised with some skill, indeed better than many European nations. Ashantiland was far more than a grouping of iron-age forest tribes, as he had imagined, but a sophisticated and complex society. He looked up as Akron raised his voice in excitement.

"There are the Linguists, Major Windrush! See? The Asantahene's Linguists!"

Three men sat under yet another splendid umbrella with a bundle of golden rods in front of them.

"Linguists? Are you not one of the king's Linguists?"

"I am not," Akron spoke in hushed tones. "The Linguists are the men who can bridge the gap between the dead and the living."

Jack nodded. "They are a sort of priest, then?"

"Yes. The Linguists have great powers." Akron looked away as one of the Linguists glanced in his direction.

"And you, Akron," Jack said quickly, aware that King Kofi was coming closer. "What are you?"

"A humble translator," Akron said.

The Asantahene was looking at them. The scarlet umbrella was no longer moving.

"Did King Kofi send you to spy on us?" Jack asked quickly.

"I am an interpreter," Akron said.

While the king waited under his umbrella, Jack realised that a troop of muscular slaves carried the king in an ornate cradle, like the body of a coach. The slaves looked sleek and well cared for, while leopard-skin and red velvet lined the cradle. The king wore a long leopard-skin cloak, with a necklace of silver bullets.

"Why is the necklace only silver and not gold?" Jack asked softly.

"The bullets are a sign the nation is at war," Akron said. "Please don't talk any more, Major, unless at the Asantahene's request."

A body of chiefs or sub-kings stepped clear of their crimson hammocks and approached the Asantahene, each chief with his bodyguard of captains, each with a gold-handled sword.

Jack estimated King Kofi at around 40 years old, sitting in great dignity with a thin gold band around his head and the silver bullets prominent around his neck. Beside the king was a tall man holding a sword with a gold handle, and then one of the nobles stepped in front, blocking Jack's vision.

Shift, damn you, Jack said to himself, but the moment was passed.

Behind the king, a group of royal females was also present. Slender women with a dignity equal to the king's and with necklaces of fine gold, they looked over the assembly with calm eyes, ignored Jack and the 2nd West entirely and spoke only to each other.

The king lifted a single finger towards Akron, who approached immediately. When the king pointed to Jack and the West Indians, Akron launched into a long speech, evidently explaining who Jack was and his purpose in Kumasi. King Kofi lifted his hand, and Akron returned. The King gave a soft order, and a few moments later, a body of Kumi Okese's white striped warriors separated Jack from his men.

"Keep your heads up, lads!" Jack shouted as the warriors hustled him down the street, with the crowd parting before them.

"Yes, sir!" That was Private Coffin. "The Lord will look after us!"

Glancing over his shoulder, Jack saw Wickham call his men to attention as a company of warriors escorted them in the opposite direction. "Good luck, 2nd Wests!" Jack shouted, and then his escort pushed him inside one of the large houses. A warrior cracked him over the head with a musket butt, another poked him in the back, and he sprawled on the floor.

Chapter Ten

Jack's first impression was of a large open chamber, with a tall Ashanti warrior staring down at him, and then Kumi Okese stepped close, with Akron at his side.

"These are Kumi Okese's words, Major Windrush, not mine," Akron sounded almost apologetic.

"Just translate honestly," Jack rose to his feet, dusting himself down. When two white-striped warriors levelled their muskets, Kumi Okese gestured them back.

"Kumi says that if it were up to him, he would decapitate you right away and decorate the walls of his house with your head," Akron said. "You are fortunate that the king wishes you to live."

Jack nodded. "Tell Kumi Okese that I appreciate the kindness of the Asanta-hene and his loyalty to the king's wishes."

Kumi Okese glowered at Jack as Akron translated the words.

"Kumi Okese says that if you try to escape, he will personally cut off your head."

Jack forced a smile. "Tell Kumi Okese that if he chooses to disregard the wishes of the Asantahene, that is his choice. Tell him that my sovereign Queen Victoria, expects her subjects to be well treated and will be displeased if you abuse my men or me."

When Akron passed the message, Kumi Okese touched one hand to the gold hilt of his sword, leaned closer to Jack and stormed from the house. The two warriors took hold of Jack, dragged him from the front room into a back chamber and tied him to a bolt on the wall. Landing a few parting kicks, the warriors left Jack lying on the ground and walked away.

"Don't you harm my men!" Jack shouted, knowing the Ashantis would not understand his words. He struggled with his bonds, while a single rat emerged from a corner of the room to explore his feet. Outside the house, the singing, intermittent musket shots, blaring of horns and the constant thunder of the drums continued. Jack knew that for the remainder of his life, he would remember these Ashanti drums.

* * *

Jack did not know how much time passed as he lay in the gloomy hut. The drumming died away and stopped, rats explored his legs, and the light faded. He tried to sleep, dozed fitfully, fought the cords around his wrist and worried about his men. It might have been ten hours or two days when somebody entered his room.

Jack looked up. "What's happening?"

Akron looked nervous as he unfastened Jack's bonds. "Get up slowly, Major Windrush. You have a visitor."

Kumi Okese was wearing the full ceremonial clothes of an Ashanti war captain, from the cap and feathers to the baggy red trousers and gold-hilted sword. A group of warriors had followed him into Jack's room.

"Kumi Okese wishes you to watch the ceremony," Akron said.

"Which ceremony is it this time?" Jack heard the blowing of horns and the inevitable tapping of drums.

"The British killed one of the king's nephews during the battle outside Elmina," Akron reminded. "And four chiefs. This ceremony is for one of the chiefs to ensure he has slaves to look after him in the afterlife."

"Oh?" Jack did not resist when three stalwart Ashantis dragged him to a front room and held him secure, with one clamping a firm hand across his jaw. It was the first time Jack could see the street in its entirety, with elegant substantial houses with palm-thatched roofs, stately banyan trees for shade and cleanliness that would do credit to any town in Europe.

Growling something, Kumi Okese stalked away, with his eagle feathers bouncing beside his head and his sword hanging from his waist. Akron remained in the room, although he kept his distance from the warriors.

Hundreds of people filled the street, children, women and men of every rank from the lowest to the royal officials. The Ashanti nobles were dressed in their finery as they gathered, with their followers and warriors surrounding them. Both men and women wore bright costumes, talking animatedly as if on some public holiday. Remembering the starvation in Cape Coast, Jack pondered on the difference between the flamboyance of the aggressor and misery of the victims.

"You see," Akron spoke as if three men were not holding Jack rigid, "when people enter the next world, they retain the same rank they did in this one. That means that a king will be a king, and a slave will still be a slave, and a king will need his wives and slaves to look after him."

"Ah," Jack nodded as best he could. "That's interesting." He remembered the Islamic belief that when a man died a martyr, seventy-two virgins and a palace awaited him in paradise, while the ancient Norse thought they would ascend to Valhalla, a place of feasting and battle. Every religion had its beliefs and traditions. Jack watched as the nobles drank from a gourd, pointed their muskets upwards and fired a volley, to the delight of the crowd. White smoke coiled around the street. After a few moments, the nobles moved to the next house and repeated the whole drinking and firing procedure.

"This is a sign of respect for the dead man," Akron said. "They are only firing powder, not ball ammunition."

The nobles continued along the main street, drinking and firing in front of each house. With so much beer consumed, the warriors became increasingly inebriated so that Jack wondered if somebody might load with ball and kill one of the bystanders. *If I'm lucky, they'll blow Kumi Okese's head right off his shoulders.*

When they reached a house diagonally opposite to Jack's, the procession halted, with the gun smoke slowly lifting. Four drummers walked slowly down the street, each leading a burly man with a large black cap. The drummers beat a slow, sinister rhythm that Jack guessed was the precursor of something more extreme than a drunken celebration. When the black-capped men joined the head of the procession, they spoke together for a few moments before moving into the crowd.

"They are the executioners," Akron said. "They're searching for the correct people to accompany the king's nephew into the next world."

"I see," Jack said. "Does that mean they're going to find people to murder?"

"Those the executioners choose are called the ochres of the deceased," Akron spoke in hushed tones, as befitted a funeral.

Jack struggled with the warriors holding him. "Can you get these lads to let go of me? I'm not going anywhere."

After a few words from Akron, the warriors released Jack and moved aside, although they still watched him from the corner of their eyes.

"Do the executions know who they are choosing?" Jack asked. "Or is it a random selection?"

"I don't know," Akron said. "They will choose which slaves they think best for the dead chiefs."

The crowd's chatter rose when the executioners dragged out a struggling young man. The executioners tied their victims' arms behind him, with the crowd watching in tense excitement. The youngster protested violently, screaming for help until one of the executioners thrust a knife through his face, in the right cheek and out the left. War-hardened though he was, Jack could not repress a shudder of horror as the executioner added a second knife in the right cheek, pushing it right through until it came out the left, with bright blood flowing from the ochre's face.

"Oh, dear God," Jack said as the crowd watched in apparent approval, with a few horns blaring against the constant hammer of the drums.

Working slowly, the executioners looped the youngster's lips over the point of each knife, then cut off his left ear and carried it, dripping blood, in front of him. A second executioner slashed at the ochre's right ear but failed to severe it, so it hung on a flap of skin.

As Jack watched in sick horror, one of the executions bored a hole through the ochre's nose, passed a thin cord through and pulled him along, while others pushed a long blade under each of his shoulder blades and, seemingly at random, slashed his back.

"Is this part of the ceremony?" Jack asked.

Akron nodded, seemingly unable to look away from the ongoing horror. "Yes, Major Windrush."

The executioners found a second man, and a third and then a woman, until a row of prisoners, male and female, stood, bound, knife-gagged and bleeding in the centre of the street. The crowd shouted at them, some jeering or making loud comments. When Jack tried to look away, two of the Ashanti warriors took hold of him, forcing him to watch every second.

After a few moments, the executioners grabbed the nearest ochre and, to the intense interest of the crowd, forced him to his knees. While one man held him, another lifted his large, clumsy-looking sword, and hacked at the victim's neck. Although he must have had a good deal of experience, the executioner took three attempts to remove the man's head. The struggles of the second victim proved unavailing as two of the executioners held him secure while a third wielded the sword.

"Dear God in heaven," Jack said. He noted that his Ashanti guards watched avidly.

"It's a sign of respect for the deceased," Akron explained, without diverting his gaze from the executions. "The higher the rank, the more slaves should accompany them. It would be very disrespectful not to provide slaves for the afterlife."

"There appear to be hundreds of slaves in Kumasi. Where do they come from?" Jack was grateful for anything that provided a diversion from the executions.

"The slave market," Akron sounded surprised that Jack should ask such a question.

"Who brings them there?" Jack pressed further. "Are they criminals to be made into slaves?"

"The army captures them, Major Windrush," Akron said. "The Ashanti raid all around for slaves to ensure a ready supply for work and sacrifice." He paused for a moment. "Unlike your terrible societies, men here are not born into slavery."

Jack made no reply. *Akron has confirmed what we thought. No wonder the Fanti are afraid of the Ashanti.* He looked up as Kumi Okese strode into view, with half a dozen of his striped warriors at his back. Kumi Okese stared deliberately at Jack before clapping his hands and giving a rapid order. Jack felt Akron stiffen at his side.

"What's happening, Akron."

"Nothing," Akron's voice was strained. "It would be best if you closed your eyes, Major Windrush." When Akron said something to the warriors, they again gripped Jack.

"What's happening, damn you?" Rather than withdraw, Jack stepped forward. "What did Kumi Okese say?"

"Look away, Major Windrush," Akron pleaded. "Look away."

The crowd shifted, looking up the street as the executioners trotted away. Umbrellas rose and twirled, with people talking in high, excited tones until the executioners returned, dragging another victim with them.

"That's one of my men," Jack saw the West's uniform. "Oh, dear God," Jack said as the executioners hauled Private Manning to Kumi Okese. Jack raised his voice to a shout. "Leave that man alone! He's a British soldier, damn your murdering hides! He's escorting a diplomatic mission." Jack struggled to escape his guards. "Tell them, Akron. For God's sake, tell them they can't murder a British soldier."

With the sweat running down his face, Akron shook his head. "I dare not."

"You dare not? That's Stanley Manning! That's one of my men!" Jack scraped his nailed boots down the shin of a guard and broke free when the man yelled and jerked backwards. Taken by surprise, the second warrior's lunge was ineffective, and Jack leapt for the door, only for the third guard to crack the hilt of his knife over Jack's head, temporarily stunning him. Jack fell swearing.

Grabbing him, the guards dragged Jack back to the window, forcing him to watch. Two executioners held the struggling Private Manning.

"Manning!" Jack shouted. "Stanley! We are the 2nd Wests!"

For a second Private Manning looked up. "2nd Wests!" He saw Jack at the window. "God save the queen!"

"Good man," Jack whispered. "Good man indeed." He straightened to attention as two executioners thrust Manning onto his knees and a third poised his sword. "Make it quick," Jack said softly. "Please, God, make it quick."

Mercifully, the executioner swung his sword. Private Manning's head sprung from his body to roll on the ground and lie, eyes open, staring at the impassive Kumi Okese. Jack's guards relaxed their grip, stepping back now the entertainment had finished.

"You're a murdering hound Kumi Okese," Jack shouted into the sudden hush. "Tell him, Akron, tell Kumi that he's a dirty murdering hound and I'll see him dead for murdering one of my men."

"I dare not."

Grabbing Akron by the front of his robe, Jack crashed him against the wall of the house. "Tell him, Akron, or by the living God I'll kill you here and now."

The guards hauled Jack roughly away, shouting at him as they rammed him against the window.

"Kumi Okese!" Jack roared. "You murdering bastard! Come here and fight me!" When Kumi looked over, Jack was sure he had a faint smile on his face. He looked directly at Jack, said something to the executioner and lifted Private Manning's head by the hair before striding to Jack's house.

"Come here, Kumi Okese!" The guards stopped Jack's lunge for the door, holding him secure as Kumi Okese stepped inside, still with Manning's dripping head hanging from his fingers. "You're a dirty murdering hound!" Jack said. "Translate, Akron, tell the bastard what I think of him."

"I am sure he can tell what you think of him," Akron said.

"Tell him anyway!" Jack shouted. "He murdered one of my men!"

As Akron spoke a few halting phrases, Kumi Okese stepped closer to Jack, and Akron translated again.

"You are alive only because the Asantahene wishes it, Major Windrush. When the Asantahene tires of you…" Kumi Okese did not need to complete the sentence. The head he deposited at Jack's feet was completion enough.

Jack grunted. "Your time will come, Kumi, I promise you that." He prodded Akron. "Tell him what I said."

Looking at his feet, Akron said something, and Kumi Okese gave a short, barking laugh. "If you try to leave Kumasi," Kumi Okese spoke through Akron. "I will hand all your soldiers to the executioners." He stalked away, with his warriors and Akron at his heels, leaving Jack alone in the house.

Across the road, the executioners lifted what was left of Private Manning and threw him with the other bodies. Already the vultures were busy, their beaks tearing at the eyes and bellies of the dead.

"I'm not leaving you there," Jack spoke to himself as he stalked outside, ignoring the dissipating crowd. "Come on, Stanley," he lifted Manning's head. "I can't do much for you except give you a decent burial." Walking over to the pile of bodies, Jack lifted Manning, balanced him over his back and carried him to the outskirts of the town, holding the head under his arm. A squad of Ashanti warriors followed, muskets ready in case Jack tried to escape.

The earth beside the marsh was sufficiently soft for Jack to scrape a hole with his hands, with the Ashantis watching him curiously. Knowing they would not kill him without the king's permission, Jack turned his back and continued to dig. He looked up in surprise when a little girl joined him, delving into the earth with a small hoe.

"Thank you," Jack gave what he hoped was a smile.

"Are you digging a grave?" The girl spoke in nearly perfect English, albeit with an accent Jack had never heard before.

"Yes," Jack said. "For my friend."

"I'll help." The girl was on her hands and knees, digging energetically.

"Where did you learn to speak English?" Jack could not hide his surprise.

"Mrs Ramsayer taught me," the girl said. "Is that deep enough?"

"It is," Jack looked at the hole. It was only a shallow pit, but better than nothing.

Carrying Private Manning over, Jack laid the body down and placed the head where it belonged. When he began to push back the earth, the little girl joined in.

"Are you going to say a prayer?"

Jack stared at her. "Did Mrs Ramsayer teach you about prayers as well?"

"Yes." The girl waited for Jack's reply.

"I'm not very good with prayers." Jack had seen soldiers buried from Burma to Berwick and from Canada to the Crimea. Each death was a personal tragedy, yet he felt worse over Private Manning's murder than any of the others.

"I know some," the girl said.

"I am sure Stanley would appreciate that," Jack said.

"Was that his name?" The girl did not look disturbed about the presence of a corpse. Living in Kumasi, Jack reasoned, had probably conditioned her to such sights. "My name is Abena." The girl stood beside the grave, closed her eyes and bowed her head. "Go with God, Stanley and Jesus will take you in his arms; Amen." She opened her eyes. "How was that?"

"You did very well," Jack said. "Thank you, Abena." He looked up as a sharp female voice sounded from the outskirts of Kumasi.

"Abena! What are you doing here?"

Chapter Eleven

"I am sorry if Abena is causing you concern." The woman was blonde and too sun-bronzed to be even remotely fashionable, while her clothing was patched beyond recognition. Jack could not begin to guess her age.

"Abena is helping me," Jack said. "You must be Mrs Ramsayer."

"I am Elda Becker." The newcomer said, slightly coolly, Jack thought. "Abena! Off you go!"

"Yes, Miss Becker!" Giving a small curtsey, Abena scampered away.

"I am sorry about the death of your soldier," Elda said. "The execution ceremony was not an edifying sight, was it?"

"It was repulsive," Jack said.

Elda nodded. "Not all the Ashanti culture is like that. They are very advanced in other matters. I won't give up trying to change them." Her smile was unexpected. "You are Major Windrush, aren't you?"

"Major Jack Windrush, 113th Foot, attached to the 2nd West India Regiment, at your service, madam." Jack gave a polite bow. "I am sorry to see a woman in such circumstances."

Elda's accent was heavily German. "The Lord sent me here for a purpose, Major. I am alive, as are you, unlike these poor unfortunate people we saw killed today."

"That is true," Jack said. "May I ask how the Ashantis are treating you?"

"Tolerably well, Major," Elda said, then looked away. "Most of the Ashantis are kind, despite the executions and there is one man who helps me." She lifted her chin as if expecting Jack to criticise her.

Jack nodded. "It is good to have a friend in a strange place."

Elda gave a small smile. "Not everybody would agree with my choice of friends, Major. His ideas are different from those in Europe." Again, she lifted her chin.

Jack did not take the bait. "I hope he can keep you safe after you while you are here."

"I also hope that," Elda said. "What brought you to Kumasi, Major?"

"My original mission was to try and gain your release." Jack gave a wry smile. "I did not expect to become a hostage myself."

"Man proposes," Elda said, "but the Lord disposes. Are the authorities in Cape Coast Castle in touch with the Asantahene?"

Jack patted her arm. "Now don't you fret, the Ashantis have attacked the British at Elmina and are threatening Cape Coast Castle. That's a declaration of war if I ever heard one so we could see a British army marching through Kumasi before long."

"You haven't seen the power of the Ashantis," Elda said. "You have not seen the number of men they can muster, or how they fight. They're unbeatable in the forest."

"They have never met British infantry," Jack tried to calm her down.

"You can't beat them," Elda repeated.

"I've had my share of forest fighting," Jack said. "In Burma and India. The British soldier is the most adaptable in the world." He tried to sound confident.

"Are you going back into Kumasi?" Elda asked.

"Soon. I'll put a cross on Private Manning's grave first." Jack looked at the human skeletons on the tree nearby. "It will give him some protection."

Elda nodded. "He's in the Lord's hands now. The Ashanti won't allow a cross to remain."

"I'll know I've placed it," Jack said, "and so will Manning." *Mary would wish me to,* Jack told himself. Why was it that he always felt more religious when in these terrible places, yet when he was back in safety, he rarely attended church? The old seaman on *Lady Luck* was right, there were no atheists in a storm, either in a storm of waves at sea, or a storm of blood and horror in this forest.

At least Mary was safe. She might even be home now, back in Herefordshire or Berwick, with David, unaware of the troubles her husband was enduring.

The Ashanti warriors watched as Jack made a simple cross out of two tree branches, and then, shouting, they grabbed him.

"I'll look for you, Elda," Jack said as the warriors hustled him back to Kumasi. "Don't give up hope."

The warriors half guided, half dragged Jack to a small house in a side street, where they threw him into the front room and left him there.

* * *

"This is the man," Abena's small voice sounded in Jack's ear. "He's a soldier."

Jack looked up to see a circle of people around him. One elderly, bearded man helped him to his feet.

"You are welcome to our house," the elderly man said in a thick German accent. "Although the Lord knows we have little to offer in the way of hospitality."

"The fact you are here is sufficient," Jack said. "I am Major Jack Windrush, 113th Foot, temporarily attached to the 2nd West India Regiment. You must be the missionary hostages."

"Yes." The elderly man nodded. "I am Mr Kuhne, one of the Basle missionaries." He seemed eager to speak. "Are you here with good news? Are the British trying to release us from this dreadful place?"

"The British are aware of your plight," Jack said. "I was sent to try and persuade King Kofi to release you." He looked down at himself. "I was not very successful, as you see."

"We are the Ramseyers," a calm-eyed man said, gesturing to his wife and the two children who stared, wide-eyed, at Jack. "There is also a Frenchman named Bonnet. The Ashantis hold him in a different house."

"I didn't know about the Frenchman," Jack said.

The missionaries glanced at each other before Mrs Ramseyer spoke. "He was a gun dealer," she said. "He was bringing the Ashantis a consignment of muskets when they seized him and his guns."

Jack grunted. "I've no time for gunrunners," he said, "but it seems like the Ashantis have killed the goose that lays the golden eggs."

The missionaries crowded around, asking a dozen questions about the latest developments on the Gold Coast. They all looked haggard, with shaded eyes and lined faces. Jack could only guess what horrors they had witnessed in their years of confinement, never sure when the Ashantis might decide to sacrifice them.

"Major Windrush, will the British come to rescue us?" Mr Kuhne stroked Jack's uniform jacket as if it were a talisman.

"Soon," Jack said. "They will be here soon. General Wolseley, one of the best generals in the army, is coming to Africa, and reinforcements are already at sea. Once they arrive, General Wolseley will be in a better position to pursue the war. Hold on to your faith; only a few more months."

Mrs Ramseyer could not hold back her tears. "A few more months!"

When Mr Ramseyer put an arm around her, speaking in German, Jack turned away. "Does Elda Becker also live here?"

"No." Kuhne was almost abrupt. "She lives elsewhere."

The missionaries glanced at each other. "We don't like to discuss Elda Becker," Mr Kuhne said quietly. "She is different from us."

"Are you not all Christian?" Jack asked.

"We are." Mrs Ramseyer put her arm around Abena. "I am not sure if Miss Becker is."

Jack nodded without understanding. "All right," he said. "I have no intention of waiting here to be executed, or for a British army to maybe come sometime. We seem to have an element of freedom. Are we allowed to go into the streets? Or are we shot on sight?"

"We have freedom," Kuhne said, "as long as we don't leave Kumasi."

"How are they treating you apart from that?" Jack asked.

"Well enough by their lights," Kuhne said. "The king allows us a monthly allowance of gold dust to buy food, while the mission at the Gold Coast sends us money and clothes from time to time."

Jack nodded. When he first heard about the hostages, he imagined much worse confinement with chains and tiny cells. "When I get back, I'll let the people in Cape Coast know."

Kuhne shook his head. "The Ashantis won't let you go, Major. They will detain you here for years."

Jack grunted. "Perhaps. Do any of you know where the Ashantis hold my men?"

"I do," Abena held up her hand like a schoolgirl.

Jack smiled. "I thought you might, Abena. Can you take me there without getting into trouble?"

"Yes!" Abena seemed pleased to help.

"Come on, then." Jack held out his hand for the little girl.

"Major Windrush," Kuhne said. "What are you going to do?"

"Get out of Kumasi. Somehow."

As Abena led him from the missionaries' house, Jack was surprised how attractive Kumasi was. Sitting in the middle of a gloomy forest, he had expected only a large village with ramshackle huts with thousands of near-naked people. Kumasi, Jack allowed, was nothing like that. The town was as sizeable as many in Britain, with brightness and vitality everywhere he looked. Each nobleman seemed determined to outdo his neighbours, wearing colourful clothes similar to the Roman toga. The women looked sophisticated, with necklaces of aggry beads, gold ankle rings, bright sandals, and gold bands around their knees, while handsome slave boys followed them.

Although the people stared as Jack walked past, nobody tried to stop him. He had experienced more unfriendliness in many English towns.

"Your men are along here, Major Windrush." Abena tugged Jack into a side street, quieter than the main thoroughfare although still busy with people. Men laughed together, women walked, balancing burdens on top of their head and a single nobleman strode under his umbrella with his gold-handled swords thrust carelessly into a leopard-skin sheath. Behind him, his entourage of shapely young women walked as if in a missionary school crocodile, except for the last in line, who stared at Jack.

"Your soldiers are up here," Abena pulled at Jack's sleeve.

"How far, Abena?"

"Not far, Major Windrush." Abena stopped at the smallest house in the street. Even if Abena had not shown him, Jack would have known his men were inside, for there were two Ashanti guards at the door, each armed with a musket and sword.

Jack stood outside, trying to peer in the small window. The guards looked at him with a mixture of boredom and suspicion.

"Halloa! Second Wests!" Jack shouted. "Are you in there?"

When one of the sentries gestured angrily, Abena shouted at him, waving her hand. After a few moments, Sergeant Wickham appeared at a small window beside the door. "Major Windrush?"

"Is everybody all right in there?"

"Yes, sir." Other faces joined Wickham's. "Except for Private Manning, Sir."

"I know about Manning," Jack said. "How are they treating you?"

"Well, sir."

"Don't give up," Jack said. "Things will get better."

"Major," Abena pulled at Jack's sleeve. "Look."

A dozen warriors were marching toward them, white-striped faces set into ferocious scowls.

"Thank you, Abena," Jack said. Raising his hand in quick farewell to the Wests, he moved away.

Now I know where my men are held. I have to work out how to free them and get back to Cape Coast Castle, though a hundred and forty miles of Ashanti-controlled forest, with no map and a single track.

* * *

"Major Windrush," Mr Kuhne spoke quietly. "Please come here. You may find it interesting."

Jack stepped to the window beside Kuhne. The yellow umbrella moved slowly up the street, announcing to all the world that Kumi Okese was coming. As well as the umbrella bearer, there were two bodyguards, one with a long musket, and the other with a long, gold hilted knife at his belt. Behind them, beyond the shelter of the umbrella, a small train of slaves walked, heads down. Kumi Okese strode in the shade of the umbrella, straight-backed and proud, with his leopard-skin cap on his head and his colourful robes covering him from neck to knees. At his side, wearing a simple Ashanti robe and with a thin gold chain around her neck, Elda walked with all the grace and dignity of an Ashanti noblewoman.

"What the devil?"

"That is why Elda Becker is not with us," Kuhne said. "She has gone native. She has left our community to live with that Ashanti chief."

Jack nodded, trying to control his anger. "That's Kumi Okese."

Elda's husband or not, I am going to kill him the first opportunity I get.

"I would have no objection to Elda's man being African," the missionary said, "except that Elda has rejected Christianity to adopt fetish worship." He dropped his voice. "She has even bought a slave from the slave market."

Jack shivered at that. "I did not know that." He watched Elda walk past. She did not look healthy, and he wondered if she had chosen Kumi Okese out of self-preservation rather than affection. How genuine was she?

"They are coming here." Kuhne's voice rose in alarm.

The Ashanti warriors burst through the door in a body, pointing their muskets at the missionaries.

"Major Windrush," Akron stepped to the front. "You are greatly honoured. The Asantahene wants to see you in the Bantummah."

Chapter Twelve

"Thank you!" The warriors formed around Jack, pushing him out of the house and up the street. "Thank you!"

Kumi Okese watched, unsmiling, then marched in front, with his followers at his back.

"You are greatly honoured," Akron repeated. "Very few foreigners meet the Asantahene."

At that moment, Jack only felt apprehension as he stumbled through Kumasi towards the Bantummah, the king's palace, at the northern side of the town. Jack's escort propelled him down a narrow street with a foul odour that may have emanated from the deep ditch that ran down the centre until they came to a large, flat-roofed building.

At first glance, Jack thought the palace gates appeared like the entrance to some Lancashire factory, except for the gaudily-dressed sentries. The fence was of bamboo, somewhat imposing but not threatening. The palace itself was fairly large, with shutters open on an array of windows.

Akron stepped back. "What do you think?"

"It's an impressive building," Jack watched as the escort spread out, some evidently in awe at their surroundings.

"The Asantahene has many uses for his palace," Akron enthused. "As well as living here, he has some of his wives, his royal treasury and an armoury."

"Some of his wives?" Jack queried. "I have enough trouble with one! How many does King Kofi have?"

"Three thousand, three hundred and thirty-three," Akron said. "It is a magical figure to protect the life of the king." He lowered his voice as they entered the outer courtyard. "Most of the king's wives live at a palace called Barramang."

"We would call that a harem," Jack said. "It must be a large building."

"It is," Akron said.

"Have you been there?"

Akron shook his head. "No. I have heard it is built of stone, with a lot of big rooms."

"I see." Jack thought it best to say no more.

They moved on, inside the palace gates as Jack surveyed his surroundings. He knew that any scrap of information might help him escape, although he could not think how to get through the forest between Kumasi and the coast. *The Ashantis don't need to imprison their hostages,* Jack told himself. *The jungle is a greater barrier than shackles and stone walls.*

To Jack's eyes, Bantummah was not a single building, but a group with a well-built two-storey stone tower in one corner. In common with the best houses of Kumasi, the palace was composed of several courtyards, all beautifully worked in painted stucco, with diamond and scrollwork on the red-and-white walls. One courtyard led to another, some with rounded, others square columns with pediments and capitals, but all with alcoves filled with various items.

"Is that the king's treasure?"

"His treasury and his stores," Akron replied.

Some of the alcoves held European swords, others held gold ornaments, carelessly piled together as though they were of less value than the ivory horns or colourful silk umbrellas. Jack stopped involuntarily at the alcove that held a collection of war drums, each one dark with blood, while human jaw-bones and skulls decorated the sides. It was an image that remained with Jack as Akron ushered him into the stone tower where the king had his private chambers. As he hesitated, two guards stepped closer, each with a sword at his belt, while a third prodded the muzzle of his musket hard into Jack's spine.

"Better to come this way, Major Windrush," Akron headed up a flight of stairs, with Jack a few steps behind.

The upper storey of the tower was like a cornucopia of everything the royal family had collected for generations, from Persian rugs to silver dinner services, gold masks to necklaces of aggry beads.

Akron pushed Jack in front. "Hurry, Major Windrush. The king is waiting."

The guards stepped closer as Jack approached the chamber in which the king waited. He could feel Akron's reverence when they entered the room.

"Very few foreigners are allowed into the palace," Akron spoke in hushed tones. "You are very privileged."

Jack thought of his long line of ancestors, most of whom had achieved a higher rank than he ever would, yet he doubted if any had met an African king. Whatever happened next, he would have something to boast about to his grandchildren, provided he survived.

King Kofi Karikari sat on a carved throne, with a bevy of noblemen at his back, Yaa Asantewaa in the corner and a second throne at his side. On the second throne sat what Jack guessed was the famous Golden Stool. He studied it for a moment, seeing a squat, highly carved piece of dark craftsmanship, adorned with golden plates and ornaments. It was like nothing he had seen before, yet he could feel the power emanating from that ornate piece of furniture.

As Jack looked, he became aware that in the centre of the nobles, Kumi Okese stood, with his smoky eyes glaring at Jack. Kumi Okese's fingers tapped the hilt of his sword, and he thrust his head very slightly forward.

King Kofi looked Jack up and down. "Who are you?" Akron translated the king's words.

"Major Jack Windrush of the 113th Foot, attached to the 2nd West India Regiment, Your Majesty." Jack bowed politely.

King Kofi half rose from his throne, with his mild voice at odds with his stern eyes. "Why are you in my kingdom?"

Aware that his life, and the lives of his men, depended on his answers, Jack gave a direct answer. "Your army brought me into your kingdom, Your Majesty. I had not intended to cross the Prah."

"You came to my army, which was in my territory. The Ashantis own all the land as far as the coast."

Jack knew it was not the time to dispute the boundaries of the Asantahene's kingdom. "I was sent to talk to General Amanquatia, to ask about the captive missionaries and ask if Your Majesty will release them."

"And if I do not?" King Kofi gave the hint of a smile, without a trace of humour.

Jack took a deep breath. "My sovereign, Queen Victoria of the United Kingdom of Great Britain and Ireland, will be displeased," Jack took it upon himself to expand upon his original mission. "She may decide to send an army across the Prah."

King Kofi gave a bark of laughter, which the gathering chose to mean they should laugh as well until the Asantahene raised one hand. Instant silence descended. King Kofi leaned slightly closer to Jack, with Akron still translating his words. "The people of your queen have occupied my fort of Elmina without paying tribute."

Jack had anticipated that statement. "My queen bought Elmina and the adjacent land from the previous owners, the Dutch. There was no mention of payment to your Majesty." Jack waited until Akron translated his words before he continued.

King Kofi smiled. "You say your queen may send her army against me. Do white men know how to travel to fight? You need black men to carry you."

Jack thought of the fever-ravaged traders in Cape Coast who had the local men carry them on litters as if they were either invalids or too important to walk.

"British soldiers can march anywhere," Jack said boldly. "From the snows of Canada to the mountains of Afghanistan. I have fought the queen's enemies in the Burmese forest and the plains of Russia."

King Kofi nodded solemnly. "So you say, Major Jack Windrush, yet I can see the marks of Ashanti shackles on your wrists. It is only by the kindness of our women that you are free."

"Yaa Asantewaa is indeed a generous lady and a true friend to Great Britain. Her counsel is wise." Jack floundered for words.

King Kofi laughed again, with the nobles joining in as if Jack had said something uproariously amusing. "You know little about Ashanti women, Major Jack Windrush."

"What man knows anything about any woman?" Jack countered. "I barely understand my wife!"

The king spoke again in his soft, polite voice, with Akron bowing as he translated. "Elmina is mine, and I will come and retake it by the sword. My ancestors ate and drank at Elmina, and they got whatever they wanted there. Tell your queen to pay tribute for my fort of Elmina, or I will send my armies to destroy that fort and Cape Coast Castle."

Fully aware that Colonel Harley had no intention of paying anything to King Kofi, Jack knew he could only play for time, which had been his original mission.

"I will take his Majesty's message back to my superiors," Jack hinted that he expected to get back to Cape Coast Castle soon. "Will your Majesty restrain his armies until he receives a reply?" He saw Kumi Okese inch forward, with his fist closing on the hilt of his sword.

King Kofi said something that made Kumi Okese glance at Jack with something like triumph. Akron hesitated before he translated. "The Asantahene has asked Kumi Okese to show you the power of his tribe as a warning to your queen."

What the devil does that mean? "Tell the Asantahene that I will be honoured to review Kumi Okese's warriors," Jack watched the king's face as Akron translated his words.

When King Kofi snapped an order flicked his fingers, the guards hustled Jack away, with Akron hurrying beside him and Kumi Okese a few paces behind, still gripping his sword.

About five minutes' walk from the palace, they came to an area of tall rushes around a misshapen tree, where scores of birds fought in ear-piercing disharmony. The sickly-sweet stench warned Jack there were dead bodies nearby.

"What's this?" Jack asked. "Does Kumi Okese intend to kill me, now?"

"This is the fetish tree," Akron said. "Kumi Okese wished to show you where we leave the bodies of the sacrificed."

"Oh, dear God in heaven." Jack gasped as he parted the reeds. The tree looked even uglier when Jack knew its purpose, with scores of strange fetish objects dangling from the branches. Uncounted dead bodies were scattered around, some recent, all in various stages of decomposition and many mere skeletons, with skulls lying in untidy, sun-bleached heaps. The stench was appalling, and the birds, vultures prominent among them, continued to tear at their feast despite the presence of the humans.

Kumi Okese spoke, pointing to the birds. Akron shook his head until Jack said: "Tell me what he said, Akron."

"Kumi Okese said to tell you that if he had his way you and all the hostages would end up here."

Jack faced Kumi Okese. "Tell him that we are enemies after he murdered my soldier."

Akron took a deep breath before he related Jack's words. Kumi Okese nodded grimly, growled something and stepped away.

"Kumi Okese says that if the British invade his country, he will personally feed the hostages to the birds," Akron said.

Jack forced a grin. "Dead men can't do that," he said, "and I promise that I will kill him the first chance I get."

"We have to go to the central square," Akron took hold of Jack's sleeve. "Please Major. The Asantahene ordered it."

Jack nodded. "Take me," he said.

War-hardened as Jack was, the remains of dead men did not bother him unduly. Rather it was the manner and futility of their death that sickened him. Only when the rattle of drums caught his attention did he look up.

Kumi Okese stood under his yellow umbrella with rank after rank of white-striped warriors behind him.

"How many of Kumi Okese's Edwesu warriors are there?" Jack asked.

"Some say two thousand," Akron said. "Some say five thousand."

At a word from Kumi Okese, a pair of drummers began a slow beat, with two horn-players blasting at their side. The entire force began to march, company after company of warriors, each man painted with white stripes, and each man carrying a long musket, some beautifully inlaid with gold.

Staring straight ahead, the warriors were uniformly tall and surprisingly silent for African troops. Kumi Okese watched, wordless, as his men marched past, not in step but undoubtedly disciplined until Jack reckoned that 2,500 warriors had passed him. Behind them came half a dozen policemen. Distinctive figures with their half-shaved heads and a fringe of hair over their foreheads, the policemen carried either a short lance or the whips Jack remembered from the journey from the coast. The hairstyle stirred a memory from Jack's school days when he had toiled over Homer's *The Illiad* where,

The sprinting Abantes followed hard at his heels,
Their forelocks cropped, hair grown long at the back.

Pushing the memory away, Jack glanced at the hundred women who followed the warriors, carrying powder horns and large staffs. He thought they looked every bit as formidable as the men. When they had all passed, and the drumming and blare of the horns faded away, Kumi Okese faced Jack again, spoke a few words and followed his men.

"Kumi Okese said that he will wash his warrior's feet in the blood of the British," Akron said.

"That may be so," Jack replied. "That may well be so."

Tonight, Jack promised himself. *I'll see if I can get the men out tonight and head for the coast. If we get a decent lead, I defy the Ashanti to catch us, however good they think they are.*

* * *

"Yaa Asantewaa wishes to see you." Akron's voice sounded through the darkness of the room. Jack heard the missionaries stirring in the house. He was already awake, ready to leave the house to try and rescue his men.

"I'm coming," he called.

"Hurry, Major Windrush!"

"I doubt I have any choice in the matter." Jack looked down at himself, wishing he had a candle. "Give me a minute, and I'll put on my dress uniform." He fumbled to change his uniform.

"Hurry!" Akron said. "Yaa Asantewaa is waiting!"

Dressed in his crumpled and soiled best, Jack followed Akron out of the house. Two guards fell in behind them, long muskets and knives prominent. Starlight illuminated the night-time streets, with a small patrol of police staring at them until they recognised Akron and looked hurriedly away. Somewhere a dog barked, the staccato sound echoing eerily.

"This way, Major." Yaa Asantewaa's house was at an intersection of two streets, square-built, with the shutters open and a light behind the windows. The guards hesitated outside until Akron snapped at them and they took position on either side of the door.

"I told them that you are an English gentleman," Akron said. "You do not hurt ladies."

Jack nodded. "Thank you, Akron."

Yaa Asantewaa greeted Jack with great courtesy at the open front room. "Welcome to this house," she said. "I do not normally live here, you understand." She waited for Akron to translate, "Kumasi is not my home."

Jack bowed deeply. He respected this woman, although he suspected she had no liking for him.

"This way," Yaa Asantewaa led Jack to an inner courtyard, where a banyan tree soared upward. "There is more privacy here." Her stern face relaxed in a smile. "We can talk without prying ears."

When Jack glanced at Akron, Yaa Asantewaa shook her head. "Akron occupies a very privileged position here. He will say nothing. Will you, Akron?"

"I never reveal any conversation," Akron said.

"If you did, I'd have your head," Yaa Asantewaa said without any change of expression on her face.

"I know that." Akron was equally expressionless.

"I also have a guard with us." Yaa Asantewaa indicated a broad-shouldered sentinel who appeared from the shadow of the banyan. "He knows his orders." Sitting on a beautifully carved stool, she gestured that Jack should do likewise. "I know you have spoken to the king, but I want you to tell me what the British want in our lands."

"Peace and trade, my lady," Jack said as Yaa Asantewaa's steady gaze scrutinised his face.

"Peace, trade and conquest," Yaa Asantewaa corrected. "And money. Europeans, white men, think of everything in terms of how much money they can make. They would sell their souls for money and take our Golden Stool for its monetary value."

Jack shifted uneasily, knowing there was truth in Yaa Asantewaa's words. British businessmen would sell their mothers for half a sovereign and think the bargain worthwhile, while Britain was notorious for appropriating the national symbols of other nations.

"You look askance at our dress and culture," Yaa Asantewaa spoke like a school teacher lecturing a backward pupil.

"Your ways are different from ours," Jack said, warily. He thought of the murder of Private Manning and the horror around the Fetish Tree.

"Perhaps not so different as you imagine," Yaa Asantewaa said. "We have bands to welcome our royalty. Does your Queen Victoria not have music to welcome her?"

Jack thought of the military brass bands, the flutes and drums and the highland bag-pipers. While the Ashanti soldiers had fired muskets in the air, the British and other Europeans fired 21-gun salutes; there was little difference. He had to admit Yaa Asantewaa had a point. "She does," Jack said.

"We are an empire that absorbs people and makes them into Ashantis," Yaa continued her reasoned discourse. "The British Empire also absorbs people and makes them British, as we see with your West Indian soldiers. What is the difference?"

Jack thought of the components of the British Empire; from the Inuit of Canada to the Aborigines of Australia, all were subject to the same queen. Britain itself had been formed by the union of Scotland with England and Wales and had attached Ireland in 1801. "You have a point," he admitted. He thought of his grandmother, Indian by birth, who had contributed her blood to the Windrush line, and of Mary, his Eurasian wife, mother to his quarter-Indian son.

"You do not approve of our religion," Yaa Asantewaa pointed to the fetishes that hung from the banyan tree in the courtyard.

"I do not," Jack said.

"Yet you worship a man who the Romans executed, and the very symbol of that execution is holy to your religion."

Jack could not argue. One of the principles that senior officers hammered into him when he was an ensign was to respect the religion of the people of the empire. Yet the British had crushed Thugee, an Indian religion based on killing travellers, and had ended the practice of Sati, where widows were burned on their husband's funeral pyres. Where did humanity end and religious tolerance begin?

"Our war captains wear colourful uniforms," Yaa Asantewaa said. "Don't yours?"

Jack thought of the plumes, gold braid and tassels of British officers on parade and decided that there was not much difference in military finery. He smiled. "If you saw the officers of a Highland regiment in all their glory," he said, "you'd wonder how they are ever able to fight."

"Our king and his officers of state wear gold to prove their status," Yaa ignored Jack's comments. "Does your Queen Victoria not have a crown adorned with gold and jewels?"

Jack nodded. "She has two," he said. "One in London and one in Edinburgh."

Yaa Asantewaa gave a small smile, her point proven. She shifted slightly, leaning closer to Jack. "And you think us barbaric for having a Captain for Royal Executions and an Official Executioner."

"It would be thought unusual in Europe." Jack tried to be diplomatic.

"Is the Lord Chief Justice of England not the same as a Captain for Royal Executions? He has the power to order executions or to lock up men and women for all their lives, which is torture that endures for years."

Again, Jack had to admit that Yaa was correct. "There is a similarity, Yaa Asantewaa." He held his patience, wondering why Yaa had summoned him. Akron translated diligently, standing at the side.

Yaa Asantewaa continued, pressing home her points with undeniable logic. "You also have a chief executioner, although you hide him away and pretend he is something abhorrent, yet on him depends the ultimate sanction of your law."

Jack remembered William Calcraft, only the latest in a line of official English hangmen that stretched back to the Elizabethan Jack Ketch and no doubt much further. Jack had never witnessed an execution in England but knew that public hangings had only ended a few years before, partly out of official moral indignation over the crowds of thousands who considered the spectacle to be free entertainment. Jack thought of the fetish tree. It was a repulsive sight, but not much worse than the merry old English practice of gibbeting, placing executed men in a metal frame and leaving them to rot at crossroads and other public places. It was only forty years since that monstrosity ended.

"The Golden Stool," Yaa said, smiling as she realised she was winning her argument. "Do you find that strange?"

"It is outside my experience," Jack said, cautiously.

"Yet your Queen Victoria is anointed by God, and sits on the sacred Stone of Destiny." Yaa waited a second. "A stone that one of your many aggressive kings stole from a neighbouring country."

Once again, Jack could not disagree.

"You see?" Yaa Asantewaa said, "we are more alike than not. Except the Ashantis do not have the same lust for conquest and money as white men do."

"You have slaves," Jack said. "We abolished slavery decades ago."

Yaa Asantewaa shook her head. "We treat our slaves well," she said. "Many men marry their slaves and have them as honoured wives. In your country, are there not children and men who work in dark underground mines all their lives? And women, children and men work in mills and factories, kept away from daylight and the sounds of nature?"

"There are."

"That is worse than any slavery that even our prisoners of war have to endure," Yaa said. "We would not make our children suffer in that manner."

Jack kept his temper, reminding himself of his original mission. He was here to delay any Ashanti attack on Cape Coast Castle, and to find out about the hostages. "We're not all bad," he said.

Some soldier's instinct made him turn around an instant before somebody kicked over the lantern, plunging the room into darkness. Jack saw the blur of movement, the flash of steel and the dark shape wielding the knife and then the guard was writhing on the ground with blood pumping from his throat. He heard Yaa Asantewaa gasp as the intruder jumped on her, knife held blade upmost.

"Enough!" Jack launched himself forward.

Blocking the blade with his left forearm, Jack jabbed a fist to the intruder's chin, rocking him back. The man was strong and agile, recovered quickly and tried to push Jack aside. In the dark, Jack could only see the flash of bared teeth and the glint of wide eyes. He slammed the man onto the floor, saw him roll away and leap to his feet, still holding the knife.

There was no sound except the harsh gasps of Jack and the attacker, and little whimpers from Akron, who had stepped back with both hands to his mouth.

The intruder tried to shoulder Jack out of the way, lunging at Yaa Asantewaa with the knife until Jack jabbed at the man's elbow with the heel of his hand, deflecting the blow. From the corner of his eye, he saw Yaa lift a heavy gold figurine from the back of the room and step forward.

"Keep back, Yaa!" Jack snapped, landing another punch that rocked the intruder and sprayed blood across the room. Following up with a kick from his steel-shod boots, Jack saw the intruder scramble away to the door from where he had entered. Throwing himself forward, Jack reached the door at the same time as a guard carrying a blazing torch.

For a fraction of a second, Jack and the intruder stared at each other, both panting for breath. Sergeant Wickham's eyes were narrow, with blood dribbling from his mouth where Jack's fist had cut his lip, and then he dashed away, pushing past the guard as though he was not there.

Yaa Asantewaa was breathing hard as she joined Jack, still holding the golden figurine. She pointed to Akron, who translated in a shaky voice. "Did you see who that was? Did you see his face?"

"Not clearly enough to identify him," Jack lied. "Are you all right."

"He meant to kill me." Yaa Asantewaa sat down, cradling the ornament on her lap.

"I believe he did," Jack said.

"You saved my life."

Jack nodded. "Perhaps."

"Why did you save me?"

"I don't believe in killing women," Jack said truthfully. "I am here on a diplomatic mission to try and bring peace to our empires, and I was a guest in your house."

Yaa Asantewaa gave Jack a sideways look. "Many British soldiers would have allowed that man to kill me."

"Some, perhaps. I think that most officers would have acted as I did."

Nodding, Yaa Asantewaa pushed past Jack, stepping over the body of the guard. She gave a string of orders that saw a score of warriors appear outside the house and spread out on the streets. One or two stared at Jack until Yaa waved them impatiently away.

"Yaa Asantewaa has ordered a search for the intruder," Akron said. "When they find him they'll kill him and enslave his family."

Jack nodded, expecting no less. *If the Ashantis catch Sergeant Wickham, they'll likely murder all my men.*

Yaa Asantewaa watched as a captain appeared with a squad of men behind him. "If you had not helped me, Major Windrush," she said, "I would have suspected the British had ordered me killed."

"We don't operate like that," Jack recalled that his superiors in London had once ordered him to assassinate a foreign agent. This unexpected visit to Africa was forcing him to face some uncomfortable truths.

Yaa Asantewaa gave him a sideways look. "I think the British are capable of anything if it furthers their cause. They will convince themselves they are right, whatever they do." When she leaned closer to Jack, he saw the deep intelligence in her eyes; this woman understood the British mentality far too well.

"I know the history of your people, Major Windrush," Yaa said quietly. "I know how you arrive with promises of trade and friendship, then expand and take over, always with a plausible excuse and a smile to hide the gunboats and bayonets."

"As far as I am aware," Jack said carefully, "Great Britain has no intention of taking over the Ashanti lands."

Yaa Asantewaa's eyes narrowed slightly. "You say the words Great Britain as if you were not part of it, yet you are a British officer, Major Windrush." She gasped with sudden shrewd insight. "No! You are not wholly British, are you?"

"I am as British as anybody can be," Jack said.

Shifting away from Jack, Yaa Asantewaa paced the length of the chamber with her hands working at her sides. "What are you, Major Windrush?" She turned abruptly to face him again. "You don't burn in the sun as other British do."

"My mother was half Indian," Jack felt his chin lift as if in defiance.

"I knew it!" Yaa Asantewaa said. "I knew you were different from the other cold-eyed Northerners." She gave one of her rare smiles. "Because you saved my life, Major Windrush, I'm going to send you back to Cape Coast Castle with a message from the Ashanti people."

Jack felt a lift of elation, quickly tempered by worry. "If you free me, you must also free my men," Jack said. "And the hostages."

"We have no hostages," Yaa Asantewaa said. "We do have some white guests, who will remain with us."

"And my men?" Jack wondered about Sergeant Wickham.

"They will go with you," Yaa Asantewaa said.

"Thank you." Jack did not press for the release of the hostages. He had seen them, they were reasonably safe and well, while freeing them was probably beyond Yaa Asantewaa's power.

"Here is my message," Yaa Asantewaa still spoke through Akron although Jack knew by the tone of her voice that she was sincere. "You may add it to anything that the Asantahene says. The Ashanti lands may be small to you, but they are our home, and your ways are not our ways. You are occupying our lands and interfering with our trade."

Jack nodded. He expected that scores of native tribes and small kingdoms around the globe had thought the same when the British, or the Dutch, or the Americans, Burmese, Moghuls or even Ashantis had encroached on their territory. "I will pass your message on."

Yaa Asantewaa continued. "Then also tell Colonel Harley, your Administrator- General this, Major Windrush. Tell him that we will fight to hold our lands, and fight to preserve our freedom. We have thousands of men and a barrier of forest through which white men cannot penetrate." Yaa Asantewaa stepped closer and lowered her voice so that although Akron translated in a monotone, her words still carried sincere intent. "And if our men will not fight, then I will gather the women of Ashanti together to fight for our land."

Jack had met warrior queens before, notably Jayanti during the Indian Mutiny, but Yaa Asantewaa impressed him with her sincerity. For a minute, he felt like applauding her, and then a whiff of the decaying bodies from the fetish tree came to him, and he recalled the horrific scenes of execution. *Be careful, Jack, and get your men out safe.*

"I will relay your message to my superiors," Jack said. "If we get safely to the coast."

"I will arrange for a party of warriors to escort you," Yaa Asantewaa said. She stepped back inside her house. The sun was rising now, tinging the tops of the trees and sending near-horizontal shafts of sunlight along the streets. "I do not like you, Major Windrush. I do not like the British. You do not belong in the land of the Ashantis, and you do not belong in Africa."

Jack nodded. "If the Ashantis did not raid the Fantis, the British would not make war on the Ashantis."

"The British make war on everybody," Yaa Asantewaa's tone altered. "They make war on their neighbours, and everywhere their ships can sail." She stepped back. "Although I will permit you and your men to leave, Major Windrush, I will give one warning. If you return, I will hand you over to the executioners."

"I will endeavour to avoid that," Jack said.

Chapter Thirteen

Sergeant Wickham called his men to attention when Jack entered their house.

"We're going back to the coast, lads," Jack saw that Wickham's lips were swollen and knew one of his blows had taken effect, "under an Ashanti escort, so don't do anything to antagonise them."

"What about our rifles, sir?" Private Daley asked.

"We'll be lucky to get out with our heads," Jack said. "I don't think we'll see our weapons again." He nodded to Wickham. "I need to speak to you alone, Sergeant. You lads get yourselves ready."

Jack took Wickham outside. "Explain, Sergeant?"

"Sir?" Wickham tried to look innocent.

"Don't play the old soldier with me! Why did you attempt to murder Yaa Asantewaa?"

Sergeant Wickham opened his eyes wide as if surprised by the question. "I am a British soldier, sir. Yaa Asantewaa is the enemy. It's my duty to kill the enemy."

"Don't take me for a fool, Sergeant. Why?"

When Wickham dropped his eyes, Jack took hold of his jacket. "Tell me why, Sergeant!"

Wickham straightened his shoulders. "It's a long story, sir."

"Give me the short version."

"Yaa Asantewaa is Ashanti of the Edwesu people, as is Kumi Okese. I am of the Denkyira."

Jack frowned. "And?"

For a moment, Wickham's eyes registered something like contempt, and then he resumed the habitual blank stare of a ranker talking to an officer. "The Denkyira are the true tribe of this area. We were the dominant people before the Ashanti moved in. We are enemies."

"I see." Jack knew that Wickham was not telling the whole story. "Was that not a long time ago? Are you not all the same now?"

"Do you think we are all the same because we are all black African?" Wickham had a bite in his voice. "Are white men all the same because they are from Europe? Are the French the same as the Dutch and the Scots the same as the English?"

Jack conceded that point. "You are not African, Sergeant. You are from Jamaica."

"My ancestors were carried over to Jamaica as slaves," Wickham was fighting to control his emotions. "They were slaves in the British plantations for decades before emancipation."

Jack nodded. "Your ancestors experienced rough times, Sergeant, but now you have a career in a fine regiment."

"You don't understand what it's like to be treated as an inferior all your life."

"Perhaps better than you think," Jack murmured. "Why try to kill Yaa Asantewaa?"

Wickham stiffened. "It was an Edwesu slave party of the Ashantis that raided our village and sold my ancestors to the white men as slaves."

"Ah." Jack nodded, thinking about the decades of degradation Wickham's family must have suffered as British slaves. "I understand, Wickham, but Yaa Asantewaa was not involved. She was not born then."

"It is about blood, sir."

Is it not always about blood and family? The wars between nations are only part of it. The real rivalries, the real hatreds are between families and within families.

"All right, Wickham. Your actions put your men in danger." Jack pondered for a moment. He had intended to strip Wickham of his sergeant's stripes, but he would need his expertise on the journey back to the coast.

"Yes, sir," Wickham said. "Sir, in Africa, I'd prefer to be known by my real name. I am Kwabena Badu."

For a moment, Jack was unsure of what to say. "That may well be so," he said at last, "but you enlisted as Albert Wickham, and that is the name I shall call you."

"I am more than just a sergeant in the Second West Indians," Wickham said. "I am also Kwabena Badu of the Denkyira."

"When you're time served," Jack said, "let me know. I will help you return here if that is what you wish."

Wickham's eyes were wild. "The Edwesu Ashanti are the enemies of the Denkyira people."

"If you had succeeded in murdering Yaa Asantewaa," Jack tried to keep his voice level, "the Ashanti would have killed all your men. Whatever your ancestors were, you are a sergeant in the British Army, with your primary responsibility to look after your soldiers." Jack's anger overcame him, and he raised his voice.

"You put some ancient feud before your duty, Sergeant! When we get back to Cape Coast, I will order a court-martial to see what becomes of you, but no NCO under my command will put his men in danger over a private dispute. Dismiss!"

The privates looked up as Jack and Wickham returned, neither hiding their anger. Jack took a deep breath. "Steady, lads. We'll be leaving this hellish place soon."

The Ashanti escort lined up in the street, twenty men with long muskets, twenty men who did not look in the least pleased at their task. They hurried Jack's party out of Kumasi and onto the track that led back to the coast.

"Thank you," they said, pushing the Wests along. "Thank you!"

"Major Windrush!" Abena stood under a tall tree. "Come back and see us."

Jack only had time to give Abena a wave before Mrs Ramsayer hustled her away.

As they crossed the area of marshland on the southern border of Kumasi, Jack paused for a moment to look behind him. He felt an overwhelming sense of relief to leave Kumasi. Although he had visited many terrible places in his career, none had worshipped death in such a fashion. Jack shivered, thinking of the awful end of Private Manning. As Abena had warned, somebody had removed the cross he had placed on Manning's grave.

The wave of hatred was so intense that Jack felt dizzy. Manning had been his man, and Kumi Okese had ordered him butchered for some warped religious ceremony. That had not been a soldier's death.

"I won't forget you, Stanley," Jack promised, 'I'll make Kumi Okese pay for your murder, I swear. Somehow, I'll make him pay. Yes, Abena, I'll be back, and I'll bring a whole blasted army with me!"

"Thank you!" the Ashanti escort shoved Jack in the back. "Thank you!"

"I'll see you later," Jack warned with the anger still hot inside him.

The Ashanti pushed him again, digging the butt of his musket into the small of Jack's back. "Thank you!"

Jack moved on, splashing through the marsh to the rising ground beyond, knowing he would remember Kumasi with a shiver of horror. The escort set a fast pace, which Jack was pleased to accept. *I'll write you the moment I return to Cape Coast Castle, Mary*, he said, willing himself to march along the horribly familiar road.

"Straighten up, lads," Jack snapped. "We're British soldiers, not Bushmen in uniform!" That had been Manning's phrase, and again Jack felt the twist of anger within him. "Get these feet moving! Show these Bushmen how real soldiers can march."

The Wests responded with a will, banging down their feet on the damp path as they overtook their escort, so the Ashantis had to jog to keep pace with them.

"That's my men," Jack stared at the gap where Manning should be. "That's my 2nd Wests!"

On the third day, Sergeant Wickham vanished. Jack did not see him leave. One minute he was at the rear of the Wests, the next he had gone.

"The forest took him." Private Daley said, with his eyes wide. "It swallowed him up."

Jack looked around at the forest. "Sergeant Wickham was a good soldier," he said. "Hopefully he will join us at a later date." *He's deserted*, Jack thought. *I should not have told him about the court-martial. Rather than face the disgrace, he has run. That's two men I've lost to the Ashantis. That's two scores I have to settle.*

* * *

As soon as the West Indians waded to the southern bank of the Prah, the escort turned back to Kumasi. Only then did the drumming begin, as if the entire Ashanti nation had waited until the invaders had left.

"This way Wests," Jack led his men south, still forcing the pace, thinking as much of Mary as of his duty. "Only a few days now. Keep alert for stray Ashantis."

Banging down their boots, partly relieved that they were safe but angry and guilty at the loss of Manning and Wickham, the Wests nearly double marched towards the coast.

"Halloa!" The sound of a British voice was welcome.

Jack looked up to see a shirt-sleeved man with a Havelock hanging from his forage cap, and sweat beading his face. "Halloa; what the devil are you doing so near to Ashanti land? You look like a civilian."

The man wiped the sweat from his forehead with the back of his hand. "Civilian yourself! I am Lieutenant Gordon, 98th Foot, surveying a road for the infantry. Who are you? And who are these scarecrows?"

"Major Jack Windrush, 113th Foot, with Privates Stair, Coffin, Ogston and Daley of the 2nd West India Regiment," Jack said, "returned from Kumasi in Ashantiland."

"Good God, man! What were you doing there?"

"Just talking to the king," Jack tried to sound nonchalant, "watching a few human sacrifices, the usual sort of thing."

Gordon lifted his head as the sound of voices travelled from down the track. "There's my boys now. Have to get them to work. Glad you're back safely, sir although you look awful."

Jack grinned. "Thank you, Gordon. I wouldn't cross the Prah if I were you, the Ashantis don't like visitors."

Gordon lifted a single eyebrow. "What the Ashantis want and what they're going to get are two different things, Sir."

Jack nodded, looking over his men. "Aye."

The further south Jack moved, the busier the road became as parties of workmen laboured under the direction of harassed engineers. He kept the Wests moving, fighting his fatigue, forcing himself to keep marching, thinking of Private Manning, thinking of Mary, thinking of revenge.

Chapter Fourteen

As Jack led his men into Cape Coast Castle, a fitful breeze flapped the union flag against a grey sky. With their stained uniforms hanging on emaciated bodies and their faces drawn and haggard, the Wests looked like men returning from the other side of hell. Yet when Jack inspected them, he was intensely proud; they marched with their backs straight and heads up, their arms swinging and eyes level. *They may be disarmed and battered*, Jack thought, *but by the Gods of War, these are men, and as good soldiers, as any I have known.*

"You lads get along to the hospital, get examined, and get some food and rest." Jack watched them march away, smiling as he contemplated a hot bath and writing a letter to Mary.

"Good afternoon, sir." Captain Brett looked tense. "Welcome back. Colonel Harley requests your presence."

"He can wait," Jack refused to lose his dream of a hot bath.

Brett shook his head. 'Sorry, sir. He's insistent." He put his hand on Jack's shoulder. "I'm sorry, Windrush, I really am."

"Sorry?" Jack said, but Brett was already three steps in front, heading for the Administrator's office.

* * *

Colonel Harley sat in a deep chair with his beard unkempt and deep lines around his eyes and nose. He looked up, unsmiling when Jack entered.

"Sit down, Major Windrush."

Jack sat on a hard chair, hoping that the Administrator-General did not keep him long. That bath was more appealing by the minute, while if he wrote a letter today, he could catch the next ship for Britain. He could imagine Mary's expression as she read about his adventures in Kumasi.

"I imagine you have had some interesting times, Major Windrush." Colonel Harley spoke formally.

"I would agree, sir," Jack said cautiously.

Harley looked away for a moment. "I won't ask for a report, yet, Major." He hesitated again. "I am afraid I have some bad news for you."

"Indeed, sir?" Jack straightened in his chair.

"It is your wife," Harley held Jack's eyes in an expressionless gaze. "We had a message about her."

"Mary?" Jack felt sudden concern. "She will be safe in England now."

Harley took a deep breath. "I am sorry, Windrush. I only wish that were the case."

Jack could only stare at the Administrator-General as the fear mounted within him. "What has happened, sir? Where is my wife?"

"Oh, my dear fellow," Harley changed from a stuffy, straight-faced official weighed down with responsibility to a caring human being. "I am so sorry."

"Sorry?" Jack could only repeat the word. He felt sick.

"Oh, my dear fellow," Harley repeated.

"What's happened to Mary?" Jack half rose from his seat. At that second, he could not have cared less about the fate of the Gold Coast Colony. The Ashantis could have it, and all the rest of Africa, as long as Mary was safe.

"There was a severe water shortage in Cape Coast Castle while you were away and some unfortunate people, the Fanti refugees, were in a bad way."

Jack nodded. "Mary got involved," he forced all emotion from his voice. Mary would have been the first to help.

"Mrs Windrush got involved," Harley confirmed. "She badgered me to send a section to fetch water from one of the small rivers." He gave a small smile. "Mrs Windrush is the most persistent of ladies."

"She is," Jack agreed. He grasped Harley's use of the present tense. "Is? Is she still alive?"

Harley gave a brief nod. "I believe so, Major Windrush."

Immediate apprehension replaced Jack's surge of relief. "You believe so? You're not sure?"

"Let me finish, Major." Harley held up his hand. "I sent out men to fetch water, and Mrs Windrush accompanied them herself, to supervise, as she said."

"I can imagine Mary doing that," Jack could not hide the pride in his voice even as he hated the dangers to which Mary exposed herself.

"The first trip was a success, but the Ashantis must have been watching. They ambushed the second patrol."

Jack stiffened. "And?"

"The Ashanti captured two men and Mrs Windrush." Harley looked away. "The Ashantis took their prisoners into the bush. I sent out strong patrols to search as soon as the news reached us."

Jack waited, unable to say anything.

"One of the patrols found the two soldiers, both decapitated," Harley spoke so quietly that Jack could hardly hear him.

"And Mary?" Jack had to struggle for breath.

"We heard nothing until this morning when one of our spies told us that Mrs Windrush had been held captive at Effutu and was now with the other hostages in Kumasi."

Jack flinched. "Held in Kumasi? Dear God, I've just left that place! If I had known that!" He thought of the human sacrifices and the fetish trees. Kumasi was the last place on earth that he wanted Mary to be.

No; the missionaries there are decent people. They will look after her. She is alive and in no immediate danger.

"Don't you fret, Windrush. We'll get her back. I'm a married man myself; I know how you must be feeling." Colonel Harley leaned back in his chair. "I have made it a point to demand the release of all King Kofi's hostages, and Mrs Windrush will be included."

Jack stood up. "Sir; give me a company of good men. With a hundred Wests and Royal Marines, I'll hammer through to Kumasi and free the hostages!"

"And get yourself and your men killed in the process," Harley said, shaking his head with a sad smile. "I can't allow that, I'm afraid, not against such redoubtable forest warriors as the Ashanti. No, Windrush. Careful planning is the way to defeat the Ashanti, not a madcap dash through Africa."

Jack took a deep breath, knowing he had allowed his emotions to control his sense. Harley was correct; the Ashantis would destroy anything less than an army. "When are we attacking Kumasi, sir?"

"I cannot answer that, Windrush. As you may be aware, I am being replaced. Major General Wolseley is on his way to Cape Coast, and he has his own ring of officers."

"If he does not want me on the expedition," Jack said. "Then I'll hand in my papers and go as a blasted war correspondent. I'm damned if I'll let Mary stay in that hellish place one hour longer than necessary."

"Calm yourself, Windrush," Harley said. "I am sure General Wolseley will always find a use for such a resourceful officer as you have proved to be."

Jack took a deep breath. "Thank you, sir."

"In the meantime, keep yourself busy. I am sure the Wests would appreciate your help. Go home, get some rest, write your report and in a day or so I wish you to resume your duties. The 2nd Wests are short of officers so I'll officially second you to them."

Jack knew Harley was trying to be kind, although at the minute he could not think of anything except Mary in Kumasi.

* * *

Jack viewed the company he now commanded, nodding to the familiar faces and wishing that Sergeant Wickham was still with him. A good NCO was worth his weight in gold in any military unit. Private Stair greeted him with a very undisciplined grin, while Coffin looked as professional as any Guardsman. Jack did not approach Ogston in case the rum fumes should knock him down.

"Right, lads. In a few weeks, we'll be going up against some of the fiercest and most experienced forest fighters in Africa in their domain. They know the forest, and how it works, so we have to be better than them."

C Company, 2nd West Indian Regiment listened intently, with the veterans nodding agreement. Daley was shaking slightly, either with fever or nervousness.

Jack spoke slowly, allowing the men time to absorb his words. "The Ashantis have the advantages of knowing the terrain and how it works. We have the advantages of better weapons, better discipline and," Jack paused for effect, "we have the advantage of being the 2nd West."

While a British regiment might have cheered at those words, the West Indians remained silent, with only the men who returned from Kumasi allowing even a smile to crease their faces. *I'll have to do something about esprit de corps,* Jack thought.

"Until today," Jack said. "You have used the muzzle-loading Enfield Rifle. Today I'll introduce you to the breech-loading Snider," Jack said, "and when you are all familiar with it, we'll practice skirmishing and bush warfare."

Again, the response was muted. Daley looked decidedly nervous as if he lacked the confidence to learn anything new.

"I have managed to obtain sufficient Sniders for us," Jack beckoned to a corporal, who handed him a rifle.

"The Snider will be your weapon for the remainder of the campaign. It is 54 inches long and weighs nine pounds three ounces, so it is slightly longer and heavier than the Enfield. It has a range of 1000 yards, although when you're fighting in the bush, you'll be much closer to the enemy. I want you all to take a few moments to familiarise yourself with the weight and feel."

As the West Indians examined the weapon, Jack explained the technical details. "Unlike your old Enfield, the Snider is breech-loading, so your rate of fire will be faster. Once you gain experience, you'll be able to fire perhaps ten rounds a minute compared to two with the Enfield." Jack held up a Snider cartridge. "The bullet has a detonator cap within the base, dispensing with the need for a percussion cap." Jack watched his men. "These are major advantages. You can fire five shots to the Ashanti's one, and your bullets are infinitely more powerful than his slugs. You don't need to fear him, even in the forest."

"We don't fear him, Sir," Ogston said, with the rum working in his system. "The Ashantis murdered Stan Manning and Sergeant Wickham. I want to get back at them."

"So do I Ogston," Jack said, waving back the shocked corporal who wanted to blast Ogston into silence for his impertinence. "And the more skilled we are with the Snider, the better chance we'll have of victory, so pay attention!"

"Yes, sir!" Ogston shouted.

With the men settled down, Jack demonstrated the use of the rifle, noting the West Indians were quick to understand the new procedure of loading through the breech rather than the old way by the muzzle.

"We'll have a few practise rounds." Jack glanced over his men. "As I explained, with the Snider, we already have an immense superiority in firepower over the Ashanti. With better skirmishing, we will be able to meet them in their own forests. I have heard good things about the fighting ability of the 2nd West, and I have seen some of you in action; I want us to be the best company in Wolseley's army!"

Private Stair grinned at Jack's words. He opened his mouth to speak, thought better of it, and said nothing.

"Target practise," Jack said. "We start now."

Leading his company to the beach, Jack set up a row of sand-filled sacks as targets.

"These sacks are about the size of a man's body," he said. "We'll practise shooting until every man of you can hit them eight times out of ten at a hundred yards, and then we'll try at a hundred and fifty yards, and so on."

As the men lined up to fire, Jack walked behind them, correcting the angle of their rifles. "Aim low," he said. "If you can see your target, aim for the broadest part of their body, where the belt buckle would be. If you can't see a belt aim where you think one should be."

When they fired, only the veterans were close to the target, with the others jerking at the triggers as if they could force out the bullet by sheer force. One by one, Jack corrected the faults, although, by the time he had the majority of them hitting the target, daylight was fading.

Jack wiped the sweat from his forehead. "Not bad, lads. You're a lot better than you were this morning."

The men looked at him, some smiling, others tired.

"Daley, you did very well." Jack encouraged the most nervous man in the company. "Carry on like that, and the Russians would run away from you, let alone the Ashantis."

"They'd run because he so ugly, sir." Stair said.

"I not ugly!" Daley said. "You ugly, man!"

Lieutenant Hopringle sauntered up. "Good evening, sir."

"Evening, Hopringle," Jack said.

"I wondered what all the noise was," Hopringle said. "Excuse me for saying, sir, but is training musketry not an NCO's job?"

"I like to keep myself busy," Jack said. *If I don't, I'll be worrying myself to distraction over Mary.*

"Yes, sir,' Hopringle said. "I was sorry to hear about Mrs Windrush, Sir."

"Thank you," Jack said curtly. "I think my lads are tired of shooting for now. I'll show them some skirmishing tomorrow, how we did it against the Plastun Cossacks."

"I'm sorry to be the bearer of bad tidings, sir, but you won't be skirmishing tomorrow."

"Why is that, Hopringle?"

"General Wolseley is arriving at Cape Coast soon, sir, and Colonel Harley has appointed you to command the guard of honour."

"What?" Jack looked around in alarm. "I want my men to be fighting troops, not parade ground soldiers. When does Wolseley arrive?"

"The day after tomorrow, sir, so you'd better curtail your shooting and skirmishing drill and get your men ready for something much more important, like looking pretty for the commander."

Chapter Fifteen

"I don't have time to mount a guard of honour, sir," Jack tried to control his frustration. "I need to train these men, so they are fit to fight the Ashantis."

"You'll have time, Windrush," Colonel Harley said. "I can't see General Wolseley landing on Monday and attacking Kumasi on Tuesday. He's a methodical man. In the meantime, we need to welcome him to the Gold Coast, and you'll be the first officer he sees."

Jack took a deep breath, thinking of Mary under the Ashantis' power. "I'd rather get the men ready for fighting, sir."

"I have given my orders, Windrush."

"Yes, sir. You mean I have to provide the guard of honour at the landing stage and Government House?"

"That's right old boy. We don't have sufficient men for both." Colonel Harley smiled. "If the Ashantis knew we only held this territory by bluff and smoke, they would waltz right in and depose us tomorrow."

"It's the same in many of our colonies," Jack spoke to calm himself down. "We hold Canada with a handful of regiments and a half-trained militia, Australia with less and I doubt we have enough fit men in all West Africa to fill one full-strength battalion."

"Quite right. We rule half the world by brazen cheek, and the navy." Harley said. "And you'll have to use that same strategy to provide two guards of honour with one company of Wests. I simply don't have enough men to spare you more, and the general will expect all the trimmings."

"I was hoping to train my company in skirmishing," Jack said.

"I selected your company because you train them so assiduously," Harley said. "The general arrives on *Ambriz* the day after tomorrow." He nodded to the door. "That does not give you any time to waste."

* * *

"Right, men," Jack addressed his company. "Colonel Harley has chosen us to be the Guard of Honour for Sir Garnet Wolseley in two places in succession. That is impossible for any regiment, except for the 2nd West India."

The men looked pleased with the praise. Stair nodded as if he was giving his approval.

"We'll have to look our best, lads, and move quickly."

For the full next day, Jack drove his company hard, having them stand at attention at the landing stage, then double to Government House and parade again. In the evening, he ensured their uniforms were at their best, brushed, pressed, and clean.

"You'll do," Jack was nearly dropping with weariness when, at last, he believed them ready. "It's an important day tomorrow, lads. Make yourselves proud."

Only when he returned to Green Lettuce Lane did Jack think of his own dress uniform. Dragging it from the cupboard, he sighed at the damage and set to work as best he could.

* * *

Through his binoculars, Jack saw a seagull perched on the masthead of the African Steamship Company's *Ambriz*. "Ready men,'" Jack said softly. "If I heard right about General Wolseley, he'll have his telescope trained on us to note every defect in our uniform and bearing."

As *Ambriz* eased closer, Jack watched her progress towards Cape Coast Castle. Knowing the strain of standing at attention for prolonged periods, Jack waited until he could see the crown superimposed on the red cross of the company flag before he called his men to attention. Only a few of the crowd bothered to look at the West Indians as they lined the landing-place, for the arrival of the new governor was more interesting than a company of soldiers.

"Here he comes, men!" Hoping Wolseley did not inspect his battered dress uniform too carefully; Jack called C Company to attention. Major General Wolseley disembarked with a core of selected 'special service' officers around him. Thin faced with a neat moustache, the general marched past the West Indians with an appreciative glance. He stopped at Sergeant Mathews at the end of the line. "Good show," he said. "Very smart," and moved on to Government House with his entourage following.

The moment Wolseley was out of sight, Jack ordered his men to move at the double, avoiding the general's route as they nearly ran through the narrow streets of Cape Coast to Government House, where Colonel Harley waited anxiously at the head of the long garden.

"Same routine, men," Jack said, noting some of the Wests were panting with exertion. "The general will be here in a minute. You're looking fine, Daley. Ogston, try not to breathe too hard, we don't want General Wolseley reeling drunk before he's properly arrived. Stop smiling Stair."

"Here he comes, sir," Sergeant Mathews said.

Once again, Wolseley spared a few moments to inspect the West Indians before entering the house. Once again, he stopped before the immaculate Sergeant Mathews. "Excellent turnout," he said and stepped inside the large building. "Your 2nd Wests are a credit to the army in dress and appearance," he said to Jack.

"Thank you, sir."

"It's a pity your uniform lets your men down," Wolseley said quietly. "I'd get a better servant, Major."

Jack had known Wolseley as a young officer in the Crimea, but promotion had been rapid, and now Wolseley arrived as major-general and Governor of the Gold Coast while Jack was only a major.

Leaving Jack feeling foolish, Wolseley greeted Harley with a handshake and entered the wide doorway of Government House. A heavily moustached captain stopped briefly beside Jack.

"Don't take it hard, sir. Sir Garnet always hates sea voyages. They bring out the worst in him."

"You'd best come inside, Windrush," Colonel Harley said. "Dismiss your men."

Still irritated at the loss of time on what he considered a pointless exercise, Jack entered Government House with all its opulence as his men returned to their austere barracks.

Even before all the officers and officials filed into the great hall, Wolseley read his letter of appointment, with the Chief Justice of the colony looking suitably self-important in his barrister's wig and gown, so unsuitable for the climate. Near the back of the gathering, the captain who had spoken to Jack introduced himself.

"Redvers Buller," he said. "60th Rifles."

"I know the name," Jack said. "You were with Wolseley in the Red River Expedition."

"I was," Buller was about 35, with a bluff appearance and a slight West Country burr to his voice.

"Jack Windrush," Jack said. "113th Foot."

Buller looked at Jack with his head on one side. "Fighting Jack?"

"That's one name they called me."

Buller nodded. "Careful, the general is coming." He stepped aside.

With the ceremony complete, Wolseley immediately became business-like, pushing past the civilians to speak to his circle of officers.

"Buller," he said, "I want you in charge of intelligence gathering."

"Yes, sir," Buller nodded as if he expected nothing less.

Wolseley pulled Jack aside. "You were the officer with the Guard of Honour."

"I was, sir." Jack waited for more criticism.

"I noticed the same faces on guard at the landing stage and here," Wolseley said.

Jack nodded. Sir Garnet Wolseley was a vastly experienced fighting man and nobody's fool.

"Are we that short of men, Major? How many fighting men do we have in the colony?"

"Less than a thousand, sir," Jack replied. "Including the West Indians and Marines."

"Good God." Wolseley frowned. "I know your face. Who are you?"

"Major Jack Windrush, sir, 113th Foot."

"That's right," Wolseley nodded. 'I remember you from the Crimea. How many men exactly, Major?"

Jack had already ascertained the number. "Seven hundred soldiers of the 2nd West India regiment, sir, with only 398 fit for field service and 102 in Cape Coast Castle. Captain Thompson of the Queen's Bays informs me he has ten fit men of the Fanti police fit for service."

Wolseley raised his eyebrows slightly. "And our native allies?"

"I don't think there are many, sir. Colonel Glover has some up-country, with the Hausas."

"I'll speak to you later, Windrush," Wolseley ordered. "I'll send for you when I want you."

I have an unknown length of time to train my company.

Chapter Sixteen

"All right, men," Jack paced in front of C Company. "I've led some of you in your first action, and your lack of experience showed."

The men looked at him, some sullen under his admonishing tone, others expressionless. Daley looked as if was he was about to burst into tears.

"Outside Elmina, you did better than the Hausas, but not as well as the Royal Marines, and they are mostly children, and part-time sailors, not professional soldiers like you."

Jack paced the length of the West Indian line and returned, aware that every man was watching him, waiting for his next words.

"Now you have met the enemy; some few of you have seen their capital city with all the horrors of human sacrifice." Jack paused beside Ogston. "You know the Ashantis murdered Private Manning." As he hoped, his words brought a low growl from the men. He waited until the sound ended before he continued.

"You also know how the Ashantis fight and you know you are better than them."

Some of the men looked a bit brighter at those words. Stair tightened his grip on his Snider.

"I intend to make you better than the Royal Marines, better than any of the regular British regiments that may land here and, by God, better even than the Brigade of Guards. When I have finished, in times to come, men will say with pride that they marched and fought beside the 2nd West India Regiment!"

Now even Daley was smiling.

"But first we have to work at it," Jack said. "Sergeant Mathews, I will need your expertise."

Jack knew he had to push them to their limit, for although they were brave as any men he had fought beside, they knew little about skirmishing, their firing, although improved, was not as good as he wished, and their discipline was poor.

"You have a lot to learn," Jack said. "And I am just the man to teach you." He also had to work himself hard, for the moment he stopped, he thought of Mary trapped inside Kumasi, and in constant danger. Acutely aware that worrying did not help anything, Jack concentrated on training his company. The harder they trained, the better soldiers they would be and the more effective in fighting the Ashanti and therefore in rescuing Mary.

I'm not going into that forest with a company of half-trained soldiers. I will drill these men and train them until they are as good as any soldiers in the world.

After ensuring his company could fire at stationary targets, Jack asked for two volunteers.

"Why, sir?" Coffin asked.

"You will be pulling moving targets for the others," Jack said. "I'll show you." Fastening a long rope onto a six-foot-long log, he hauled it across the beach. "The log is the target, not the men pulling." He knew that Stair would step forward. "You and me then, Stair."

"Aim at the logs," Jack ordered. "Pretend it's an Ashanti!"

Nobody hit the target at the first attempt, Jack rotated the men pulling, demonstrated what he expected and kept the men working. The Wests fired by sections and then individually until they could all hit the target four times out of five.

"Better," Jack said as the echoes of the firing faded with the last of the sun. "You can hit your mark and no casualties. Tomorrow we'll progress to the next stage, avoiding being shot."

The Wests watched him, listening, all aware of the spectators who had gathered to watch Jack's novel ideas of training. "Dismiss."

Nights were the worst, when Jack lay awake, worrying about Mary. He tried whisky, which made him feel worse and tried pacing the ramparts until the sentries grew used to his company. Leaving his house, he lived in the Officer's Mess, sleeping on a cane chair and growing morose and ill-tempered, living only to train his men.

"If the enemy can see you, he has a better chance of shooting you," Jack said as the skies greyed with the dawn. "So you have to learn to take cover."

The Wests listened, slowly learning the skills that Jack had garnered over two decades of soldiering.

"Forget the parade ground soldiering," Jack said. "The Ashantis don't fight like the French at Waterloo. Fight to survive; fight to win." He paced the ranks, "I don't want you to defeat the enemy. I want you to destroy them."

With Colonel Wood of the 90th Foot mounting patrols to keep away any prowling Ashantis, Jack had space in which to train his men. He gave them instructions in the Ashanti way of fighting and showed them how to counter ambushes, either firing from behind cover or charging forward. The men responded with a will, although Jack still thought their fire discipline was poor.

Recruiting a hundred local Fanti tribesmen, Jack had them cut battle-paths alongside a local forest path and gave each man a captured musket with powder but no ball. Speaking through a local Krooman, he gave the Fantis orders.

"You men are to be the enemy," he said. "You are armed with blanks so you can't hurt anybody. Ambush my company."

The Fantis stared at him in complete confusion.

"Tell them they are to try to ambush my men without being seen," Jack told the translator. When the Fantis got the idea, they grinned and scampered away. Allowing the Fantis ten minutes to arrange themselves, Jack addressed C Company.

"Ready, lads?" Jack led his men to the closest patch of forest where a narrow path sliced between the trees. "You have blank ammunition in case you fire at each other." Without mentioning the Fantis, he gave his orders. "Keep apart as I trained you, and march along the path. React to any surprises." Jack issued instructions, divided his men into sections of ten and sent the first section into the bush.

As soon as the Wests were fairly on the path, Jack joined the Fantis. Recalling fighting the Mutineers and Cossacks, Jack walked slowly, avoided twigs and loose branches, and slid beneath creepers. He followed the Fantis' battle path, stopped behind a brightly flowering bush and watched his men.

As he expected, the first section of Wests had bunched together as soon as they rounded the first bend. They were laughing and talking as they walked, not taking the exercise seriously.

"Right you Fantis," Jack spoke through his translator. "On my word, fire at the men."

Waiting until the section was level, Jack had his Fantis fire a volley, with the powder- smoke nearly filling the track. As the Wests recoiled in confusion, Jack leapt out, grabbed the last man and dragged him into the forest. Before Private Adams had time to react, Jack stuffed a gag in his mouth and had two grinning Fantis tie him up.

"Keep alert next time," Jack growled in Adams' ear.

By now, the section was firing wildly and shouting orders to each other. Leaving them to it, Jack led his Fantis and their reluctant prisoner away, crossed the main path higher up and waited in a second ambush site.

When the section eventually stopped firing, they moved on in better discipline although shaken by the loss of one of their men and not sure what was happening. Jack lay low, holding a loop of rope. Again he waited until the last man was passing, threw the loop over his trailing leg, tripped him and dragged him, yelling into the forest. Now thoroughly alarmed, the section again opened a wild fire as the Fantis fired a volley and scampered along the battle path.

After a quarter of an hour, the section was firing at every movement, so Jack carried his prisoners back to the starting point, released them and had Sergeant Mathews bring the discomfited men back to the beach.

"You see what happens when you disobey orders?" He railed at the shame-faced men. "Next time, stay in skirmishing formation, each man watching over his mate. Watch for ambushes and only fire when you're sure of a target." He pointed to the next section. "Now Sergeant Mathews will lead you in."

Jack stood back. Throughout the training, he had one overriding idea; he wanted to ensure these men could out-march, out-shoot, and out-fight the Ashantis. Every Ashanti they killed was one less to harm Mary.

With the example of the shamed section before them, Mathews' men fared better, obeying orders to stay apart and responding to the ambush with controlled fire.

"Now the next section," Jack said, and doubled the number of ambushes, varying his technique each time to keep his men guessing.

For three days, Jack hammered his company in fighting off ambushes, then on the fourth, he marched them to the beach, firing from various positions, standing, kneeling and lying.

"Look for whatever cover you can," Jack said. "If the enemy can't see you, he can't shoot you." He watched them stare across the sandy expanse. "Aye, it's easy enough in the forest, but not here, eh? Look for dead ground, dunes or anything that can keep you alive."

"We were always taught that soldiers stood straight and proud," Private Ogston sounded confused.

"In this campaign, and under my command," Jack said, "I want you to hide behind trees or rocks or bushes. Immerse yourself up to your nose in a swamp if you need to, as long as you can kill the enemy before he kills you. The Ashantis have developed a technique of fighting that works in their forests, so we'll use it against them, but better." He stepped closer to Ogston until their faces were nearly touching. "I want you to stay alive, Edward!" He doubted that any officer or NCO had ever called Ogston by his first name before.

I want you to stay alive, Edward Ogston, so you can help me get Mary back.

"I want you to live to tell your grandchildren about the days you fought and defeated the Bushmen, the savage Ashantis."

When the men gave a nervous grin at that, Jack knew he was training them harder than they had ever worked in their lives.

He continued, driving them on when they wanted to collapse, training them in concealing themselves by making them take cover and throwing stones at any part of them that he could see. Every evening he had them post sentries, and checked each man, then sent small parties out with orders to sneak up to the sentinels without being seen. He stopped that particular exercise after Private Stair fired his rifle, called out the guard and woke half the Cape Coast Castle garrison. When half a dozen irate senior officers returned to their bed, grumbling about being awakened by "damned uppity majors and damned jumpy sentries," Jack sought out the abashed private.

"Well done, Stair," Jack said. "You did exactly what an alert sentry is supposed to do. Any fault lies with me, not you."

Stair gave a wide smile. "I've never seen a colonel wearing a night-cap before, sir. It was worth it just for that."

Jack hid his grin. "Yes, Stair. It was." *You'll go far Stair. I only wish privates in the Wests could earn commissions. You'd brighten up any officers' Mess.*

After a week, a servant delivered a small booklet to Jack's house. Entitled *The Soldier's Pocket Book*, General Wolseley had written it especially for the forthcoming campaign. When Jack read through the notes, he nodded at the advice, and the next day passed the best on to his men.

They stood on the beach with the offshore breeze pleasant and the usual gathering of spectators waving to the Wests.

"Ignore your admirers," Jack said. "Especially you, Stair. I can see three young women who want to make you their own."

Jack paraphrased Wolseley's book, adding modifications from his own experience. "We'll divide the company into four sections, with an officer or NCO in command of each. Once Lieutenant Hopringle recovers from the fever he'll have One Section; I'll take Two Section, Sergeants Mathews and Roberts will take Three and Four." *That made sense when fighting in such close country. Wolseley knows his job.*

"These sections will remain together and perform all details, except pickets, which half-sections will perform."

Jack looked around the men. They were paying attention, some nodding at all the correct places.

"When we are in action," Jack spoke slowly to press home his points. "Three sections of the company will be extended, with the fourth in support of the skirmishing line. All fighting against the Ashantis will be in skirmishing order with the files two, three or four paces apart, as we have been practising this last week."

Some men nodded, with the veterans beginning to understand what Jack had been trying to drive home.

"Remember, when in action, with the smoke and noise confusing you, and wounded men lying on the ground, the support section must not lag. Stay in sight of the skirmishing line, even in thick bush. You will be in two-man files, and always keep together to support each other."

As Jack had expected, the men looked at their opposite numbers, to check they had not suddenly run away.

"Two more things, men," Jack said. "You know that the Ashanti fight with ambushes in the bush. When they ambush us, and they will, find cover and aim low where you see the smoke. Don't waste ammunition. The bearers will have to carry every bullet we fire."

From the beach, Jack led them on another drill in the forest, with platoon against platoon and section against section, pushing deeper into the bush to familiarise his men with the environment.

"Sir!" Private Coffin gestured with his head. "I can see something ahead."

"Halt!" When Jack gave the quiet order, the company stopped at once, waiting. "What can you see, Coffin?"

"I'm not sure, sir." Coffin spoke quietly. "There's something ahead, off the path."

Drawing his revolver, Jack instinctively checked it was loaded. "You men find cover and keep alert. Coffin show me."

The instant Coffin pointed ahead with his chin, Jack saw the flash of gold. He stepped carefully forward and removed the purple-and-gold scarf from the bush in which it had become entangled.

"You are right, Coffin," Jack said. "This does not belong here." He held it close, remembering Mary buying that scarf from a bazaar in Gondabad. Either the Ashantis had taken her this way, or they had stolen her scarf and dropped it. "Well done, Coffin."

Jack held the scarf for a long minute before tucking it inside his tunic. Taking a deep breath, he turned to his men. "That's us for the day, Wests." He knew he could not concentrate on his duty at that moment.

I cannot sit in the castle, waiting for something to happen. If I am not active, I will go crazy with worry. I'll continue to train my men, but they need battle experience.

With C Company safely inside Cape Coast Castle, Jack turned to face the forest. The sun eased in the west, gloriously orange, then slid away as velvet darkness spread across Africa. Jack held Mary's scarf in both hands.

"Hold on, Mary," he said. "I'm coming for you. I'm training my men so nothing will stand in our way. Whatever happens, stay alive."

The darkness was sinister, silent except for the hush and suck of the surf and the distant rustle of trees. Only when Jack turned away did the drums start with a slow, repetitive beat.

Chapter Seventeen

"Ah, Major Jack Windrush!" General Sir Garnet Wolseley held out his hand.

Wolseley was young for his rank, with a small moustache enhancing his eager face, but it was his cheerful demeanour that attracted men to him.

"Yes, sir."

They were in Government House, with a cool breeze easing through the window and two busy secretaries at the other end of the room. Lieutenant Wood, Wolseley's aide-de-camp, stood at attention behind the desk, looking every bit the aristocrat that he was.

"We were in the Crimea together twenty years ago," Wolseley remembered. "You were a good soldier, Windrush. I don't understand how you have not advanced beyond your present rank."

"I couldn't say, sir."

"Perhaps this campaign will be the springboard." Wolseley nodded as the door opened and Hook walked in. "You know General Hook, I believe."

"I do, sir."

"Oh, don't mind me, you fellows." Hook took a seat, crossed his legs and lit a cheroot. "Pretend I am not here."

Wolseley continued, addressing Jack. "You were in Kumasi, Windrush."

"I was, sir."

"And returned with most of your men." Wolseley gestured to Jack to sit opposite him.

"I lost two men, sir." Jack kept his voice level. "The Ashanti executed Private Manning, and Sergeant Wickham disappeared on the journey home."

134

"Executed?" Wolseley raised his eyebrows.

"They sacrificed him, sir. They chopped off his head."

"Did they, by God? A British soldier." Wolseley's expression sharpened. "You'll want to return to Kumasi then, Major."

"Yes, sir. My wife is there."

"I know," Wolseley said softly. "We'll get her back, Windrush, don't you fear."

"Yes, sir," Jack said.

Wolseley smoothed his moustache. "I plan to march my army from Cape Coast Castle to Prahsu, about 70 miles inland, cross the Prah and continue to Kumasi."

"Yes, sir," Jack said. "When do we start?"

Wolseley gave a small smile. "Not until I am ready, Windrush. In this part of the world, the organisation is everything. I will raise a force of natives, stiffened with British officers, and whatever men I have here." Nodding to Wood, Wolseley said. "Take notes, Lieutenant while Windrush tells me about the road, the conditions our troops are likely to face, if you think the Ashantis will fight and what sort of warriors they are."

Taking a deep breath, Jack gave details of his enforced journey to Kumasi and what he had seen of the Ashantis.

"Tell me of the Ashantis battle tactics, Windrush." The general listened as Jack explained about the war captains and the umbrellas, the ambushes, muskets and few modern rifles.

"Ambuscade, then," Wolseley ensured that Wood scribbled more notes. "They form a horseshoe around their enemy and hit the flanks. That tallies with my previous information. Continue, Windrush."

"Yes, sir. When we were fighting in the bush outside Elmina, I noticed that the Ashanti seemed to appear and disappear at will." Jack noticed that Wolseley was listening carefully, as was Hook. "The warriors had made small paths through the forest, only big enough for one man to use at a time, running parallel to the road."

"Is that how they ambush their enemies?" Hook asked.

"Yes, sir."

"Clever." Hook said. "Did you learn anything else?"

"Yes, sir. I have a message from an Ashanti noblewoman," Jack said. "A lady named Yaa Asantewaa."

"A woman?" Wolseley half-smiled. "Is she important?"

"The Ashanti are a matrilineal society, sir," Jack said. "Their royal line descents from the female side. Yaa Asantewaa is the equivalent of a duchess of the royal blood in Britain."

"Oh," Wolseley did not look impressed. "What does this Yaa woman have to say for herself?"

Jack brought Yaa Asantewaa's words to his mind. "She said that the Ashanti lands might be small to us, but they are their home, and our ways are not their ways. She said that we are occupying their lands and interfering with their trade."

"Did she indeed? This woman has strong opinions." Wolseley nodded. "Carry on."

"Yaa Asantewaa also said that the Ashanti would fight to hold their lands, and preserve their freedom." Jack could sense that Wolseley was not impressed. "She said they have thousands of men and a barrier of thick forest through which white men cannot penetrate."

Wolseley looked up. "The Ashantis greatest defence is the forest, climate and disease. That is why I intend to raise a local army. Only if that proves impossible will I have to prove that white men, or British soldiers at least, can penetrate their forest and fight them in their heartland."

"Unless we do, sir, they will never feel defeated," Jack said. "We beat them on the plain outside Elmina, but they believe they are invincible in the forest."

"Yes, indeed," Wolseley said. "If I must use British soldiers, I'll march to Kumasi in the dry season, between December and February. With or without tribal help, I'm going to invade Ashantiland, Windrush. I have the Rifles, the 23rd Foot and the 42nd Highlanders standing by. Will the Ashanti warriors fight British regulars?"

"Yes, sir, they'll fight. They don't have a high opinion of us as soldiers."

Wolseley pondered for a few moments before replying. "You'll know I have brought out several special service officers, including young Wood here, Viscount Halifax's son, don't you know."

"Yes, sir."

Wolseley smiled. "The press calls them the Wolseley Gang. Well Windrush, if you acquit yourself well out here, you may join us."

With Wolseley as the rising star of the military establishment, being included in his immediate entourage would mean almost certain promotion. "Thank you, sir."

Jack heard Hook clear his throat and scrape a boot across the floor.

"Did Yaa Asantewaa say anything else?" Hook asked.

"Yes, sir. She said that if the Ashanti men did not fight, then she would use the Ashanti women."

Jack expected Wolseley to ridicule the notion of Ashanti women fighting regular British soldiers. Instead, the general raised his eyebrows, with Hook bending forward.

"Is she as determined as her words sound, Windrush?" Hook asked.

"I believe so, sir. The Ashanti are a proud people."

Wolseley drummed his fingers on the desk. "You have experience of fighting the Ashantis, and you know them well. I'm going to use you, Windrush."

"Thank you, sir." Jack had a mental vision of the executioner slicing off Manning's head, and of Mary struggling in the hands of two white-striped warriors.

"It will be a hard fight, Sir. Can you guarantee the lives of the hostages when we invade?" From the corner of his eye, Jack saw Hook shake his head in warning. Special Service officers were there to support the general, not put obstacles in the path of his plans.

"There are no guarantees in war, Windrush."

"No, sir," Jack said.

"Even if I cannot raise local levies here," Wolseley continued, "I'll have Captain Glover and Captain Butler leading native forces from different directions to split the Ashanti army." He looked up. "The coastal kings hope to sit down quietly with their rum bottles and yams, while Queen Victoria's soldiers defeat the Ashantis. Well, Windrush, I won't let that happen."

Again, Jack said nothing. He could not guess what the local kings thought.

"Thank you, Windrush. That will be all for the present." Wolseley said.

It was an abrupt dismissal that left Jack feeling vaguely uncomfortable. "When are we attacking, sir?"

"When I am ready, Windrush," Wolseley said, "and when I have some experience of defeating the Ashanti." When he lowered his voice, Jack saw the steel behind this methodical soldier. "With only have a few weeks in which to reach Kumasi, Windrush, I must leave nothing to chance."

"Jack," Hook rose from his chair. 'Never fear. We have not forgotten your wife. Her predicament is in my mind. We will endeavour to free her."

"Thank you, sir."

"Oh, Windrush," Wolseley looked up from his papers. "It's best if you employ yourself rather than fret over your wife, so I'll endeavour to keep you busy. I'm calling the local chiefs to a palaver. Once that's complete, take your Wests and have a look at the road building, will you? Lieutenant Gordon was complaining that the Ashantis were harassing his men."

"Yes, sir." *Thank God. I'd go crazy doing nothing when Mary is in danger.*

Chapter Eighteen

Moving with impressive speed, Wolseley called together the chiefs and kings to a palaver the next day. Rather than squeeze the kings into Government House, Wolseley had ordered the servants to erect a large marquee on the grounds.

"It's a bit like the umbrellas of the Ashantis," Jack remembered the colourful gatherings at Kumasi. *Perhaps we are even more similar than Yaa Asantewaa thought.*

"On this coast,' Wolseley said, "They call such a gathering a palaver. Old India hands such as myself know it better as a durbar, where we meet the local kings, rajahs and whatnots, listen to their points of view and then tell them what we're going to do."

Jack thought that Wolseley seemed very sure of himself for a man so new to the coast. "I've attended a few durbars myself," he said. "Mostly on the Frontier."

Wolseley gave Jack a sharp look. "We must treat these people with respect and dignity," Wolseley said. "Remember, they were here long before us."

Meeting Jack's eye, Hook winked.

In mid-afternoon, the kings arrived from all around, each with his entourage of followers. Some had sword-bearers or men with gold-topped canes. Many sheltered under the umbrellas which denoted their status, and others marked their approach by beating drums. All filed into the marquee and perched on beautifully carved stools, pompous with self-importance like the senior class at a public school or newly appointed politicians in the House of Commons.

Some chiefs were too intent on their own affairs to notice anything else, while others studied the raised dais where Wolseley waited with Lieutenant Wood pristine at his side.

"Bring them up," Wolseley stood up. "One at a time."

As a mere major, Jack stood in the background as the kings ascended the dais to shake Wolseley's hand. The general greeted each with great cordiality, smiling as the translator repeated the king's words. Wolseley remained on his feet until all the chiefs had returned to their seats before he addressed them. Speaking slowly through the translator, Wolseley reminded the chiefs of the continuing threat from the Ashantis and asked them to call up their men for mutual defence.

"May as well ask them to whistle down the moon," Buller whispered.

Nodding politely and giving promises of co-operation and help, the kings accepted Wolseley's gifts of gin, traditional for West Africa and filed away as noisily as they had arrived.

"And that's the last we'll see of them," Buller lit a cheroot, passing one over to Jack. "All smiles and promises."

"Aye," Jack agreed. "I don't think they'll raise their men. Why should they fight for themselves when we're here to do the fighting for them?"

"They are very divided," Buller said. "The native peoples here are split into hundreds of small clans, tribes and nations. In the east, there are Awoonah, Krepe, Akeamu, Accra, Akim and others. To the north or west are Wassaws, Amanaheas, Denkyiras and Assins, with Fantis and Kroomen along the coast." He puffed on his cheroot, "and that's only the tribes I know about."

"I've heard some of these names," Jack said.

"Exactly so. Each small clan thinks of itself only, knowing it cannot face the mighty Ashanti Empire, so why should it try? The Ashantis don't stay on the coast long, so the tribes run away or hide and hope the Ashantis attack somebody else."

"Aye," Jack did not care about local politics. He only wanted to rescue Mary.

"Ashanti land is about the same size as Scotland," Buller said. "It extends northward from our coastal fringe to about three hundred miles inland."

Jack nodded. "I've been there, remember."

"I know you've visited," Buller said. "I'm hoping you can correct any gaps in my intelligence gathering."

"Oh, my pleasure," Jack said. "Carry on, Macduff."

"I have it written that the river Prah divides the country in about the middle, which flows east to west in its upper reaches, then at a place called Prahsu, it alters course towards the south and reaches the sea to the west of Cape Coast Castle."

"That sounds accurate, as far as I know," Jack said.

"My people have been feeding me information about the Ashanti," Buller said, "and I send it to your fellow Hook as well as to General Wolseley."

"Indeed?"

"They have a very experienced general in Amanquatia and an up-and-coming chief named Kumi Okese. He seems to be the Ashanti equivalent of our Sir Garnet, a man destined to go places in the Ashanti world."

Jack stiffened. "I've met Kumi Okese."

"Tell me about him." Buller took out a notebook. "Any detail, however insignificant could be useful."

Jack related all he knew of Kumi Okese and his Edwesu warriors as Buller scribbled notes. "Thank you, Windrush," Buller said. "I believe that when we invade, and we will, Amanquatia and this Kumi Okese fellow will be defending."

"Kumi Okese is a dangerous man," Jack said.

"You want another crack at him, do you?"

"He ordered one of my men murdered," Jack did not give more details.

"Ah," Buller nodded understandingly, adding to his notes. "I heard that." He paused reflectively. "Do you realise that we're making history here? When these Fanti fellows refuse to fight, as they will, Sir Garnet will call in British regulars. We'll be the first European army ever to land on the west coast of Africa."

Jack thought of the dense Ashanti forest and the number of men already sick with fever. "Let's hope we all come out again."

"Amen to that," Buller dropped his smile. "Amen to that."

* * *

As Wolseley attempted to raise local levies, Lieutenant Gordon of the 98th foot continued to work. To secure the security of Cape Coast Castle and Elmina, he built a couple of defensive redoubts a few miles inland, garrisoned them with whatever men Cape Coast Castle could scrape up and began work on the road to the Prah. Using local labour, good humour and bad language, Gordon had already widened the old track northwards from Cape Coast to the village of Mansu, where Jack met him.

"Good afternoon, Gordon!" With Hopringle back with them, although still weak after a bout of fever, Jack marched C Company along the new road.

"Is that you again?" Gordon gave a grin, wiping away the sweat from his forehead. "You're in better shape than last time I saw you."

Jack nodded. "So is your road, Gordon."

"Aye, but I've heard a shave that Sir Garnet intends bringing in a genuine Royal Engineer to replace me." Gordon shrugged. "Until then, I'll carry on."

"Were the Ashantis giving you trouble?"

"They were unsettling my people," Gordon said. "They appear from time to time, watch, fire the occasional shot and vanish again. They've never hit anybody yet, but I'd appreciate a military presence."

Glad of something active to do, Jack divided his men into their sections and had them patrol both sides of the road.

"Keep in skirmishing formation," he said, "and remember what I taught you. Hopringle, you take your men on the east side. Sergeants Roberts and Mathews take the west."

"Sir."

"I'll go ahead with my section." Jack moved off at a fast pace, following the route that Gordon had surveyed. *I want to meet the Ashantis. I want to destroy the men who kidnapped my wife.*

Twice Jack heard movement in the bush on either side of the path, and each time he extended his section, hoping for a confrontation, wanting to kill. He had never felt this eager to fight since he viewed the Well at Cawnpore, where the Mutineers had massacred British women and children. *Come out. Show yourselves!* He led Number Two Section into an area of thick bush, with low vegetation below tall trees, where creepers swung over the cleared path, and a cloud of insects hung as if suspended from slanting beams of green-tinged sunlight.

"There's somebody ahead, sir," Ogston said. "I can smell them."

"Ashantis?"

"Yes, sir."

"Find cover." Jack did not have to emphasise the words. Sliding behind a tree, he glanced around him, looking for his men. He saw sunlight gleaming on scarlet. "Coffin! I can see you!"

Coffin moved a fraction until vegetation covered him. Jack nodded, vaguely satisfied. "Load. Don't fire until I give the word."

Drawing his revolver, Jack checked it was fully loaded, controlled his nerves and waited.

The first Ashanti warrior appeared at a bend in the path, carrying a long musket and with a bandolier of ammunition across his shoulder. He moved confidently, with a score of men at his back, nearly trotting between the trees.

Jack waited until the leading man was parallel with Coffin. "Fire!" He squeezed the trigger of his revolver, missed with his first shot, saw his target, a lanky warrior in the middle of the Ashantis, swing his musket to his shoulder, and fired again. The Ashanti staggered as Jack's bullet crashed into his hip-bone. He fell, trying to balance on the ground with his forearm. Jack fired a third time, with the shot taking the warrior in the top of his skull, smashing the bone and spraying his brains over the ground.

Taken by surprise, few of the Ashantis had time to respond before the Wests fired another volley of .577 bullets, felling more men to add to the six casualties from the initial attack.

"Keep firing!" Jack shouted. Although these were not the white striped men of Kumi Okese's tribe, Jack still wanted to dispose of as many as possible. He cursed when he saw a Snider bullet knock a splinter from an overhanging branch. "Fire low! Don't waste ammunition!"

The Ashantis were reeling, some lying down, a few turning to run and the bravest aiming at the bush to return fire from this invisible enemy.

"Finish them off!" Jack ignored the slug that thumped into the tree in front of him. He emptied his revolver at one of the more stubborn of the Ashantis, saw Stair take deliberate aim at a running man and knock him clean off his feet, reloaded, and then it was over. The road was empty except for dead and wounded Ashantis.

"Anybody hurt?"

With no casualties among his Wests, Jack had them take the weapons from the enemy, dragged the wounded into the shelter of the trees and left them there. "Good work, men."

That was it. A successful ambush that had disposed of eleven of an enemy that numbered around fifty thousand, and wounded four more. The skirmish would not even dent the fighting power of the Ashantis, but it would raise his men's morale, it proved the Wests could defeat the enemy in their own forests and may help defend the road engineers.

Gordon looked agitated when Jack led his men back. "I heard firing."

"We found an Ashanti patrol," Jack indicated their haul of muskets.

"I see." Gordon looked relieved. "I was a bit concerned."

Jack raised his voice to enable all his men to hear. "No need for concern, Gordon. The 2nd Wests are here. We can handle a few Bushmen."

The road-building continued steadily, mile by slow mile as the engineers progressed toward the Prah. With every yard, the invasion of Ashantiland and the rescue of Mary became more of a possibility.

Jack continued with the patrols, each time probing further north, closer to the Prah. Sergeant Mathews had another brush with the enemy two days later, again with no casualties among the Wests and a few Ashanti dead. After that, the Ashantis left the engineers severely alone. Felling trees, Gordon's men built bridges and created camps at regular intervals, so when the army eventually arrived, the men could have proper shelter.

"The Romans called them marching camps," Gordon said. "If they are already in place when we invade, the lads won't be so tired and fewer will succumb to heat exhaustion."

Jack approved. "Wolseley has things well worked out."

As well as broadening the path, the engineers placed tree trunks across the worst of the marshes like a corduroy to give marching men sure footing. Jack watched one team of workers manoeuvre a log into position.

"You're using women as labourers," Jack said.

"Yes," Gordon said. "Only as far as Mansu, which used to be the Fantis slave market."

Jack watched Private Coffin jump to help as a slender Fanti woman staggered under her load.

"Good man, Coffin!" Jack forestalled Sergeant Mathews' rebuke. "Sergeant; our men can help these ladies as long as we are here."

"Yes, sir."

"Why are you using women, Gordon? Where are the men?"

The engineer shrugged. "As far as I can see, the men are anywhere except where they might meet the Ashantis. It makes me wonder what we're fighting for."

"I often wonder that," Jack said. "Is it the politicians who cause these wars or the businessmen who want to make money?" He watched Coffin hefting a log as if it was nothing.

"Did you hear the latest shave, Windrush?"

"What was that?"

"King Kofi has said that if the British ever cross the Prah, he will sacrifice all the hostages."

Jack felt nausea rise in his throat. "No,' he said. 'I had not heard that."

"It might only be a rumour," Gordon said.

"It had better be," Jack looked north with his fingers curling around Mary's scarf. At that moment, he felt further apart from Mary than he had ever done in his life and utterly useless.

Chapter Nineteen

As the days passed without any gathering of Fanti warriors, Wolseley became frustrated. "The women in this land have more courage than the men," he said.

Thinking of Yaa Asantewaa and the women building the road northward, Jack nodded. "That may be so, sir."

Wolseley rose from his desk, scattering the piled papers across the floor. "All right then, we'll call a palaver with the women, and see if they can encourage their men." He swayed slightly but pushed away Jack's helping hand. "I'm all right, Windrush, damn it!"

You're catching fever, General. You don't know the signs yet, but the Gold Coast is fighting back.

It was perhaps the most unusual meeting that Jack had ever attended as Major General Wolseley presided over scores of wives and mothers of Fanti chiefs and kings. The women arrived with fewer attendants than their men had, yet with equal solemnity. All had paid strict attention to their hair, all wore a profusion of gold rings and most had shawls and robes adorned with golden ornaments that would have put a European princess to shame.

They listened attentively to Wolseley, promised to send their men to war and returned home.

"Now we'll see," Wolseley said, as Hook lifted a glass of brandy to his lips, smiled his slow smile and walked to the window.

"You'd better get the British regiments ready," Hook said. "You're going to need them before this is over."

"Oh, ye of little faith," Wolseley said.

"Little faith?" Hook said quietly. "I never had much and lost that many years ago."

After a few days, Jack knew that Hook was correct. There was no surge of warriors eager to fight the Ashanti. Wolseley's gamble in trying to recruit the Fanti women had failed. As so often in the past, Britain had to turn to the underpaid, hard-used men in scarlet.

* * *

They stood on the wall of Cape Coast Castle, smoking cheroots and looking northward into the interior of Africa. Buller sighed, pulled on his cheroot and blew out a ribbon of blue smoke.

"There is no gathering of the clans, then."

"No," Jack said. "Perhaps we should send out the fiery cross?"

Buller grinned. "It looks like we'll have to fight these people's war for them with what we have, and whatever force Sir Garnet can manage to scrape up back home."

"Aye, but it's a bad country for white men," Jack said.

Buller laughed. "When I asked people's advice on what kit I would require for the Gold Coast, one old West Africa hand gave me a dirty look. 'Take a coffin,' he said. 'It's all you'll need'."

Jack pulled on his cheroot, raised his eyebrows and said nothing.

Buller nodded. "We've no choice now, Windrush if we've to cane King Kofi. Sir Garnet has failed to raise any sizeable force among the coastal Fantis, despite threats and promises. Now he's sent Captain Nicol of the Hampshire Militia up the Rivers Bonny and Opobo on a recruiting drive."

"That would be a change from Hampshire," Jack said.

"I would imagine so," Buller said. "Nicol was successful though, and brought back some decent warriors, while Lieutenant Bolton of the 1st Wests did the same at Winnebah."

Jack stared to the gloomy north. "The more we recruit, the better, although I doubt the levies will stand for even a single Ashanti volley."

Buller smiled. "Wolseley formed these new men into two regiments, one with Colonel Wood of the 90th in command, and the other under Major Russell of the 13th Hussars."

"God help us," Jack said, "a major of a crack cavalry regiment commanding irregular African infantry. Wellington would turn in his grave."

Buller suddenly cleared his throat, dropped his cheroot and stood at attention. "Sorry, sir, I didn't know you were there."

Wolseley stood a yard away, with Hook at his side.

"I've just arrived, Buller. What's that you were saying, Windrush?"

Jack stubbed out his cheroot. "I hope we are attacking the enemy soon, sir."

Wolseley gave a faint smile. "All in good time, Windrush."

"Perhaps Major Windrush is becoming frustrated at waiting," Hook said smoothly. "According to Buller's reports," he nodded to Buller, "General Amanquatia still has some twenty thousand Ashanti warriors in the field."

Wolseley did not look even slightly concerned at the news. "I'd better do something about it then, hadn't I?"

"Give me a resume of the present situation, Buller." Hook said. "A brief resume."

Buller stood at attention. "The Ashantis are obtaining help from a chain of small villages on the coast near Elmina. The villagers send food and supplies to Essaman, about four miles inland amidst pretty dense jungle, where Amanquatia boasts about building a town as a base for the next invasion."

"Does he, indeed," Wolseley said quietly.

"That's what their General Amanquatia said, sir, according to my spies." Buller gave a small cough. "I think it was Napoleon who said an army marched on its stomach."

"I believe it was," Hook said.

"Well, if we cut the supplies, the Ashanti army won't be secure," Buller said. "They'll have to withdraw to Ashantiland."

"Thank you for your opinion, Buller." Hook's voice was ominously quiet. "Stick to the facts, if you please."

"Yes, sir. Colonel Wood demanded that the chiefs report to him at Elmina. Rather than obey, they asked Amanquatia what they should do."

"The small villages are caught between the devil and the deep blue sea," Hook said. "Between the Ashanti Empire, that they fear, and the British Empire, which to the best of their knowledge is a handful of West Indian infantry and some sickly European civilians."

"You've developed an efficient intelligence service, Buller," Jack said.

"Bribery helps," Buller said.

"What was Amanquatia's reply to the village chiefs?" Hook returned to the main topic.

"Amanquatia ordered the chiefs not to attend. He said the Ashantis would protect the villages as the white men would not go into the forest."

"We keep hearing that," Wolseley murmured.

Hook nodded. "We do. What did the Fanti chiefs say to Colonel Wood, Buller?"

Buller frowned. "I wrote all this in my report, sir."

"Remind me, Captain." Hook's voice was like silk.

"Yes, Sir. The Ampenee chief did not reply at all," Buller said, "while the Amquana chief told Colonel Wood that he had smallpox that day, but he would come the next."

"The insolent beggar!" Hook smiled. "Did he come the next day?"

Buller shook his head. "No, sir. He fled to the Ashantis. The chief at Essaman was worse. He challenged Colonel Wood to come and fetch him, adding the usual taunt that white men don't dare to go into the bush."

"Cheeky blighter," Jack said, although he had a sneaking admiration for a petty chief who challenged the British Empire.

Wolseley paced away with his hands behind his back and his fingers intertwining. Hook met Jack's eye, winked and gave a small shake of his head.

"Sir Garnet is thinking," Hook said.

Wolseley stopped as if he had reached a decision. When he returned, his face was animated. "You have given me much to consider, Captain Buller."

Buller nodded. "That is my job, sir."

Wolseley smiled. "Gentlemen, you will agree that the Ashanti are growing bolder, day by day."

"They are," Hook agreed.

Wolseley nodded to Jack. "Windrush here has daunted their attacks on our engineering parties cutting roads, but now we have Buller's intelligence about the chiefs at Essaman and such places." Wolseley's smile was unexpected. "Gentlemen!" He rubbed his hands together. "It is time we gathered the press. I expect you all to attend."

Jack shook his head as Wolseley marched away, closely followed by Hook.

"What the devil is Sir Garnet planning? He detests the press," Jack grunted. "All us old Crimea hands detest reporters. They told the Russians all our moves before we made them.' Jack kept the bitterness from his voice as he recalled the chaos of the Crimean campaign. "I'm surprised that Wolseley even allows reporters into the colony."

* * *

Henry Morton Stanley was the first journalist to enter. The Welshman who had discovered Livingstone, he strode to a seat near the front of the room. Winwood Reade, a minor African explorer, was next, looking as if he wished to tell Wolseley his job, while the bearded George Henty of the *Standard* already scribbled notes as he took his seat.

"Here they are," Buller said, "parasites all, hoping for death and suffering to fill their columns. Let's pray that Sir Garnet gives them a swift kick up the trousers."

"Gentlemen of the press," Wolseley said, with some of the Irish accent still in his speech, "you will be aware that Colonel Glover is leading a force of native levies up the flank to menace Ashantiland."

The journalists nodded, taking solemn notes as Jack and Buller glanced at each other.

"I have some rather unsettling news, I am afraid."

Jack felt the ripple of interest as the journalists scribbled on their pads.

Wolseley continued. "I regret to say that the Awoonas, allies of the Ashantis have trapped Glover at Addah, on the right bank of the Volta River. I am going to lead a force to Glover's rescue." Wolseley glanced around the room. "Are there any questions?"

"Yes, Sir Garnet," Stanley stood, looking around to ensure everybody could see him. "Why are we taking such a passive stance? We know Ashantis are hovering around in British territory. Why do you not attack them right away?"

Wolseley looked slightly annoyed at the question. "Until reinforcements arrive, Mr Stanley, I have only a limited number of men available to defend the colony."

"You have sailors and Marines on the Royal Navy ships," Stanley said.

"The naval personnel are only available if the Ashanti attack the settlements," Wolseley explained. "I must use my small force to the best effect I can." He raised his voice slightly. "I trust you all not to release the intelligence I have just given you."

When the journalists raced out to write their copy, Wolseley smiled. "Now they will spread that news out to all and sundry, and the Ashantis will hear and hopefully act accordingly. Prepare your men, gentlemen, for we are leaving for Elmina this evening. He glanced at Jack and Captain Brett. "Windrush, I want your C Company to embark on HMS *Bittern* at six. Brett, you take A Company."

"I presume we are not going to help Colonel Glover, sir," Jack said.

"Why would we do that?" Wolseley asked, innocent as a baby. "He's in no trouble."

Chapter Twenty

As the tropical light faded and the surf crashed silver onto the beach, Jack chivvied his men onto HM gunboat *Decoy*. The Wests filed on board, chattering happily, finding spaces below deck and preparing for a voyage into the unknown. Once they settled, Jack stood on deck to watch the bustle, with boats conveying the Royal Marines and Royal Marine Artillery to HMS *Barracoutta*. With its usual efficiency, the navy sent Captain Peel and a landing party of fifty sailors ashore to man the outlying posts of Cape Coast Castle.

"Sir Garnet's taking a risk, denuding Cape Coast of all its defenders except a handful of tarry jacks," Hopringle sounded nervous.

"Aye," Jack agreed. "But he knows what he's doing."

"Does he?"

"I've never known such a meticulous planner," Jack said. "He's one of the best commanders I've served under."

Hopringle sipped from a pewter hip flask. "I've heard men say that Sir Garnet is the best general since Wellington."

Jack considered for a while. "Not in my experience. I think Colin Campbell, Lord Clyde, was the best, but Wolseley comes close. He is undoubtedly well organised."

Hopringle moved aside as a sailor rolled forward. "You were in the Mutiny weren't you, Windrush? How about Havelock?"

Jack remembered those desperate days when Havelock led his 113th to the relief of Lucknow. "Havelock would have attacked by now," Jack said. "He'd have taken every man in the colony, soldier, sailor, Marine, policeman and Uncle Tom Cobley and all, and charged straight for Kumasi. He was the right man in the right place in the Mutiny." Jack considered for a moment, "I don't think these tactics would work here."

It was nine in the evening before Wolseley, and his staff boarded *Barracoutta*, where the journalists were already waiting. Never having met this breed of man before, Jack examined them through his binoculars, watching them drinking naval grog before settling down under an awning for the night.

Hopringle grinned. "Watching the writers are you, Windrush? Making sure they don't signal our supposed plans to the Ashantis?"

"I don't trust them," Jack said.

"There are Ashanti spies everywhere," Hopringle said. "So I heard."

At half-past one, with the stars brilliant above, the flotilla weighed anchor for the short voyage to Elmina. A heavy swell rocked the ships from side to side, which did not bother the island-bred West Indians, who understood the sea as well as anybody.

"I say, sir, could you ensure your Wests are off the deck for a while?" Jack did not know the officer who spoke.

"Why is that?"

"I want to train my Hausas," the man was young and eager. "They've never fired an Enfield before."

"Good God!" Jack was genuinely startled. "We'll keep the deck clear for you." He watched as the Hausas lined up on deck, chattering happily as their officers holding up Enfield rifles.

Dear Lord, Jack thought. *What chance have these unfortunate Hausas got in action? No wonder they made a poor showing at Elmina if nobody had trained them.*

The Hausas looked clumsy with the Enfields, although they were keen to learn. They copied the officers' movements, repeating the words by rote as they squeezed days and weeks of training into a couple of hours.

"Good luck, lads," Jack said as their training finished and the Hausas clumped off below. "Aim low and shoot straight."

With the deck clear, Jack checked his men and lay on the deck to sleep. At three o'clock in a dark morning, with an onshore breeze flicking spindrift from the sea and moaning through the rigging, they arrived at Elmina, and the men began to disembark. Jack loaded his revolver, felt his tension rising and watched as Wolseley and Captain Freemantle were first ashore, with half a dozen seamen rowing their gig into the entrance of the Benya River.

"Right, lads," Jack had shaved by lantern light with a mirror propped on the sea-knife of a grinning sailor. He dabbed at the blood that seeped from a cut. "We're marching inland soon. Don't leave any kit behind. Sergeants, make sure your men are ready."

As the Wests queued on deck to board the shore-bound boats, Jack checked their equipment: Rifle, 70 rounds of ball ammunition, greatcoat, haversack, water purifier and water bottle. They filed past him, the men he had trained, the young faces and older faces, the brash and the nervous, his men going to war. *Good luck, lads; I hope my training helped keep you alive.*

"Make sure your water bottles are full!" Jack roared as *Decoy* rose and fell alarmingly with the swell. "If we have to fight, you'll need water desperately. There is nothing more thirst-inducing than powder smoke."

The men swung onto the ladder, ready to descend into the boats, with the swell so high that one minute they were ten feet above the sea, then the next thigh-deep in the water.

"Keep your rifles dry!" Jack roared. "You'll need them later!"

The navy had provided steam launches that towed the boats, with fifty soldiers crammed into each vessel and sailors wielding oars to help the engines. Private Coffin sang a spiritual song that Jack did not know, and others joined in as they jerked and soared toward the coast, dimly seen as a line of white surf against the dark background. St George's Castle' lights seemed to float in the sky like an ethereal construction on the coast, a tenuous European fingerprint on a hostile continent. High above, the stars were bright in a moonless sky, Jupiter and Venus prominent. Jack looked up briefly, knowing that Mary would be watching the same stars, only a hundred and sixty miles away yet in a different world.

The steam-launch eased toward the bar at the narrow mouth of the Benya River, with the familiar bulk of St George's Castle loomed to port. Supporting the 2nd West, boats from *Barracoutta* carried Marines and bluejackets, together with a rocket tube and a cannon. Jack could smell a whiff of tobacco from the sailors, although in the dark, he could not see their bearded faces. More obvious were the white helmets and puggaries of the Marines, and Jack wondered if the Ashantis would relish the excellent targets that splash of light made in the green gloom of the forest.

As the boats hovered offshore, a small flotilla of boats rowed up to them, with local Kroomen paddling beside the bluejackets.

The sailors' voices sounded clearly through the night. "On you come, lobster-backs! We'll take you ashore! You'll have to change boats now. It's low water here, and if you try the bar fully loaded, the surf will capsize you, sure as eggs is bacon."

Once again the West Indians proved their skills as they leapt from boat to boat, laughing and joking as the larger flotilla headed for the breakers. With the water hissing around them and spilling inboard, Jack shouted orders.

"Keep your rifles and ammunition dry, lads! Hold them up! We don't know how many Ashantis are waiting for us." Following his own advice, Jack took off his pistol belt and the fifty rounds he carried, holding it clear of the water that splashed inboard. The surf lifted his boat high, carried it forward and deposited it with a grinding crash on the sand, still waist-deep in water.

"Stay here, lobsters!" The sailors shouted cheerfully as they and the Kroomen jumped overboard to haul the boat to shallower water.

"Off we get, lads!' Forming C Company up, Jack marched them up the hill to St George's Castle, acknowledging the salutes of the Hausa policemen who guarded the entrance. "Check your ammunition," he ordered, "make sure your rifles are dry and oiled." He walked along the ranks, inspecting each man, giving a word of encouragement to the young, calming down the nervous, exchanging jokes with the old soldiers and the men who had been with him in Kumasi.

"Are we going to avenge Stan Manning, sir?" Ogston asked.

"We will, Ogston, we will," Jack promised.

The night eased away; the stars faded and a wan band of light filtered into the eastern sky. Birds called in the trees to the constant background of surf hammering on the shore.

"Marines! Leave your greatcoats behind!" A stentorian roar temporarily silenced the birds.

Jack saw the Royal Marines thankfully drop their heavy coats. He gave the same order to his West Indians. If twenty years of military experience and four wars had taught him anything, it was that the less burden a soldier carried, the faster he could move and the higher his chance of survival.

The bluejackets of the Naval Brigade gathered in small groups, their bearded faces laughing, short cutlasses prominent at their belts. Jack had met their like in the Crimea and India and knew them to be the most willing of fighting men.

The Hausas in their blue serge and scarlet fezzes swapped anecdotes with the seamen, each speaking in their native language yet seeming to make themselves understood.

Wolseley appeared in the courtyard, erect and dapper, with Lieutenant Colonel Wood at his side. Jack had never met Wood but knew him as a fighting officer, if unlucky with wounds. The Colonel was in nominal command of the column, which must have been hard with Wolseley overlooking everything he did.

When Wood snapped an order, the small army formed up, with Lieutenants Richmond and Woodgate in command of the Hausas. The Hausas looked well, but Jack remembered their far-too-brief training with the Enfields. As they had only come over from Nigeria a few days ago, they had hardly acclimatised to the Gold Coast. *It's unfair to bring these unprepared men to fight the Ashantis.*

With an old wound troubling him, Wolseley was hardly able to walk, so four men carried him in a hammock.

"That will make Sir Garnet a target for every Ashanti with a musket," Hopringle murmured.

Jack lit a cheroot, wishing they were advancing on Kumasi rather than skirmishing around the fringes of the colony. "Aye; it won't be healthy around the general."

"Windrush," Wood said, "take half your company and follow the Hausas. The rest can join the main body of the 2nd in the rear guard."

"You'll be with the rear guard, Hopringle." Jack hurried forward with two sections of Wests, while a ragged group of Fantis clustered around.

"These Bushmen look fierce enough to scare off the devil himself," Daley said.

"We'll see if they are fierce when the fighting starts," Ogston tapped the breech of his Snider. "I'll put my faith in old Snidey, here."

Immediately behind Jack's Wests came a group of local volunteers and sailors with the artillery, a solitary seven pounder plus two rocket tubes with rockets and ammunition. Captain Freemantle of *Barracouta* commanded the Naval Brigade, who swaggered along, joking with brawny native labourers who carried broad-bladed axes.

Behind the axemen marched Captain Crean's Marines. A solid block of blue, they moved with a determined stride as if nothing, not Russians, Frenchmen and definitely not Ashantis, would stop them.

The porters were next, near-naked natives with great bundles balanced on their heads containing ammunition, some food and hammocks for the expected wounded. Finally, Captain Brett and the remainder of the 2nd Wests made up the rearguard. Hopringle trotted up to Jack.

"Captain Brett said I've to stay with you, sir, if you send Sergeant Mathews to take my place."

"Off you go, Mathews," Jack said.

"Brett says I'll be more useful here," Hopringle explained.

"You may well be. This is a long column," Jack knew he would be happier with more fighting men and fewer porters. "Single file lads, and keep alert."

As the dawn light strengthened, the little army began to march along the coast, with every step sinking ankle-deep in sand, the sky clear above and bird-call sweetening the air. Jack remembered the landing in the Crimea and how that ended in carnage and chaos. *Here we go and may God help us.*

Chapter Twenty-One

Ten minutes later, the column headed inland, past the lagoon, with a good view of St George's Fort and the bridge that Jack and the 2nd West had held. Then it was over marshland with a stink that made the men gag. On either flank, the Hausas searched clumps of bushland, with the shouts of the officers as clear as their Elwood helmets and white puggarees.

"Here's the first village," Colonel Wood said. "It's deserted now, but the Ashanti used it as a base only a few weeks ago."

By now, Jack was familiar with the local villages. The brushwood huts were flimsy, offering protection from the sun and little else. When the inhabitants fled, they left only a few odds and ends on the ground. "Not even a gold nugget," a Marine grumbled. "I thought this was the Gold Coast, not the Mosquito Coast."

The column marched on, deeper into the bush. After another fifteen minutes, Jack looked behind him, where smoke smudged the treeline, and the occasional orange flame raised high.

"Somebody's set the village on fire," he said.

"No bad thing." Hopringle scratched at his leg, "I'm sure I caught fleas there."

They strode over a plain of thin scrubland intersected by occasional dense bush that cut visibility to only a few feet. "Careful here, lads," Jack said as he heard the deep boom of an Ashanti musket from ahead. "Remember your skirmishing drill if we go into action."

"We will, sir," Stair said. "Shall we join the Hausas?"

"Don't be too eager, Stair. Trouble will find us when it wants to."

As they entered an area of thick forest, Jack ordered the men into skirmishing formation, had them watch all around and probe the bush. He knew he was making himself unpopular as he slowed down the column, but the safety of his men was paramount. With shrubs at head height and creepers coiled around the trees, the forest could be deadly, despite the melodious bird sounds all around. Jack breathed deeply when they emerged without any incident.

"No Ashantis this time," Jack said.

"I'm sorry, sir," Ogston said, "but it wasn't a bird calling to us."

"What do you mean?" Jack asked.

"We didn't see any Ashantis," Ogston said, "but they saw us. They are watching everything that we do."

Daley nodded, licking his lips. "That's right, sir. I sensed them in there. And they're here too, hiding in the grassland."

The track was wending through shoulder-high grass, yellow under the sun, and specked with areas of forest and enlivened by bright flowers. It was undoubtedly beautiful but could conceal all kinds of predators.

Mary would love these flowers. "Come on!" Jack snarled at his men. "Pick the pace up!" He loosened the pistol in its holster. "I'll give a half-sovereign to the first man to sight an Ashanti warrior!" Thinking of Mary had rekindled his anger, awakening a desire to kill. He closed his eyes, struggling with the images that raced through his mind. He seemed to hear the throb of Ashanti drums and share the bloodlust of that terrible city.

"Push on!" Jack forced himself to stride ahead, with the grass swishing on both sides and his men looking around, Sniders poised.

Hold on, Mary. Hold on. Do anything you can to stay alive.

Despite the promised reward, none of his men saw an Ashanti as they left the tall grass for an area of swampland, where black ooze clutched at their feet and legs. They plodded on, step after sucking step, with Jack dreading the thought of water snakes, and insects clouding around their heads.

Colonel Wood called a halt when they left the swamp, and Jack posted sentries at hundred-yard intervals around his half-company. "Keep your eyes open," he said, altering the angle of his pith helmet, so the brim shaded his eyes from the now burning sun.

"We're approaching territory where the Ashantis are known to operate," Wood said. "I'd like all the Hausas in skirmishing order."

Jack waited hopefully for the order to deploy his men. It did not come, and after a hurried breakfast, they moved on.

With the Hausas and the Fanti tribesmen fanned out around the column, they moved forward with more caution, surrounding each patch of dense bushland and carefully probing as they advanced. Jack extended his Wests further, each man covering his neighbour.

"Sir!" Private Coffin lifted an arm. "I think I saw somebody up there." The hill rose from the surrounding bushland, with the summit cleared for agriculture.

"Stair, run back to Colonel Wood. Tell him, with my compliments, that there may be Ashantis on that hill."

Willing as always, Stair hurried to the middle of the column, returning ten minutes later with his usual smile. "The colonel says it's in hand, sir."

Within a few moments, Lieutenant Woodgate and a dozen Hausas left the column. While they doubled around the back of the hill, Lieutenant Graves led a further twelve Hausas to the base.

"Where's your Ashanti, Windrush?" Colonel Wood pushed through the column to speak to Jack.

"There's a village there," Jack studied the hill through his binoculars. 'I see it a couple of hundred yards to the right of the clearing, in the jungle. I can't see any movement at present, but this is Ashanti country, and one of my men saw somebody hereabouts."

"Can you trust his word?" Wood asked.

Jack knew his men were listening. "Implicitly, sir."

"Very good," Wood said. "Richmond," he spoke the commander of the Hausas. "Take the rest of your Hausas and inspect that village. Windrush, you and your Wests jog along in reserve."

"Yes, sir. Come on, lads. Form a skirmishing line and follow me." Feeling his old familiar mixture of excitement and trepidation, Jack advanced with his men in extended order, rifles ready.

The Hausas were in front, too bunched up for Jack's taste. He knew that on the North-West Frontier, the Pashtuns would have cut them down with ease and he suspected the Ashantis were as dangerous.

"Keep spread out," Jack ordered, as the Wests also began to creep closer together. Jack knew it was natural to seek company, but that it was false security that increased the target area for enemy marksmen. Reaching the base of the hill, they began to climb, with the tension rising when they entered the trees.

"The village is empty!" Lieutenant Graves reported. "The Ashanti have left."

"They're watching us," Ogston said. "What's that on the ground?"

It was the body of a man, stark naked, with a sword wound to the chest. "He's a Hausa," Ogston said at once. 'Not one of our men. The Ashantis must have had him as a slave and killed him for fetish."

Jack viewed the dead man for a moment, seeing him as a mute reminder of the tragedy of human existence. He wondered how the Hausa had come to be a slave, and who missed him in his homeland.

"Set fire to the village," Colonel Wood ordered, and soon orange flames and blue smoke smudged the sky. The explosion took everybody by surprise, with men ducking or crouching down. Two of the Hausas fired without aiming, and Hopringle's section knelt, slamming their Sniders into their shoulders.

"Hold your fire," Jack shouted. "That's a barrel of gunpowder exploding! The Ashanti must have stored it in the village as they did in Elmina."

Slightly shame-faced, the Wests clambered back to their feet. "Better luck next time, lads," Jack said.

Leaving the village in flames behind them, the British moved on, still without having seen a single Ashanti.

"They're all around us," Ogston said. "Watching us every step of the way."

Jack felt the eyes on him before he saw the grass move against the wind. The Ashanti stood still, with his striped face and arms perfect camouflage amidst the tall grass, and then he stepped back, the grass closed and he was gone.

"I saw him too, Windrush," Wood said quietly. "Where there is one, there will be more."

"That was one of Kumi Okese's Edwesus," Jack said. "They're the best warriors the Ashanti has."

"Royal Marines!" Wood ordered. "I want a section of Marines skirmishing on either flank. The Ashantis are here."

To their left, the open land altered as the patches of forest became more extensive and more frequent, perfect country to hide Ashantis. The column moved slower, with the native levies checking the bush and Jack's men spread out, ready to fire. On the flanks, the Marines held their rifles at the high port as the sun reflected from their white hats.

Good luck, lads.

As the Marines passed an area of tangled jungle, Jack heard a single thud, deeper than a Snider.

"That's an Ashanti musket," he said. 'Skirmish positions, men, ready your rifles!'

A second shot followed, with the sound echoing against the forest, and then a third, with white powder-smoke rising to the left and in front.

"It's an ambush!" Ogston yelled.

"Fire!" Wood gave the first order, which officers repeated along the column, like an echo.

The Marines fired a volley, the sharp crack of the Sniders contrasting with the deep, ugly thuds of the Ashanti's Tower muskets.

"Steady, Marines!" A young officer shouted. "Take your time! Don't throw away your shots!"

A hundred yards in front, the Hausas also fired, their musketry wild as they shot into the trees or anything that might be an Ashanti warrior.

Lieutenant Graves lifted his voice. "Don't fire at random, Hausas! Pick your targets!"

"Come on, lads!" Jack led his Wests forward. "Stay with me. We're supporting the Hausas." The Marines were mostly very young, but Jack had more faith in their steadiness than he had in the Hausa police. White smoke jetted from Jack's right, with the wind of a slug hissing past him. An inch to the left and it would have struck him in the right temple. Shrugging he carried on; it was only another miss.

"Marines!" Graves shouted again. "Take ground to the left!"

"Put the gun on its carriage!" A calm officer said. "Load and bring it forward. Give the lads some support."

The Ashantis had adopted their favoured horseshoe formation, firing on the British column from the front and both flanks. Jack watched his men, knowing that it was the first time most had been in action and no amount of training could prepare them for the real thing. They retained their formation, lying or crouching behind cover as they fired steadily.

"Aim at the smoke," Jack walked along the skirmish line, letting his men see him and fighting his desire to duck. "Don't waste your bullets." He flinched as something slammed into the tree beside his head, saw the gleam of the metal slug against the bark, and walked on. "Make sure you don't fire at your own men. The Marines are out there."

Stair was shouting something, his Jamaican accent thickening with excitement as he stood up for a clearer shot.

"Take your time, Stair!" Jack pushed him back into cover. "Keep your fool head down!"

The concentrated fire of muskets, Sniders and Enfields echoed around the forest, with bullets and slugs hissing and crackling in all directions. Gunsmoke coiled between the branches, writhing around the creepers, stinging the eyes and noses of all the men. Above the hammer of musketry, Jack heard the yells of the wounded, but whether friend or enemy he could not tell.

Colonel Wood stepped forward, with Wolseley at his side, as calm as if they were on the parade square at Aldershot. "Over there, I think," Wood indicated a piece of rising ground a little to the left of their present position.

"Take the high ground!" Wolseley ordered. "Hold it until we see what's happening out there." He glanced at Jack. "Windrush, you and your Wests push back the enemy."

"Yes, sir. Up you get lads! Let's show the world how good we are."

The Wests rose, some taking a parting shot at the Ashantis, others loading. Coffin was muttering a prayer as he thumbed a cartridge into the breech of his rifle.

"Maintain your discipline," Jack said, "no running. NCOs, keep your men in formation." He saw some of the Hausas charge forward, while others fired wildly at the trees.

"Aim before you fire, Jackson!" Jack grabbed the rifle from a yelling young soldier. "You're wasting ammunition!'

Keeping his men as a cover for the main British force, Jack led them to the front of the rising ground, where thick, shoulder-high bush offered shelter for any Ashantis.

"Halt!" Jack ordered. "Form a firing line." He peered through the smoke, ensuring that his men obeyed, pulled back two of the most eager and checked his surroundings.

To the left of the Wests, an area of tall grass extended for about three hundred yards, ending in a steep bush-covered ridge. Jack's Wests and the Hausas were in an extended line in front of the British force, firing at the puffs of smoke in the trees. The Hausas were yelling in excitement, yanking the triggers, so their bullets endangered everybody except the Ashantis.

When the jets of smoke from the forest lessened, Jack raised a hand. The deep booming of Ashanti muskets had stopped entirely.

"Cease fire!" Jack shouted. "Cease fire!"

One by one, his men stopped, looking at each other in evident pleasure, satisfied that they had shown their martial prowess and forced the Ashantis back. Jack grunted; some had acted like the untried recruits, many of them were excited and ill-disciplined, but not a single man had run. They had the makings of soldiers, once they learned to control their zeal.

The Hausa officers were busy stopping their men from firing so gradually silence descended on the slopes. Jack swore, as one of the rearguard shouted "Ashanti," and the firing started again.

"Hold your fire!" Jack snarled to his men. "Only fire if I give the order."

The noise ended, and silence returned, with gunsmoke drifting from the British position towards the surrounding woodland. A bird called, and another as nature recovered from the disruption. Jack saw a single leaf fall from a tree, to drift slowly to the ground, unheeded by everybody except him.

Colonel Wood scanned the forest with his binoculars before giving quiet orders that saw Captain Freemantle with the Naval Brigade drag the rocket tubes and seven-pounder toward the trees beyond the grassland on the left flank. At the same time, the men of the Royal Marine Artillery headed for the right.

Jack saw the movement behind the leaves. "It's not finished yet, boys. The Ashantis have shifted their position, that's all."

The Ashantis proved Jack right when they replied to the threat to their flanks by firing ineffectual volleys from the trees.

"You're out of range, you lubbers!" A tattooed seaman jeered.

One of the seamen was cracking jokes, with his mates laughed, adding lewd comments that spread the humour, while a section of Hausas began to chant Islamic verses. Hearing the words of the Koran, Coffin retaliated with a psalm, so it was a strange medley of sounds that greeted the Ashanti ambush.

There are no drums, Jack thought. *Why are there no drums today?*

"They're at extreme range for their muskets," Jack said. "Number One section, fire when you see a target. Number Two Section, hold your fire."

The firefight continued for a few moments, with the Ashanti fire gradually diminishing.

"Lieutenants Graves and Woodgate, take a platoon of Hausas each and skirmish lower down the slopes." Wolseley gave rapid orders. "The rest of the Hausas and Windrush's West Indians, follow the main path into the valley past that hill."

We're the bait, Jack thought. *Wolseley is sending us along the path to tempt the Ashanti into attacking so the rockets and artillery can catch them.* "Come on, boys! You heard the general! Follow me!"

As the British moved, the Ashanti fire began again, with the forest fighters concentrating on the flanking parties.

"These Ashanti know their stuff," Jack said to Hopringle. "They recognise that the main threat comes from the flanks."

In his first real action, Hopringle gave a nervous grin, ducking as an Ashanti slug whizzed past his head.

"You'll get used to it," Jack said. "You'll never get to like it, but you'll put on a mask, as the rest of us do."

The Wests were becoming noisy, shouting threats at the Ashanti and bunching until Jack ordered silence. "Skirmishing order," he reminded. "Keep apart and don't offer yourselves as targets for the enemy."

The firing from the trees increased, and Jack felt a tug on his jacket. He looked down to see an ironstone slug embedded in the fabric on a level with his ribs. *If that had been a bullet, I'd be dead,* he told himself. "Keep moving forward, C Company! Only fire if you are sure of your target!"

Judging by the response from the Wests, many were very sure of their target. They fired, loaded and fired again, moving forward from cover to cover as Jack had trained them. Jack grunted, knowing the psychological strain of being under fire without hitting back. It was better to retaliate, even if the possibility of hitting the enemy was remote. Only the best-disciplined troops could receive fire without responding. Slipping his hand inside his tunic, he touched Mary's scarf for luck.

"Keep moving!" Seeing movement in a bush ahead, Jack fired two rounds, sidestepped as something buzzed past him and stepped on. Knowing that he was a conspicuous target in the scarlet uniform of the 113th, he had to fight his nerves. *Once this expedition is over, I'll see if Wolseley allows my men to wear something more neutral.*

Jack flinched as one of the Hausas staggered under the impact of a slug, then a second smashed into the man's face. As the Hausa crumpled, two more Ashantis fired, with the Hausas body jerking at each strike. He lay, groaning on the ground, trying to pluck something from inside his jacket.

"Lie still, man," Jack stepped to the wounded man. "The bearers will take you back."

The Hausa looked at Jack with the light fading from his eyes, still reaching inside his jacket.

"What do you want?" Jack opened the Hausa's tunic. When a small copy of the Koran slid out, Jack pushed the book into the man's hand. "Rest easy, Hausa," Jack said, patted his shoulder and stood up.

C Company had advanced fifteen yards while Jack had been with the wounded man. Stepping across a trailing branch, Jack moved forward. The Hausas and his Wests were firing, with the sharp crackle of musketry marking their route. With so many Ashanti warriors around them, the British seemed to be moving through a tunnel of smoke so dense it nearly hid the trees.

The Hausas ahead were erratic, running in all directions, loading and firing without taking aim and ignoring the frantic orders of their officers. *That's not surprising, with their lack of training.*

"Keep moving!" Jack said. "Aim and fire only when you have a target! Don't waste ammunition!"

He saw a small clearing in the forest, with a sizeable village under the pall of drifting white smoke. *That must be Essaman.* The palm-leaf roofs looked very peaceful amidst the din of battle, and Jack hoped the woman and children had escaped to safety. He grunted as a score of Ashanti warriors emerged from the houses, firing towards the advancing British. *These Ashanti lads are game.* Suddenly aware of movement to his left, Jack saw the Hausas retiring, one by one and then in a great body of open-mouthed men. Half a dozen discarded fezzes remained, red against the green bush, to show how far the Hausas had advanced. The sharp notes of a bugle tried to recall the Hausas, failed and tried again.

"Stay with me, C Company!" Jack lifted a hand to Hopringle, who stood erect amidst his men, daring the Ashantis to fire. "Hopringle! Keep your fool head down!"

Glancing behind him, Jack saw the Hausas Lieutenant Woodgate retiring with only his bugler, swearing like a Marine on a drunken binge.

"These Hausas don't have your training," Jack shouted to his men. "Come on, 2nd West! Show them how true soldiers behave!"

All around him, Jack heard heavy firing, from the deep thuds of the Ashantis' muskets to the regulated, sharper crack of the Sniders. Behind the musketry, he heard the shrilling of British bugles and the throbbing of Ashanti war-drums and blare of their horns. Powder-smoke filled the air, the hoarse shouts of men and the occasional shriek as a shot slammed home. *This is getting hot, but my lads are holding up well.*

A sinister whoosh intruded into the sounds of battle. Jack looked up to see Captain Freemantle's rocket fly over the palm-thatch roofs of the village, trailing a ribbon of smoke and sparks. He had heard that rockets unsettled the Ashantis, but evidently, nobody had told that to the defenders of Essaman. They stood their ground, loading and firing from the shelter of houses as rockets soared past.

As the rocketeers and the Ashanti exchanged fire, Captain Freemantle pushed forward the nine-pounder, with Captain Bullen of the Marines at his side and the seamen and Kroomen struggling with the weight. A group of Ashantis emerged from the forest and opened a steady fire on the gunners, momentarily exposing themselves.

"Get these men!" Jack pointed to the Ashantis.

Captain Bullen staggered as a slug hit the compass case around his neck, while a bullet passed through Captain Freemantle's arm, spinning him in a complete circle.

"Force them back, lads! Hopringle! Your section is closer, protect the gunners." Even as he directed his men, Jack admired the skill of the enemy. *Good tactics of these Ashantis, targeting the officers.*

With blood seeping from his arm, Freemantle tore a handkerchief from his pocket, wrapped it around his arm, tied it with his teeth and carried on.

"Hopringle! Defend the artillery. We'll press on here." Jack's section and the remaining Hausas advanced steadily. Again the Ashantis aimed at the officers, with another spent slug winding Jack as it struck him under the breast bone, and a bold warrior stepping clear of the forest to shoot Colonel McNeill. As the colonel collapsed with blood gushing from his lacerated arm, Ogston took steady aim and shot the Ashanti marksman.

"Well done, Ogston!" Jack praised. He saw the flash of white teeth as Ogston grinned at him through the smoke.

With many of the officers down, Wolseley took direct command, ordering Jack's Wests to attack Essaman in front as the Marines closed in on each flank.

"Both your sections, Windrush!"

A frontal attack against steady infantry was one of the most perilous manoeuvres, so Jack knew he had to set an example to his inexperienced troops.

"Come on the Wests!" Loading as he marched, Jack advanced in front of his men. "Come on, C Company!"

Immediately aware that the pincer movement would squeeze them in a cross-fire, the Ashantis fired a final farewell and fled into the jungle, leaving Jack dizzy with relief. He gripped Mary's scarf. *We survived that action, Mary.*

"We've captured Essaman!" Somebody shouted in a broad Devon accent as the Marines' flanking sections met in the centre of the village. "Stand and fight, you beggars!"

"Well done, Wests!" Jack praised as his company grinned at each other. "Make sure you're loaded in case the Ashantis return."

Throwing off any final shred of discipline, the Hausas ran into Essaman, yelling and shrieking, as they began to loot the village of anything they could carry. Jack realised that some of his men were looking at him hopefully. He shook his head. "We're the 2nd Wests," he said, "not Bushmen in uniform." He knew that looting had been a soldier's perquisite since time immemorial, but he wanted his Wests to maintain their discipline until he knew it was safe.

"Torch it!" The word spread. "Put Essaman to the flames."

"Not yet!" Coffin yelled. "There's somebody inside that house!"

"Hold!" Jack shouted as a bearded sailor lifted a blazing torch. "Check inside, Coffin. Cover him Ogston."

Holding his rifle ready, Coffin dived inside the hut, emerging a moment later with a terrified little boy. "What do I do with this wild Ashanti warrior, sir?"

"I'll take that beggar off your hands, soldier," Captain Crean said, lifted the child and promptly handed him over to a group of eager Marines. "Here, men, do something with this little chap."

"A recruit!" The Marines welcomed the youngster with grins and extended arms.

"My missus always wanted a little boy," a grizzled sergeant said. "If she sees this little tyke we'll never get rid of the blighter."

"Now can I burn the house, sir?" The bearded sailor asked plaintively, with his torch dripping sparks.

"Yes, on you go," Jack said.

When the flames took hold of Essaman, with the now-expected explosions from casks of gunpowder, Wolseley ordered the buglers to blow assembly, and his small army gathered in a nearby clearing, some laughing, others quiet, as the officers checked the casualties. "Thirty-two wounded, one dead."

Jack had two of his Wests injured, none seriously. "That's your first action, lads," he said. "You did well." His men grinned to him, with Daley shaking with reaction as Ogston put an arm around him.

The Marines looked exhausted, some lying flat on the ground, others in a state of shock. Except for the NCOs, Jack doubted if any of them were twenty years old, and many much younger. They were little more than boys, first-year recruits who had proved themselves in this very alien environment. Now some were severely wounded and may die before they had properly matured.

"I heard they were dragged from Devon and sent here before their training was complete," Hopringle noticed Jack studying the Marines. "I wonder how many regret taking the Queen's Shilling now."

"I think most soldiers have regrets after their first action," Jack said. "Then it becomes part of life. Regrets are part of the soldiers' bargain. And the Marines' bargain."

Although Jack had taken part in much bloodier expeditions, he wondered if the results were worth the casualties. The British had destroyed a couple of villages that the Ashantis could rebuild in a few days and had killed a few dozen warriors from an army of many thousand.

"That's a good day's work so far, Windrush." Colonel Wood did not agree with Jack's assessment. "We've proved that British soldiers can face and defeat the Ashantis in their own forests."

Jack nodded. "It's a start, sir." He was more interested in the behaviour of his West Indians, and the safety of Mary. If he was going to Kumasi, he wanted his men to be thoroughly trained and better disciplined. *They are not ready yet. I need a crack company to fight the Ashantis. I need to get my company into action again.*

Chapter Twenty-Two

IN THE BUSH NOVEMBER 1873

With a section of Wests escorting the wounded back to Cape Coast Castle, Wolseley ordered the column to march on. Jack adjusted his pith helmet, ensured his men were loaded and led them across a plain where patches of scrub and forest could give the enemy plenty cover. Now aware how stubborn the Ashantis' defence would be, Wolseley sent skirmishers in front, with Jack's company supporting the Hausas.

"Don't shoot unless you see an enemy," Jack emphasised. "Remember that the porters have to carry every cartridge, and the further we march, the more scarce ammunition will become."

He thought of Mary and that hellish fetish tree. "Aim before you fire," he said for at least the fiftieth time, "and make every shot count. We are not here to loot the enemy's villages. We are here to destroy their empire and free the hostages."

After an hour of slow progress, Wolseley called a halt outside another small village, from which the inhabitants had fled. A quick search revealed no women or children, only a couple of kegs of gunpowder and a vintage French musket, abandoned by a fleeing warrior.

Jack glanced up. Although there was no sound of drums, he could feel the menace all around.

"Torch the place," Wolseley spoke from his hammock. As the flames rose, he called the officers together. "We've marched far enough inland to make our point, gentlemen. The Ashanti now know we can defeat them in the forest. It's time to remove the enemy from our coast."

The column left the village blazing behind them and plunged into an area of forest so dense that Jack could hardly see two yards on either flank.

"Wait here, lads." Borrowing a cutlass from a seaman, Jack hacked into the bush beside the track.

"What are you doing, sir?" Hopringle asked.

"Searching for an Ashanti battle path," Jack said. "They cut them parallel to the main track to ambush us." After a few moments, with sweat bursting from every pore, he knew that not even the Ashanti could cut a secondary path in such impenetrable jungle.

"We're safe from ambush here," Jack told his waiting Wests, "but don't relax. Keep alert, keep in extended order and keep your rifles loaded. There might be a stray Ashanti, somewhere."

The path narrowed further, forcing the column into single file, a long line of men all wondering if the Ashantis had infiltrated the thick trees on their flanks. Shortly after, they had other worries, for even walking was difficult. With this track the only route, thousands of travellers had worn a deep cleft in the ground, which nature had filled with a particularly glutinous mud. Men cursed as the mud sucked the boots from their feet and insects clouded around their heads.

"It's bloody hot," a flame-haired young Marine took his helmet off to wipe sweat from his face. "I never knew it would be this hot."

"Put your helmet back on!" Jack snarled. "The sun is as deadly as any Ashanti bullet." He looked up as a shift in the wind carried a low rumbling to them. "That's gunfire," he said. "Heavy stuff, not musketry."

As they staggered and limped along the track, starting at every hint of possible Ashanti ambush, the booming of heavy guns became more distinct.

"What's happening, sir?" Hopringle sounded nervous.

"I'm blessed if I know," Jack said.

"Don't you lobster-backs worry," a smiling Navy lieutenant said. "The navy's here to look after you. That noise you hear will be *Argus* and *Decoy* shelling the enemy." He looked southward as if he could see the sea through miles of forest. "I know the sound of British gunboats anywhere, even in the middle of the African jungle."

"Thank you, lieutenant," Jack nodded, thinking that Wolseley was the most organised general he had ever met, ensuring that the navy bombarded the enemy in conjunction with an attack by the army.

"Oh, always happy to oblige, old chap. Any time you lobsters need educated, just ask a sailor."

"Pick the pace up!" Wolseley shouted from his hammock. "We want to reach the villages soon after the Navy has finished with them."

Hopringle looked confused. "I thought we were returning to Cape Coast. Which villages did the general mean?"

"Amguna, Akimfoo and Ampeenee," Jack said. "They've been helping the Ashantis."

Hopringle shrugged. "We'd best have a look, then."

After a few hours inland, it was a relief to come to the freshness of the coast, although a fringe of cocoa-not grass and palm trees blocked any view of the sea. The cannonade grew louder as the column marched to Amguna, with the regular boom of naval artillery an alien intrusion into the natural sounds of Africa.

Colonel Wood lifted his voice. "Windrush, take a section ahead, ensure there are no Ashantis in Amguna."

"Come on, lads," Jack jogged ahead, with his men at his heels. "Skirmishing order!" They moved at a fast pace across the sand, with the wind pleasant on hot faces and palm trees rustling beside them. Always aware the Ashantis would target him first, Jack forced himself to stand tall, encouraging his men.

Amguna was similar to the villages inland, except for the belt of cocoa- nut trees and the fresh sea breeze. Jack saw a flicker of movement across a doorway. "Careful, lads, in case there are musket men."

Now veterans, the Wests obeyed at once, stretching into a line that out-flanked Amguna on both sides. As they approached the village, a dozen people fled, taking their children, animals and some household possessions with them. There was no musketry and no sign of any Ashanti warriors as the bleating of goats gradually faded.

"Follow me," Jack moved cautiously between the houses, kicking open doors to see if anybody was inside. After ten minutes, he ordered Ogston back to the column. "My compliments to General Wolseley," he said, "and Amguna is clear of the enemy."

"Burn the place down," Wolseley ordered from his hammock.

Moving away a few hundred yards from the burning village, the British halted, with coconut trees protecting them from the worst of the afternoon sun. Again, the young Marines collapsed on the greyish sand, seeking shade as sweat eased from faces already burned brick-red.

"Look up there!" Stair pointed upwards, where green coconuts bunched under the leaves.

"Get some down, Sam!" Ogston urged, lifting a fallen branch.

Grinning, Stair climbed part way up the tree, reached up with the branch and dislodged a dozen nuts.

"What's this?" A young Marine lifted a coconut curiously. "What's it do?"

"It's a coconut, Johnnie," Private Coffin explained. He showed the Marine how to open the shell, using his bayonet to slice away the green rind and gouging a hole in the nut.

"Drink the milk, Johnnie," Ogston demonstrated. "It's good."

At first hesitant at this novel food, the Marine tasted the contents, nodded and swallowed the contents before passing the news on to his mates. Within a few moments Marines and bluejackets joined the West Indians and Hausas in drinking coconut milk, laughing together under the swaying palms with the sound of the surf in the background. Jack thought it could be an Elysian scene, except for the smoke from the burning village, the grumble of naval gunfire and the preponderance of weapons.

"You, men." Jack pointed to Number Two section. "You're on sentry duty. Go a hundred yards outside the camp and watch for Ashantis."

"The Marines aren't on picket," Jackson protested, with coconut milk dripping from his chin.

"You're better than them," Jack said. "You're the 2nd West." He looked at the Marines. Despite the refreshing coconuts and the sea-breeze, most of the young men lay supine, sweat-streaked and exhausted. Some were sleeping, others just lying prone, trying to draw deep breaths of air. *These lads won't go much longer.*

Wolseley and Colonel Wood seemed to come to the same conclusion. "The youngsters are about done," Wolseley said.

"Best leave them here for the navy to collect, I think, sir," Wood said. "The Hausas and the 2nd West are better acclimatised to the conditions."

"I'll see if there are any volunteers," Wolseley said. "You never know with Royal Marines. They always have the capacity to surprise."

When Wood said he was "looking for twenty Marine volunteers to continue the march," he was nearly knocked down in the rush. Smooth-faced boys who had been prone with exhaustion a moment before declared their willingness to continue.

"Take me, sir! I'll show these Shanties what for!"

"I'm your man, sir," said a boy who looked as if he should still be in school.

"I'm tough stuff, Colonel! I'm coming!"

Wood smiled. "Good boys," he said, visibly moved, "brave, brave boys." Selecting twenty of the fittest, he ordered the surgeon to examine them and sent the remainder as an escort for the dozen hammocks of wounded men. "Take them to Elmina," Wood pointed along the coast. "It's only a few miles away."

Jack's Wests marched with the main body in the opposite direction, with each footstep sinking and sliding in soft sand and the sun glaring above, reflecting from the sea as the breakers crashed beside them. After an hour, HMS *Decoy* came close inshore and sent her boats full of fresh bluejackets and Marines.

"You couldn't do without us, could you?" Captain Luxmore said, grinning as his men swarmed ashore through the surf. "Typical army, full of colour and shine until things get difficult and then what is it? Send for the navy!"

"Not quite," Jack shouted back. "My 2nd Wests wanted to show the bluejackets how real warriors fight, not shellbacks who spend all night in comfortable bunks and all day swanning about in cool breezes." He felt, rather than saw, his men's pleasure at his words.

"We've brought water," Luxmore's smile did not fade, "and a case of claret for the Marines. Can't have the lads going thirsty, can we?"

"Well met, Captain," Jack said, as the newly arrived bluejackets and 2nd West sized each other up.

A bugle blared, bringing the men back to the ranks and they marched on, sometimes with the sea in view and the navy patrolling as if in a different world, and at other times with tall trees screening them on both sides. When they approached another village, the inhabitants fled, some carrying household goods, others driving fowls or goats before them.

"Shall we torch the houses, sir?" An eager midshipman asked.

"Not this time," Wolseley said. "They have not fired on us, and we've had no reports of this village supporting the Ashantis." He raised his voice. "No looting here and no souvenir hunting! We do not hurt our friends."

Blinking away the sweat that dripped into his eyes, Jack marched on, until they reached another, larger village that a stretch of coconut grass, twelve feet high, had protected from the navy. Even naval gunners could not bombard a target they could not see.

"What's this place called?" Hopringle slumped down with his back to a tall palm.

Jack checked his notes. "I'm not sure."

"Burn it," Wolseley said without hesitation, "and march on."

Once again, the flames rose, orange-red and ugly, while dirty smoke smudged the bright sky.

"They'll remember us on this coast," Hopringle said.

"Aye." Jack took a pull at his water bottle. "For all the wrong reasons. We're the men who destroyed their homes." He ignored Hopringle's curious look, for this work of destruction depressed him.

"They can build the houses again, sir," Ogston must have understood Jack's thoughts. "Better burning houses than enslaving the inhabitants."

Jack trudged on, head down, hating himself. *I should be rescuing Mary, not burning huts scores of miles from Kumasi.* "Pick up your feet, C Company!" He roared. "This is not a blasted picnic!"

They forded an ankle-deep stream, with the water muddy and foul as it flowed from a lagoon, and with insects hovering near the surface.

"Don't drink that," Jack snarled as some of the Marines scooped up water with their helmets. "God only knows what diseases it harbours."

"God knows everything," Coffin said quietly.

"Windrush," Colonel Wood gave a quiet order. "Take your Wests and scout ahead, for Ampanee."

Glad to be active, Jack led his men forward, all his fatigue forgotten in the energy of movement. After another quarter-mile, Stair gestured ahead.

"Sir," Stair said, "a flag."

Green, black and yellow, the Ashanti flag hung from a tall flag post in defiance of General Wolseley, Queen Victoria and the entire British Empire. Jack drew his revolver. "They would not display that flag unless they intended to fight. Skirmishing order, lads, and be prepared for an ambush."

The Wests moved on, more warily now, tense, expecting trouble, with their heart-beat increasing and the breath harsh in their throats. Ampanee huddled behind tall grass, with thick forest fifty yards to the rear. As he came closer, Jack saw the village was a collection of simple huts no different to all the others on this coast, except for the flag.

"Take One Section ahead, Hopringle." Jack knew it would do the lieutenant good to lead his men in action.

The group of Ashanti warriors that clustered beneath the flag were too intent on watching a coastal gunboat to notice C Company's advance. Jack pushed his section in support of Hopringle, who had taken to cover a hundred yards from the village.

"Extended skirmishing formation, lads!" Jack ordered.

"Sir!" Coffin pointed to the figure on the base of the flagstaff. "That's a man."

Stark naked, the man was spread-eagled upside down against the staff. He lacked his head, which lay on the sand a few yards away. Whether he had been sacrificed to a fetish or killed because he sympathised with the British, his death would have been terrifying.

Once again, Jack thought of Mary in the hands of the Ashanti and choked on his next words. He was tempted to charge straight in, killing, but twenty years of military experience tempered his ardour with caution.

"Hopringle, notify Colonel Wood what we have here." Jack fingered the chamber of his revolver. "Watch over these Ashantis, lads." He posted his men in the best places he could, having to push three into cover.

"Sir! We're soldiers," Jackson protested. "We're not scared of the Bushmen. We stand in the open to fight! We don't skulk behind trees!"

"Do as you are ordered," Jack snarled. "A dead soldier is no good to anybody." He slammed Jackson behind a tree. "Stay there and obey orders!"

Jackson's movement had alerted the Ashanti, with some moving in single file towards this new British threat on their flank.

"Right, boys. Fire when they get in range. Make sure of your target and aim low." Jack cursed when more of the enemy appeared. Rather than a dozen warriors, there were scores, in the village or emerging from the forest fringe. "Ampanee must be one of the Ashantis' main bases!"

"Shall we withdraw, sir?" Hopringle asked.

"No!" Jack snarled the word. "We stand fast and hold them."

With some Ashantis giving covering fire from the village, scores of others advanced towards Jack's thin line, ducking into cover like trained soldiers and coming steadily closer despite their casualties.

"Fire at will, Wests!" Jack flinched as something thudded into the sand beside him. *That was a bullet from a Snider or an Enfield. This is not pleasant.*

The whoosh and fiery trail was welcome as Wolseley put three rockets into the village and then sent forward the Naval Brigade. At the sight of rockets, the Ashantis faltered. "Rapid-fire, boys!" Jack roared. "They're wavering!"

The Naval Brigade passed through the 2nd Wests' position with the usual exchange of banter and a genuine request, "don't fire at us, Wests! We're on your side!"

"Cease fire!" Jack shouted. "Let the tarry-backs do their work!" He grabbed Jackson's rifle. "You too, Jackson!"

Drawing their cutlasses, the sailors charged forward, chased the Ashantis out of the village and took up defensive positions facing the bush.

"Follow the sailors, boys," Jack led them into Ampanee, "the Bushmen aren't done yet."

After a few moments of relative quiet, the Ashanti opened a heavy fire from the trees, with slugs hammering against the huts and scarring the trees.

"Get around their flanks," a beefy naval lieutenant ordered and the seamen moved in single file to the left, when a horde of Ashantis burst from the trees, yelling and waving muskets and long knives.

For a terrible second, Jack thought the Ashantis would massacre the seamen, but without waiting for an order, the sailors dropped to their knees and opened rapid fire. The Snider bullets felled the first wave of Ashantis, while the rest wavered.

"One Section," Jack said, "be prepared to support the seamen." He could not fire for fear of hitting the sailors. "Fix bayonets!" Although he had not had time to train his company in bayonet drill, he hoped their natural aggression would be enough. He saw Stair inch forward. "Wait for my order, damn it!"

Miraculously surviving the hail of Snider bullets, a tall, rangy Ashanti with a long white cloak ran for a petty officer with his knife. The petty officer fired, missed, dropped his rifle and drew his cutlass. Without a word, he squared up to the charging warrior, feinted left, cut right and thrust straight for the Ashanti's throat.

"And that's done for you, my lad," the petty officer said, wiped his blade on the Ashanti's cloak, sheathed his cutlass, picked up his rifle, loaded it and carried on as if nothing had happened.

"Hold!" Jack said. "The navy doesn't need us this time."

As the surviving Ashantis retreated into the forest, a second group charged at the British right flank.

"Here they come again, boys," Jack shouted. "Keep calm, shoot low and take your time." He heard Captain Crean give his Marines similar instructions. The initial volley from the British staggered the Ashanti charge, and when Jack ordered independent firing, the volume of bullets increased in direct proportion to a decrease in accuracy.

"Remember your training! Take your time, men!" Jack admonished again. "Aim before you fire!"

The concentrated fire of Wests, Hausas, Marines and the Naval Brigade forced the Ashantis back, still firing but with their long muzzle-loaders giving them a significant disadvantage when facing breech-loaders in the open. Leaving a scatter of bodies on the ground, the Ashantis retreated to the forest and continued to fire.

"Lie down," Jack ordered as two of his men staggered under the impact of Ashanti slugs. "Get behind cover!"

Jackson looked at the blood seeping from his shoulder. "We're soldiers, sir. We fight in the open!"

"You'll be dead soldiers if an Ashanti slug hits you in the head! Get under cover! I'm not losing good men!"

Eventually, the firing died away. Gunsmoke drifted out to sea as Marines, seamen and West Indians grinned to each other as comrades in arms. A sailor passed over a twist of tobacco to Ogston, who responded with a smile.

"Have a swig, Jack," Ogston handed over his water bottle.

The sailor took a drink, gasped and took another. "By God, lobster, that's better than water! Where did you get it?"

"Jamaican rum!" Ogston said. "We make it!"

"I'll have to get a transfer to your mob," the sailor said in pure Somerset.

Ogston grinned. "Bring your tobacco with you."

"Burn the place down," Wolseley ordered from the hammock.

When the seamen thrust torches into the thatched roofs, hundreds of rats and bats swarmed from the huts and around the column. The seamen made game of them, competing to see who could kill most with their cutlasses as the Wests watched, cheering on their favourites. It was just another minor incident in a campaign that Jack wished would end. He could not see this process of skirmishes and village burning, defeating King Kofi or freeing Mary.

"That was a good start, gentlemen," Wolseley said. "We have shown the Ashanti that we can fight in their terrain and punished some of their villages." Gathering his staff, he sailed back to Cape Coast Castle on *Decoy*.

"Sir Garnet has his life well organised," Hopringle said.

"His life is all Sir Garnet," a navy lieutenant said.

"Everything is well then," Hopringle said. "All Sir Garnet."

"We're heading back to Elmina!" Colonel Wood said cheerfully. "Step along, men!"

"Come on, C Company!" Jack roared. "You're veterans now! You faced and defeated the Ashantis."

That may be so, Jack told himself, *but we're no closer to rescuing Mary and every day in Kumasi is dangerous for her. When are we going to march?*

Chapter Twenty-Three

"That's all Sir Garnet, then,' Hopringle said. "The chiefs of Essaman and Amperee have sworn allegiance to the queen. We're turning the tide."

Jack nodded. The phrase "all Sir Garnet" was entering slang, meaning that everything was perfect. "I heard as much. Might is right, and the chiefs do what they must to protect themselves. If the British seem to be the stronger, they'll attach themselves to us. If the Ashantis are in the ascendancy, the chiefs will be cheering on the Asantahene." Jack lit a cheroot as he stared over the wall. "We can't blame them for seeking self-preservation."

The defection of the two chiefs was not the only success of Wolseley's raid, for Buller's spies reported that Amanquatia had ordered a withdrawal to Ashantiland. Jack was unsure if Wolseley's expedition was the direct cause of the Ashanti retreat, or if sickness in Amanquatia's army was the real reason. Whatever the truth, the people of the Gold Coast breathed a collective sigh of relief.

"Amanquatia has retreated to Mampon," Hopringle said. 'Sir Garnet should gather every man he can and hit him now. Smash the Ashantis when they are in retreat!"

"What with?" Jack blew smoke into the air. "Sir Garnet has no more men now than he had a month ago."

"We defeated the Ashantis at Essaman," Hopringle said.

"We defeated a small local force," Jack said, "after some pretty stiff fighting. Wolseley's trick with the journalists worked, or Amanquatia would have reinforced his army at Essaman. Amanquatia has the cream of the Ashanti army, thousands of seasoned veterans including Kumi Okese's Edwesus. I have no doubt our scraped up few hundred would fight well, but..." Jack shrugged. "Remember McCarthy? The Ashantis defeated him and used his skull as a drinking cup. I have no desire for King Kofi to slurp his Earl Grey from my head."

"Your wife is in Kumasi," Hopringle said.

"I know that," Jack whispered savagely. "You'd better be getting on with your duties, Lieutenant, or I'll knock you down."

He turned away, considering the implications of Amanquatia's withdrawal. With the Ashanti army concentrated in its homeland, Kumasi would be better defended. Remembering the forested Adansi Hills that lay between the coast and Kumasi, Jack thought of the difficulties of pushing a British army through miles of Ashanti ambushes. It may have been better to keep the Ashantis less concentrated near the coast, where the British could thin out their numbers in a series of encounters rather than risking everything on a single push into the Ashanti homeland.

Jack fingered Mary's scarf that he wore around his neck. *Stay alive, Mary, that's all I ask. Stay alive, and I'll come for you.*

* * *

"I don't normally agree with interfering with the religious beliefs of other people," Wolseley faced Jack across the width of the desk. "However, in the case of the Ashantis, I am prepared to stretch a point. For health and climatic reasons, we cannot risk a prolonged campaign in West Africa, so I must think of some way of augmenting our military superiority."

Jack guessed what was coming next.

"You may know that the Ashanti kings each have a stool in which they hold their ancestral spirits," Wolseley said. "I will retain you as commander of C Company of the Second Wests, Windrush and when we go to Kumasi, I wish you to find King Kofi's Golden Stool. If I have that, the Ashanti people will know that Great Britain is their master in spiritual as well as military matters." Wolseley shuffled the papers in front of him. "I have chosen you for this task, Windrush, because you know Kumasi better than any of my officers. I want you to make the capture of the Golden Stool your priority."

"My wife is also in Kumasi, sir," Jack reminded.

"I have not forgotten, Windrush," Wolseley said. "I have sent numerous messages to King Kofi demanding that he release all the hostages, including Mrs Windrush."

"Thank you, sir," Jack said. "Are the British regiments on their way?" He felt his heartbeat increase. If King Kofi released the hostages, his emotional nightmare would end, and he could concentrate on his duty.

"I expect them to arrive in early December," Wolseley said. "One battalion each of the Rifles, the 23rd Foot and the 42nd Highlanders, with Royal Artillery and Royal Engineers."

Jack nodded. "It's a full-scale war, then."

"It's war." Wolseley looked up. "Kumasi will burn, depend on it."

"That's good news, sir. I hope your diplomacy works and the hostages are released."

"The Golden Stool would be a fitting prize for this campaign, Windrush. I rely on your discretion to keep the mission to yourself." Wolseley nearly smiled. "General Hook told me you were the best man for this sort of work."

"Thank you, sir." Jack could hardly think of capturing the Golden Stool. He thought of Mary in Kumasi and hoped that Wolseley's diplomacy, on top of the success of the recent expedition, could bring her back.

* * *

Despite all Wolseley's best efforts, the Fanti chiefs failed to provide warriors in either quantity or quality. Only a few hundred turned up, and to Jack's eyes, used to the superb fighting men of the Indian sub-continent, the chiefs had sent their dregs.

"The Ashanti warriors will eat these men for breakfast." Jack watched Colonel Wood trying to train the recruits, while the Wests laughed with unhidden scorn.

"Oh?" Buller raised his eyebrows. "I didn't realise the Ashanti were cannibals." He grinned. "One more reason to destroy them."

"We'll not destroy them with that bunch," Jack pointed to the Fantis. "They'll run at first sight of a proper Ashanti warrior."

"It's all up to us then," Buller said. "As usual."

"Aye," Jack said. "As usual."

As Jack continued to train his men, Wolseley used what forces he had to harass the retreating Ashantis. He sent Colonel Wood on a reconnaissance from Elmina, while he arranged an expedition inland.

"The Ashantis are retreating," Wolseley said. "I want to hurry them along. Bring a half company of your Wests, Windrush."

"Yes, sir." Jack was already fretting to do something rather than waiting in Cape Coast.

Although some of his men were down with fever, Jack selected Numbers One and Two sections, filled the gaps with volunteers from Three and Four sections and joined the expedition. The engineers had improved the road beyond compare, so the column made good time, stopping at wayside stations where well-built huts sheltered them, and military police kept order.

"We're already civilising the country," Buller said.

"We are," Jack agreed. "The quicker, the better."

The Marines already looked more mature than on the previous expedition, while the sailors were the same willing warriors as ever. Russell's regiment of men from half a dozen tribes took the van, with Jack's Wests watching them with the suspicion of professional soldiers eyeing amateurs.

"Are we attacking Kumasi?" Stair asked.

"Not this time," Jack told him.

"Oh," Stair looked disappointed. "The women there were gorgeous."

They marched through the night, with a full moon throwing nearly ghostly light on low scrubland, while the occasional patch of tall forest plunging them into sudden darkness where sounds and smells prevailed. When the night eased, they marched through the hottest day Jack had yet experienced in Africa, with two Marines collapsing through sunstroke.

"Isn't this fun, Windrush?" Buller wiped the sweat from his forehead as they halted in the evening. "Wandering across Africa chasing shadows."

"Any more intelligence?" Jack had not seen a single enemy yet. His men were bored with marching without reason, and he felt the same.

"I am here with a report for Sir Garnet," Buller tried to sound important.

"Damn Sir Garnet. Have you any news of Mary, of the hostages? Has King Kofi released them, yet?"

"Not yet," Buller shook his head with genuine sympathy. "I'll contact you the second I hear anything, Windrush." He lowered his voice. "Getting information from within Kumasi is not easy. King Kofi has a new man in charge of internal security there, and he executed one of my spies."

Jack could picture the scene. "Do you know who?"

"A man you already know," Buller said. "Kumi Okese."

Jack felt his stomach churn. "That's unfortunate," he said. "He's a most efficient man and a fine fighter, the Sir Garnet of the Ashantis. He'd be an asset to any army."

Buller lit another cigar. "Is that so? Maybe we'll recruit him after we complete this business." He grinned. "We seem to get out best soldiers from the ranks of ex-enemies, Sikhs, Gurkhas, Highlanders *et al.* Why not a regiment of Ashantis?"

"Maybe," Jack could not smile, "although I doubt Kumi Okese would join us. He's an Ashanti to his bones and as dangerous an enemy as we will ever face."

"We're moving again," a young midshipman said with great excitement. "General Wolseley sends his compliments, Major Windrush, and could your West Indians take the rearguard, please."

"It's a chase now, Windrush," Buller said. "We've got Amanquatia on the run."

"We're like a terrier dog chasing a lion," Jack said. "The Ashanti have split into several armies, each one much larger than ours. Wolseley wants to catch one of them on the flank around our garrison at Abrakrampa."

Their march took them across a plain with patches of forest and scrub, to a deep forest broken by areas of knee-deep swamp. Although Wolseley's old wound had prevented him from marching on the previous expedition, the creepers and low branches on this track negated the use of a hammock. Wolseley had to walk, disguising the pain of his injured leg. Jack's old Burma wound also played up, so he limped, fought the pain and curled Mary's scarf around his fist.

Hold on, Mary.

With around 300 houses and huts, plus a Wesleyan chapel at one end of the town, Abrakrampa was sizeable by local standards, with a static garrison of mixed British and native defenders. Wolseley arrived as moonlight glowed behind static clouds and nervous sentries sent a challenge.

"Who goes there?" The words hollow in the dark.

"General Wolseley!" A brass-lunged naval lieutenant replied.

"Enter, sir!"

Although cleared of Ashantis, the inhabitants of Abrakrampa were in dread, jumping at small sounds and continually checking the surrounding forest. "They think the Ashantis are all around them," Buller said, "blocking the roads."

Wolseley's little force rested for an hour and set off again, heading for an Ashanti gathering at the village of Assanchi. Clouds shrouded the moon, so the British patrolled in the dark, with lantern-light bouncing against the surrounding trees and casting weird shadows.

"The Ashantis are waiting for us," Daley said.

Jack felt the same. He could taste the men's nervousness, smell the fear in their sweat. Wolseley's recent successes had only given a temporary respite; the dread of the Ashantis was too deep-rooted for one victorious skirmish to remove. Night passed into day, and the sun rose in glorious dawn that turned into a stiflingly hot morning. The men marched on into Africa, waiting for the dull thud of Ashanti muskets or the ominous hammer of the war drums.

They reached the village of Assanchi, to find the Ashantis had already left. The heat and conditions drained the Marines' strength, so they lay in the shade, gasping for breath. Even the Wests reached for their water bottles and cursed the sun that beat down upon them.

"The Ashantis are leading us into a trap," Daley said. "They'll draw us deeper and deeper into Africa and then cut us off and kill us."

"The officers are too stupid to see their plan," Jackson glowered at Wolseley, nursing his still aching arm. "We should run the army, not them."

Jack ignored the grumbling. Soldiers had groused since armies were invented and would continue to complain until the ploughshare drove the sword from the globe. Like looting a captured town, it was one of their perquisites. Grumbling was a safety valve that did little harm unless it spread and deepened. Jack had no reason to believe that would happen in the 2nd Wests, but he kept his ears open, ready to squash any persistent complaints.

After a fruitless night chasing empty rumours, Wolseley lifted his hand. "I think that's sufficient marching for the day. The Ashantis are well gone now." He rubbed at his sore leg. "Back to Abrakrampa."

It was early morning when they passed the clearing around Abrakrampa, to find Buller was waiting for them, surrounded by a bevy of his native spies. "No luck then, Windrush?"

"Not a whisper of the enemy," Jack watched as dozens of the Marines slumped to the ground, overcome by the heat or suffering from their ill-fitting boots.

Buller shook his head. "You were with the wrong column, old man. Colonel Festing took out 700 men and clashed with the Ashanti at Iscabio. I don't know the enemy casualties, but Festing had five killed and 47 wounded, including himself."

Jack nodded. "I fought under Festing at Elmina. He's a good man." *All the same*, he thought to himself, *these encounters are only pinpricks that do nothing to free Mary.* Every day that passed, Mary was in danger, and if these small defeats annoyed King Kofi, he might well decide to sacrifice the hostages in revenge. The sooner the British regiments arrived, the quicker they could attack Kumasi.

"If the general had more men, he could follow up his successes," Buller said.

"Aye, and if wishes came true, I'd have been born a belted earl," Jack retorted. "You are right, though, Buller. Given a couple of regular British regiments and some artillery, Wolseley could chase Amanquatia back to Kumasi. He could squash the Ashantis before they had time to organise their defence."

"Thank God for the Navy," Buller said. "So far we've fought this campaign with untrained natives, a part battalion of West Indians, Marines who should still be with their mummies and sailors on land. If King Kofi knew how weak we were, he'd whistle up all his men and sweep us into the sea."

"All the more reason to keep pressing him," Jack said. "King Kofi must have spies in Cape Coast and Elmina. Keep him on the run, or he'll regroup and come back at us. We'll just have to manage with what we have until then."

The British regiments aren't due until late December, Jack thought. *Even if they marched as soon as they arrived, the British regiments could not possibly reach Kumasi until early February. Kumi Okese had weeks to organise his defence.*

Jack heard the firing at seven that morning. He was on his feet in a second, buckling on his revolver and shouting for his men.

"Stand to, Wests!"

Bugles blared the Alarm as Jack's men ran to their posts, some fully dressed, others in a state of near-nudity, but all carrying their rifles and ammunition, which was the mark of a soldier.

The musketry continued for a few moments, sputtered up again and died out. Silence returned, save for the usual sounds of the bush.

"Only skirmishers," Buller said.

"They're still out there," Ogston said. "Waiting."

"I can feel them," Jack said. The menace was palpable, the sensation of thousands of fierce forest warriors within a mile or so of the village.

Limping heavily, Wolseley toured the defences. "Windrush, you reinforce Abrakrampa with your Wests. I'm hunting Amanquatia." The general gave crisp orders as he led his column away.

The defenders watched Wolseley march out, and then silence descended, except for the croak of circling vultures.

* * *

Abrakrampa baked under the sun, with the defenders knowing they were all alone. If the Ashanti decided to attack, there was no sizeable army to come to their aid until the British regiments finally arrived. Jack lifted his head as he heard drums muttering in the distance. They beat for half an hour and stopped, leaving a silence that seemed to press down upon them.

"They know the general has gone," Jack said to Lieutenant Gordon, who had strengthened the defences of the village.

"We have a good position," Gordon said, quietly, "with Captain Grant and ninety men of the Wests, Lieutenant Wells and 50 Marines and bluejackets, 100 Hausas, assorted Fantis, Sierra Leone Volunteers and Kosoos, plus the local king with a few hundred Ambras."

"Will they fight?" Jack knew that numbers mattered less than spirit when the battle started.

Gordon shrugged and smiled at the same time. "Time will tell."

Gordon had transformed the chapel into a small fortress by removing the thatched roof and strengthening the upper story to support the weight of a rocket trough and an ancient cannon. "The Marines and sailors garrison the chapel," Gordon said. "It's like their ship in the forest." He grinned, a likeable man in an unlikely situation. "The cannon is Dutch and probably as reliable as a snyde shilling, but the bluejackets call it Nelly and keep it polished."

Jack looked over the chapel, noting the sandbags that fortified the windows and the Marines and seamen lounging inside, smoking pipes, chewing tobacco and exchanging jokes that would blister the ears of any respectable chapelgoer. "That place is in good hands."

A wooden palisade surrounded most of Abrakrampa, with defensive trenches along the sides, while determined men guarded loopholed houses.

Gordon had created a killing ground around the village by clearing away the trees yet leaving sufficient low bushes to hamper any attempt at a full charge.

"You've done a good job, Gordon," Jack approved.

"If the Ashantis come, they'll break their regiments against our defences," Gordon said, "providing the men hold firm." He lowered his voice. "I'd give a hundred guineas for half a battalion of British regulars, though."

Major Baker Russell, the garrison commander, greeted Jack cordially. "You've been under siege before, I hear, Windrush."

"Yes, sir. At Lucknow."

"Well, place your men wherever you think best. Your experience will be useful." Russell hesitated. "Do you know our local fighters?"

"Not well sir, except for the Ashantis."

"Permit me to enlighten you. The Hausas are Mohammedans, brave soldiers, but a bit undisciplined. The Kossoos are fierce swordsmen from the Sherbro River, courageous to a fault. You'll like them."

"I'm sure I will," Jack said.

The drums started at noon, distant yet menacing, throwing their threats over the garrison of Abrakrampa.

"Our neighbours are bidding us good afternoon," Russell said. "They're at Anasmadi, about a mile away." He grinned. "My Kossoos like to catch any stray Ashantis and chop them up."

The drums muttered away in the background all day, unnerving until Jack grew used to the sound, and then he ignored it. Village life continued. Using the opportunity, Jack trained his men in the rudiments of defensive warfare, with the Kossoos and Hausas watching, and the seamen giving bawdy advice. The tension mounted in Abrakrampa as people awaited the inevitable attack.

On the 2nd November, Russell sent out Jack with a mixed party to reconnoitre Anasmadi. With Winnebah tribesmen in front, Kossoos acting as scouts and the Hausas marching eagerly, Jack ordered his Wests to keep alert.

"I have no idea how these tribesmen will behave if we meet the enemy."

"I can hear the Bushmen," Ogston said. "I can smell them."

"Where?" Jack fingered the butt of his revolver.

A musket boomed ahead, quickly followed by the crack of a rifle. A moment later, the Winnebah tribesmen rushed back, nearly flattening Jack in their panic to escape from the Ashantis.

"So much for our allies," Jack said. "Stay with me, men." Sliding behind a tree, he waited for the Ashantis to appear. After five minutes, when the Hausas fired in every direction, things calmed down without a single Ashanti approaching them.

"Let's have a look," Jack said. "Ogston and Stair, you're with me." A hundred yards deeper into the forest, they found the Ashanti camp. Cooking fires were unattended, huts left vacant and bits of clothing scattered. "It looks as if our scouts met their scouts and the Ashantis ran as fast as the Winnebahs," Jack said.

"Bloody Bushmen," Stair said. "They must know the 2nd Wests are here."

Jack nodded. "That's what it must have been. There's nothing here for us, so we'd better return to Abrakrampa."

"Sir," Ogston said. "Can you hear that?" He lifted his rifle. "It sounds as if something's dragging on the ground."

"I hear it." Jack half-crouched, watching for some Ashanti trick. The silence was oppressive as if Africa waited to pounce.

"Sir!" Ogston pointed his rifle at the woman who crawled towards them, hauling a six-foot-long log. "The Bushmen left a slave behind."

"Cover me," Jack crouched beside the woman, who stared at him through wide, terrified eyes. "The Ashanti have clamped the poor woman to this log."

"I'll get it, sir." Drawing his bayonet, Ogston prised the clamp from the wood. "There we go, my pretty."

"Bring her with us," Jack said as the woman broke into a long speech in Fanti. "She might have some useful information."

"How about the Winnebahs, sir?" Ogston asked.

Jack grunted. "They can make their own way back."

* * *

"What have we here?" Using his working knowledge of Fanti, Major Russell listened to the woman's story. "This unhappy woman is Amba Firitumba. She was in her village outside Cape Coast a few months ago when the Ashanti enslaved her and her three children. She hasn't seen her little ones since."

"Poor woman," Jack said.

"One of many, I'm afraid," Russell said. "She is a reminder of why we are here. Of more immediate concern, Amba told me that Amanquatia is going to attack Abrakrampa."

"Amanquatia is still around, is he?" Jack glanced at his surroundings. "I hoped he was halfway back to Kumasi by now."

"So did I." Russell shook his head. "No matter, we'll keep the defences up to scratch," Russell said. "Although we can discount the Winnebahs."

The Ashantis returned that evening, remaining within the forest as they circled Abrakrampa, talking in loud voices, occasionally showing themselves to the sentries, laughing and immediately withdrawing to the shelter of the trees.

"They're trying to unnerve us," Jack said. "Letting us know they're there, tempting the frightened to desert and weakening our resolve."

"Well, Windrush," Russell said, "Sir Garnet has weakened us without any help from the Ashantis. First, we lose the Winnebahs, and now the general has ordered our Naval Brigade to Esseboo."

"They're some of our best men," Jack said. "After the 2nd West."

"Aye," Russell gave a wry smile. "We'll miss them."

The Naval Brigade took the news phlegmatically, with Lieutenant Wells ordering them to pack up their gear and prepare the artillery for transport. The seamen and Marines worked with a will, squaring away all their kit within an hour.

"I'll send a section of Wests to defend the church, Russell," Jack said. "If you can persuade the Navy to leave Nelly the cannon behind, I'm sure we can work out how to fire the blasted thing."

Russell grunted. "Thank you, Windrush."

The firing came without warning, hundreds of muskets in a great arc around the west side of the village around the church.

"Well now," Russell drawled the words as a hail of slugs rattled around Abrakrampa. "It looks like our Naval Brigade is going nowhere. The attack has begun."

Chapter Twenty-Four

Without waiting for orders, the seamen and Marines raced to their old positions. Backing the Ashanti musketry, drums and war horns sounded all around Abrakrampa, with a chorus of the chilling Ashanti war song.

"What the devil," Jack said as a lone defender left the village and stepped into the clearing, half-seen in the fading light. "Who is that idiot?"

"That's no idiot," Russell said. "That's the King of Arbra, the local tribe."

"Is it indeed? Well, he's either going to desert to the enemy with all his men, or surrender."

"No, Windrush," Russell said. "Have a little faith."

Raising his hands, the king shouted something, with Russell translating to Jack. "I am the king of this country; come on if you are coming!"

"Brave man," Jack altered his opinion of the king.

Less impressed than Jack, the Ashantis responded with a volley that kicked up the dirt and grass around the king, who turned and withdrew with a dignity that Jack could only admire.

"Well, he tried," Russell said. "Naval Brigade, show these Ashanti what you can do."

"Aye, aye, sir!" A seaman bellowed, and the Naval Brigade immediately fired Nelly. The sound was like nothing Jack had heard before, a stupendous bang that shook the church as a cloud of blue-white smoke enveloped the sailors.

"That's from the navy, boys!" The seamen yelled in evident glee.

The Ashanti musketry continued, with the defenders replying, Sniders and Enfields cracking all around the village perimeter. As so often in Africa, the moon glowed strongly, highlighting the surrounding trees and casting wavering shadows on the cleared space. The Ashanti drums throbbed incessantly, with war horns blaring to the sky.

"Don't' waste ammunition," Jack snapped as Stair began rapid fire. "Don't shoot unless you're sure of your target."

"It's all right, old man," Russell said. "I made sure we're well supplied." He laughed as a slug landed at his feet. "The enemy will run out of men before Abrakrampa runs out of ammunition."

The seamen were in their element, loading Nelly with handfuls of bullets and firing them at any concentration of the enemy. "Give them a broadside, lads, the bloody land pirates!"

"Away you lubbers! The navy's here!"

Every so often, a group of Ashantis would venture from the forest onto the clearing, when the Navy would fire one of their scarce rockets. The group would scatter, yelling, to the cheers of the sailors and Marines. On one occasion moonlight fell squarely on a particularly bold group, revealing the white stripes down their faces and arms.

"Pot those men," Jack ordered. "That's Kumi Okese's Edwesus." Taking the rifle from Daley, he took careful aim for the tallest, fired, rode the kick and saw his target stagger. "That's one less," he said, to the cheers of the Wests. He felt no satisfaction in his little victory as he reloaded and fired again. The Edwesus melted into the bush, a second before a rocket hissed over where they had stood.

"Only fire when you see their gunsmoke," Jack walked behind his men, knowing the Ashanti would aim for him but hoping the darkness and distance would minimise their accuracy.

"They're not very good," Ogston said. "If they were the French at Waterloo, they would have attacked by now. We beat the French, and we'll beat the Bushmen, too."

"Good man, Ogston," Jack said. "If the Wests were at Waterloo, we'd have beat the French all the quicker!"

"That's right, sir!" Ogston aimed and fired. "I wish the Ashanti would show themselves."

"So do I, Ogston." Jack agreed. It was unnerving fighting an invisible enemy.

At about four in the morning, the drums altered their beat, and the Ashanti fire suddenly ceased. As the moon waned, Russell ordered lanterns lit around the perimeter of the village, each one casting an arc of yellow light into the clearing, with the forest a dark smudge on the periphery.

"Now what are the Ashantis up to?" Russell asked.

"I'm blessed if I know, sir," Jack said.

"Maybe they've run."

"Not these lads," Jack shook his head. "These men won't run." He stepped over to his Wests. "I want every third man to remain on sentry," he said. "The others grab what sleep you can."

The pre-dawn dark intensified, with the sounds of night slowly diminishing. Jack patrolled his section of the perimeter, peering across the clearing. *If this was the Frontier,* he told himself, *the Pashtun would be massing to attack our most vulnerable spot. In Crimea, the Plastun Cossacks would use the dark to crawl across the killing area. What are the Ashantis planning?*

"The Bushmen are scared to come," Ogston said.

"Can we attack them, sir?" Stair asked.

"We sit tight," Jack said. "At least until daylight."

"What do you think, Windrush?" Captain Grant's Scottish accent was somehow reassuring in the dark.

"I think you and I should get some rest while we can," Jack said. "Tomorrow might be a long day."

* * *

Dawn was majestic above the trees, creating a sense of peace that Jack always relished. He lay on the ground, stretched, listened to the bird calls and fell back asleep with his fist curled around Mary's scarf.

"Windrush." Grant leaned over him. "Your men need you."

"What time is it?" Jack pushed himself upright, remembering where he was. He pushed Mary's scarf out of sight within his tunic.

"Breakfast," Grant said.

Still sleep-confused, Jack ate, washed and shaved while watching his men change the guard with as little fuss as veterans. Coffin was nearest to him, humming a hymn as he peered over the plain at the dark smear of the forest beyond.

"There's a weakness in our defences," Jack said, after another circuit. He pointed to a slope beyond the church, yellow grass illuminated by the rising sun. "If the Ashantis occupied that hill, they could fire onto our gunners."

Russell nodded. "Captain Grant said the same. Could a section of your men hold the hill in the open?" Both ducked as the Ashanti opened fire, the slugs pattering onto Abrakrampa's houses like hail on a window. "Here we go again!"

By now used to being under fire, the Wests acted coolly, only responding when they were sure of their target.

"Here they come!" Ogston pointed to a group of Ashantis mustering opposite C Company, just outside the forest. "They're going to rush us."

"Bayonets, boys," Jack checked his revolver was fully loaded. "Let's show them West Indian steel! Two Section come with me. Hopringle, stay here with One Section, provide covering fire if the Ashantis drive us back." He waited until the Ashantis were well into the clearing, then vaulted the parapet and ran forward, cheering, with the Wests at his back.

Not used to seeing men run at them, the Ashanti attack faltered at the sight of a score of determined West Indians behind long glittering bayonets.

"At them, Two Section!" Jack fired his revolver as his Wests slammed into the Ashantis, bayonets stabbing, men roaring, gasping, fighting their fear as they lunged into the kill. Jack shot at the leading warrior, ducked the slash of a sword and saw the Ashantis almost immediately recoil. Rather than face the Wests, they turned to run.

"After the Bushmen!' Stair shouted, bounding five paces in front of his colleagues.

"No! Get back, Stair!" Jack knew that the Ashantis might be waiting in ambush among the trees. "Get back! That's an order, Private!"

As the Ashantis retreated, Jack's men were left vulnerable in the open plain, with the warriors within the trees having an excellent target. Even before the last Ashanti slid into the forest, the firing began. Jack saw Ogston stagger, clutching at his chest. "Back, lads!"

Stair stopped, shouted at the hidden warriors and joined the withdrawal, with Number One section providing covering fire. The entire affair had only taken five minutes and left four Ashantis lying on the ground. Ogston rubbed at his chest. "That slug surely stung," he said.

"Let me see," Jack opened Ogston's tunic. The bruise spread across the left side of Ogston's chest. "Nothing's broken," Jack said. "You're made of tough stuff."

"I'm from Jamaica!" Ogston said.

"That explains it," Jack closed the tunic. "Take care of yourself, Ogston."

The day continued, with the defenders keeping behind cover and the Ashantis firing from the trees. When the Ashantis launched an occasional rush into the clearing, the defenders responded with a counter-attack that pushed them back. In mid-morning, the Ashantis finally occupied the hill above the church and targeted the Naval Brigade.

"I can take a section and remove them," Jack offered.

"That's in hand, Windrush," Russell said. "You can't have all the fun."

At two in the afternoon with no warning, Captain Grant led his section of Wests in a mad assault at the Ashantis.

"Charge!" Grant roared, drew his sword and ran uphill with his men behind him.

"Bloody crazy Sawnie," Jack said, shaking his head. "Thank God they're on our side."

As soon as the Wests closed, the Ashantis turned to run, with Grant slashing at them with his sword, chasing them to the forest. His Wests took no prisoners, stabbing their bayonets into any Ashanti who tried to fight.

"You see?" Russell said, smiling, "Captain Grant has it all in hand."

After Grant's attack, the Ashantis remained within the forest wall, never venturing into the open. The firing continued until the evening, sometimes sporadic, sometimes intense but seldom effective against the barricades and houses of Abrakrampa.

"We've held them off," Hopringle sounded surprised.

"Somebody is coming," Ogston said, still rubbing at his chest where the slug had hit him.

Jack had learned to trust his men, so was not surprised ten minutes later when Wolseley marched into the village with a body of seamen and Marines, and a company of native levies.

"Aye, come now the fighting's over, Sir Garnet," Grant said.

Jack nodded. "As long as he came," he said.

It might have been the arrival of Wolseley that persuaded the Ashantis to retreat, for there was no firing that night. Next morning, cautious patrols found only the dead and wounded in the forest and on the road.

"Follow them up, Windrush," Wolseley ordered. "Dog their rearguard, harass them back to the Prah."

"Yes, sir," Jack said. "Come on, boys; we're on the road again."

Marching in the wake of the Ashantis, Jack found the track and surrounding countryside a litter of discarded gear. As well as powder-kegs and muskets, there were brass pans and beautifully carved stools, a chicken coop complete with chickens that Coffin swore belonged to Amanquatia himself, and flasks of rum that Ogston appropriated.

"Sir," Coffin pointed to the bodies that lay beside the road. Most were Ashanti warriors, dead or dying from wounds or disease; others were Fanti slaves, killed by the retreating army.

Only once did the Ashantis throw out a rearguard, firing their muskets too early to do any damage.

Jack grunted at the familiar drift of powder smoke. "Hopringle, take your section and engage them on the road. Number Two Section come with me."

Moving into the forest, Jack hacked a passage a hundred yards deep and then moved towards the Ashanti. As soon as they saw the Wests menacing their flank, the Ashantis withdrew, as Jack had intended.

"Right boys, on we go! If you see the enemy, fire at once!"

There was something deeply exhilarating in moving at speed along the track, passing the occasional Ashanti casualty or escaped Fanti prisoner. For the first time in weeks, Jack began to feel optimistic. The Ashantis were on the run; he was in command of half a company of quality infantry, and the road to the Prah was clear. All he had to do was press on, hope the British reinforcements arrived soon, and this war would be over.

On the third day of the pursuit, a messenger ran to Jack as he strode onwards at the head of his men.

"Major Windrush!" The midshipman was heavily perspiring. "I have urgent news."

Jack opened up the paper the midshipman handed to him, read the contents with disbelief and swore. All his high hopes vanished like snow on a warm day.

General Wolseley is ill with fever, the message said. *You are ordered to discontinue any offensive actions until the position is clarified. Return with C Company, 2nd West Indian Regiment to Cape Coast Castle.*

"Is there a reply, sir?" The messenger asked.

"No, no reply," Jack said. He looked onward up the track, where the debris of the retreating Ashantis covered the ground, crumpled up the note and threw it away. "No reply at all."

Chapter Twenty-Five

Two months. It was two months since the siege of Abrakrampa and the short but exciting chase that followed. Two months of frustration, waiting for Sir Garnet to recover and gather sufficient bearers for the march. Two months more for Mary to languish in captivity in Kumasi.

Jack stood on the beach at Cape Coast Castle, clenching his teeth on the butt of a cheroot as the British regulars arrived. They sat in ordered ranks in the broad-beamed surf boats as the Kroomen guided them through the rollers and onto the white sands. Rather than the traditional bright scarlet that had made British soldiers such good targets on campaign, the men wore uniforms of neutral grey, which would be far more suitable for action in the African forests. Jack nodded, *well done Wolseley, all Sir Garnet indeed.*

"You know,' Windrush," Buller spoke around his cigar, "if that beach were in England, it would be crowded with holidaymakers, every summer."

"That might happen once we civilise the place,' Jack watched as the 23rd Foot disembarked, each man staring at the unfamiliar scenery, the bright sand and the white Cape Coast Castle. Although some were young, they looked more mature than the Royal Marines with whom Colonel Festing had defended Elmina. The 23rd carried themselves like professional fighting men, confident, slightly arrogant yet wary. "I can't see many people coming here from Birmingham or Glasgow if it's full of human sacrifice and fetishes. Margate is bad enough in all conscience, but the Gold Coast is beyond the pale."

"Aye, maybe," Buller puffed out a perfect smoke ring. "Although for some, it may even be an attraction. Get rid of the mother-in-law, don't you think?

Hand her over to King Kofi's executioners and have her head hung from the old fetish tree? That would be a change from music halls and publics."

Jack forced a smile. "That might be an attraction, indeed." He watched as the soldiers marched up the beach, their uniforms drab, baggy and unsightly under the bright sun. "I must be getting old,' Jack said. 'When I started soldiering, everybody except the Rifle Brigade wore scarlet. Now we're wearing grey and khaki, looking like workmen rather than soldiers. It's more sensible, yet it detracts, somehow."

"Aye, you're right," Buller said. "There's no glamour left in this profession. We should all wear bright uniforms, march towards the enemy in dense columns and die gloriously as they shoot us to pieces. Wouldn't the Ashanti just love that?"

"I'm sure they would," Jack had already ordered grey uniforms for his company. He watched the 23rd Foot, the Royal Welch Fusiliers march past, with the goat at their head looking very confused. "A couple of weeks ago these men were in a British winter and in another couple of weeks they'll be fighting in the middle of a tropical forest. No wonder we lose so many men to heatstroke and disease."

"Disease has hit half the officers who arrived with Wolseley," Buller looked at Jack from the side of his eyes. "I imagine you're better equipped with your half-Indian mother."

Jack stiffened. "That must be it," he said. "I didn't know you knew."

"It's common knowledge, old boy," Buller said, returning his attention to the landing infantry. "Fighting Jack Windrush from India."

Unsure if Buller was insulting him, Jack said nothing.

"Others just call you Fighting Jack, the lucky major with the charming wife." Buller smiled. "How did you land such a beauty?"

"That beauty is still in Kumasi," Jack said.

"I know," Buller said softly. "You're taking your company to Prahsu on the Prah River very shortly, Major. Then you'll be in striking distance of Kumasi."

"How do you know that?"

"It's my job, old boy, it's my job."

* * *

Once again on the road north, Jack felt a new purpose as he marched his men onward. With no baggage train, he had to rely on porters, who became more unsettled with every mile. However, the state of the road more than made up for a few disgruntled porters, for the engineers had completed the route from Cape Coast to Prahsu. Jack thought the road was probably the best in sub-Saharan Africa, broad and well-surfaced, with nearly 240 newly-constructed bridges and eight carefully designed camping grounds complete with huts and a hospital.

Jack watched his men swing along in their new Norfolk grey uniforms, with pith helmets replacing the turbans, Sniders on their shoulders and pocket filters to cleanse the river water. Jack was impressed by these new devices, simple tubes of charcoal, but having experienced the foul water in the forest, he knew the filters could be as essential as a rifle.

They're looking good, Jack said to himself. *My company of Wests are looking very good.*

"Here we are, lads," Jack said when they reached Accroful. "Our first stop."

Day after day, they moved on, eating well and as fit as any soldier in West Africa could be. For the first four stages, the road strode over scrubland with few trees to break the impact of the sun, and then they were in the forest, with massive trees on either side and interlaced branches filtering the rays of the sun. It took six days to march the 74 miles to Prahsu, and when they arrived, Jack could hardly believe the difference. Where once had been virgin forest, the engineers had created a formidably large camp, with military quarters, solid huts for men and officers and a flagpole from which the Union flag draped.

Jack grunted, as a crudely painted notice caught his attention. *The Forlorn Hope*, it read, above the doorway of the hospital. Shaking his head, Jack strode to the river. He had crossed the Prah twice already, once in each direction. It may be the sacred river of the Ashantis, but now there was a British camp on its banks and British, African, and West Indian voices echoing across its dark brown, somehow sinister water.

"We're crossing the Prah tomorrow," Jack told his men. "We don't know how the Ashantis will act, but I'll guarantee they won't greet us with open arms and bottles of rum. Not even you, Ogston."

"I don't need their rum, sir," Ogston said. "I got my own."

"Well, don't tell the sailors, or they'll want some," Jack replied.

"We trade regularly," Ogston said, laughing.

As Jack looked across the swirling river, the Naval Brigade gathered around the campfire, utterly careless of any Ashanti, Russian or anybody else as they roared out songs born on ships from the Arctic to Cape Horn. The seamen had built a massive fire, adding entire tree trunks to keep the blaze alight, fighting the dark, forcing away any fears of what tomorrow might bring.

As the last of the bawdy nautical songs died away, a lone Marine stood up and sang in broad Cockney.

> "*Vith the fair sex, bless 'em, need I say*
> *That I am number Von*
> *It's really quite a bore to me*
> *The way the girls do run*
> *Not away from me, but after me*
> *Hah, you may laugh and scoff*
> *But I can tell yer that the girls*
> *Think me Immensekoff.*"

Girls, Jack thought. *Girls or drink; that's the mainstay of military men, and I am no different.* He returned to the side of the Prah.

"I'm coming for you Kumi Okese. You murdered Private Manning, and I'm going to kill you." He fingered Mary's scarf. "And I'm coming for you, Mary." For a second, he pondered the possibility that Mary could be dead, then shook his head. No. No; he would have felt something if she died. A final log fell on the fire, scattering sparks, and the ember-glow faded until the night was as dark as Jack's thoughts.

"I'm coming, Mary," Jack wrapped Mary's scarf around his fist. He felt closer to her than he had for months, although he knew the Ashantis would fight and had been granted months in which to prepare a defence.

"Aye, you'll be waiting for us," Jack said as he peered across to the northern forests. "But you've never met British infantry before." He did not move when an Ashanti warrior emerged from the trees a few hundred yards on the northern side of the river. As the man approached, Jack saw that he wore the full uniform of a war-captain, except for the eagle feathers.

"Kumi Okese!" Jack said and reached for his revolver.

Three more Ashanti warriors stepped from the trees, all with the white stripes of Kumi Okese's Edwesus. They formed around Kumi Okese, as the war captain returned Jack's gaze, unflinching.

"Sir!" Hopringle trotted up to Jack. "Jesus! That's an Ashanti!" Without a thought, Hopringle pulled out his revolver, but by that time, Kumi Okese and his bodyguard had gone.

"That was Kumi Okese himself," Jack remained where he was, staring north until Buller sauntered up in a cloud of tobacco smoke.

"Come along, old boy. You'll wear out the trees, glaring at them like that." Buller lowered his voice. "You'll get her back, never fear."

"Aye," Jack realised his hand was tight around the butt of his pistol. "Aye, I will."

General Wolseley sat outside his hut as Jack returned. "Ah, anything happening, Windrush?"

"Nothing of note, sir," Jack said. "Kumi Okese was looking us over, so we know the Ashantis will defend the road to Kumasi."

"Splendid," Wolseley said. "That way we can smash them and prove that British soldiers are a match for the fiercest warriors in West Africa."

* * *

The army crossed the 200-foot long bridge over the Prah by stages, with Russell's Regiment and Lord Gifford's Scouts probing first. On the 13th January, the 2nd Wests crossed, leaving behind a camp hospital already full of fever-struck men.

Meeting no opposition, the British gradually moved north, investigating each village as they approached the Adansi Hills.

Hopringle gave a small laugh. "It looks like King Kofi is not even going to fight. We've crossed their blessed Prah and not an Ashanti to be seen."

"They'll fight," Jack produced two cheroots, handed one to Hopringle and lit both. "We think the Prah is the boundary of Ashantiland, but north of these Adansi Hills is their real homeland. To the south, the land we are on now belonged to the Assin, a tribe the Ashanti conquered."

"What's beyond the hills?" Hopringle stopped for breath, and to ease his aching muscles.

Jack recalled the route. "Forests and mud swamps," he said. "Half a dozen villages, then the small town of Amoaful, and the Ordah River. The Ashantis might contest any or all of them, and finally, there is the marsh around Kumasi where I buried Private Manning, and the city itself."

"The city of gold," Hopringle whispered.

"It is a city of death," Jack replied. "A city of dreadful death."

As they came closer to the hills, the drums began a deep throbbing from the surrounding forest, punctuated by the blare of Ashanti horns.

"I detest that sound," Jack said. "When I leave Africa, I will hear these drums in my worst nightmares.'

"Sir!' Coffin said. "On the summit of the hill!"

Dressed in the full uniform of a war captain, Kumi Okese stood in front of his three-man bodyguard, with Akron at his side. When Kumi Okese held up his hand, the drums stopped, and the Ashantis looked down on the long British column that toiled up their guardian hills.

Kumi Okese said something in his deep voice, with Akron roaring out the words, so his voice echoed through the trees.

"British soldiers! Return home, British soldiers. You will die if you cross these hills!"

The words seemed to linger, a threat in themselves.

"No white man will return alive!" Kumi Okese stood on the apex of the hill, with the sun catching the gold bands around his arms and the long, gold-handled knife at his waist. A breeze rattled the fetish objects that adorned his chest. The bodyguards behind him each cradled an Enfield rifle, possibly the weapons taken from Jack's men when they were prisoners.

"No white man will cross our hills and return alive!"

"Ho! Bushman!" Private Stair shouted back. "How about us? How about C Company of the 2nd West? We are all black men!"

Jack's company laughed at that, with one or two glancing at Jack.

"You're white sir,' Private Stair said, greatly daring. "Maybe we'd best leave you behind on the north side of these hills while we defeat the Ashantis without you?"

Pleased at the reaction of his men, Jack ignored the insolence. "And when I'm with you lads, I am entirely West Indian!"

When the men nearby smiled or cheered, Jack wondered if such a simple statement helped morale more than all his training. Yet it was true. When he was with these men, he was part of a unit; he and his men fought and died together; they were C Company, 2nd West Indians, the best company in the British Army or any other army, damn you!

Jack did not see Kumi Okese move. One moment the Ashanti captain was prominent on the forest track, and the next he was gone.

"Fire!" Belatedly, Jack came to his senses. "Shoot that fellow."

As if awakening from a dream, the West Indians fired a volley, with bullets thudding into trees and flicking leaves from the branches. Stair reloaded hastily, stepped into the bush beside the path and fired again. "I'll get him, sir!"

"Come back, Stair!" Jack ordered. "Cease fire. He's gone."

The column struggled to the summit of the hill, with creepers brushing against their shoulders and the occasional bright flower a reminder of English cottage gardens and a life that was not constant toil and the ever-present threat of ambush. Despite their altitude, the heat was stifling, pressing down on them, squeezing the breath from their lungs, forcing the British soldiers to struggle for each lungful of oxygen.

They toiled up the steep southward facing slopes of the hills with the men gasping in the heat and swatting at clouding flies, slashing at creepers that overhung the path and alert for any Ashanti ambush. Every time they crested a hill, Jack looked north into what seemed a never-ending forest, with mist coiling around the tops of trees, still with an aura of mystery and menace. Yet every step brought him closer to Mary, just as every mile the British advanced put Mary in more danger of retaliation from King Kofi.

Reaching every summit was a small victory, with the northward slopes gentler, easing them downward towards Kumasi. Once again, Jack wondered why the Ashanti were not contesting this frontier.

"If I were the Ashanti commander," a captain of the Rifles said, puffing on a cheroot, "I'd place ambushes on every hill slope. We are most vulnerable when we're climbing up, concentrating on the path rather than the trees."

"Aye," Jack agreed. "I can't help thinking we'll pay for this yet. A few threats and the odd musket shot isn't much of a defence."

"You were in Kumasi, I hear," the Rifleman said.

"I was," Jack admitted.

"What do you think they are doing up there?"

Jack looked ahead. "I wish I knew," he said.

"Maybe they've given up," Lieutenant Wood said. As Wolseley's aide-de-camp, he had no business to be away from his master, Jack thought sourly. "Maybe the Ashantis know they can't stand against the British army and they've all run away." He lifted his revolver. "I hope not! I want a crack at the devils!"

Jack pushed Lieutenant Wood's revolver until the muzzle faced the ground. "Careful of that thing, son. You might blow somebody's head off, and the way you handle it, probably one of my men."

"I want to fight them."

"I think you'll get your chance later. Just now your position is with the general. Trot along to his side now, there's a good chap.!"

The Rifles' captain grunted as Wood ran back down the column. "I'm Moore, by the way."

"Windrush," Jack nodded to the Rifles. "Your men look a handy bunch, Captain."

"Some are twenty-year veterans," Moore said. "They've been with the regiment since the Crimea. Others?" He shrugged. "We have far too many young boys in the army now with the short service rules. We hardly have time to train them up before they leave."

"I noticed the Marines were the same," Jack said. "Half grown boys with little stamina or experience in handling their weapons. It hardly seems right pitting them against seasoned Forest fighters."

Moore looked over his men, shaking his head. "When I joined up, the men were ten, twenty, even thirty-year veterans who had seen it all. They were tough as teak. Now we depend too much on children, drill and superior weapons. One day we'll meet an enemy with weapons and discipline to match ours. And then we'll pay for our expectations of superiority."

Jack nodded. "Let's hope it's not on this campaign." He looked northward, thinking of Mary.

"Oh well, best be marching on!" Moore gave a weak smile. "Kingdoms to conquer and all that, don't you know?"

"Aye, kingdoms to conquer," Jack agreed.

At the top of the final hill, they halted, with the older men and youths sinking at the base of trees, reaching for their water bottles. Jack frowned, recognising his surroundings. They stood in a clearing, with a group of three trees together, hung with low creepers and with a group of bright red flowers peeping from a broad-leafed plant.

This spot was where Yaa Asantewaa had ordered my manacles removed on my previous journey to Kumasi. This spot was where I had my first view of the strange land of the Ashanti.

"Last time I came this way I was in chains." Jack rubbed his wrists in painful memory.

Hopringle was breathing hard. "This time you have the best general in the army and thousands of British and West Indian soldiers with you."

Jack compared his situation then as a shackled prisoner, and now as part of a British column striking at the heart of the Ashanti kingdom. Curling his fist around Mary's scarf, he thought of Mary with manacles around her ankles and shivered. *Why am I resting here?* "Pick it up, boys! We've a long way to go yet. I think the Bushmen will be waiting for us."

Kumi Okese has missed a trick, Jack told himself. *The Ashanti should have defended this range of hills. The Afridi or any other Pashtun tribe would have made us fight for every yard we gained in such a territory.* The Ashanti were forest fighters and brave men, of that he had no doubt, but they lacked the tactical and strategical skills of the Pashtun.

Unless, Jack thought, and the idea chilled him unless they were allowing the British column to penetrate so deep into the forest that they could never fight their way out. Unless the Ashanti were already around them in their favoured horseshoe position, watching everything Wolseley and his men did. Unless the Ashanti had them in a trap.

"Keep alert, 2nd Wests," Jack put a hand on the butt of his pistol "If you see anything suspicious, anything that should not be there, let me know at once."

"We always do," Jackson murmured, sotto voice.

"Are you all right, sir?" Hopringle unbuttoned his holster. "Have you seen something?"

"It's too quiet," Jack said. "The Ashantis are too passive. They are bold warriors, and we are in their territory. Why don't they strike? Why are they waiting?" Jack pointed to Hopringle's holster. "Keep that unfastened all the time, and check you don't drop your revolver. If you need it, you'll need it quickly."

"Go back, white men!" The voice floated towards them. "Go back, white men! You'll never see your homeland again."

"Who said that?" Hopringle said, staring all around.

"I doubt we'll ever know," Jack said.

They walked on, easing down the gentle slope until they saw the old woman at the side of the track as if she were waiting for them.

"This could be trouble," Jack said as the woman stepped square into the middle of the path. Jack put a hand on the butt of his revolver as the woman pointed at him with a long-nailed finger and spoke in a high, cracked voice.

"I doubt that's a blessing," Hopringle said.

"More likely a curse," Jack checked the men at his back. Daley looked a little shaken, while Coffin was unruffled.

"Pagan Bushman religion," Coffin said. "We are better than such superstition."

"I hope so," Jack said. "It seems as if the Ashantis are using religion and psychological warfare against us."

"We'll use Sniders against them," Coffin said.

Leaving the old woman beside the path, they marched on, with the summit of the hills protruding above a hazy green-tinted mist and the trees seeming to glower at them with cold hatred.

"Message from Sir Garnet for Major Windrush!" Lieutenant Wood was eager as a puppy.

"Here I am, Lieutenant"

"Major!" Wood jumped to attention and saluted so hard he nearly knocked off his pith helmet. "Sir Garnet Wolseley sends his compliments, sir, and could you take your men and join the Rifle Brigade."

"Thank you, Wood," Jack said formally. "Pray convey my compliments to Sir Garnet and inform him I will be there directly."

Jack had served alongside the Rifles in earlier campaigns and knew their techniques. He signalled to his men "Come on, boys! There's no finer regiment for this sort of terrain."

The sun was half-way to the horizon when Jack led his company to the hard-bitten Rifles. A veteran NCO looked askance as the Wests formed up at their side. "Don't you Wests make us a target," he snarled. "We've no time for Johnny Raws here."

"Yes, sergeant. How long have you been in Africa?" Sergeant Mathews asked.

"Three weeks in Africa, but we've got more battle honours on our colours than nearly any other regiment." The Rifles' sergeant said with justifiable pride.

"Three weeks?" Mathews scoffed. "We've been here for three years! Don't let us down, Johnny Raw in Africa!"

Jack stifled his smile. Regimental rivalry was one of the strengths of the army, and it was good to hear his men holding their own with soldiers of a crack British regiment.

"Windrush!" Hopringle nearly tugged Jack's sleeve with excitement. "Did you hear the news?"

"What news was that?"

"King Kofi has released the hostages!"

"What?" Jack was not sure which emotion was uppermost, elation, relief or disbelief. "What? Where?"

Hopringle could not contain his grin. "I thought you'd be pleased, sir. I don't know the details, Windrush, but they're coming down the path from Kumasi, and there are women amongst them."

"Women?" *It must be Mary.* Not stopping to listen to any more, Jack ordered Hopringle to take charge of his men as he ran up the path.

Oh, God, please let it be true! Let Mary be safe.

Chapter Twenty-Six

ACROSS THE PRAH JANUARY 1874

With no thought for his dignity as a British officer, Jack ran past the troops, barely acknowledging the salutes of the men, and surged ahead. Buller stood on his own, talking to a group of his spies.

"The released hostage?" Jack asked. "Where are they?"

Buller shook his head. "They're not here yet, Windrush. Sorry old chap. You'll have to wait for them. It's not safe to go on. The Ashantis are a bit treacherous, don't you know?"

"To the devil with the Ashantis," Jack said. "I'm going up the track."

"I wouldn't if I were you," Buller said, as Jack loped ahead, part running, part striding, and unheedful of any possible Ashanti ambush.

Mary, dear God, I hope you are safe! Jack tried to control his rising excitement as he thought of taking his wife in his arms once more and losing his nagging dread.

He saw the group approaching, walking slowly with a small Ashanti escort. "Mary!" Yelling her name, Jack broke into a full run, splashing through a small stream without pause. "Mary!"

On sight of a British soldier running towards them, the Ashanti warriors levelled their muskets, then turned them upside down as a sign of peace. Jack ignored them completely as he scanned the released hostages.

"Mary?" He asked. "Where's Mary Windrush, my wife?"

He knew the hostages from his time in Kumasi. Mr Kuhne and the Ramsayers lifted their heads when they saw him, while an Ashanti ambassador, resplendent with his golden breastplate, hurried past to seek Wolseley. Mary was not with this group. *She must be beyond that bend in the track.*

Mr Ramsayer greeted Jack like an old friend. "Major Windrush! My dear fellow." He held out his hand. "You said you'd be back to rescue us and here you are."

With his mind full of Mary, Jack had little time for pleasantries. "My wife was in Kumasi, Mr Ramsayer. Is she coming? Did you see her?"

Ramsayer's expression altered. "Your wife?" He shook his head. "Oh, my dear fellow. That lovely lady. Of course, Mrs Windrush; I had not thought she would be your wife. Oh, I am sorry."

"Have you seen her? How is she?" Jack grabbed Ramsayer's arms, shaking the missionary in his anxiety. "Is she with you?"

"I've seen her," Ramsayer said. "She is alive." He smiled, trying to soothe Jack's anxiety. "She did not come with us."

"Why not?" Jack asked sharply.

Ramsayer glanced at his wife before he replied. "I cannot say," he said.

Jack knew he was lying. "Why not?" He did not turn around when he heard the clump of footsteps behind him. He knew it was two of his Wests.

Mrs Ramsayer stepped beside her husband. "One of the Ashanti nobles refused to let her go," she said, quietly.

Jack felt as if somebody was squeezing the blood from his heart. "Why?" He almost whispered the word.

"I'm dreadfully sorry to say this, Major Windrush," Mrs Ramsayer placed a hand on Jack's shoulder. "But he wanted a white slave."

Jack felt as near to fainting as he ever had in his life. "What?"

"Kumi Okese wants a white slave," Mrs Ramsayer said. "That was his intention with Elda Becker, but they married, Ashanti style, so now he has your wife."

"Dear God in heaven," Jack whispered. "Mary, a slave? Will this nightmare ever end?"

"I apologise for bringing you bad news," Mrs Ramsayer said.

"Thank you," Jack stood still as the missionaries hurried toward Prahsu. He stared northward, momentarily unable to move. *Mary was a slave of Kumi Okese.*

"Sir?" Ogston stood behind him, with Coffin at his side. "Are you all right?"

Jack took a deep breath of the humid air. "Yes, thank you, Ogston. I'm all right."

"We heard the lady," Coffin said. "We'll get Mrs Major Windrush back."

"Thank you," Jack said. "Please tell Lieutenant Hopringle I will return shortly." Without another word, Jack walked northward, keeping to the middle of the track. After a dozen steps, he pulled the revolver from his holster.

Come on, Ashantis, he pleaded, *ambush me now. I want to kill. I want to kill every one of you and destroy your entire bloody empire! Oh, God, preserve my wife. Whatever else happens, protect my wife.*

Chapter Twenty-Seven

"We're moving out, Windrush. We're reconnoitring a village three miles ahead."

Jack lifted a hand, acknowledged the order, and rose from his cot. Shouting at his men to wake, he gesturing to them to join him as the Naval Brigade trotted ahead, with A Company of the Rifles jogging in skirmishing order, rifles at the trail.

"Keep up with the Rifles," Jack said, "study them; they're the best in the business at this kind of soldiering."

The Wests nodded, following Jack's lead. By now, every man in C Company knew that the Ashantis held Mary as a slave. They acted with silent sympathy, obeying orders without question, not knowing that Jack understood and appreciated their support.

The figure in white loomed out of the dark with his arms upraised.

"It's a priest," Daley said.

"A false priest," Coffin raised his voice. "May I shoot him, sir?"

"No," Jack said. "He's an unarmed civilian."

The Rifles and Wests marched past the priest, who retained his stance, shouting, until a Rifles sergeant gave him a shove. "Go and bother somebody else, old fellow," the sergeant said. "You're wasting your time with us."

"Sir," Stair pointed to a white thread stretched across the path in front of them. "That's a fetish thread sir, to stop us passing."

Jack grunted. "Is it by God? We're the 2nd Wests, not some superstitious bunch of blasted Bushmen!"

Kicking the thread aside, Jack marched on, as his men pointed out other fetish signs, with various animals sacrificed and left beside the road and once the naked body of a man, castrated, mutilated and impaled.

"Keep moving," Jack ordered, thinking of Mary. "Let's destroy these people."

Dawn arrived at the same time they came in sight of the next village. The Rifles opened into extended order, outflanking the settlement as Jack's C Company and the Naval Brigade advanced towards the front.

"Keep alert, men," Jack held his revolver ready, hoping for resistance. He felt no fear for himself, only a desire to fight, to kill, to destroy.

The orange flash of muzzle-flares augmented the growing light as half a dozen Ashanti warriors opened fire, with the slugs going nowhere, then the defenders quickly retired when the Rifles closed from the flanks.

"Search the houses," Jack ordered as his West Indians pushed forward, side by side with the bluejackets. "Watch out for hidden marksmen," On the North-West Frontier, the Afridi could pretend to retreat while leaving a few men to shoot unwary British soldiers. Jack was sure the Ashantis could be every bit as devious. He watched his men spread out as he had trained them, keeping in pairs, covering each other as they kicked open doors and checked inside.

"The village is empty, sir," Sergeant Roberts gave a smart salute.

We didn't kill a single Ashanti.

"Take up defence positions, in case the enemy return," Jack ordered, watching the men of the Rifle Brigade move outside the village to shelter behind fallen trees. "Watch how the Rifles move and learn from them."

"Now, what, sir?" Hopringle asked.

"Now we wait for orders," Jack said.

The drumming began an hour later. At first, it was only a slight throbbing, and then it increased in volume, minute by minute until every man was alert. The Rifles began to patrol deeper into the forest, moving silently, grey ghosts through the trees.

"Keep alert," Jack felt his palm sticky with sweat as he gripped his revolver. "I've heard that rhythm on the drums before. I'm sure it's a message of some sort."

"Ashanti drums summon men to war, sir," Ogston said. "They also send some messages."

Jack nodded. "Do you know what these drums are saying?"

"No, sir," Ogston smiled. "Maybe they are saying we surrender now that the 2nd West are here?"

"Perhaps they are,' Jack forced a smile. "Keep alert. The drumming might signal an attack on the village."

Taking out his binoculars, Jack scanned the forest, looking for unusual movement, when he saw the man staring directly at him. White stripes down the warrior's face and arms revealed his tribe, while he carried an Enfield rifle. Without hesitating, Jack lifted his revolver and fired, with Stair's Snider cracking out simultaneously. When neither shot took effect, Jack fired again, with Ogston and Jackson joining him. Two bullets ploughed into the warrior, knocking him backwards and onto the ground at the side of the path.

"Cover my back, lads," Jack ordered. "I want that Enfield." Without waiting for a reply, Jack ran across the road, weaving to disrupt the aim of any Ashanti marksman, and slid down beside the injured warrior. The man was severely hit, yet did not make a sound as he lay on top of a creeper.

Jack lifted the Enfield. "Ours, I believe," he said, and stopped as the silver Celtic Cross caught his gaze. "Where the devil did you get this?" The Ashanti had attached the cross to the butt of the rifle, so it hung loose like a pagan fetish charm. "That's Mary's! That belongs to my wife!"

Ripping the cross free, Jack held it tight. He remembered buying that cross from a jeweller outside the priory on the Holy Island of Lindisfarne. Mary had held it up to the light, laughing. "Where did you get it?"

The Ashanti stared at him, uncomprehending as blood from his wounds seeped into the ground.

"Where's my wife, damn you?" Lifting the man, Jack shouted in his face, shaking him until droplets of blood scattered, some landing on Jack. "Tell me, you murdering bastard!"

"Sir!' Coffin was at Jack's side. "Sir, you're making a target of yourself."

"This bastard has my wife's cross! He'll tell me where she is, damn him!" Lifting his revolver, Jack rammed it into the Ashanti's mouth.

"He can't tell you, sir," Coffin tried to ease the Ashanti from Jack's hands. "He's dead. Come away now!"

"Dead?" Jack looked up, suddenly aware of the Ashanti slugs that were bouncing around him. The warrior's head lolled backwards. Jack tried to control the fear that had threatened him ever since he learned the Ashanti had captured Mary. He knew that he was hovering on the edge of insanity, and for a moment, he had crossed that precarious threshold into madness. "Thank you, Coffin."

"Come away, sir!"

The Wests were waiting for him, firing at the Ashanti gunsmoke. Jack held Mary's cross in his hand. "Shoot them," he said softly, as the drums stopped, so for a moment, there was a deadly hush, with even the birds silent. The smoke drifted away, leaving nothing except the crumpled corpse of the Edwesu warrior, and the cross in Jack's hand.

"What are we waiting for, sir?" Hopringle asked.

"Orders, Hopringle," Jack said. "Orders."

* * *

The drums began again, drowning out the music of nature, making thought difficult, dominating everything, the resonance of native, untamed Africa. Watching the great trees all around, Jack thought that the British occupied the land they stood on and could dominate as far as the range of their rifles. Beyond that, Africa remained much as it always had been, watching, waiting, knowing the British presence was as temporary as a footstep in soft mud.

"We've got two prisoners," a patrol of the Rifles returned, with the men looking far more at home in the Forest than Jack had expected. The London accent was reassuring in this alien environment.

A runner panted up, looking over his shoulder. "Colonel Wood's compliments, sir, and could you return to the column."

The withdrawal was without incident, although Ogston saw warriors dogging them just beyond the forest fringe. Jack did not know when the drumming stopped. The noise seemed to fade away rather than ending in a crescendo, and the bird song continued, yet as Jack threaded along the path southward, the rhythm of the drums remained within his head. They were a threat, he knew, a personal threat from Kumi Okese to him. He felt sick heading away from Kumasi as if he was betraying Mary.

Can we push on from here? Can we move quickly now, before it's too late and the Ashantis murder Mary, or worse, enslave her and disappear forever? That thought brought nausea to Jack's throat.

And the rhythm of the drums returned, throbbing through Jack's head as he lay on his hammock that night. He curbed his impatience, checked his revolver, and grasped Mary's cross in his fist, with anxiety fighting his reasoning. He wondered if he should leave the column and head for Kumasi on his own, but shook his head. With unknown thousands of Ashantis between him and Mary, he must stay with the column. A dead man could not help anybody.

He woke without leaving his nightmare, gave automatic orders and roamed around the camp.

"It's all right, sir," Coffin said quietly. "The Lord will look after her." Coffin's eyes were steady. "Mrs Windrush is a good woman."

"Thank you, Coffin," Jack felt the silent sympathy of his men as he stared up the path to Kumasi.

That day was pure frustration as Wolseley ordered C Company, and the Rifles to remain in camp. He could only watch as the Naval Brigade rolled past, chewing tobacco and exchanging banter with the soldiers.

"You have a nice rest, boys, and let the navy do the work," a bearded petty officer said.

"Away you tarry-arsed bastards! We'll be there when the real fighting begins!"

A company of the 23rd Fusiliers were next, led by their regimental goat as they marched northward.

"You're going the wrong way, Welshmen," the Rifles jeered. "There are no sheep up there in Ashantiland!"

"I'll see you later, boy, and you'll not be smart with no teeth in your mouth."

Fighting his frustration as he watched others march to the front, Jack checked his men, ensured their rifles were clean and oiled, and all had sufficient ammunition. He listened as a section of Rifles preparing for picket duty as a youngster voiced his opinion about the campaign.

"These old soldiers moan about the trenches in the Crimea. They weren't in it compared to this."

Jack moved on, remembering the months of misery in the frozen trenches before Sebastopol. These young soldiers might find it hard in the heat and mud of the tropical forest, but this campaign would only last a few weeks, then they would be home. It had to be quick, for when the rains came, every stream would be a river, every river a torrent and every patch of swamp would double or quadruple in size until they were impassable.

I am getting old, he told himself, *reminiscing over past campaigns.* Remembering the jungle in Burma, he wondered how this new generation of soldiers would cope with the swampy bush, humid heat and swarming insects and flies.

As he had before, Jack tried to accept the green gloominess as sunlight struggled to seep through the forest canopy.

Push on, Sir Garnet; push on!

It was good to hear the bugle calls resound through the trees, with each company having its call, good to have British Army organisation amidst the primeval chaos of the forest. Jack checked his revolver for the twentieth time, aware he was only trying to distract himself from agonising about Mary. The bugle called again, his company's call.

"That's us, boys!" Jack shouted. "We're with the Rifles again."

They marched, with Jack's men keeping pace with the crack British infantry, the 42nd, the Rifle Brigade and 23rd, one Scottish, one English and one Welsh regiment, a union brigade probing into the forest.

"We cannae fight in the forest, can we no'?" A Black Watch private said, glowering hopefully at the green gloom. "Come on then and see, you Shantees!" With the red buckle on his helmet the only sign he was from the Black Watch, the private thrust on, sweat pouring down his freckled face and determination in the line of his jaw.

Jack nodded. Whatever King Kofi and Kumi Okese chose to believe, the Ashantis would find the British regiments, the most versatile infantry in the world, more than willing to face them in the forest, or anywhere else.

They marched that day, and on the next, the 29th of January. Jack's company and the Rifles set off again half an hour before dawn, with the sound of their boots loud through the forest.

"Hopringle," Jack said. "Send Ogston and Coffin out as scouts, they're steady men."

Where are the Ashantis? Why does Kumi Okese not fight?

They marched on, nearly silent except for the thudding of their boots as they waited for an Ashanti ambush. Ogston trotted back towards them, carrying his Snider at the trail and with Coffin guarding his back. "Somebody's coming down the track towards us, sir."

Jack nodded. "Thank you, Ogston." He could feel the vibrations, the steady tramp of feet that told him that British soldiers, not Ashantis, were approaching. Even so, Jack raised his voice. "Keep your rifles ready."

Five minutes later the Naval Brigade met them head-on, with the 23rd Foot a few minutes behind them, marching in column of four, red-faced and unhappy.

"Nothing to see up there, Westies," the Welshmen of the 23rd said. "Only more bloody trees. The Ashantis have hooked it."

"Where are you headed?" Jack asked.

"Another village in the middle of bugger all,' the Welshman replied. "We've to count the trees and make sure they're not Ashantis in disguise. Some bloody campaign this, marching up and down all bloody day. The Grand old Duke's not in it!"

Now near the front of the straggling column, Jack's West Indians pushed on, finding the road narrowing the further north they marched, and the ground rougher. The drumming continued, now rising, now falling, passing messages around all of Ashantiland.

"They're gathering their men," Jack guessed. "They'll be waiting for us up ahead somewhere." He touched the butt of his revolver. *The bastards are going to try and stop me from rescuing Mary.*

The column marched down a slope and halted at a small clearing. With the ground too uneven for the tents, Jack posted sentries and ordered his men to clear away the bush, as the Rifles, a hundred yards away, did the same. The forest crowded all around, with Jack feeling as though the trees were watching. Twice he thought he saw movement and once he could have sworn a white-striped Edwesu warrior stared at him from the shelter of a bush. The birds were calling, insects humming, and everything seemed normal, yet he could not shake off the feeling that something was wrong.

"The forest demons are there," Daley shared Jack's forebodings.

"Aye, maybe. Double sentries tonight," Jack ordered. "And NCOs to patrol regularly. Ensure each man studies the ground in front of him, so he immediately knows if anything changes."

"You're feeling the same way, then," Captain Moore of the Rifles accepted one of Jack's cheroots. "The Ashantis are out there."

"I'm certain of it," Jack said. "Although I haven't even smelled one and my sentries haven't seen any."

"Nor have mine," Moore said. "I felt the same before the Russians attacked at Inkerman. It was a sort of hush as if the earth knew something was going to happen. In this case, it's the forest."

Jack nodded. "I remember that hush at Inkerman."

Moore gave him a doubting look. "I can't remember the Wests being in the Crimea."

"I was with the 113th Foot."

"Ah, the old Baby Butchers." The Rifleman dragged at his cheroot. "I remember them at Inkerman." His eyes narrowed. "What's your name again? Windrush?"

"That's me."

"Jack Windrush, Fighting Jack." Moore extended his hand. "I did not realise that you were that Windrush. A pleasure to meet another Crimea veteran."

"Likewise," Jack shook the Rifleman's hand. They stood side by side with the sounds of the daytime forest sinking with the light. The infantrymen settled down with murmured conversations.

"You'll be checking your men tonight?" Jack asked.

"I think neither of us will get much sleep," Moore said.

Jack nodded. "Aye. That's all part of the soldier's bargain."

They parted, each with his duty to do as the night closed with that remarkable swiftness of the tropics. Jack took a deep breath. Uncomfortable as it was, waiting for the Ashantis to attack was soldiering that he understood. He much preferred this, with an honest enemy who wished to kill him for an honourable end, to the subtle half-truths and downright lies of diplomacy and spying. Regimental soldiering was the life he chose, and he could accept the hardships and challenges with an easy mind.

Oh, God, Mary, I hope that you are all right. If the Ashantis have hurt you, I swear I will not rest until I have torn their empire piece by piece and tree by bloody, fetish-ridden tree. I'll destroy their golden stool, kill Kumi Okese and burn their towns to the ground.

Jack stopped himself. He knew he could not do any of these things. He took a last draw of his cheroot to calm his nerves and tried to push any thoughts of Mary to the back of his mind. He would need all his concentration for the ordeal to come, for the Ashanti were gathering, of that he was sure.

Chapter Twenty-Eight

"Sir," Ogston whispered. "Something's not right."

Jack squinted into the dark. With dawn at least half an hour yet, he could barely see the edge of the forest let alone anybody moving out there. "What's wrong, Ogston?"

"I'm not sure, sir," Ogston said. "I've been watching the trees." He looked away, as if afraid to say more.

Jack sighed. "What's wrong with the trees?"

"They're moving, sir," Ogston said. "They say there are demons in the forest."

There are worse things than demons out here.

"Could it be the wind?"

"There's no wind, sir."

Although Jack focussed his binoculars, he could not make out details in the dark. "I'm going forward, Ogston. Don't shoot me!"

Feeling very vulnerable, Jack stepped forward, depending on his night vision as he focussed on one tree that stood behind a darker belt of bush. After a moment, Jack blinked as the tree seemed to have moved further away from the shrubbery.

Forest demons? I don't believe in such things.

"Jesus!" Jack breathed. He was wrong; the tree was not sliding away from the bushes; the bushes were creeping closer to him. He concentrated, watching as the bushes moved again, sliding noiselessly towards the British camp. Backing away, with his heart pounding inside his chest, Jack returned to Ogston.

"Wake the men," he said urgently. He kicked Sergeant Mathews awake. "Mathews! Get everybody into firing positions, as quietly as they can. Don't bother getting dressed, just grab a rifle and ammunition. Hurry man! As quietly as you can!"

Jack checked again. He was right; it was no illusion caused by overwrought nerves. The bushes were undoubtedly closer.

"The forest is alive!" Daley said. "It's coming for us! The Fantis said there were forest spirits and we've angered them by coming here."

"It's not the forest." Fighting his jangling nerves, Jack checked to see his men were coming into position, some fully dressed, others only in their shirts and Stair naked except his rifle and ammunition. "It's the Ashantis hiding behind palm leaves and bushes. Load!"

Even before his men were all in position, Jack gave the order. "Aim for the bushes, boys. Aim low and fire at will."

The sudden crackle of musketry awoke the rest of the sleeping camp, with the Rifles bugler blasting the alert and the Riflemen running to their positions. The Wests' muzzle flares revealed vignettes of the surroundings, with Ashanti warriors frozen in time as they emerged from behind their sheltering bushes to return the Wests' fire, or falling under the searching Snider bullets. White smoke jetted as the Ashantis fired from behind their screens of leaves and small bushes.

"The forest is attacking us!" Daley repeated until Sergeant Mathews shoved him hard down on the ground.

"Shut your mouth and shoot!" Mathews snarled.

Standing tall so his men could see him, Jack felt an Ashanti slug zip past his face. "This is foolish," he told himself and fired three rounds into the smoke-tinged dark. Long jets of flame showed the position of the Ashanti musket men, so many that he could not count them.

"Aim for the muzzle flares," Jack ordered, swearing when the hammer of his revolver clicked on an empty chamber. He reloaded hastily, surprised that his fingers obeyed his brain without fumbling.

When Coffin chanted the first line of a revivalist hymn, others joined in, singing the words in deep, melodious voices, so Christian hymns battled against the din of gunfire and hoarse cries of fighting men.

Jack realised he was shooting at nothing. There was no return fire from the forest. "Cease fire! Cease fire!"

In the excitement of battle, some of his men continued to load and fire until Jack and the NCOs physically stopped them. The Rifles had already ceased fire, so only the dying strains of the hymn and the harsh panting of scared men filled the air. A leaf dropped, landing with an audible rustle that drew two more shots.

"I said cease fire, damn it!" Jack said. "They've gone." He checked his watch, startled to see that they had been firing for nearly an hour. It seemed like only a couple of minutes.

"Casualties?" A calm voice sounded from the Rifle's ranks. "Any casualties?"

Jack asked the same question. One man had been grazed by a slug; another had a minor wound in his leg.

"Keep alert," Jack said. "Sergeant Roberts, take over here; the men not on duty, get back to bed. Stair, there are no women to impress, so get dressed. Ogston and Coffin come with me."

Ensuring his revolver was loaded, Jack inspected the ground in front of the 2nd West's positions. He counted twelve Ashanti dead and judging by the trails of flattened grass and broken undergrowth, others had been wounded, but in the half-light of approaching morning, Jack could not even guess how many. He nodded in grim satisfaction when he saw three of the casualties had the Edwesus' white stripes.

"You did well, lads," Jack said when he wakened his men for breakfast. "The Ashantis won't try another night attack on the 2nd Wests."

But Jack knew that the worst was still ahead. With warriors such as Kumi Okese and inspirational women like Yaa Asantewaa, the Ashanti would contest every yard of territory. The fight for Kumasi was only beginning.

* * *

Jack lifted his head at the unmistakable wail of bagpipes. The sound brought back a host of memories, from the 93rd Highlanders of the Thin Red Line at Balaclava to Campbell's pipes that signalled the relief of Lucknow. Jack remembered what a Highland corporal had told him about the pipes. "The pipes warn the enemy that the Highlanders are coming," the corporal had said. "They tell the enemy how long they have to live."

"Here come the kilties," Jack said.

"Bloody Sawnie bastards," a bitter-faced Rifle private said. "They get all the glory. Bloody Queen Victoria's pets."

When the 42nd Highlanders, the Black Watch, swaggered along the forest path as if they owned the place, Jack was slightly disappointed they did not wear kilts but were in the same grey uniforms as the other regiments. He knew the alteration of uniform was sensible in the forest, but there was something particularly martial about a Highland regiment in kilts.

"All right, lads," Jack said as the Wests cheered the 42nd. "On we go."

They marched on through the swampy bush, now with the Black Watch in the van and C Company further back with the Rifles, swatting insects and watching the flanks. Then Private Jackson vanished without a sound.

"Sir!" Daley doubled up to Jack, slithering on the greasy mud-covered track. "Jackson has gone!"

"Gone?" Jack checked his men; there was a gap in the ranks where Jackson should have been. "When?"

"A minute ago, sir. He was walking and then he wasn't. The forest took him, sir. The forest spirits!" Daley looked over his shoulder as if afraid a tree would reach over to him.

"It was the Ashantis, not the forest. Show me exactly where it happened."

"Over here," Daley guided Jack fifty yards down the trail, eyeing the overhanging creepers with deep suspicion.

Jack saw the trail of broken vegetation where the Ashantis had dragged Jackson into the bush. Unholstering his revolver, he ordered Sergeant Mathews and Ogston to follow and eased into the forest. Immediately Jack did so, the atmosphere altered as the foliage closed around him. Within ten steps, he could have been a mile from the column, and after twenty, the entire British Army seemed like a different world. He stopped to examine the trail. A trio of colourful butterflies rose from the ground, where Jack saw scuffed earth and flattened grass.

"The Ashanti dragged Jackson here." Jack followed the spoor until he came to one of the Ashanti battle paths parallel to the main track. Scores of footprints headed north.

"The Ashanti are moving beside the column," Jack increased his speed, hoping to overtake the Ashantis before they killed Jackson. The battle path ran in a series of curves, then turned abruptly to the left at a patch of mahogany trees.

With sweat dampening his palms, Jack motioned for Mathews and Ogston to wait. He listened for the enemy, wondering if they were watching him. When he heard nothing, he moved forward, step by cautious step, following the trail that stretched as far as a fast-flowing stream and then disappeared altogether. Mathews and Ogston followed, silent as creeping night.

A drift of conversation came to Jack and he held up his hand. His men halted, rifles ready, as a group of Ashantis entered a clearing on the opposite side of the stream. Jack counted them, reaching fifteen before the last man appeared.

Fifteen Ashantis against three Wests. A sudden attack might panic them.

"There's Jackson!" Mathews gestured with his chin.

When Jack saw Jackson's body lying underneath the largest of the trees, minus his head, his anger mounted. *That was one of my men!* A sudden sound made him turn around, to see Coffin and Stair behind him, with Sergeant Roberts and three more Wests.

"What the devil are you doing here?"

"We thought you might need help," Roberts said.

Jack bit back his angry retort. "These Ashantis have killed Jackson. Form a skirmishing line and on my word, shoot the bastards flat."

That was the kind of order the Wests understood. Spreading out, they lay behind cover, extended their rifles and waited.

"Fire," Jack said when the Ashantis bunched up.

The fusillade ripped into the unsuspecting Ashantis, scattering those who were not immediately hit. Jack emptied his revolver, reloaded and emptied it again before he realised the enemy had vanished. The Ashanti casualties lay in the undignified postures of death, some with expressions of surprise on their face, others with a frown. Jack counted them. Seven, of whom five wore the Edwesu white stripes. Seven deaths to avenge a private of the Wests.

"Retrieve Jackson's body," he said. "We'll bury it here and now. Dig a grave with your bayonets. Coffin, I want you to say the appropriate words. Sergeant Mathews, you and Ogston stand guard."

Jack felt cold. Apart from sorrow at Jackson's death, he felt no emotion at having killed seven men. There was neither elation nor guilt. This skirmish had been only another incident in a war in which he should not be involved.

* * *

On the morning of 30th January, Captain Moore appeared with intelligence. "I hear that the Ashantis are massing. They have warriors beside the track all the way to the town of Amoaful."

"Amoaful," Jack remembered the place. "That's a sizeable settlement on the north side of a steep-sided gulley. If I were Kumi Okese or Amanquatia, I would make my stand there."

Moore grunted. "We'll soon see if they agree with you, Windrush."

As the track ran along level ground, the column moved faster, with the soldiers stopping to fill their water bottles from the numerous streams of bright water.

"Don't forget to filter the water before you drink," Jack warned. "It might look clean, but you don't know what impurities it contains." Ensuring the NCOs enforced his orders, Jack walked around his men, talking to them one by one.

Sergeant Mathews saw the object before anybody else. It was stuck on a pole in the track, with the eyes open and staring at them.

"That's Private Jackson," he said.

"It is." Jack took the head down at once, in case it unsettled his men, yet the word spread within minutes. Where he expected superstitious fear and a loss of morale, he found a surge of anger and a desire for revenge instead. Jack could feel the tension rising. When Coffin sang a soft psalm, others joined in, until Stair began a chant of "blood, blood, blood," which spread through the ranks.

"Sir," Sergeant Roberts said, "the men want to march at the head of the column. We want to get back at the Ashantis for what they did to Jackson."

"I feel the same way," Jack said. "We'll obey orders though, and remember Hubert Jackson when next we fight. And we won't forget Stanley Manning."

"Yes, sir," Roberts saluted. Jack heard the news circulate C Company.

Jack wrapped Mary's scarf around his fist, looked at the silver cross he had fastened to his pistol holster for luck and marched on. He knew that the Ashantis would fight at Amoaful. Jack did not doubt that. He only hoped the British could inflict a sufficiently signal defeat to end the war.

We're coming, Mary. Every day brings us closer.

Chapter Twenty-Nine

"Check your ammunition," Jack said. "There will be a battle today. Make sure your rifles are clean and oiled, and your water bottles are full of filtered water." He walked the ranks of C Company as they stood at ease.

"You are as good as any regiment in the British Army," Jack said, "and better than most, so I know you will fight well."

The men listened, straight-faced but proud.

"General Wolseley has issued his order of battle," Jack said. "It is nothing less than the traditional British regimental square."

"That's the one we used to defeat Napoleon," a hopefully anonymous voice from the ranks said.

"That's correct, Ogston," Jack said. "But in our case, the square will be inside the forest. The general has arranged the army into four columns, with Brigadier General Sir Archibald Alison commanding the first column, which will be the front of the square. Colonel McLeod of the 42nd has the left flank, Lieutenant Colonel Wood the right flank and Lieutenant Colonel Warren of the Rifle Brigade the rear."

The Wests listened. Jack knew that few officers ever bothered to explain tactics to the men, whose duty was only to follow orders, but he remembered how it felt to fight without knowing the full picture.

"At present, we are with the Rifles," Jack said. "There is no knowing where the fortunes of battle may send us. Wherever it is, I know you will add lustre to the name of the 2nd West Indians."

For once, C Company cheered, with Jack responding with a wave. He remembered his military history studies, when Publius Flavius Vegetius Renatus, 1500 years earlier recommended forming a square when the troops were superior in morale and quality to the enemy. Jack did not doubt that the British soldiers held both cards, while the Ashantis had the advantage in numbers and knowledge of the terrain. The coming day would decide who held the aces.

The 42nd Highlanders led the column. They started marching with the breaking dawn, the splashes of red on their helmets reminders of past glories and the swagger of their shoulders a warning not to oppose them. Jack's C Company was next, with the Rifle Brigade immediately behind.

"The Ashantis are out there," Sergeant Mathews said. "I can smell them."

"You and Manning came from the same island, didn't you?" After four months in their company, Jack knew his men.

"Yes, sir. We're Bajans, from Barbados, the pride of the West Indies." Mathews said.

"Then you can avenge him, today," Jack said. Both men lifted their heads when they heard the spatter of musketry.

"That's it started," Jack checked his watch. "Nearly eight o'clock. Lord Gifford's African scouts will be clearing the village of Egginassie."

At the sound of gunfire, the Highlanders quickened their step. "Come on, lads!" A Perthshire voice roared. "Hurry it up, or there'll be nane left for us!"

A couple of wounded scouts staggered past and made their way to the rear, dripping blood.

"Pick it up!' A Black Watch lieutenant shouted, and the Highlanders increased their pace until they were doubling as they came to Egginassie, a wretched place beside the road. Lord Gifford, slim and dapper, was there with his wild-looking tribesmen. He waved to the hurrying column.

Passing through the village, the British nearly trotted along the forest path with Sergeant Mathews growing more eager by the yard.

"I hope the Ashantis fight, sir," Mathews patted the lock of his Snider.

So do I. I want to smash them. "Amanquatia and Kumi Okese command them," Jack said. "They are both fighting men."

"I knew the Bushmen would cause trouble today," Sergeant Mathews said as the Ashanti battle cries sounded without the accompaniment of war drums.

"Make sure your rifles are loaded!" Jack ordered. They were still marching along the narrow track with the forest pressing on both sides. With a hundred trees overhanging the path, Jack felt as though he was travelling through a long green tunnel.

"Skirmishing order," Jack shouted, and the Wests spread out like the veterans they now were. As the left flank pushed into the forest on either side of the path, it stumbled into what had been the Ashantis encampment, with small huts thatched with plantain leaves. "Be careful of ambushes," Jack ordered, but the huts held no warriors, only low bamboo bedsteads and cooking pots.

"Sir!" Mathews said. "Listen to the firing! They've started the battle without us."

An unmistakable volley sounded, with the deep boom of the Ashanti muskets echoing in the green gloom of the trees. After the gunfire came the singing, thousands of voices chanting the Ashanti war-song, a noise that lifted the hairs on the back of Jack's neck. He had heard British regiments singing on the march, and the Warriors of God on the Frontier shout "Allah Akbar," but he had never heard anything as impressive as the Ashanti chorus that day. The sound came from all around them, a theatre of music with the British as the audience.

After a few minutes, the horns joined in, all with different tones, a weird accompaniment and then, finally, the roar of war drums, with the three sounds combining in an unnerving harmony.

The silence, when it came, seemed to paralyse the British advance as the men stood in their ranks, staring at the trees. The red hackle of the Black Watch looked like miniature spots of blood against the sombre green of the forest.

"Well, bugger this, lads, eh?" A Dundonian voice sounded. "Come on, let's get intae they Shanty bastards, eh?"

The Ashantis responded with a tremendous volley that ripped into the British ranks, knocking down a dozen of the 42nd. Jack saw Highlanders stagger back, holding faces, arms and chests as the slugs smashed at them from close range.

Colonel McLeod of the Black Watch roared above the chaos of battle. "The 42nd will fire by companies, front rank to the right, rear rank to the left!"

The Highlanders moved on, firing as men dropped. "A Company, front rank, fire! Rear rank, fire!"

"Advance!" Major Duncan MacPherson shouted. The Black Watch responded, crashing through the trees. They fired a volley of their own, the painful crack of the Snider meeting the deep boom of the muzzle-loaders as the Highlanders loaded, fired and advanced, heedless of casualties.

The Ashanti's fire continued, erupting from the trees all around the 42nd as thousands of muskets fired together.

"Amanquatia has gathered every Ashanti in the world here," Hopringle said, staring at the clouds of smoke, through which orange muzzle-flares gleamed.

"Advance!" Major MacPherson shouted again, then crumpled as a slug smashed into his leg.

"The Shanties have got Big Duncae, eh?" The Dundonian voice sounded again. "Ye've hud it, noo, ya Shanty bastards!"

Major MacPherson rose, tied a handkerchief around the bleeding gash in his leg and shouted again. "Advance!"

Jack saw a piper with the 42nd, encouraging the men as the thin wail of his pipes rose above the hellish racket of battle.

"Double," Jack ordered. "We're the 2nd West! If the Sawnies need us, we'll be there."

"Who are the Sawnies, sir?" When Sergeant Mathews looked confused, Jack remembered his company had never fought alongside regular British infantry before. "The Sawnies are any Scottish regiment. The 42nd is also known as the Black Watch, or the Forty-twa." He moved on, "Never mind, just follow my orders, sergeant."

The Ashanti army held the heavily wooded slopes that slid down to a swampy valley and then rose again to the sizeable village of Amoaful. As Jack led his company forward, he saw white powder smoke wreathed both slopes, with myriad muzzle-flares all around. Standing exposed on the path and extended into the trees, the Black Watch was firing back, volley after volley of Snider bullets that hissed and crackled through the trees, with every so often Major MacPherson shouting "advance" and pushing the men forward. Casualties were everywhere as the Highlanders, necessarily exposed as they moved, fell to the concealed Ashanti marksmen.

"Now we'll see if British soldiers can face the Ashanti in the bush," Hopringle said.

"That's the Black Watch," Jack said. "I saw them at the Alma and in the Mutiny. They'll face anybody, anywhere."

"Advance!" Major MacPherson said, and the Highlanders moved again, ignoring their casualties as they fired and pushed forward into the dense undergrowth.

"They're all around us!" Sir Archibald Alison had fought under Sir Colin Campbell in the Indian Mutiny, where he lost an arm. Now he commanded the advance, where two companies of the Black Watch were in action. "Bring up another company!"

"It's how they fight, sir," Jack came beside the colonel. "They adopt a horse-shoe formation to ambush their prey."

"We're the 42nd, damn them. We're nobody's prey." Sir Archibald stroked his whiskers, evidently wanting to draw his claymore and charge forward with his men.

"Yes, sir. I've brought a company of the 2nd West in support. Where do you want us?"

"Support the Forty-twa, Major! Take the left flank of the frontal assault and keep out of the Highlanders' path."

Nodding, Jack returned to his men. He did not know Sir Archibald, so could not compare him to the many splendid Scottish soldiers he had met, from Lord Clyde to Hugh Rose. Jack did not doubt the man's courage, for nobody could command Scottish infantry unless they were brave, but on first impressions, he thought Alison blinkered and tactically naïve.

The Ashanti fire was increasing as a third company of Black Watch arrived, with the pipers playing as they doubled forward. The sound of the pipes heard through the crackle of musketry, the incessant thunder of the drums and the harsh shouts of fighting men, was one of the strangest things Jack had ever heard.

"The Ashantis are trying to turn the flank," Jack said.

Sir Archibald nodded to Jack. "So I believe, Major." Without a qualm, he nodded to a stocky major. "Baird, take two companies along to the left, will you? The Royal Engineers will go along with you to widen the path." Despite Jack's misgivings, Sir Archibald was as calm as anybody there. "You know the general's instructions."

The fighting intensified, with some Ashanti waiting in the branches of the tall trees to fire down on the advancing British.

"Wests," Jack said. "Aim for these men, and for God's sake don't hit the Forty Second!" Now was the opportunity to test his musketry training.

As he moved slowly forward, Jack could see the virtue of Wolseley's classic square, for the Ashantis were unable to outflank the British. Whichever the Ashantis advanced, they faced a wall of Sniders and determined men. Three hundred yards out on each flank, engineers hacked out forest paths in the manner of the Ashantis, along which the infantry marched, under constant fire.

Wolseley had collected the reserve ammunition, the hammocks and the bearers within the centre of the square, where the infantry could protect them. Jack's appreciation of Wolseley as a commander increased; in Jack's estimation, Wolseley was proving himself the best Irish-born general since the Duke of Wellington. He had countered the Ashantis' battle tactics, now all depended on the steadiness of the troops.

Jack had no doubts about the British regiments, with the Black Watch, the 23rd and the Rifles amongst the best soldiers anywhere, and he knew his company of the 2nd West would hold their own. He was less sure about the Hausas and hoped they were not in the line if the Ashantis launched a serious attack.

"Advance," Major MacPherson ordered yet again, staggered from loss of blood, grabbed a stick to support him and moved on with his men.

"Listen to that bloody tune!" The Dundonian voice sounded again, distinct above the battle. "The pipie's playing *The Campbells are Coming*! Does he think we're the bloody Argylls?"

One heavily bearded lance-sergeant grunted as an Ashanti slug hit him. He looked at the blood soaking through his chest, grunted again and pushed on into the trees. "Come on, lads!"

"Good man, Sergeant McGaw," Major MacPherson said, limping on with his stick.

Jack nodded. "Aye; you were wrong, Amanquatia. British infantry can face your Ashantis in the bush. Come on, C Company!"

As the British cut through the forest to form Wolseley's square, Jack led his Wests to the front left, where the 42nd continued to advance on either side of the track. The Black Watch had pushed the enemy down the slope, so Jack saw wounded Highlanders amidst a host of Ashanti dead and injured. As he slid downhill in the wake of the 42nd, Jack noticed that many of the Ashantis had white stripes down their faces. Kumi Okese's Edwesus were resisting bravely, as expected.

Fighting all the way, the Black Watch reached the ugly swamp at the bottom of the gully. The fringe of bright flowers seemed out of place in this scene of slaughter and strife.

Beyond the swamp, the ground rose to a heavily wooded ridge, curling towards the British left flank. Gunsmoke from the ridge proved that the Ashanti musketeers were there in numbers.

"Come on, men," Major Baird shouted. "The enemy on that ridge is blocking our advance." Leading from the front, he splashed into the swamp with slugs kicking up mud all around. With Sergeant McGaw and the cheering Black Watch a few steps behind, Major Baird began the ascent of the wooded slope.

"Come on, the Wests!" Jack shouted, following in close support.

As the Highlanders and West Indians crossed the swamp, Jack realised there was a river as an additional barrier, while the Ashantis were reinforcing their numbers by the minute. He shuddered; Amanquatia had chosen a position similar to the Russians at the Alma, forcing the British to cross a river and climb a slope in the face of defensive fire.

The stream at the bottom of the ravine was shallow, reaching only to Jack's knees, but as soon as he burst from cover, half a dozen Ashantis fired, with the slugs tearing the surface of the water all around.

"Come on, 2nd West!" Jack fired his revolver at the nearest musket smoke. "Skirmishing order! Open your ranks, fire at the smoke and support one another!"

Somewhere to his right, Jack heard the pipes screaming above the constant fusillade of Snider fire and the thuds of Ashanti muskets. Looking to left and right, he saw the 42nd advance, company by company and section by section, never halting for long, but still in too close formation for his liking. "Open their ranks, for God's sake," Jack pleaded, but the Highland officers kept their men together, offering targets for the thousands of enemy marksmen. In the thick bush, entire sections of the Highlanders vanished from Jack's view, with only the crackle of the Sniders, the hoarse orders of officers and NCOs and the wailing pipes signalling their presence.

The sheer volume of enemy fire showed that the Ashantis far outnumbered the 42nd. Jack saw Highlanders fall in ones and twos, most to rise and stagger onward, some with horrendous facial wounds from the Ashanti slugs, others holding limbs or trunk where dark blood seeped through the sweat-stained grey cloth. Despite the casualties, the remainder never faltered, pushing the Ashantis back yard by hard-won yard.

"Follow my orders, C Company!" Jack beckoned to the bugler. "Listen for the regimental calls." He inched forward, checking his men, firing whenever he thought he saw the enemy.

A new outbreak of musketry erupted from the left. "The Ashantis are still trying to outflank us!" A hard-faced highland major shouted.

The 42nd companies on the left flank immediately shifted their attack to the front. "We cannae get through the bastards that way," one tousle-haired corporal roared, tying a handkerchief around an arm that streamed with blood. "So let's go right down their throat! Come on the Forty-twa!" Hefting his rifle, he plunged into the bushes, snapped a shot, loaded, swore when a slug sliced at his leg and carried on with the red hackles of his men bobbing in his wake.

"That's the way, Rab!" Sergeant McGaw roared, ignoring the blood that soaked his uniform. "Show them your cap badge, Forty-twa! Take the bayonet to them!"

"Keep going, 2nd Wests!" Jack shouted. "Follow the Highlanders!" Taking a deep breath, Jack plunged forward. He knew his men were behind him, saw a flicker of movement to his right and left as the Black Watch forced their way on, stepped over the slowly-writhing body of a wounded Highlander and shouted again.

"This way, the Wests!"

Jack knew the British musketry must be taking effect, but for every Ashanti the Highlanders and West Indians shot, half a dozen took their place, so resistance stiffened as they pushed up the hill. Jack swore as a slug hammered into a tree he sheltered behind, ducked as something hummed through the air above his head and fired at a gush of smoke a few yards to his left. He had been in a score of battles from Pegu in 1852 and Inkerman to the Ridgeway fight Canada, but he swore he had never experienced such a volume of fire as in that African forest.

Even when Wolseley sent a company of Rifles to reinforce the 42nd, the British were losing men for every five yards of ground they gained. The advance stalled, with panting Highlanders glaring uphill and the Rifles and Wests exchanging Snider bullets for Ashanti slugs as the battle reached its crucial point.

"We're losing too many men," Hopringle said.

"It's not finished yet," Jack ducked as a dozen shots screamed overhead. "Those were Snider bullets. We're firing at ourselves."

"Here's the artillery coming!" Captain Moore of the Rifles said.

"Give the gunners covering fire," Jack ordered.

Although the 42nd and Rifles had advanced a considerable distance up the slope, the Ashantis still managed to harass Rait's artillerymen. Busily firing at the enemy, Jack had little time to watch as the Hausas, and Royal Artillerymen manoeuvred their steel nine-pounder across the swamp and river. The men struggled, sweat trickling down their faces as they pushed the cannon, flinching as Ashanti slugs rattled off the gun barrel, swearing to manoeuvre reluctant wheels through clinging mud.

"That's hard work for the gunners," Moore said.

"Support the artillery!" Jack yelled. "Keep these blasted Ashanti musket men down!"

When he reached a relatively flat area, Rait stepped clear of the gun, ignored the Ashanti slugs, and scanned the hillside. Noting a dense patch of forest where the Ashanti gun smoke was thickest, he aimed his nine-pounder. The Hausa gun-crew were smart, loading in seconds and firing at once. Jack saw the case-shot rip into the trees, again and again, as Rait altered the angle of aim slightly each time. When the artillery fire ceased, a company of the 42nd charged forward, bayonets fixed and the pipes screaming in support.

"Come on, 2nd West," Jack rose from his cover. "Follow the Black Watch!"

The West Indians advanced without hesitation, scrambling up the slope as slugs tore leaves from the trees and hammered into the ground.

"Go on, the Westies!" A wounded Black Watch private shouted encouragement. "Give them hell!"

By the time Jack's men arrived, there was nobody left to fight. The bayonets of the 42nd had completed the artillery's work, with shattered Ashanti bodies scattered around and a lone Black Watch private sitting against a tree, smoking and muttering to himself, tears in his young eyes.

"They're breaking," a Black Watch lieutenant shouted as the Ashanti firing began to ease. "Push on, the Forty-twa!"

When the 42nd penetrated their centre, the Ashanti on the flanks crumbled. Too preoccupied with his own fight, Jack had no time to watch the action elsewhere. On the left, the British had cut through to the crest of the ridge. Once there, the artillery fired rockets at an Ashanti encampment, forcing them away. On the right, Colonel Wood and the Naval Brigade had made progress until heavy Ashanti fire pinned them down. Too careful of his men's lives to engage in a frontal attack, Wood ordered his men to lie down and fire back, depending on the superior firepower of the Sniders to overcome the Ashanti numbers.

"Come on!" Jack followed the Black Watch over the ridge, where the Ashantis were now fleeing from their camp. For the first time that day, Jack saw a live Ashanti as Amanquatia formed up his battered regiments in the village of Amoaful. Kumi Okese was there, prominent under his yellow umbrella as he addressed his white-striped Edwesus.

This time the British did not allow the Ashantis to form a proper defence. Rait's artillery blasted case shot into Amoaful, sweeping into the Ashanti ranks like a broom, felling dozens and scattering the others. Panting with effort, Jack watched. "Form up, C Company," he ordered. "Take a roll call, Hopringle."

"Capture that village," Sir Archibald Alison ordered, and the Black Watch, angered by their casualties in the slogging advance, gave a cheer and charged in with the bayonet. Jack's Wests followed, with the Rifle Brigade company soon after, scattering the remaining defenders and firing at the warriors as they fled into the trees. The battle for the village was short and fierce, ending in the Ashantis total rout.

"We've done it," Sergeant Mathews said, rubbing at his chest.

"We've broken through and captured Amoaful," Jack checked his watch. One thirty. It had taken the British five and a half hours to press the Ashantis back, yet he still heard heavy firing from the British right flank and further down the column. The Ashantis were not done yet.

"They're devils, these Ashantis," Captain Moore leaned on a tree, wiping sweat and blood from his forehead. "But they're brave devils."

"They're as persistent as the Pashtun," Jack said.

"The 42nd took heavy casualties," Moore said. "Their tactics were all wrong, advancing in sections as they did."

Although he agreed, Jack did not comment. Criticising any regiment's tactics was a sure way to create bad blood, and the Highlanders had fought with their customary bravery.

Sir Archibald Alison looked over the men in Amoaful. Some were lying exhausted, others drinking from water bottles. A few men tied makeshift bandages around wounds, while others checked their ammunition or swapped stories about the fighting. Sergeant McGaw was checking his section, ignoring his bloodstained tunic.

"Windrush," Alison spoke in an educated Edinburgh accent. "How are your Wests?"

"They did well, sir," Jack said.

"How many casualties?"

"I have three wounded, one seriously. I sent the badly hurt man back." Jack said.

"So few?" Alison raised his eyebrows.

"I taught them to fire from cover, sir, rather than expose themselves need-lessly," Jack defended his men, feeling that Alison was attacking them for not taking more casualties.

Jack looked back down the hill as heavy firing broke out. "What's happening down there?"

Captain Moore joined them. "The Ashantis are attacking the column, trying to break the supply lines,"

"They're resilient; I'll grant them that," Alison said.

"Shall I take my Wests down and help the column out, sir?"

"Stay put," Alison said. "I may need you here."

It was nearly three in the afternoon before the last sputter of fire died out, and relative peace returned to the forest. The British had four killed and 173 wounded, mostly from the 42nd, who had taken the brunt of the fighting. Jack leaned against a tree in the middle of the village and lit a cheroot, surprised he was not shaking with reaction.

"How many men did the Ashantis lose?" Hopringle asked.

"We'll never know," Jack said. "The bodies will be out there in the forest. If you want to go and count them, help yourself."

"I'd say we shot thousands," Hopringle said. "We taught them no end of a lesson."

"You may be right," Jack said, "although my estimate would be about five or six hundred if we're lucky. The Ashantis are expert at keeping behind cover. Now go and check your section, ensure your men are fed and watered and have sufficient ammunition. We won a battle, not the whole war."

"Yes, sir," Hopringle injected a little resentment into his reply. Although Jack knew the lieutenant wanted to talk about his first action, he had no desire to listen to a Johnny Raw's ideas. He wanted to be alone. No, Jack corrected him-self as he curled Mary's scarf around his fist. That was not true. He wanted to be with his wife.

The remainder of the Rifles and the baggage entered Amoaful later that afternoon, tired and glad to have somewhere to rest. Wolseley set up a field hospital in the village, where busy surgeons treated the casualties before an escort took them back to the coast. Towards evening, Wolseley sent two companies of the Rifles and a section of the Wests to a nearby village, leaving Jack's men where they were.

"Bed down, lads," Jack ordered. "Three section, you take the first watch." Crawling into a hut, he lay down. As always after a battle, a hundred scenes and incidents crowded into his mind as the day's events unfolded. He closed his eyes, mentally and emotionally drained, yet sleep evaded him. Sometime after midnight, he heard the sputter of musketry as the Rifles and Wests combined to repel an Ashanti attack on the village.

"Come on, lads," Jack ordered as his men emerged with rifles in their hands. "Defensive positions."

After half an hour, the firing died away, without a serious attack on his men. "Number Three Section, get some sleep. Two Section, take their place."

Remaining outside the hut, Jack lay on his back, staring at the sky and hoping that Mary was all right. It was always worse at night, for during the day he had a host of problems to keep his mind occupied. At night, when he lay alone, he had time to worry. The images of the battle no longer troubled him. Now, he only saw Mary in chains, with Kumi Okese leering at her through his smoky eyes.

Chapter Thirty

ON TO THE ORDAH FEBRUARY 1874

Jack awoke with a slight ache in his head and a bitter taste in his mouth from the previous day's powder-smoke.

"Are we pressing on to Kumasi?" He asked hopefully, watching Wolseley give orders.

"It seems not," Captain Moore said. "I think Wolseley is consolidating first."

"What is there to consolidate?" Jack asked. "We beat them fair and square on ground of their choosing! Now is the time to double march to Kumasi."

Moore grinned. "Shall I go and tell the general your opinion? I'm sure Sir Garnet will listen to your advice."

Biting back his impatience, Jack checked his men, ensured they all had full water-bottles and got their fair share of provisions, set out sentries from One Section and tried not to think of Mary. While the Rifles patrolled two miles southward to ensure the baggage came through safely, the 42nd and a few of the 23rd engaged in punitive expeditions, Jack and the West remained in Amoaful, baking in the heat.

"One thing's for sure," Captain Moore said. "The Ashanti won't be starved to death."

Cunning hands had woven palm leaves into large containers, which held a mixture of flour and maize. The British soldiers tasted the contents cautiously, some thinking they may have been poisoned.

"It's fresh as a Sunday morning," Coffin said, smiling. "Far better than army rations."

"Well done, lads!" Jack approved. "Dig in!"

As Jack watched his Wests enhance their rations with this free food, the Rifle other ranks discussed Kumasi.

"It's true, I tell you," one private said. "King Kofi pays his men in gold, and solid nuggets are lying about the streets."

"You're talking nonsense, man," another said.

"I'm telling you!" The first soldier shouted to prove his words. "That's why this place is called the Gold Coast! The king has a great gold crown and sits on a golden stool. And all his wives, he's got thousands of them, all his wives wear great gold chains and nothing else."

"Nothing else?" A quiet man showed sudden interest. "Nothing at all?"

"Only gold chains."

Shaking his head, Jack walked away. The soldiers were in for a disappointment if they expected to pick up lumps of gold from the streets of Kumasi.

"Ah, Windrush," Buller appeared, cigar in hand and looking as immaculate as if he were squiring women in Hyde Park rather than facing Ashantis in the African forest. "Did you hear the news? No, then I'll tell you. We disposed of your old adversary in the late battle."

"Who? Kumi Okese?"

"Oh, no, the general himself, Amanquatia. Your Okese fellow must be in charge of the Ashanti army now." Buller drifted away, waving a languid hand at soldiers who saluted him.

Kumi Okese in charge? Jack pondered. If so, he was not with Mary, which could only be good. *If I see him, I will kill him*, Jack promised, wrapping Mary's scarf around his fist.

After a day's frustrating rest, Wolseley ordered the army to march again. With Russell's local levies scouting ahead, Colonel McLeod commanded the advance guard, while Rait's men transported the nine-pounder.

"We're at the head today," Captain Moore trotted past with H and C Companies of the Rifle Brigade, who moved further back after their exploits at Amoaful.

"We'll support you, Moore," Jack said. "Come on, C Company! We're travelling light. Take your rifle, ammunition and three days rations in your haversack. Nothing else."

The Wests obeyed without question.

"No tents?" Hopringle asked.

"It looks like we're finally dashing for Kumasi," Jack said. "Three days, maybe even two, and we should be there." *Hold on Mary; I'm coming.*

* * *

Even after their defeat two days previously, the Ashantis showed their spirit. Only an hour after leaving Amoaful, Jack heard the first deep thuds of Ashanti musketry. *Here we go again.* He touched the silver cross on his holster.

"Keep in formation, boys!" Jack said. "Make sure you're loaded and ready." He did not alter the speed of the march as he heard the slow spatter of aimed rifle fire and knew the Rifles were responding. Within a few moments the firing died away, and a quarter of a mile up the track they passed a bullet-scarred tree trunk with the dead body of an Ashanti warrior crumpled on top. The Wests barely paused to look; they had all seen dead warriors before. Jack noted the man's white stripes. *Kumi Okese is not finished yet.*

There was more musketry half an hour later, and again the column barely paused.

"We're pushing them aside now," Jack said. "Maybe we'll have a rapid march to Kumasi." *Two days, stay alive, Mary!*

This time two Ashanti warriors lay dead beside the road, while another with a splintered leg glowered at the marching column.

The rain started then, easing through the canopy above to patter on the road, drip on men's heads and quickly turn the hard-packed earth into mud.

"This rain might swell the rivers," Jack said, worrying.

"We'll get her back," Hopringle tried to reassure him.

Another hour of hard marching found them in a small deserted village. The only living thing was a half-starved dog, which one of the Rifles immediately fed with a biscuit. Jack saw a cooking fire outside a hut, with maize-meal bubbling in the pot on top.

"Not bad!" Coffin said, after a quick taste. "What a waste to leave it here."

"The Ashanti must be rattled now to leave in so much of a hurry," Hopringle said. "We've beaten them."

"They're on the run, for sure," Jack said.

Hold on, Mary, Jack thought. *Not long now. I'm coming for you.*

An outbreak of firing ahead halted the column, denting Jack hopes. "Front rank face right," he ordered. "Rear rank face left."

The Wests swung around, ready to repel any ambush until Colonel McLeod ordered them up to support the Rifles.

"With me, lads!" Although Jack marched C Company at the double, by the time they reached the front, the Rifles had already cleared away the Ashantis.

"You're not needed, after all, Windrush," McLeod said. "The Rifles did the job. Good skirmishers, these men."

"Yes, sir," Jack said. "If the Forty Second had adopted the Rifles' fighting style, they might have taken fewer casualties at Amoaful." He ignored McLeod's hard glare, for he disliked seeing unfortunate leadership waste good soldiers.

There was another deserted village a few miles further on, and two streams of clear water running across a bed flecked with iron pyrites.

"Gold!" A young Rifle said, to the jeers of his companions.

The column continued for half an hour and then halted, sweltering in the heat. The Rifles' adopted dog slowly wafted its tail, enjoying its unaccustomed popularity as Jack looked ahead, calculating the distance to Kumasi.

"What's happening, sir?" Jack felt his frustration mounting, knowing that Mary was only a few dozen miles ahead.

"We're waiting for Sir Garnet," Colonel McLeod said, "and the rest of the column."

"I could take my Wests and push on sir," Jack offered. "We're used to this sort of terrain."

"Stay with the column, Windrush," McLeod said. "The Ashantis may have more ambushes ahead."

Knowing McLeod was correct, Jack nodded. "Yes, sir."

"Rest while you can, fill your bottles and remember to filter the water," Jack said. The Wests scattered to find shade from the sun, except for the unlucky half-section Jack posted as sentries. Insects buzzed around the men, irritating everybody. A cloud brought light rain, which increased as the day wore on.

Wolseley arrived with four stalwart men carrying him on a litter, while his Black Watch bodyguard exchanged pleasantries and insults with the Rifle Brigade. "Feed the men," Wolseley descended from his perch, gasped as he put his weight on his wounded leg and limped around the village, "and the Rifles will advance to the next village."

Jack looked up. "Permission to accompany the Rifles, sir?"

Wolseley nodded. "Yes, Windrush. Take your Wests."

Gathering his men, Jack followed in the wake of the hurrying Rifles without encountering a single Ashanti warrior. A solitary woman sat under a tree in the village of Aggemmamu, pointing to the British soldiers as they splashed through the spreading puddles.

"King Kofi is a bad man," she said in English, repeating herself three times as laughing porters gathered around her, brave in the presence of British soldiers.

Captain Moore ordered the woman to be taken to a hut and guarded. "If we don't look after her," he said, "either one of these bold lads will put a knife through her, or she'll cut somebody's throat and disappear into the bush."

"Aye," Jack said, remembering the women along the North-West Frontier. "Like as not, Moore."

By evening the rain had eased away. The Wests collected dry wood and built a fire in the centre of Aggemmamu, with most removing their clothes to dry them. Some had disappeared into the huts to sleep when somebody shouted: "Ashanti!"

Jack did not see who started the panic, but within seconds all the porters and many of the native levies were on their feet, yelling "Shantee" and running down the path, southward, towards the far distant coast. The Rifles sergeant on guard tried to stop them, and half the Rifles and Wests poured out of the huts, Sniders in hand, to see a disorderly mob fleeing in panic.

"Now we have no porters," Jack told his men. "We'll have to travel without anything except what we can carry."

The Wests nodded. Daley lifted his chin. "We don't need these bloody Bushmen." He looked at Jack. "We're the 2nd Wests."

Jack looked upwards as the sky wept again, large drops of rain dropping from unseen clouds.

* * *

Jack peered into the rain that bounced from the track and dripped from the trees, hoping the weather would not slow their progress. His company marched immediately behind the Rifles, sloshing along the muddy path, miserable yet determined.

"We're nearing the River Ordah," Jack said. "That's the last major obstacle before Kumasi, so watch for ambushes," he gave the order to his men, knowing they were veterans now and needed no warning.

"Maybe the Ashantis have all run," Coffin said hopefully, a moment before the deep thud of a musket proved the opposite.

"No. They're still there," Sergeant Roberts said, immediately firing at the jet of powder smoke.

"Front rank face right," Jack ordered, "rear rank face left. Fire."

The Wests fired a volley, waited to see if the Ashantis retaliated and marched on. Nobody commented, such small scale ambushes were part of the routine of the column and seldom did any harm. Birds called unheeded from the trees as insects continued to plague the column. When they came to a rise, one of the few remaining porters carrying Rait's gun stumbled so the wooden framework on which the nine-pounder sat tipped to the left. An artillery corporal rushed up to straighten things up, and they continued, step by step along the narrow track on a march that seemed never-ending.

The rain ended suddenly as if God had turned off the tap of heaven and the Wests lifted their shoulders slightly. Coffin hummed a hymn, stumbled, recovered and marched on.

Frequent firing ahead proved the Rifles were in contact with the Ashantis, but the column continued at the same pace, the Sniders clearing the way. Jack felt the sweat soaking his tunic, thought of Mary and scanned the trees on either side of the path. The desultory firing continued, culminating in a sharp outbreak that, for once, slowed the column.

"Number One section," Jack shouted. "You're with me!' He was about to hurry forward when the firing ended, and a Cockney voice shouted.

"Who's that?"

Flicking away the sweat that beaded on his eyebrows, Jack ordered Sergeant Mathews to take command of the section and hurried forward to the Rifles position.

"It's a flag of truce!" Captain Moore passed the news down the column. "The beggars are surrendering!"

"Not them," Jack said. "It's some sort of ruse." He joined the Rifles' officers at the front of the column, with the native levies looking scared and the Riflemen fingering their triggers as they stood or crouched behind cover.

The elderly Ashanti stood on the path, with an ambassador's gold breastplate on his chest, and apprehension on his face. Beside him, a familiar figure carried a flag of truce.

"Akron," Jack said quietly.

"I know the fellow in the breastplate," Captain Moore said. "He's an ambassador from King Kofi. We gave him a guard of honour back in Fomanah."

"I know his companion," Jack said quietly.

"Send them to the general," McLeod took charge. "They're ambassadors! Treat them with respect." He glanced at Jack. "Major Windrush, take a section to escort the Ashantis."

"This way, gentlemen," Jack said, forming Number One section around the two ambassadors. "Akron; how is my wife?"

Akron looked astonished. "Your wife, Major?"

"Your people hold her prisoner in Kumasi," Jack said. "How is she?"

Akron and the ambassador struggled to keep paste with the Wests. "The Indian woman? Kumi Okese's new slave?"

"Is she well?" Jack asked.

"She is well cared for," Akron said.

"Where is she held?"

"Kumi Okese has her in his slave quarters," Akron said.

"Where is that?"

"Behind his house."

About to ask more, Jack stopped as Wolseley, imperious on his hammock, demanded the letters the ambassador held. Wolseley scanned the paper, grunted and gave a small snort of impatience. "King Kofi wishes me to halt my advance. What do you say, Windrush? You're the only man here who has met his Ashanti Majesty."

Jack glanced at Akron, who stood impassive as if he did not understand a word. "I'd say push on harder than ever, sir. I would not believe King Kofi's if he told me it snowed at the North Pole." Jack looked up as another shower of rain spattered them. "The rainy season is due, sir. The longer we delay, the more chance there is of a constant downpour, and we have the Ordah River to cross, and the swamp that guards Kumasi. If they are swollen, they will delay our progress, and seriously impede our withdrawal."

Wolseley smiled. "You speak with great eloquence, Windrush. Do either of these gentlemen speak English?"

"Yes, sir. Akron, the man with the flag, is fluent."

"Then, Mr Akron," Wolseley said, "pray tell the Asantahene that we will not halt. That is all."

"Thank you, sir."

"You have not forgotten the charge I laid upon you, Windrush," Wolseley said.

"No, sir. I have not." *But your blessed Golden Stool can wait until I've found Mary, Sir Garnet.*

As the ambassadors returned up the column, the Ashanti started firing again, with slugs whistling from the forest. "So much for the flag of truce, Akron," Jack said. "I want to speak to you before you return."

"Yes, Major." Akron ducked as a slug ripped into his flag. His companion with the gold breastplate gave a little whimper and began to hurry along the path, shouting something. The firing intensified, with one Rifleman grunting and falling, to rise shortly after, looking at the slow spread of blood on his leg. He swore, lifted his Snider, aimed and fired back.

"I'm Joe Briggs!" he shouted. "You'll not see me die in a hurry! We're tough stuff in Whitechapel!"

Despite the situation, Jack gave a grim smile. He knew the Ashantis were capable warriors, but British soldiers could hold their own against anybody. At the next shot, the ambassador backed away, and Jack was sure he would have fled to Wolseley if a Rifles' corporal had not ushered him to the front of the column.

"There you go, chum," the corporal said. "Go and join your mates." He looked at Jack, "can I boot him up the backside, sir? Help him on his way, like?"

"That's not very diplomatic, corporal," Jack placed his hand on Akron's arm. "Could you imagine doing that to a British diplomat?"

The corporal considered for a moment and his grin widened. "Oh, yes, sir. It would do them a world of good. They start the wars and beggars like us, and these Ashanti lads do the fighting."

Jack nodded. "That's very true." He swore as Akron slipped, twisted free and ran up the path as though his life depended on it. "Come back!" he shouted in vain, watching as both Ashantis revealed an amazing turn of speed.

Well, now I know that Mary is alive and where the Ashantis hold her. This time tomorrow I could be with her.

The firing sputtered away and then increased all around the advance guard. "The devils are stubborn today," Captain Moore said.

"They don't want us to cross the Ordah," Jack fired his revolver into a patch of woodland, ducked behind the trunk of a tree and hastily reloaded. 'It's the last barrier before Kumasi."

"Good," Captain Moore said. "All the sweeter when we cross."

As the firing grew even more intense, the Rifles sent patrols into the forest to seek for the Ashantis. Jack watched them leave the path, exchanging dark jokes as they slid under the leaves.

"Sir?" Sergeant Mathews sounded hopeful. "Can we not hunt the Ashantis too?"

"No," Jack said emphatically. "I'll need all of you when we get to Kumasi. I don't want unnecessary casualties."

"Yes, sir." Mathews looked disappointed.

"Get into cover," Jack said. "Only fire when you are sure it's an Ashanti. Remember that the Rifles are out there too." He heard the tussle in the bush, the deep thuds of the muskets and the returning crackle of the Sniders and then the Rifles' patrols returned with wounded men.

"We got three of the devils," one long-faced sergeant said, sending his two wounded back down the column. "Maybe four. Big beggars with white stripes down their faces. They thought they were facing parade ground soldiers, not the Rifles!"

Jack nodded agreement. The common perception of the British soldier was the scarlet-coated Guards, with their spit-and-polish and immaculate drill. The reality was here, the men from London slums and the back-streets of Dundee, men brought up in the harsh climate of Highland Scotland, or with the tyranny of the soil in English shires. These men faced adversity with a curse and dark humour. Death might claim them, but nothing could defeat them. Jack felt a sudden surge of pride, tinged with a shame he did not understand.

The column moved on again, with the Ashantis contesting every yard, so the British marched through drifting powder-smoke, with slugs pattering around them. At one stage, where a swamp spread at the base of a wooded rise, the Ashanti fought behind a barricade until the artillery and the Rifles forced them out. A quarter of a mile further back, Jack's Wests listened to the battle in growing frustration. Only when the Rifles cleared the route could the march continue, with Jack aware of growing dampness burdening the atmosphere.

"The rains are gathering," he said. "We'd better get a move on."

"This is still the dry season," Hopringle protested.

Jack grunted, saying nothing as they rounded a bend, and the column came to a halt.

"There's the Ordah." Excitement tinged Hopringle's quiet voice as he pointed to the slow brown river that slithered between dipping green trees.

Jack nodded. Once across that river, Ashanti resistance should either stiffen or collapse. The column halted, with the Rifles' skirmishers taking up defensive positions along the banks.

"Number One Section, face your front, extended order," Jack snapped. "Number Two Section, front rank face right, rear rank face left. Number Three and Four Sections, you're in reserve."

"I thought they'd have put up a better defence here," Jack said, as the musketry died away. "I thought they'd have at least a screen of musket men." He stepped to the river bank, very aware a score of Ashantis could be aiming at him.

"So did I," Hopringle stood slightly further back, holding his revolver. "I was expecting a contested river crossing."

At thirty yards wide, the Ordah was as more of a psychological as a physical barrier, with the water not sufficiently deep to halt a determined advance. "King Kofi bathes here once a year," Jack remembered something that Akron had told him. "The Ashantis think the Ordah is sacred."

"The Ashantis seem to think that every river is sacred," Captain Moore said grimly. "Here comes the general."

"Camp here," Wolseley ordered. "The engineers can build a bridge. That will be easier for the porters and wounded to cross, and when the rains come, a swollen river won't delay our return."

Biting back his frustration at the thought that Mary was only a few miles down the road, Jack took C Company to form a defensive perimeter. He watched the engineers felling trees with a controlled frenzy as they constructed the first bridge the Ordah had ever seen. Despite his desire to charge ahead, Jack knew that Wolseley was correct. If they had to withdraw at speed, having a rain-swollen river behind them would be dangerous, especially if Ashanti musket men filled the woods.

"I don't think I've ever properly appreciated the engineers before," Captain Moore said.

"Nor have I," Jack admitted. "They're a Godsend."

"Aye, or a Wolseleysend!"

As the day eased, the rain began again, with the Wests and Rifles using tree boughs and leaves to build shelters while the Engineers toiled by torchlight. At eight in the evening, a supply officer brought up a keg of Jamaican rum, which proved popular with the men.

"That's not bad stuff," Ogston said.

"You should know, Oggy," a Rifle corporal said. "You make the best there is."

After creating a guard rota for the night, Jack tried to sleep, although the rush of the river and thoughts of Mary restricted his rest. He woke before dawn, realised he lay in a muddy puddle, swore soundly and rose to check the sentries. The rain teemed down over the new bridge, pattered in the river and dripped from the surrounding trees.

"Welcome to Africa," Jack pulled up his collar and hauled his pith helmet over his head.

"That's Kumasi joined to civilisation for the first time in its history," Captain Moore joined Jack, a wet cigar between his teeth. "I can hear the Ashantis celebrating already."

The sound drifted towards them, a myriad voices, the monotonous grumble of the drums and an occasional yell.

Jack nodded. "Aye." He said no more as he checked his revolver was loaded. He did not feel like talking that morning. *By tomorrow evening*, he told himself, *I will be with Mary, or I'll be dead.*

Chapter Thirty-One

The Wests moved an hour before dawn, thundering across the bridge as the rain eased to a reluctant stop. Water dripped from the overhanging leaves, the only sound in the ominous hush as if the country was shocked at this foreign army invading the empire that had caused so much fear.

"Orders from the general!" Lieutenant Wood shouted. "The advance party is not to fire first! King Kofi might want to negotiate."

Jack watched the young officer run back, all his dignity gone as he passed on what he must have considered a critical order.

"Bugger that," one of the Riflemen said.

"Did you hear that boys?" Jack said to his men. "If you see an Ashanti pointing his musket at you, don't fire. Greet him nicely and say how do ye do?"

When only Sergeant Mathews smiled at the irony, Jack continued with a warning. "Keep alert, lads. The Ashantis won't be happy today."

Jack had barely finished speaking before the muskets roared. Once again, Jack had his men take cover and fire back, blasting every jet of smoke and muzzle flash with bullets as Russell's Bonny natives and the Rifle Brigade led the advance, firing and moving, pushing slowly forward.

"Is that the Ashantis negotiating, sir?" Hopringle asked.

Behind Jack's company, the 42nd lined the length of the road to keep communications open and guard the baggage, with musketry continuous and the occasional casualty as Ashanti slugs found their mark.

"Maybe we should invite the politicians here," Jack said. "Show them the reality of Imperial diplomacy."

The track rose towards the village of Ordahsu, which the Ashantis seemed determined to hold. The firing increased with every yard, forcing the column to halt and return fire.

Jack grunted. "This is getting hot!" confined to the road, the column fired into the forest, taking casualties, aiming at spurts of smoke, men cursing, groaning, shouting, helping their colleagues and performing acts of unrecorded heroism.

"Keep moving!" Still carried on his litter, a target for every Ashanti musket within range, Wolseley gave orders without flinching from the slugs that whistled past him. "Press on!"

Walking amongst his men, Jack beckoned them forwards. "Come on, lads! Support the Rifles!"

Heading the column, the Rifles surged into Ordahsu. The Ashantis met them with a torrent of musketry, making every hut a strongpoint and every house a redoubt. In an unfamiliar town gritty with concealing smoke, the Rifles fought through the streets, kneeling to fire, finding cover where they could, cursing as they met the Ashantis head-on.

"With me, boys!" Jack pushed up his Wests, charging towards a hut where two musket men were reloading. Firing as he ran, Jack's first two shots missed, and only his third caught an Ashanti in the stomach. The man doubled up, while his companion lifted his musket by the barrel and swung it at Jack.

Stair leapt past, thrusting with his bayonet as he shouted: "Second Wests!" He turned to Jack with the Ashantis blood spattered over his face. "That Bushman's dead sir," he casually bayonetted the wounded man and ran on to the next hut as Jack reloaded his revolver.

The crack of artillery made Jack flinch as the nine-pounder added to the noise, with the gunners targeting the most stubborn areas of Ashanti defence.

"You!" Colonel McLeod pointed to a Rifleman who sheltered at the corner of a hut to fire at the Ashantis. "Are you afraid of the enemy that you must hide from them?"

The Rifleman turned around, surprise on his face. "No, sir. I am not afraid, but if I did not take cover, I should expect to be marked for extra drill."

"Good answer, Rifleman," Jack encouraged as McLeod stormed away. "Come on, lads!" Revolver in hand, he led a rush towards the right side of the village, where a group of Ashanti were sheltering behind the doorway of a substantial house, firing up the main street at the Rifles.

Bullets kicked up dust at Jack's feet, and a slug cracked against his jacket, temporarily winding him. He gasped, sinking to his knees as he struggled to catch his breath.

"Sir?" Sergeant Mathews stopped at his side. "Sir?"

"I'm all right," Jack said. "Go on! Take that hut."

Rolling onto his side, Jack recovered his breath, stood up and staggered forward. The Wests and Rifles had cleared the village and were searching the houses for any stragglers. Rifle and West wounded sat side by side in the shade, while a score of dead Edwesus lay in their own blood, mature warriors killed defending their country, the white stripes bright in the sunlight. A dozen native porters also lay on the ground, some whimpering in fear.

"Well done, lads," Jack recovered his breath. "Now we'll have to wait and see what happens next."

As the British consolidated their hold on Ordahsu, the Ashanti launched a surprise counter-attack, yelling as they rushed from the forest. For a few moments, the position was precarious as the outlying Rifle pickets withdrew.

"Force them back!" Jack fired and reloaded as his men joined the Rifles. The high crack of Sniders drowned all other sounds as the Ashanti attack faltered before it reached the village. They fell back, sullenly. Silence descended, save for a few isolated shots that did no harm.

"They're getting desperate," Hopringle said.

"They knew we've got them beat." Jack counted his revolver cartridges. He had twenty left and no way to replenish until nightfall. He waited, with the tension mounting inside him. Although Jack knew the British had mauled the Ashanti army, Kumi Okese might have some nasty surprises yet. Now that he was no close to Mary, he did not want to die in a sordid ambush.

"Why are we waiting?" Hopringle echoed Jack's thoughts. "We've got the Ashantis on the run; we should push them hard."

"Didn't you hear?" Captain Moore had dried blood down one side of his face. "Sir Garnet, in his wisdom, has decided that the 42nd should have the honour of being first to enter Kumasi."

Jack swore silently. "So we have to wait until they march to the front of the column."

"That's right, Windrush, we wait while the Ashantis gather their forces again."

Jack fretted with impatience, wondering if he should leave his men and strike off alone to find Mary. With the Ashanti army in retreat, the danger would not be as great. He calculated the odds. He knew where Kumi Okese held Mary, so once he entered Kumasi, he could find her. However, a lone white face in an enemy capital city would make him vulnerable. With scores, possibly hundreds of disgruntled Ashanti warriors in the streets, it was unlikely he would survive for long. It would be better to wait. A dead husband was no good to Mary, and getting her killed while trying to rescue her, was not intelligent. However... Jack was still deliberating when he heard the sound of pipes.

"Bloody Sawnies," a Rifles sergeant said. "We've led the advance for three days. We should be first into Kumasi, not the Forty-bloody-second."

Jack listened as the Rifles greeted the 42nd with insults and jeers, to which the 42nd responded in kind. For a moment, Jack thought there would be a full-scale inter-regimental brawl until things simmered down into mutual glowers.

"Take us into Kumasi, 42nd," McLeod ordered, and the Black Watch marched ahead.

"Windrush!" Wolseley beckoned him forward. "You have a mission to accomplish."

"Yes, sir," Jack said. "Come on, lads, we'll follow the Forty-second!"

For the first mile, the British met no opposition, but after that, the Ashantis had recovered. Their first volley wounded seven men. The 42nd returned fire, hammering the trees, bushes and all that hid behind them, so they forced a passage along the road, marching with the pipes screaming defiance. Colonel McLeod strode to the front, shouting orders as the Ashantis tried ambush after ambush.

"A Company, front rank, fire! Rear rank, fire!"

One private stepped ahead of the column, level with the colonel, daring the Ashantis to shoot him.

"Who's that man?" McLeod asked.

"That's Tam Adams, sir," A Fife accent came in reply.

"Good man, Adams! The Forty-second will fire by companies!"

"For old Scotland!" The Highlanders cheered as they forced the road, ignoring casualties, blasting through ambushes. Jack grunted; perhaps there was a reason that Sir Garnet put the Black Watch in the van. Their unique *elan* was better for this sort of advance than the more cautious approach of the Rifles.

Accepting casualties, they powered along the road to the scream of the pipes, smashing through each Ashanti ambush.

Can you hear the pipes, Kumasi? Can you hear the Highlanders coming? Then you're going to die. The 42nd is advancing, the Black Watch, Queen Victoria's Highland furies. You can run, or you can die.

Jack began to recognise landmarks. "Six miles to Kumasi," he said, wrapping Mary's scarf around his fist. "If the 42nd keep this speed up, we'll be there in two hours, ambushes or not."

After the weeks and months of waiting, it was exhilarating to march along in the wake of the Highlanders, brushing aside Ashanti ambushes, passing empty kegs of gunpowder and the Ashanti dead and wounded.

I'm coming, Mary!

After four miles the landscape altered, with the scrub and forest giving way to waving grass higher than the tallest man. Alert for possible ambushes, Jack ordered his Wests to spread further out even as he increased his pace. *I'm coming! Hold on, Mary, I'm coming.* Splashing through the final swamp without a care for the depth, Jack automatically replaced the cross the Ashantis had knocked from Manning's grave.

"We've not forgotten," Sergeant Mathews saw the name Jack had carved on the wood.

"Nor have I," Jack said.

They ascended the rise to the main street of Kumasi with the Highlanders before them and the wail of the pipes warning the Ashantis to keep clear. Jack looked around, seeing the familiar houses as if in a dream. After so much effort, he was back, yet it felt unreal. He wanted to run ahead and shout for Mary, yet knew he could not.

"Keep in skirmishing order," Jack said as the Wests spread out, rifles ready. He had wondered if the Ashanti warriors would make a last stand in the streets of their capital, but instead, they had joined the crowds that gathered to watch the British enter. Most warriors stood with their muskets held butt-upward as a sign of peace, while a few even offered gourds of cool water for the soldiers. It felt like an anti-climax, as though a proud empire had collapsed with a whimper. There was not even a single drum beating, not a horn sounding and no umbrellas in sight.

Was that it? No final flourish? No gallant heroes?

"Sergeant Mathews," Jack led his men away from the main streets to a quieter square, where a group of women and children watched curiously from under the dripping leaves of a banyan tree.

"Yes, sir." Mathews' eyes were never still as he surveyed his surroundings, looking for the enemy.

"I have two things to find in Kumasi."

"I know, sir," Mathews said. "The Golden Stool and Mrs Windrush."

"How the devil do you know about the Stool?" Jack knew he should not be surprised. Sergeants in the British Army had a knack of finding out everything. There was no reason that a sergeant in the 2nd West should be different.

Mathews smiled. "I hear things."

"Well, sergeant, take Number One Section and try to get into the palace; search for the Stool; it was in the upper storey of the tower when I saw it last. I am going to find my wife."

"Yes, sir." Sergeant Mathews hesitated a second. "Good luck, sir."

"Thank you," Jack said, ordered Hopringle to take over C Company and without another word, headed for Kumi Okese's house.

You had better be right about Mary, Akron. Groups of Ashantis watched him, civilians and soldiers, yet Jack knew if anybody challenged him, he would shoot without compulsion.

Jack's heart raced as he ran through the streets, trying to remember where Kumi Okese lived. When a curiously shaped banyan tree caught his eye, he knew he was on the right track, ran into the side street, and stopped with a curse.

A hundred men were milling around, pushing and shoving at each other as a section of Rifles was arguing with a large group of Ashanti warriors. Desperate to find Mary, Jack would have avoided them, but they were directly in his path.

Looking past them to Kumi Okese's house, Jack swore again "What the devil's all the commotion, Corporal?"

The corporal was Irish, severely sunburned and with a mouth like a gin-trap. "The general wants us to disarm the Shantees, sir. This bunch doesn't want to be disarmed."

"So I see." Jack saw that the Ashanti warriors were already disappearing. "Take what you can, corporal, but if any Ashanti objects, don't argue." The last thing the British needed was a mass brawl when the column was scattered about the streets and vastly outnumbered.

"Yes, sir!" The corporal stared as Jack grabbed an Enfield and a bandolier of ammunition from a surprised Ashanti.

"I'll have these, fellow!"

With the situation resolved, Jack moved on, feeling his tension mount as he neared Kumi Okese's house. "Mary!" He raised his voice, loading the Enfield in case any Ashanti showed fight. "Mary!"

There was no reply. Jack ran inside, shouting. He ran from room to room, booting open doors, holding his rifle at the ready. There was no sign of Mary and nothing to say that she had ever been there.

"Mary!" Jack felt panic surging through him as he yelled himself hoarse, peering desperately into alcoves and courtyards. Only echoes replied.

Swearing, Jack sped from the house and headed for the street where the Ashanti had held the hostages, ignoring the comments of the British soldiers he passed.

"You're in a rush, sir."

"I say," a plump major tried to stop him. "You, fellow! What's the hurry?"

The hostages' houses looked as if Jack had left them the previous day, with everything so familiar, it was hard to believe he had been involved in three expeditions since he was last here. Rushing forward, Jack entered the open front room where he had spoken to Elda.

"Mary!"

"Who are you looking for?" Elda sounded as calm as if she was in a drawing-room in her native Bohemia.

"Oh, thank God it's you, Elda!" Jack could have collapsed with relief. "I'm looking for Mary Windrush. The Ashanti took her hostage. Is she here?"

"The half-caste woman?"

"My wife," Jack belatedly remembered Elda's relationship with Kumi Okese. "Do you know where she is?"

Elda shrugged. "Yes, she was here."

"Was?" Grabbing Elda by the shoulders, Jack shook her. "What do you mean was here? Where is she now?"

"I don't know." Elda looked away.

"Yes, you do!" Abena burst into the room, her young face crumpled with anger. "You do know Miss Becker! Kumi Okese took her with him as his slave!"

"Oh, dear God in heaven!" Pushing Elda aside, Jack crouched beside Abena. "Do you know where they are now?" He tried to calm his panic. The thought of Mary in Kumi Okese's hands made him feel sick.

"Kumi Okese took her north, to his village I think," Abena said.

"You'll never find her," Elda said. "Never."

Chapter Thirty-Two

"Which village? Why? Tell me!" Terrified for Mary, Jack nearly shook Abena.

"It's called Nkaben," Abena said.

Jack stepped back. "Why has he taken her away, for God's sake?"

Elda rose from the floor, brushing herself down. "He's either going to keep her as a slave, or sacrifice her."

Jack felt the iced hand of shock grip him. "'Oh, dear God in heaven. Where is this place, Nkaben?"

As Elda gave a small smile, Abena took hold of Jack's sleeve. "I'll take you, Major Windrush."

"Hurry," Jack said. Leaving Elda standing in the middle of the house, Jack lifted his Enfield, scooped up Abena, and stormed away.

"Is there a path, Abena?"

"I'll show you," Abena said. "Past the palace, Major."

Jack nodded, rushing northward through Kumasi. He had a glimpse of Wolseley staring at him and moved on. Sir Garnet Wolseley, the British army, the war, the Golden Stool, and even the 2nd Wests, would have to do without him. Mary was more important than anything else.

"This way, Major Windrush, I think."

Following Abena's directions, Jack pushed through a crowd of Ashanti civilians and ran to the northern outskirts of Kumasi where a confusion of tracks led in various directions.

"Which one, Abena?"

Abena stopped, staring around her before she shook her head. "I don't remember," she began to cry. "There are too many roads; I don't remember."

"You!" Jack grabbed the nearest Ashanti, a warrior with a musket draped across his back. "Where is Nkaben?"

The man looked confused for a second, then his face cleared as Abena translated Jack's words.

"Nkaben," the Ashanti said, indicating one of the tracks.

"Is that where Kumi Okese is?" Jack asked, aware the man could not understand his words until Abena translated again.

"Nkaben," the warrior was about twenty years old, with clear eyes. Powder stains on his clothes and arms showed he had taken part in the recent fighting. He said something else.

"The man does not know if Kumi Okese is there," Abena said.

"Take me!" Shoving the muzzle of his Enfield into the man's chest, Jack repeated: "Take me to Nkaben!"

The warrior set off at a fast trot across the muddy ground. Jack followed, with his boots splashing through puddles and his head brushing against creepers that unleashed showers of lukewarm of water. After a few minutes, the Ashanti increased his speed and darted into the forest, leaving Jack floundering on the path and Abena a few yards behind.

"Come back!" Jack shouted, knowing his entreaties were futile. He aimed the Enfield in the direction the warrior had taken but did not fire. Taking a deep breath, Jack tried to calm himself down. He was an experienced soldier, he told himself. If he was tracking anybody else save Mary, what would he do? He certainly would not dash unheeding into the forest after an unknown number of enemies as if he were a young ensign on his first campaign.

Jack considered his position. He was alone in the Ashanti forest except for a child, chasing an enemy who had his wife and might kill her. He had no support, and he did not know the strength or position of his enemy.

Very well then, check my surroundings and see what they tell me.

"Stand still," Jack said to Abena. The ground underfoot was muddy, with falling rain deepening the puddles. Jack scouted around, looking for footprints. There were many, mostly of bare feet or sandals, yet he saw, quite distinctly, the pointed toe of a European-style boot. Kneeling, Jack put his hand against the smudged print to judge the size; it was a woman's boot, and he knew without a doubt, it was Mary's.

"Abena." Jack instinctively put out his hand and lightly squeezed when Abena responded in kind. "I'm sorry. You'd better get back to Kumasi. It might get dangerous here." He waited for her protest, but Abena only nodded, turned around and ran back the way she had come.

Hefting the Enfield, Jack strode along the track, searching for any further evidence. Twice more, he saw the impression of Mary's toe, as if she had been running. Jack speeded up, long-striding while still searching for spoor.

He was so intent on looking for Mary's footsteps that he nearly failed to notice the abrupt bend in the path. Halting at the banks of a fast stream that crossed the road, Jack saw Mary's footprint pressed into the mud and crossed over.

Nkaben squatted on a slight rise in the bend of the river. As with many African villages, a collection of well-built houses spread around a central tree, while smaller huts straggling northward and eastward to a cleared area of small fields. Jack heard the soft throbbing of the drums from three hundred yards away and slid behind a tree to watch.

The yellow umbrella was in plain sight, with Kumi Okese standing beneath it and one of his bodyguards at his side, sporting a bandage on his left arm. Around the umbrella, a hundred Ashanti warriors gathered, some brandishing muskets, others with rough bandages. These were the remnants of Edwesu fighting men who had resisted the British advance into Ashantiland, pushed back but still defiant, still undefeated. These were the warriors who had contested a modern army with outdated weapons and raw courage. Despite his situation, Jack could feel respect for them as warriors.

That feeling altered as he saw Mary, standing with shackles on her wrists and ankles. A group of men pushed her back and forward. Every time they shoved, Mary stumbled, recovered and straightened her shoulders.

"Right, you bastards," Jack said. "That's my wife you have there." He wondered if he should have brought his Wests, knew there was no time, and aimed the Enfield. "I'm going to whittle you down," he said, "and free Mary. You first Kumi Okese."

Aiming at Kumi Okese's head, Jack took a deep breath and squeezed the trigger. The Enfield gave a loud crack and bucked violently against his shoulder. *When was this thing last cleaned?* He saw a man next to Kumi Okese jerk upright and spin as the bullet took him in the shoulder. By the time the crowd had worked out what had happened, Jack had loaded. Again aiming at Kumi Okese, he adjusted for his previous miss and pressed the trigger.

"Damn!" Jack swore when another warrior stepped in his line of fire. At three hundred yards, the bullet took the warrior in the head, blowing a mess of blood and brains over Kumi Okese.

"Come on the 113th!" Jack roared, hoping that Mary would hear and understand he was there. "Cry Havelock!" He used the old slogan that the 113th had adopted during the Indian Mutiny. "Cry Havelock!"

Jack fired again as the yellow umbrella shifted, and Kumi Okese gave orders that saw his warriors fan out towards Jack's position.

Loading as quickly as he could, Jack moved to his right, outflanking the village and heading diagonally towards Mary. He could see her clearly now, standing erect, refusing even to bow her shoulders before her captors. Jack was never more proud of her than at that moment. *Show them, Mary!*

Throwing himself down behind a fallen tree, Jack aimed and fired, reloaded without waiting to see the result of his shot, yelled "113th Foot! Come on the 113th!" and ran on, still skirting the village, trying to unsettle the Ashantis so they would leave Mary unattended, trying to make the Ashantis believe a British regiment surrounded them.

The Ashanti warriors were closer now, some firing at the places Jack had already vacated, others shooting at shadows as Jack slid through the forest, using all the bushcraft he had learned in two decades of soldiering. His route had taken him closer to Mary, so now they were only separated by a hundred yards. Mary remained standing with her head high.

"Cry Havelock!" Jack roared.

"Let loose the dogs of war!" Mary joined in. "Come on, the 113th!"

Aiming, Jack fired again, knocking down a young Ashanti warrior. "Come on the 113th!" He reloaded desperately, wishing he had a breech-loading Snider rather than the old muzzle-loading Enfield. Mary would know the 113th were not part of the campaign. She would understand he was alone and unsupported. Jack fired again, rolled on his side to reload and swore when two Ashanti warriors spotted him. While one knelt to fire, the other drew a long knife and ran forward, yelling. Fumbling his reloading, Jack swore as he dropped the percussion cap, rolled away, drew his revolver and shot the charging man. The second Ashanti fired, with the slug passing so close that Jack flinched with the wind of its passage, and then the Ashanti was on his feet, hefting his musket like a club.

Waiting until the warrior was only ten paces away, Jack fired two shots. Both hit the Ashanti in the chest, knocking him back. He crumpled with an expression of surprise on his face as Jack reloaded the Enfield and his revolver. *I'm coming, Mary!*

Jack had lost sight of Kumi Okese and the yellow umbrella. Mary stood about ten yards from the fetish tree, with a shaft of sunlight reflecting from a human skull swinging from a branch. At the base of the trunk, two vultures feasted on a dismembered human body, barely pausing as the echoes of the gunfire died away. Jack could not see the bodyguard anywhere. *Now! Move now!*

"Stand fast, the 113th!" Jack shouted, took a deep breath, and ran towards Mary.

"Good evening, Captain Jack," Mary greeted him with a small curtsey that rattled her manacles.

"Good evening, Mrs Windrush," Jack said. "I don't approve of your new jewellery."

"They are rather heavy, don't you think?" Mary lifted her wrists. "I intend to hand it back at the first opportunity."

"They do look a little clumsy." Now that he was close, Jack could see the lines of strain on Mary's face and the worry in her eyes. "We'd better remove them, I think."

"Jack!" Mary screamed as Kumi Okese's bodyguard leapt from behind the tree, with his knife bare in his fist. Lifting the Enfield, Jack shot the man through the stomach, leaving him to lie, writhing on the ground.

"We only have a minute before the warriors return," Jack said. "Pray excuse my lack of manners." Ducking down, he placed Mary over his shoulder, straightened up and headed towards the forest.

Tired after days of campaigning and months of stress, Jack found Mary heavier than he expected. "You must have put on weight. Tell me if you see any Ashantis following us."

"Not yet," Mary said. "We're all right so far."

When he had first come to Africa, Jack had considered the forest a hostile place, but now it seemed a welcoming refuge as he ran over the open ground. Splashing across the river, Jack slipped on a loose stone, nearly dropped Mary and staggered into the trees. After only a few steps, he slumped down in the shelter of a tall palm and eased Mary to the ground.

"I might keep you like this," he said. "It's easier to control you."

"It's damned uncomfortable." Mary's use of bad language proved her agitation.

"Lie still and I'll try to get the shackles off you."

The manacles around Mary's wrists had a simple bolt to pull, while her ankle shackles were more complex, with a screw.

"Jack," Mary whispered as he worked the mechanism.

"We're nearly there. Be patient."

"Jack!" Mary injected more urgency into the word.

Jack looked up. "What is it?"

"Over there."

Jack saw the movement in the trees, the flicker of white cloth and the glint of sun on metal. He slid down beside Mary, still working on her shackles. "Only a few more twists, Mary."

"Jack!"

The Ashantis arrived suddenly, thrusting the muzzles of their muskets into Jack's back. Rolling over, he reached for his revolver until a hard hand grabbed his wrist and Kumi Okese snarled an order. Half a dozen Ashantis pulled Jack upright, with Mary at his side. Jack punched at the nearest warrior, felt a surge of satisfaction when the man staggered back, and then gasped as somebody cracked him across his head.

"You could have lived, Major Windrush," Elda slid beside Kumi Okese. "You could have left the woman and lived, but you had to be a hero, and of course I told Kumi you were coming." When she smiled, Jack saw the madness in her eyes. "Now Kumi will sacrifice you both."

Jack glanced at Mary, struggling between two brawny warriors. "Tell Kumi he does not need to kill the woman. I will willingly go if he sets her free."

"It's too late for that," Elda said.

"Set her free, you bastard!" Jack struggled against his captors as Kumi Okese watched, expressionless. The warriors dragged Jack and Mary to the fetish tree, with Elda following, clapping her hands. The vultures hopped further away, waiting, with blood dripping from their cruel beaks.

"Sorry, Mary," Jack said. "I failed you."

"No, you didn't," Mary tried to sound calm. "If I had not been stupid enough to get captured, we would not be in this mess."

The executioner from Kumasi stood under the tree, holding a large, slightly curved sword. He looked dispassionately as the warriors hustled Jack and Mary to him.

"Kumi Okese is sacrificing you to his ancestors," Elda explained, "and to the ancestors of his tribe." She was laughing, and Jack wondered if her long captivity in Kumasi had unhinged her mind.

Jack fought hard to retain the phlegm of a British officer. "Tell him that he can kill me if he wishes, but if he murders my wife, a British woman, Lord Wolseley will burn all of Ashantiland will. Tell Kumi Okese the British Army will hunt him down and hang him like a dog."

Jack saw Elda pale at the words and speak to Kumi Okese, who shrugged and said a few short words.

"Kumi will take that chance," Elda said.

With two Ashanti warriors forcing him onto his knees, Jack tried to grab Mary's hand, but she was just out of reach. He was aware of Elda watching, her eyes bright.

"Goodbye, Mary, old girl," Jack said. "I'll see you on the other side in a few minutes."

"Goodbye, Captain Jack. I love you." Mary began to intone the 23rd Psalm, her voice quavering at first but strengthening with each verse.

"The Lord is my shepherd; I shall not want.
He maketh me to lie down in green pastures."

Never a religious man, Jack tried to join in, then reverted to something he knew far better. "Cry Havelock!" He could see the executioner approaching, with rainwater dripping from the blade of his sword. "Come on the 113th!" He was back in India again, leading his men towards Lucknow. Then he was on Inkerman Ridge with the great grey masses of Russian infantry rolling towards him through the mist and his handful of the 113th waiting under the dripping colours.

Mary's voice strengthened as the Ashantis pushed her to her knees.

"He restoreth my soul: he leadeth me in the paths of righteousness for his name's sake.
Yea, though I walk through the valley of the shadow of death, I will fear no evil: for thou art with me; thy rod and thy staff they comfort me."

The crack of the rifle meant nothing to Jack. It seemed part of his memories until his soldier's brain analysed the sound. *That was a Snider*, he thought, *except they didn't have Sniders at Inkerman.* He heard the thump of the bullet hitting its target and saw the executioner staring in amazement at the small hole that had appeared in his side. The Snider cracked again, and the executioner's head snapped back, with blood spraying out the back of his skull.

"*Thou preparest a table before me in the presence of mine enemies: thou anointest my head with oil; my cup runneth over.*

Surely goodness and mercy shall follow me all the days of my life: and I will dwell in the house of the Lord forever. Jack?" Mary stopped her singing.

With the Ashanti guards distracted by the unknown marksman, Jack made a sudden lunge up and barged into the men holding Mary. "Run, Mary! Run!"

"Jack," Mary hesitated, waiting for him.

"Run!" Jack pushed her away, landed a punch on the jaw of the nearest Ashanti and scooped up the executioner's sword. Although it was heavy and poorly balanced, it was better than nothing. As the second Ashanti stared, Jack chopped him down. Another shot sounded, and then a roar as fifty warriors ran from the forest.

"What the devil?" Jack looked for Kumi Okese, gripping the sword as blood dribbled onto his fingers.

Mary grabbed his left hand. "Come on, Jack!"

"No! You get away, Mary!" Jack swung the sword, missed the nearest man and tried again, stepping forward to shield his wife.

The mob of men charged into the village, carrying an assortment of weapons, from swords and spears to muskets. The man at their head held an Enfield rifle with a fixed bayonet. Jack stared at him. "Sergeant Wickham."

The newcomers were attacking the Ashanti with great gusto, hacking with their swords and spears, or firing their muskets and using the butts as clubs. Sergeant Wickham stopped in front of Jack. Out of uniform, he looked every inch the African warrior. "I answer to Kwabena Badu now, Major Windrush."

"I'm glad to see you're alive, Sergeant," Jack said. "Who are these men?"

"Men of my tribe," Wickham said. "Denkyira warriors."

Jack watched two of the Denkyiras dispose of two Ashantis without difficulty, leaving the white-striped men sprawled on the ground. Yelling, Kumi Okese slashed aside three Denkyiras and strode towards Wickham. Three warriors followed their chief. Jack felt for his revolver, swore at the empty holster and hefted his sword.

"I want him, Major," Wickham said.

"So do I," Jack said softly. "He was going to murder my wife, and he murdered one of my men."

"One of my friends," Wickham drew his knife as Kumi Okese came closer.

Kumi Okese's Edwesus charged first, with the Denkyiras meeting them before they reached Jack and Wickham. Kumi Okese feinted at Wickham, sidestepped, and attacked Jack, swinging his knife at Jack's throat. He was fast and fierce, but clumsier than Jack had expected. Used to the Pashtun with their long Khyber knives, Jack dodged Okese's slash and hacked his sword at onto the Ashanti's head, splitting it in two. Kumi Okese crumpled to the ground.

That's Private Manning avenged. Yet inside, Jack felt hollow.

"Nicely done," Wickham approved.

"I thought your people were scared of the Ashanti and could not fight," Jack said.

Wickham smiled. "We fight when we want to and when we have a reason. Whatever you may pretend, the British war with the Ashanti is not our war. You want control of this part of Africa, nothing else."

Jack dropped his sword. "I suspect that you are not returning to the regiment?"

"No," Wickham said. "For three generations, my family has wanted to come home. I am home." He spread a hand to indicate the tribesmen who stood around the village, some leaning on their weapons as they watched Jack, others finishing off the Edwesu wounded. "These are my people."

Jack nodded. "I posted you as killed in action," he said. "That is accurate as Sergeant Albert Wickham no longer exists. You killed him, Kwabena Badu, and you saved our lives. Live in peace."

"I did not save your life," Kwabena Badu pointed to Abena, who appeared from behind the fetish tree. "That little girl told me what was happening." He smiled. She is Denkyira and was a slave of the Ashantis; now she will be my adopted daughter."

Mary smiled to Abena. "Thank you, Abena."

Jack looked at the bodies of Kumi Okese's warrior, lying in crumpled heaps on the ground. For a moment he thought of the proud regiment Kumi Okese had paraded through the streets of Kumasi. They were all gone now, their pride broken by Highland bayonets and the bullets of Snider rifles, their regiment destroyed at Abrakrampa, Amoaful and Ordahsu, with the survivors scattered with the taste of defeat bitter in their mouths. They had been brave men, fighting for a culture that had no place in the late 19th century.

Elda Becker body lay prone, separated from the rest. Jack did not know who killed her or why. He shook his head; she had come to Africa to do good, but Africa had proved too much for her.

Stooping, Jack lifted the yellow umbrella from the ground. For months it had been a symbol of his enemy, a thing of dread. Now it was only an umbrella, nothing more. "I've been watching this all through the campaign," he said. "'I was going to take it for the officer's mess." He handed to Kwabena. "I think you deserve it more than me."

"Keep it," Kwabena said. "I may get more."

Handing the umbrella to Abena, Jack watched as Kwabena led the Denkyiras away. "Oh, Mary," he said, "I have something else for you." Sliding a hand inside his tunic, he produced the scarf he had carried for so long and placed the Celtic cross on top.

"I wondered where those had got to." Mary tried to hide the catch in her throat. "We bought that scarf in Gondabad two days before we got married." Turning away to hide her tears, she tied it loosely around her neck. "And we bought the cross in Lindisfarne when you were based in Berwick."

"Come on, Mary," Jack heard the roughness in his voice. "We have a golden stool to find."

"I don't care about the Golden Stool or a hundred golden stools," Mary said. "We're together again, and that's all that matters."

Chapter Thirty-Three

When Jack walked into the house Wolseley had requisitioned, the general was with Lieutenant Wood, both of them admiring the lieutenant's booty. Augmenting King Kofi's state umbrella of black and crimson velvet, Wood had a beautifully carved stool with silver ornamentation. Jack knew that as aide de camp to Wolseley, Wood could be relied on to be first to the loot. Aristocrats always were; in Jack's opinion, that was how they had obtained their titles in the first place.

"I found the stool with a sergeant of the Wests," Wood said. "The beggar refused to give it up to me. I had to put him under arrest."

I'll have Sergeant Mathews free before this day is over.

"Ah, Windrush," Wolseley looked up from his study of the stool. "I ordered you to locate the Golden Stool of the Ashantis, did I not?"

"You did, sir," Jack said.

"Yet despite my direct order, you went swanning around on some personal mission, delegating your duty to a sergeant, of the West Indian Regiment at that."

"Sergeant Mathews is a good man, sir. He was good enough to fight for the queen and put his life on the line, and the West Indians are excellent soldiers."

"You put your personal interest before your duty, Windrush," Wolseley said. "I had hopes for you. I wondered why a man with your fine fighting record had not advanced beyond major, and now I see why. You neglect your duty, sir. I am not surprised that you are only a major; indeed, I am surprised that you reached that exalted rank." Wolseley was working himself into a rage. "I

266

hope you enjoy your majority, Windrush, for you will climb no higher for the remainder of your career."

About to retaliate, Jack thought of Mary. "Yes, sir, you're probably right."

"Fortunately, Lieutenant Wood here located the stool. Dismissed, Windrush."

"Yes, sir." Jack glanced at the stool, smiled and left the room.

Yaa Asantewaa was outside, standing close to a circle of Ashanti warriors. "Your general does not approve of you, Major Windrush."

"It would appear not," Jack said.

"We have a saying in our land," Yaa said. "*Enne ye medea okyina nso we dee.* It means, today is mine, tomorrow is yours. That means one day one person has a victory; the next day, his enemy will win."

Jack nodded. "Aye, Yaa, that is the way of the world."

"Today your general has won his victory over us, and you." Yaa was not smiling. "Tomorrow he may find out he does not have our Golden Stool but another. Will you tell him?"

Jack shook his head. "Not I. As far as I am concerned, the Ashanti are entitled to their Stool. They fought hard for it. I've got my wife back so I'll call the bargain square."

Yaa smiled. "You are a strange man for a British soldier, Major Windrush." She looked into his eyes. "I will guard our Golden Stool in case another British soldier wishes to steal it, and your day will come."

Jack looked over to Mary. "I think it already has," he said.

Dear reader,

We hope you enjoyed reading *The City Of Dreadful Death*. Please take a moment to leave a review, even if it's a short one. Your opinion is important to us.

Discover more books by Malcolm Archibald at
https://www.nextchapter.pub/authors/malcolm-archibald

Want to know when one of our books is free or discounted? Join the newsletter at http://eepurl.com/bqqB3H

Best regards,

Malcolm Archibald and the Next Chapter Team

Historical Notes

The slave trade was one of the most despicable events to disgrace humanity, with British slavers playing their ignoble part.

In the three centuries of European participation, an estimated six million slaves were transported from West Africa. The numbers captured in East Africa during 1800 years of Arab slaving must be staggering.

From 1807 onward the Royal Navy instituted anti-slavery patrols off the coast of West Africa, with 150,000 slaves freed from 1810 and 1864. This figure is impressive but pales into insignificance with the estimated 100,000 a year carried across to the Americas. The Royal Navy paid a high price for this humanitarian service. In 1829 alone, over 25% of the men in the West African squadron died from disease. Ships could spend up to five years off the West African coast.

The West Indian Regiment

The West Indian Regiment was part of the British Army from the late eighteenth century and has never received the publicity or recognition it deserves. The regiment participated in many expeditions against the French in the Caribbean and fought in Central America and West Africa. The senior officers who knew the soldiers had nothing but praise for them.

The Wests played a prominent part in the Ashanti Wars. Although I have included them in the occupation of Kumasi in this fictional account, they were denied that opportunity in reality. Of their bravery and devotion to duty, there is no doubt.

Yaa Asantewaa (1840-1921) is one of the most significant female figures in African history. She led the Ashanti against the British in the war of 1900 when the then British governor of the Gold Coast demanded the sacred Golden Stool so he could sit on it. Although the British eventually won the fighting, the Ashanti retained the sacred stool.

Amoaful: The deciding battle of the Ashanti War, where the British defeated a very determined Ashanti defence. Lance Sergeant McGaw won the Victoria Cross and gained promotion to sergeant. He died in Cyprus four years later.

Kumasi. Wolseley's occupation of Kumasi was astonishingly short. The British remained only a few days, looted the palace, set fire to the town and withdrew, struggling over the swollen rivers as the rains came. The Ashantis did not attack the coastal settlements again.

About the Author

Born and raised in Edinburgh, Malcolm Archibald was educated at the University of Dundee, a city to which he has a strong attachment. He has experience in many fields and writes about the Scottish whaling industry as well as historical fiction and fantasy.

Books by the Author

- Jack Windrush Series

  - Windrush

  - Windrush: Crimea

  - Windrush: Blood Price

  - Windrush: Cry Havelock

  - Windrush: Jayanti's Pawns

  - Windrush: Warriors of God

  - Windrush: Agent of the Queen

  - Windrush: The City of Dreadful Death

- A Wild Rough Lot

- Dance If Ye Can: A Dictionary of Scottish Battles

- Like The Thistle Seed: The Scots Abroad

- Our Land of Palestine

- Shadow of the Wolf

- The Swordswoman Series

  - The Swordswoman

  - The Shining One

  - Falcon Warrior

  - Melcorka of Alba

Lightning Source UK Ltd.
Milton Keynes UK
UKHW011943310820
369135UK00007B/214